THE FOREST KING'S DAUGHTER

Elly Blake

LITTLE, BROWN AND COMPANY
New York Boston

This book is a work of fiction. Names, characters, places, and incidents are the product of the author's imagination or are used fictitiously. Any resemblance to actual events, locales, or persons, living or dead, is coincidental.

Copyright © 2025 by Elly Blake

Map copyright © 2025 by Virginia Allyn

Cover art copyright © 2025 by Micaela Alcaino. Cover design by Sasha Illingworth and Patrick Hulse. Cover copyright © 2025 by Hachette Book Group, Inc. Interior design by Carla Weise.

Hachette Book Group supports the right to free expression and the value of copyright. The purpose of copyright is to encourage writers and artists to produce the creative works that enrich our culture.

The scanning, uploading, and distribution of this book without permission is a theft of the author's intellectual property. If you would like permission to use material from the book (other than for review purposes), please contact permissions@hbgusa.com. Thank you for your support of the author's rights.

Little, Brown and Company
Hachette Book Group
1290 Avenue of the Americas, New York, NY 10104
Visit us at LBYR.com

First Edition: February 2025

Little, Brown and Company is a division of Hachette Book Group, Inc. The Little, Brown name and logo are registered trademarks of Hachette Book Group, Inc.

The publisher is not responsible for websites (or their content) that are not owned by the publisher.

Little, Brown and Company books may be purchased in bulk for business, educational, or promotional use. For information, please contact your local bookseller or the Hachette Book Group Special Markets Department at special.markets@hbgusa.com.

Library of Congress Cataloging-in-Publication Data
Names: Blake, Elly, author.
Title: The Forest King's Daughter / Elly Blake.
Description: First edition. | New York : Little, Brown and Company, 2025. |
Audience: Ages 14 and up. | Summary: "A forest princess and a demon boy whose kingdoms are at war must join forces to fight a greater evil, rekindling their forbidden childhood friendship and a new romance."—Provided by publisher.
Identifiers: LCCN 2024013734 | ISBN 9780316395724 (hardcover) |
ISBN 9780316395922 (ebook)
Subjects: CYAC: Fantasy. | Forests and forestry—Fiction. | Magic—Fiction. |
Romance stories. | LCGFT: Fantasy fiction. | Romance fiction.
Classification: LCC PZ7.1.B586 Th 2025 | DDC [Fic]—dc23
LC record available at https://lccn.loc.gov/2024013734

ISBNs: 978-0-316-39572-4 (hardcover), 978-0-316-39592-2 (ebook)

Printed in Indiana, USA

LSC-C

Printing 1, 2024

To
my dad,
who said,
"Why don't
you write a book
about a forest?"

Prologue

Sylvans are our natural enemies.
That is the purest truth known to
Dracukind.

—GAXIX, DRACU PHILOSOPHER

ZERU CLOSED HIS BURNING EYES, REELING AS ALWAYS
from that first shock of brightness as he pushed his face
aboveground. He raked his hands through his hair and wiped
dirt from the twisted horns that grew from his head as he marveled at the cold, white light of the moon, so different from the
flickering torchlight of the Cryptlands. Even after a year of these
forbidden trips into Thirstwood, he still shivered as he looked at
that glowing disc. It might be the closest he'd ever get to seeing
the sun.

Patting his pocket, he made his way along the winding paths
toward the meeting place. If Cassia was late, he would pull her
hair and make her cry.

No. Even as he had the thought, he knew he wouldn't.
Though Cassia was a Sylvan, she was his friend. He looked forward to these meetings above all things.

As he reached the massive yew tree, a girl's voice called in singsong, "Dracu, Dracu!"

His scalp prickled as a thrill surged through him, but he sat himself against the trunk to wait. Not the trunk of a blood tree, though, which could trap an unwary traveler with its branches and drink them dry. More appeared every year, turning the canopy crimson with their red leaves.

Cassia's footsteps grew louder, frustration crackling in each step. "I know you're here!"

Zeru muffled a laugh.

She burst into view like a sprite, her dark golden hair tangled about her shoulders, the freckles on her nose visible in the glow of the moon. On the night they'd first met, he'd reached out to touch them, and she'd slapped his hand. That was when he knew he liked her. Despite the fact that her pointed ears and softer features had proclaimed her his enemy.

Cassia's eyes narrowed on him. Sylvans had poor night vision, which meant he could see her expression but she couldn't see his.

"Why do you always hide?" she demanded.

"Because you always find me." He shot to his feet, baring his teeth in a sharp grin. "I thought Sylvans loved to track their prey."

She looked away. "My father was going to take me hunting, but my mother said I was too young." She gave him a measuring look. "You haven't gone yet, have you?"

"Twice." Never mind that he was banned from going again.

"Where?" Her face flickered between curiosity and doubt. "It's forbidden for Dracu to hunt in our forest."

Talking to Cassia was like navigating a bramble-choked path, full of snags. He could not tell her much without endangering

⁓ 2 ⁓

himself, but he wanted to know more about her. "Everyone knows that, Sylvan. I didn't say I'd hunted here."

But of course he had. There wasn't enough game in the Cryptlands. On nights of the full moon when the trees were sleepy and the wards placed by the Sylvan king were thin, the Dracu dug their way up into Thirstwood. Zeru's father had taken him to track small game—hares and weasels, mostly, as deer and boars were rare. On the second hunt, Zeru had killed two hares. He'd stepped lightly alongside his father with a heady feeling of accomplishment at the meat he'd bring home to his family. But then they'd run into the Sylvan king's hounds. Their shining white fangs rushed closer at a terrible speed, Sylvan Huntsmen following with bows and swords drawn. Fear had rushed through Zeru's veins, freezing his feet to the ground. He'd sworn he could feel the hounds' breath before his father had swept him into the nearest escape in the ground.

At the next full moon, Zeru had begged for another chance. He'd promised to run if he heard the hounds. But no matter how he'd pleaded, his father had stood firm. He would not take Zeru again until he was older.

In stubborn defiance, Zeru had snuck out alone. The last thing he'd expected was to find a lost Sylvan girl. When he'd looked into her wide eyes and seen tears icing her cheeks, something had gripped his chest, and he'd spoken softly to her—more softly than a Dracu should ever speak to an enemy.

"What about your mother?" Cassia asked, drawing him back to the present. "Does she hunt, too?"

"Of course. Doesn't yours?"

Cassia shook her head. "My mother hates the sight of blood." She tilted her head to the side. "Tell me more about the creatures who live underground. You said there are different kinds of Azpians, but I only know about the Dracu."

Zeru didn't want to talk about anything to do with the Cryptlands. Forbidden as it was to be in Sylvan territory, it was worse to give an enemy information. Searching for a distraction, he saw a caterpillar making its way across a fallen leaf.

Picking up the leaf, he said, "I brought you something."

"What is it?" Her face lit with excitement.

Over the months, he'd given her two other gifts: a holed stone, which was supposed to bring good fortune, and a fish-bone comb he'd found while exploring. He shouldn't have. Sylvans were greedy and would come to expect more. But Cassia wore the holed stone around her neck on a string, and the comb was tucked into her hair. So, at least she appreciated his gifts.

Her smile faded as she took the leaf, blinking at the caterpillar, which had lifted its upper body in curiosity. "What do I do with it?"

He hid a grin at her confusion. "Name it."

"Zeru," she said without hesitation.

He fought an urge to slap the leaf from her hand. "Zeru is a noble name given to me by my mother. Choose another."

She wrinkled her nose, bringing the freckles closer together. "Leafy?"

He nodded, relaxing.

She stared down at the twitching creature, holding it uncertainly.

He let out a laugh. "That's not your gift."

"Oh." She set the leaf down carefully at the base of the nearest tree. "What's my real gift?"

"What about *my* gift?" he asked, stalling. "Did you bring me something?"

She blinked. "I don't know what Dracu like."

"I don't know what Sylvans like," he countered, "but I've brought you gifts. This is your third."

Stepping closer, she promised, "I'll bring you something next time."

He held in a smile. Though she was eager for the gift, she didn't understand what it meant. In Dracu tradition, a third gift sealed a connection with another person. It meant you valued this friend above others. He'd found something better than a fishbone comb this time.

"Close your eyes," he said.

She obeyed immediately, a smile still curving her lips. She was too trusting. He had an urge to drop the caterpillar into her hand. Instead, he took the ring from his pocket. The metal was misshapen, the gemstone a smooth cabochon, its dark yellow color reminding him of Cassia's hair.

As he placed the ring in her palm, her eyes opened. "Where did you get it?"

He lifted his chin defiantly. "It's mine."

She slid the ring onto her finger. "My father says Dracu lie."

The fact that she was right made him angry. He'd found it in his mother's jewelry box among so many beautiful things— opal brooches, strands of black pearls, hematite bracelets that reflected the torchlight. She wouldn't miss this plain old ring. "Give it back, then, if you don't want it." He made a swipe for the ring, his claws extended.

She yanked her hand away. "You gave it to me." The gemstone gleamed. "I'll never take it off."

Warmth fluttered in his chest, as if her hand had touched him there. "Never?"

After a hesitation, she nodded. "Never."

They stared at each other. He knew she was a Sylvan, and he was a Dracu, but they'd found each other and now he'd given her three gifts. They would remain friends.

"Remember," he said, "next time, it's your turn to bring me a gift."

"Next time . . . ," she said, trailing off.

He felt it, too. The ground was trembling and groaning like the belly of a hungry beast. The trees began to shake, raining blood leaves onto Cassia's hair.

"The hunt?" she asked, her eyes wide.

But the rumble came from below, a burbling cackle of voices blending with the earth's deep groan. It wasn't Sylvan Huntsmen. It was worse.

He grabbed her hand, and they ran, tripping over fallen logs and spiky shrubs. Branches whipped out to slice Zeru's face and catch at Cassia's clothing. Shifting and tearing free, darting like stags, they burst into a clearing enclosed by blood trees. In the center, the flat earth rounded up and up as if a mountain were being birthed.

Zeru turned away, pulling Cassia with him, but a latticework of branches blocked their escape.

"No!" He stared in disbelief, his heart frantic in his throat. He'd heard the trees could move their roots and branches like limbs, but he had never seen it.

In the center of the clearing, the earth swelled, then erupted, spewing a nightmare of beasts with weapons drawn. All the creatures of the Cryptlands were familiar to Zeru, but he had never seen so many together, and never like this—wild, violent, and out for blood. Skrattis howled battle cries as they hefted axes and cudgels. Imps flew like arrows, their tarry eyes and mouths with sawlike teeth opened wide and seeking. Pit sprites filled the air with clouds of soot that blocked the moonlight.

Cassia tried to pull her hand from Zeru's, but he held on. She was thrice-gifted, his friend for life, and he would protect her.

In the center of the chaos, the Dracu queen rose from the ripped earth, her crown of onyx spikes gouging the sky, her green hair wild, her cloak whipping behind her in a keening wind. The curving horns that rose from her head proclaimed her a Dracu, her emerald eyes daggering around the clearing. Leaves shook loose and branches snapped as she singled out Zeru and Cassia. Her voice was a tempest of accusation as she growled, "Return my Dracustone to me."

At that moment, Zeru's mother and father emerged from the earth. His father's expression made Zeru tremble almost as much as the queen's eyes. His mother's eyes rounded in horror as they fell on the small Sylvan by his side.

"Cassia," Zeru breathed, putting his palm out. "Take the ring off so I can give it to the queen."

Cassia grasped the ring, her eyes going wide. "I said I would never take it off."

He shook his head. Didn't she know this was life or death? Before he could say anything, Cassia was ripped from him. Bulbous-eyed imps with their bat-like wings flew toward her as pit sprites obscured her in a dark cloud. Zeru roared and fought to get to her, but a hand clamped his shoulder in a giant's grip.

"Leave her!" It was his father, a general in the queen's army, and Zeru felt the weight of his command. "You have done enough damage this day."

"You have ruined us," his mother said, her voice shaking. Her despair was worse than anger.

He couldn't think while his friend was at the mercy of the vilest members of the Azpian realm. The winged imps had swarmed over her, their small, coal-flat eyes lit with violence. Drakes slithered from the ground, their scaled, serpentine bodies undulating through the crowd. He saw their teeth, sharp like needles, and imagined them sinking into Cassia's skin.

"Help her!" he begged, struggling to pull from his father's grip.

A hand met his ear with a stinging clap. "You dare to ask that after what you've done?"

The shrieks of imps blended with his father's grim voice, the terrible harmony stabbing into his ears.

"What did I do?" he cried.

"The Dracustone ring," his mother wailed. "A Seer prophesied it would be vital to our people. I was charged with keeping it for the day when the queen could wear it. And you have given it to an enemy."

Zeru couldn't speak. He stared at his mother in agonized silence. How could he have known?

His neck prickled as he turned to see Huntsmen on black horses entering the clearing through a gap between trees. Their swords swung in bright arcs, their mounts' hooves trampling. Imps and Skrattis shrieked, no longer in bloodlust but in fear, fleeing and dying with gasps and gurgles. Drakes dug their way into the ground. Pit sprites dissolved into puffs of smoke, leaving the scent of brimstone.

The largest of the riders approached, steam rising from the nostrils of his stallion. His bone-white antlers announced his ownership of Thirstwood forest. The Sylvan king.

"Bring my daughter to me," he said, his voice a storm rumbling through the woods.

8

One of the Huntsmen strode forward carrying a small form. There were scratches and cuts on Cassia's cheeks, and her freckles were coated by a smearing of blood, but her chest was moving with quick breaths. Zeru's legs went weak with relief. At least she was alive.

At the same moment, the truth broke into his confused mind. Horror coursed through his body, leaving his fingers and toes tingling. He had given the Dracustone to the Sylvan king's daughter.

The king grabbed Cassia's hand. He inspected the ring with a satisfied expression that was there and gone in a heartbeat. A chill ran through Zeru's body at the cold way he let Cassia's arm fall before nodding to the Huntsman. "Take her to Scarhamm."

Zeru watched, a terrible tightness in his chest as Cassia's limp body was lain across the saddle.

"The Dracustone belongs to me," the queen said with ringing conviction. "Give it back, or by the Ancients, we war."

The king laughed, a rockslide of mirth. "The Solis Gemma was given to my daughter. Freely. It belongs to me now."

Her eyes glowed like green lamps. "The ring was not the boy's to give. Make her return it."

"I will tell her to use it," he said, leaning down to loom over the queen, "to destroy our enemies who hurt her this day."

Fog swirled from the queen's mouth as she said, "Then you have chosen war."

The king's eyes seemed to glow. "At last." He wheeled his horse and rode away.

Zeru stared as the last of the Huntsmen disappeared. Around him lay gruesome corpses of Skrattis, imps, and drakes, but all he could think of was the sight of his friend, bloodied and helpless. She was alive. But would she know that he had tried to help her?

He would meet her on the next full moon to tell her. And get the ring back. He could still fix this.

At the sound of his name, he made himself turn to face his parents. His father's voice was like claws against granite, carving each word into Zeru's mind and memory. "All of Dracukind will pay for what you have done today. And you most of all."

1

Sylvans and Dracu
By war divided,
Never now shall meet
Without bloodshed, tears, and pain.
—Excharias, Sylvan poet

Cassia thrust her arm in rapid jabs, conscious of her footwork on the layer of straw covering the training yard. Her knife was an extension of her arm. A talon, a claw. The Dracu had claws, but she had her knife.

The fortress of Scarhamm had shaken most of its snow cover, but the frozen earth lay fallow, waiting for warmth. Cassia felt like the seeds lying silent underground, full of potential, needing only the right conditions to burst free.

A few dozen Huntsmen had paired off, some practicing with heavy wooden swords, others weaponless, sparring with fists. Her two older sisters, Enora and Thea, crossed wooden swords, their clatter blending with the general din. Burke, the Second Huntsman, was perfection itself, his movements economical and relentless. Though Sylvans had many different builds, heights, skin and hair colors, their uniforms were always the same: green and brown to blend with the forest. Usually, Cassia enjoyed watching the Huntsmen spar, imagining that she might be that proficient one day. But sometimes she was struck by the memory of her mother tending honeysuckle and roses in this very spot. She remembered watching as the seeds were dropped into the rich soil. She'd always felt peaceful here at her mother's side.

Over the past ten years, most of the gardens had become training yards, the roses dug up or trampled underfoot.

Cassia was acutely aware of Tibald, the weapons master and trainer, watching her with sharp eyes. Later, he would tell her whether she had been too slow or too broad in her movements, if she'd failed to protect her weak spots. But she'd been practicing every evening for hours, and she moved through her routine with more confidence than usual. The Huntsmen were always talking about the strange joy found in battle. *The wild frenzy of it! The beauty of the fight!*

How she wanted to feel like that, to fight alongside her sisters, to prove she had as much value on the battlefield as she did wielding the ring from some safely tucked-away location.

"Go for the throat, Cass!" a small voice piped.

Cassia smiled but didn't turn, waiting until she had finished her routine before facing her younger sister, Rozie, who sat atop a rock on the edge of the yard.

"If this were a real battle," Rozie said, eyes shining, "you'd have killed at least seven Dracu. Maybe even eight."

Cassia laughed. Imaginary Dracu were easy to kill. "What about you? How many have you taken down today?"

Rozie looked at her fingernails, a mannerism she'd clearly picked up from Thea. "A dozen or so, I would think. On the way here."

Cassia grinned at her sister's careful wording. The added words, "I would think," made it not quite a lie. Sylvans valued truth above all things, believing a lie was like a broken vow, which carried dire consequences. Even trying to lie made Cassia's throat close up.

"And what did you kill them with?" Tibald shouted from across the yard.

Rozie scrunched up her face in a fearsome scowl. "I looked at them like this."

Tibald's booming laugh echoed. "That would do it!"

Their eldest sister, Enora, ruffled Rozie's curly red hair. Her own silvery blond hair was neat as a pin in a long braid coiled crown-like on her head. "We need you on patrol, Sproutling, if you can kill with a look."

"No," Thea, the second eldest, broke in, mischief in her dark eyes. Her long brown braids danced as she strode to Rozie in her long-limbed, graceful way. "Tell the truth, Sylvan, lest you choke on your lies. You felled them with your stench. You can't avoid the bath forever, you know."

"I am simply not dirty," Rozie declared, spreading her arms for inspection. Her eyes narrowed on her arm. "Except for that one spot."

Thea snorted. "Now I'm worried about your eyes as well as your nose."

As the Huntsmen laughed, Tibald shouted, "Don't listen, Rozenna! You're as clean as a snake and twice as pretty."

"Thank you!" Rozie said without a trace of irony. Her love of creatures that slithered or crawled was well known.

Sparring resumed as Enora and Thea took a break to swig from water skins. Rozie hopped off the rock and came to Cassia's side. "You've been practicing."

Cassia grinned. She glanced at Burke, who only bestowed his approval to the most proficient among the Huntsmen, but he wasn't paying any attention to her. "Did Tibald look impressed?"

Rozie frowned, pushing back a hank of hair. "He looked the same as always. Smiling. A little drunk."

"Rozie! He isn't." Cassia glanced at Tibald, who was watching the Huntsmen in his all-seeing way. She dropped her voice. "He has red cheeks, that's all." What you could see of them under that salt-and-pepper beard.

"I know," Rozie said, only slightly quieter. "I said he *looks* drunk, not that he *is*."

Cassia shook her head at her sister's irrepressible nature. "Well, if you're in the training yard, you need to train. Raise your weapon, Huntsman."

Rozie looked delighted, then made a show of looking around. "Where is my sword? Ah! How could I be so careless?" She pretended to heft a blade from the ground, complete with grunts and facial contortions.

"You need a lighter weapon," Cassia said, tucking her knife into the sheath at her waist and producing a pretend one. "Try this," she said, handing her sister an invisible dagger.

"Ah, that's much better." Rozie gave it a once-over. "A handsome weapon."

They bowed to each other, fighting smiles. At seventeen, Cassia was older than Rozie by five years, yet she spent more time with her than with their elder sisters. Though she wanted above all things to be like Enora and Thea, warrior-like and ruthless in battle, in her secret heart, Cassia envied Rozie's ability to make everything playful.

Rozie lifted her hand, blade up, and loosed a battle cry that roused birds from their nests. Cassia chuckled as she pantomimed a return slash. Rozie parried, and the fight was on. Enora and Thea laughed at their antics, and some of the Huntsmen ceased their training to watch the mock battle, shouting advice or howling at Rozie's expressions. After a minute or two, Cassia got the better of her young sister, grabbing her in a quick hold. But she failed to take the killing blow. Rozie reached behind her and sank the pretend knife into Cassia's heart.

Cassia gasped and put her hands to her chest, her eyes closing to Rozie's pleased guffaws. As she fell to the ground, a hush fell over the Huntsmen. The wooden swords went quiet. A throat cleared. Blinking the sweat from her eyes, she looked up. Looming over her was the most intimidating sight in Scarhamm.

The Sylvan king. Her father.

For a second, she lay frozen. No matter how familiar, the sight of him always shook her. He stood ten feet tall, his shoulders broad as an ancient oak, his dark eyes piercing in a face carved from granite. Antlers grew from his head, more impressive than any crown that could be crafted. It was a sense deep in her bones that mixed awe with fear whenever she looked at him. This was not only her father, but the warrior king who had saved the Sylvan people from destruction at the hands of humans.

When the Ancients had abandoned the mortal world, leaving the land folk at the mercy of humans, it was Silvanus who had become defender of his people. He alone had guided forest-dwellers of all kinds into the safety of Thirstwood, his power commanding the loyalty of the trees. Feared as much as admired, Silvanus's presence was felt by every creature of the woods, his forest magic humming through every vein, whether filled with sap or blood.

Cassia found her feet, her back straightened as if pulled by strings. She had a hot-cheeked sense of how ridiculous she must look, mussed and covered in dirt and bits of straw. Her father rarely came to watch his daughters train, but when he did, his verdicts were decisive and cutting.

"Raise your hand," he ordered.

She reached for her dagger, eager to display her hard-won proficiency.

~ 15 ~

"Your other hand, Deathringer," he barked. "The Solis Gemma."

With a silent gasp, she lifted her ringed hand, wincing as a tremor ran through it. As always, she felt the weight of the ancient artifact. Not the physical weight but the one in her mind. Everything it was supposed to be.

Deathringer. It was a name from legend, given to the last person who had wielded the Solis Gemma in battle. A champion who had slaughtered thousands in the Ancient Wars. Not only did her father believe the stories were true, but he also expected her to live up to that name. Not a day had gone by since she'd first put on the ring that she didn't feel the heaviness of this burden, the sense that she was not living up to what she was meant to be.

She *could* create a blast of light. She could cause terrible pain to Azpians, those creatures who dwelled in darkness underground, like the Dracu and Skratti. She had rendered hundreds, maybe thousands of them defenseless in that way.

But she could not kill.

"Demonstrate your power," he commanded.

She swallowed, looking up at him with a silent plea. She always trained alone with the ring, never in front of anyone else. Not because she was worried about hurting any forest-dwellers— they were unaffected by the ring's light.

What she hated was risking failure in front of an audience.

But her father's glare was implacable. She had no choice.

Shakily, she forced her will against the ring, calling on its power, pushing past the pain that ran from her heart through her limbs. The gemstone responded, its glow intensifying. As the yellow light pulsed, she had a moment of hope that she could do this. In battle, she could create a blast that would disorient enemies in a fifty-yard radius. But now, under the watchful eye of her father, with her stomach twisted and her palms sweating, the light didn't expand as it should. A middling flare pulsed a few times through the yard before dying.

Out of the corner of her eye, Cassia saw Enora and Thea give each other a look.

Embarrassment heated her skin as an owl hooted somewhere nearby. Owls were viewed as mortal representations of Noctua, the ruler of the spirit realm. The bird's call felt like a condemnation from the Ancient herself.

"A paltry display," the Sylvan king pronounced, his contempt like the crunch of dead leaves underfoot.

Cassia bent her head. How small she must seem to a warrior with so much natural power. As she stared at the ground, she could feel the eyes of the Huntsmen, these men and women who depended on her. She was a vital part of their army, as Tibald always reminded her. But she'd overheard the jokes about her. The speculation that the legends were either exaggerated or the king's daughter wasn't up to the task.

She was a disappointment. Never what they truly needed her to be—a warrior who could fell armies, not just weaken them.

Swallowing, she found the courage to look up at her father. His eyes were thunderclouds, his lips a grim slash above a squared jaw. She had a sudden urge to run into the forest to hide among the trees.

"The war room," he said as he turned and strode away, his footfalls shaking the ground.

The silence stretched until Tibald broke it. "Quit gawping and get your arses back to practice!"

With throat clearings and scuffles, the Huntsmen resumed their training. But the relaxed mood had been ruined. Even the sunlight seemed gray.

"Keep your chin up," Thea said briskly.

Cassia lifted her chin, but her stomach twisted as she followed her father.

"Why can you not master the ring?" the Sylvan king demanded, his anger shrinking the dimensions of the large chamber.

Cassia had always found the war room intimidating with its echoing size, creaking floorboards, and massive fireplace. The gray stone walls bristled with swords, axes, maces, shields, and other instruments of warfare. Her father stood at the head of the ancient oaken table, which was scarred from centuries of use. There were no chairs. The Sylvan king didn't believe in sitting when action was being decided. Flames from the fireplace behind him burnished his antlers but left his eyes in shadow.

A familiar tremble took hold of her limbs, the usual sickness coiling in her gut like a venomous snake. She hated these lectures. There was only one note, one repeated theme. No matter how hard she worked, no matter how desperately she stretched herself to her limits, to bend herself into the shape of someone worthy of his approval, she failed him. Every time.

And if she argued, if she tried to defend herself...well, that had only happened once. She had spent hours trapped alone in the dark war room, the table itself shackling her at her father's command. She'd learned not to offer excuses. But neither could she say nothing.

"I don't know," she said, hating the weakness of her reply, knowing it would stir him to greater anger.

His fist met the table, the impact rattling through the wood and into her stomach. "The Solis Gemma is a thing of great power. An artifact of the Ancients themselves! And you make a mockery of it." His voice scraped along her every nerve. "When you first wore the ring, I rejoiced that this would be our edge over the Dracu, our salvation in a stalemate that had lasted far too long. Now, ten years later, what do I have to show for it? You should be able to kill enemies outright with a blast from the gemstone! A Deathringer who brings no death is no use to me."

No use to me. The words seemed to beat against her like the wings of some great, screeching bird.

He spread his hands, a gesture that might express defeat if they weren't his massive hands, his powerful frame that spoke of consequences to anyone who didn't do what he commanded. "Day by day, their attacks increase. The Dracu draw closer to Scarhamm, to your home, the seat of your people, the last refuge of the Sylvans. And instead of applying yourself to mastering the power of the stone, the one thing that may end this war, you roll in the dirt like one of the hounds. Do you take nothing seriously?"

He had her all wrong. *I'd do anything to master the ring. How can you not see?*

But if she said that, he would hold up the many examples of proof that she didn't care enough, or at all.

"The Dracu alone outnumber us three to one," he said, "and even still they recruit from the Azpian hordes. Every day more drakes, imps, pit sprites, and Skrattis have joined their ranks. Our greatest danger is the full moon after the snows melt, when the Dracu are hungry from a long winter and the wards thin. Soon, our walls and our wards will not be enough to protect us."

Cassia stared at her father, a solid lump in her throat. In the great hall, he spoke of crushing their foes and wiping the forest of the memory of the Dracu. But here, in the hush of the war room, she heard a starker truth.

They were losing.

What about Thirstwood? she wanted to ask. The trees were loyal to the Sylvan king, the last and best protection of the forest folk. They had always been enough.

She had never seen her father this worried.

He paced, making the floorboards jump with each step. "Seer after Seer has proclaimed it: The war between Sylvans and Dracu will only end because of the Solis Gemma. We will beat our enemy decisively, but we need the ring. Do you care about your people at all, Cassia?"

She wanted to shout but spoke softly. "Of course! I—"

"Then prove your loyalty!" It was a challenge, a gauntlet thrown in her face. "Find the power within you to master that stone. Do so now, before you have no people left."

She pulled in a long breath. *Can it really depend on me?* She stared at the deep grooves in the table, biting her lip to stop its trembling. Finally, she lifted her head, knowing she must always meet his eyes when he spoke or when she spoke to him.

"I will." The words were barely a breath. "But how? I've tried everything, Father—"

He threw an arm out, the wind of his motion flinging air against her cheek like a slap. "My field is battle. Must I spoon-feed you everything? *You* are responsible for learning how to use the ring."

She reared back, recovering with squared shoulders and a stiff nod. "Yes, Father. Leave this to me."

As he stared at her, tension held the breath hostage in her chest.

"Remember," he said with solemn warning. "You are the Deathringer. It is up to you whether you live up to that name. If you fail, you fail all of us."

⌒ 20 ⌒

2

> The Old Ones were giants who sprang forth when the world was young.
> After ages alone, they longed for someone to admire what they had wrought.
> From their longing, the Ancients came to life.
>
> —FROM *THE ORIGINS OF THE LAND FOLK*

CASSIA LEFT THE WAR ROOM, HER EYES ACHING with the threat of tears. She turned, finding Enora and Thea leaning against the wall next to the doorway, their arms crossed as if waiting for her. Enora's pale gray eyes looked concerned. Not wanting to worry her sisters, Cassia rolled her eyes, trying to hide the despondency that hung over her like a dark cloud. Thea lifted a dark brow, her deep brown eyes attentive, and Cassia knew she saw through her. But Thea wasn't one to talk about feelings. In a wry tone, Thea said, "I don't suppose he hauled you in there to discuss the serious issue of the Second Huntsman's pants being too tight?"

Despite herself, Cassia let out a hoarse bark of laughter. Thea could always lighten the mood. Taking a steadying breath, she explained what her father had said about the Azpian numbers. "Add to that, the usual. I'm not using the ring to its full potential. I could master it if I took it seriously."

Why did her stomach twist so painfully? It wasn't the first time her father had lectured her. It wasn't the first time he'd expressed disappointment. Far from it. But this time, the words had stung in a new way. Perhaps because there had been an edge of urgency to them.

Why couldn't she be what he wanted her to be?

"Oh, Cass," said Enora, putting a hand on her shoulder. "No one takes things more seriously than you do. We know you're trying. Caring too little is not your problem."

Wanting to get away from the war room, Cassia started down the corridor, her sisters falling into step beside her.

"I agree." Thea jostled her shoulder, bumping her the way she had when they used to wrestle as children. "On the other hand, maybe if you'd stop staring at Burke's arse for two seconds, you'd find time to figure out your ring."

Enora's laugh was cut short by an unconvincing cough.

"I don't ogle him," Cassia protested, adding for the sake of truth, "much." Which drew more laughter. "I'm mostly jealous because it all comes so easily to him. I wish I had an ounce of his confidence."

"Arrogance, you mean," Enora said.

"It's warranted," Thea said. "He's good." The highest compliment she could give.

Cassia sighed. "Father is worried. The harsh winter gave us a break from the attacks, but the thaws will bring the Dracu back. We used to celebrate spring with revels. Now we wait to see how badly they outnumber us."

It made her chest ache when she thought of their history, the stories shared in front of the great hall's massive fireplace of a thriving people who had covered lands from sea to sea. Like other land folk, Sylvans had been pushed back by the encroachment of humans, retreating into wilder, less cultivated places like Thirstwood.

The Dracu had done the same. The difference was, the Dracu allied with fearsome creatures: the goblin-like Skratti, winged imps, and poison-tongued lizards called drakes. Though Sylvans were as tough as tree bark, most of the forest-dwellers tended to be smaller, including pixies, river folk, and wood sprites who did not have a history of battle. The Sylvan king's Huntsmen fought to protect the forest folk, but their numbers were cut with every raid, their strength culled in every fight.

"Regardless of what Father says, it's not all on your shoulders, Cass," Enora said. "Focus on the ring, and we'll be at your back on the battlefield."

Cassia forced a smile, knowing that Enora was trying to be encouraging. She only wished it were a mere matter of focus. She'd focused on nothing but the ring for years. The Sylvan king had been confounded by her lack of ability to use the gemstone as a weapon. He seemed to think it would be something she would do instinctively, the way he spoke with the trees. He had hired Seer after Seer to guide her with whatever knowledge of the ancient artifacts they possessed, cobbled together with spells.

Finally, at twelve years old, she'd created her first blast of light. Though the radius had been small, her father had immediately placed her on the battlefield to test its effect. Her second blast hadn't killed enemies, but it had incapacitated them. She would never forget watching Azpians fall to the ground, writhing helplessly as the Sylvan Huntsmen stabbed them in the chest or took their heads. She'd doubled over as the world had spun and faded to black. She'd woken in the arms of the weapons master, Tibald, as he'd rushed her away from the fighting. She'd never been allowed that close again.

After that, her father had placed her far enough away that she was out of sight, but near enough to use the blast on enemies. The current Court Seer, Veleda, had experimented with potions to increase the gemstone's range, with some success. But it wasn't enough.

"I have to push myself harder," she said aloud.

"Or find a new angle," Thea suggested. "Surely there's something you haven't tried yet. Sometimes when we're strategizing, I find just looking at the map in a different way can help me see something I missed."

Enora nodded. "Go see Veleda again. Be like Rozie. Pester her until she comes up with something."

Maybe they were right.

Thea punched her shoulder. "You'll figure it out, Deathringer. We know you will."

She felt her lips compress at the nickname, even though she appreciated Thea's faith in her. A new resolve took hold as she took the stairs down to the lowest level of the fortress.

Cassia drew up short when her foot splashed into cold wetness. Grimacing, she continued on, her boot squelching. She didn't know why Veleda chose a place where water found its way through cracks and no amount of mortar would keep it dry. Scarhamm was built in a bend of the Scar, a river that began in the snowy heights of the Ambrose Mountains to the north before meandering through marshy lowlands on its way to Thirstwood. The river provided water for the people of Scarhamm and offered protection against enemies. But it also created a constant battle against damp and rot.

When Cassia reached the Seer's familiar peeling wooden

door, she took a breath before pushing it open, knowing the smells that would hit her: pungent herbs and even more pungent odors of animal remains. She peeked her head in and was greeted by the sight of an upside-down rat skull, light flickering through its empty eye sockets. The Seer stood at her worktable with her back to the door, her arm moving as she stirred something in an iron pot. Her long dark curls were knotted with a scarf at her nape.

"Come in, Cass," Veleda said in her easy tone.

Cassia stepped into the room, calmed by Veleda's off-key humming. The space seemed more and more cluttered every time she visited. Rickety shelves groaned under the weight of dusty bottles and vials. Herbs garroted with twine dangled in haphazard bunches. There were bat wings preserved in oil and glass jugs of crickets. A stuffed boar's head stared with marble eyes from one wall, while a goat's carcass hung in a corner from a steel hook. Cassia turned away, her gorge rising.

She'd seen divination rituals performed by Court Seers over the years. Some used runes, some bones, others needed blood or raw meat for summoning spirits from the Netherwhere. Veleda tried a little of everything. She spent most of her time in these damp rooms rather than dispensing predictions from her raised seat of honor in the great hall. But she'd proven herself after her arrival from a tiny village to the north, offering more correct predictions than any Seer Scarhamm had ever had.

"What can I help you with, Cass?" Veleda asked, turning. She was a tall woman, strong of jaw and cheekbone, her full lips almost always curving up with a hint of mischief. Her eyes were a nebulous color, sometimes green, sometimes bronze. Though her face had few lines, it was hard to tell age among long-lived Sylvans. Even the king, whose great age wasn't known—not even by his daughters—had few creases on his sun-weathered skin.

"I need to learn how to control the ring," she said, the statement coming out more of a question than she'd intended.

"Is that all?" Veleda's lips twitched. "I thought it would be something difficult." She tossed some animal hides onto a table, revealing a chair.

Cassia eyed the chair, which must certainly have blood on it, before perching on its edge. "I know you've said that you can't See everything. Some things remain obscure, as is the will of the Ancients. But there must be something else we can try."

"Let me see." Veleda looked around the room, as if for inspiration. "We've read every text we could find. We've used herbs, enchantments, and divination. We've summoned spirits. We've tested potions until my fingers turned green. Almost as green as your face when the healer gave you that purgative." Her eyes twinkled at the memory.

Cassia grimaced. "I haven't forgotten."

"We even tried to find your mother's tree to ask her."

Cassia's breath stopped short at the casual reference to her mother. No one mentioned the Sylvan queen lightly.

During the war, Queen Coventina had grown listless. Year after year, she'd weakened, finally becoming so ill, she'd needed to retreat to her tree for rest.

Every Sylvan had a tree. Both energy source and sanctuary, they served as places to heal and rest.

But Cassia didn't even know where hers was, let alone her mother's. From the time they were born, her father had forbidden his daughters to have a direct connection with their trees. She didn't know why. She only knew the restless ache she'd felt for as long as she could remember.

That was what had led her into Thirstwood as a child, though it was a secret she had never revealed to anyone. When she'd first met Zeru, she had been searching for her tree.

Then she'd received the ring, and her life had changed forever. Everyone's lives had changed. That was the part that lived inside her heart like a leaking poison. Her defiance had led to her mother's illness. And to war. Every terrible thing that had happened in the past ten years was a result of Cassia's own headstrong disobedience. Her childlike conviction that it wouldn't hurt to follow her instincts. To search for the forbidden.

"Some things do not want to be known," Veleda said, spreading her hands.

"Isn't there someone else we can consult?" she asked, succumbing to that familiar ache in her chest. The secret hope that ending the war would bring her mother home. She would do anything.

Veleda's eyes sharpened. "Who do you imagine knows the truth about your ring?"

At a loss for how to answer, Cassia glanced around the room, her eyes falling on what could have been a Dracu horn. "The Dracu queen, maybe?" As she said it, she warmed to the idea. "The night I got the ring, she didn't call it the Solis Gemma. She called it the Dracustone. They must know more than we do. Maybe their Seers or some of the elders . . ."

Veleda held up a hand. "First of all, the Dracu queen will claim anything as her own, regardless of its origins or true name. If it's in the Azpian realm, it's hers. Second, how do you propose to ask her? A trip to the Cryptlands?"

Heat crept up Cassia's neck. "Of course not." No Sylvan went into the Cryptlands. At least, not if they wanted to come out. "What about summoning a Dracu spirit?"

27

The Seer chuckled, leaning her hip against her worktable. "Even if I did manage to summon one, it would be hostile to Sylvans and wouldn't tell us anything. Nothing true, at any rate. I don't have to tell you, it's dangerous to have a hostile spirit in the room."

That had happened once. One of the spirits had shaken the shelves, breaking half of Veleda's glass bottles before she'd dismissed it. It had almost managed to break through the protective circle she had drawn around Cassia.

Cassia pressed her lips together and stared at the floor. There had to be a way.

Veleda sighed and her tone softened. "Your hopes torture you. If you could be content. The blast of light debilitates the Dracu for long enough that your Huntsmen can gain an advantage."

"My Huntsmen?" Cassia repeated. "Surely they're yours, too."

"Our," Veleda corrected, inclining her head.

"My father has charged me with finding a way to use the ring to its full potential. To be able to...kill outright. Our enemies could attack any day." She looked down at her hands, which were folded in her lap, the ring's dull surface taunting her. "There has to be something. Some way to gain greater control."

"You've pushed yourself until you almost died," Veleda reminded her. "Every battle takes more out of you. Do you want to destroy yourself along with your enemies?"

This was more important than pain. Anyway, she deserved to suffer. This was her penance. For sneaking out as a child and befriending an enemy. For failing to learn how to use the ring so she could end the war. And for what the war had done to her mother.

She met Veleda's eyes. "I'd do anything to wield the ring the way our people need me to."

The Court Seer's brows lowered, and her tone sharpened. "Be careful, Cassia. A statement like that almost sounds like a vow. And I don't know if that's something to which you want to be bound."

Veleda returned to her worktable, clattering her mortar and pestle together louder than before. Cassia stared at her back for a moment, disappointed that the Seer hadn't even tried. She shut the door softly behind her before retracing her steps, careless of her boots splashing through frigid puddles and leaving wet tracks.

"Cassia, wake up!" Rozie shouted.

Cassia sat up in bed to see Rozie in the doorway, her copper hair wilder than usual, her linen nightgown a ghostly slash against the dark. "I heard shouting, and the gates are opening. The watch guards are calling for healers."

Her mind fuzzy with sleep, Cassia asked, "Who was out on night patrol?"

"I think Enora and Thea were on duty."

Cassia was on her feet in a second, the cold floor jarring her into alertness. She followed Rozie down the stairs, both of them rushing headlong for the doors. Fear chilled her as much as the wintry air as they reached the open gates. There was a confusion of shouts and orders as Huntsmen ran out to help the returning party, visible now among the trees. Crossing the bridge over the river, Cassia found herself at the edge of the forest, her eyes scanning the crowd for her sisters. Tension eased in Cassia's chest as Enora's silvery head came into view. Then she saw Thea being carried on a pallet. A swoop of stark fear hit Cassia like a blow. She put a hand to one of the trees, her palm meeting the reassuring feel of bark. For a few horrible seconds, she thought her sister might be dead. Only the silent communion between herself and the tree spirit gave her the strength to remain upright. Then Enora motioned her to come closer, her face strained but not devastated. And she knew Thea was alive.

There were several Huntsmen on pallets, but Cassia went straight to her sister's. Thea's eyes were closed, her forehead beaded with sweat. Thea who could bear more pain than anyone. One of the healers arrived, ordering everyone out of his way. Quickly, he tore the fabric of Thea's trouser leg, exposing an open wound.

Cassia turned her head to the side so the injury was out of view. "What happened?"

"Thrice-damned Dracu," Enora said, her hands fisted. "There was drake poison on his blade. Had to be."

"I have the antidote," the healer said, reaching into a satchel, "but we still need to clean the wound."

Thea's eyes opened, spearing Cassia with a feverish brown glare. "Going to slit that Dracu's throat. I'll never forget his face. Never."

"Don't vow it," Cassia said, anxiety twisting her stomach. A vow was a promise that had to be kept, regardless of the cost, even more so if you vowed to one of the Ancients. Which Thea might be furious enough to do. It was said if you broke a vow to Noctua, your death would be swift.

"I don't need to vow it." Thea took the antidote from the healer, grimacing as she drank its bitter contents in one gulp. "I'll have my revenge."

"You will," Cassia assured her, feeling helpless.

As the healer cleaned the wound, Thea said, "It's all right, Cass, go. I know you can't stand blood."

Cassia's face heated. A warrior king's daughter who couldn't

⁓ 30 ⁓

bear the sight of blood. Only her mother and her sisters knew that shameful secret. It was an aversion that Cassia and her mother had shared.

As Thea was carried to the infirmary, Cassia and Enora followed. Rozie appeared, grabbing Enora's hand. "What happened?" she demanded.

Enora took a breath and put on her elder-sister face, the reassuring one that held all her worry inside. "We were patrolling to the east thanks to a tip from one of the pixies. The Dracu ambush came out of nowhere."

"From under our feet," said Burke, the Second Huntsman, stepping alongside them. He spit on the ground as if his disgust could reach down into the Cryptlands.

Cassia ran her fingers through her hair, conscious that she was in her nightdress and mussed from sleep.

Enora's jaw firmed as she nodded. "They were hiding under leaves and sprang up to surround us. Over a dozen of them to four of us. The grace of Noctua was with me, though. Only a few scratches." She nodded to the Second Huntsman, her expression mischievous. "Burke here is all bruised up."

"Hardly," Burke said, his smooth, deep voice full of scorn. "It would take more than that to put a mark on me."

Cassia watched Burke as he strode through Scarhamm's gates, feeling the familiar blend of admiration and envy she carried for all the talented Huntsmen. And a slight warmth to her cheeks. From all the stories, he was second to none in Dracu kills. The handsome young Sylvan had risen to the position of Second Huntsman at a young age. He was only three years older than Cassia herself.

"What about the trees?" Cassia asked Enora, who walked beside her. Thirstwood should have come to the Huntsmen's aid, using branches and roots to trap their enemies. "Why didn't they protect you?"

Enora grimaced. "We were in Hexdun Valley. The Dracu are setting up a damned encampment. They've never come above so early in the season."

Cassia's breathing shallowed. Hexdun Valley was dangerous: a treeless, rocky expanse bordered by cliffs. The Dracu returned there year after year. An attack on a Sylvan's night patrol could only mean one thing: The spring campaigns were about to begin. The previous year, a hundred Huntsmen had died in the night of their first attack. How many would they lose this year?

"Those monsters are begging for a confrontation," Burke said, his voice rough with loathing.

"And we will oblige," said a voice as deep as the roots of a thousand-year-old oak.

Everyone turned, heads bowing as the Sylvan king emerged from the fortress. He looked forbidding, his dark eyes shining with determination, his antlers as sharp as sword tips.

Enora stepped forward, clasping her hands behind her back. "When, Father?"

"Three days."

"Under a full moon?" Cassia said, hearing the fear in her own voice. The full moon would mean the wards were thinnest, and the Azpians could come through them with greater ease.

The king's eyes fell darkly upon her, and she wished she hadn't spoken.

He made a gesture with his massive hand. "Enough of these small clashes. The wards will be weak, the Dracu overconfident, and the queen will show up in numbers. We take as many heads as we can." He didn't release her from his stare, and Cassia read the silent demand. She had to do more than she ever had before. The ring couldn't fail.

She could not fail.

Cassia nodded to him, her eyes speaking a promise. *I'll be ready.*

3

A Sylvan is fashioned from light and air.
A Dracu is a creature of earth and darkness.
Neither can thrive where the other abides.
—EXCHARIAS, SYLVAN POET

I'M NOT READY.

The thought ran through Cassia's mind as she surveyed the battlefield from atop a cliff overlooking Hexdun Valley, a gray bowl of war-scorched earth collared by low cliffs on two sides, with the immense forest of Thirstwood stretching out to the north and west. She wished she were closer to the trees. She had only to touch the bark and feel the life force running through each trunk to feel calmer. But it wasn't the time.

The Sylvan king, his bone-white antlers soaked in moonlight, moved through the fray on horseback like a graceful nightmare, his longsword as pitiless as a scythe at harvest. Cassia winced, filled with a mix of revulsion and admiration as her father took three Skratti heads in one swing. The Sylvan Huntsmen, well-trained and as vicious as wolves, wove between the Dracu—slashing, skewering, and beheading with efficient strokes.

Her father had been right about the Azpian hordes joining the Dracu queen's side. Their forces outnumbered the Sylvans five to one, a sea of enemies that looked as if it would swallow them whole. Not only were there Skrattis from the deepest recesses of the Cryptlands, but there were also winged imps and pit sprites—noxious clouds that flew into eyes and noses like a stinging pestilence. Enora said it was like having a handful of soot blown into your face. You couldn't see or breathe for a moment, and in that time, an axe or a mace could find your head. If enough of them converged, they could suffocate you.

Cassia watched the grisly, awful dance. The Sylvans favored the elegance of swords, while many Azpians preferred axes, cudgels, and maces—heavy weapons that showed their brute strength but were prone to clumsiness. Enora once shared a gleeful account of an imp who'd managed to get his helmet stuck on backward. The halls of Scarhamm had shaken with laughter, and even the Sylvan king had smirked.

But now there was no mirth, only fear. The odds were so much against them.

She paced the cliff's edge, her leather boots tearing up weeds and mud. When Thea appeared beside her, she jumped, having forgotten her sister's presence.

"Breathe, Cass," Thea said, putting a hand on her shoulder. "Don't spend your energy before the fight."

Cassia took a deep breath. If only she knew how to be calm.

"I should be down there," Thea said in a low tone, her irritation palpable. Her recent injury meant she'd been forced to stay behind. "I hate not being at Enora's back."

Cassia gave her sister's arm a squeeze. Enora and Thea together were more than twice as formidable as they were separate. There was something about how they read each other that worked magic.

"You're watching my back," she pointed out. "When you should be resting."

Thea made a disgusted noise. "I'll rest when the last Dracu falls."

～ 35 ～

Which was probably never. Not if Cassia couldn't slay enemies with the ring. "I'm the one who should be down there. The ring's blast would take out more enemies from up close than from way up here." She was always kept apart, never risking herself the way the Huntsmen or her sisters did. More and more, she was finding that separation intolerable.

"Cass," Thea said sharply. "You know why. We can't risk the Solis Gemma falling back into Dracu hands."

"I know." But it marked her as different. An outsider to her own people.

"You'll get your chance, Deathringer," Thea said. "When you master that thing, you're going to take out more Dracu than the rest of us combined."

Cassia tried to smile, but found little comfort in the words. It was easy for Thea to say, her reputation being established. She'd been described as a violent dance on the battlefield. Cassia once saw her and Enora cut through seven Azpians who were surrounding them. They moved and reacted to attacks in harmony, almost as if they could read each other's thoughts.

Not like Cassia. *Deathringer.* The nickname was empty. She wore a weapon of legend on her finger but dealt no death.

Cassia breathed deeply of the frostbit air, watching silently for her cue. The Azpians' numbers were taking their toll. The Huntsmen were hemmed in, ragged and flagging.

"We keep falling back," Thea said darkly. "They've slipped past our—no!"

Cassia held her breath as the Sylvan king was nearly unseated from his horse by the onrush of two Skrattis and a Dracu. He stabbed one Skratti while kicking the other away, taking a hit to his back that sent him half sprawling. But he managed to keep his

36

seat on Feria, his white stallion, and skewer the Dracu through the throat under his helm.

The Sylvan king's head turned up and toward her, and he lifted a hand. Her signal.

But the battlefield seemed so far away. Too far. What if *that* was the reason she couldn't kill with the ring? She'd resolved to push herself harder. To take risks.

Decision made, she slid down the angled cliff, grabbing weeds and rocks for purchase, the shouts and cries of battle growing louder. Thea screamed her name, probably wondering what fool idea had entered her head. But Cassia was sure of herself, for once. She had to do this.

The Skrattis were bigger than she remembered, their muscles bulging, their tusks as sharp as sword points. They fought with shrieks and cries, their eyes wide, grimacing with pointed white teeth. The Dracu moved with eerie speed, their horns pale blurs in the fray. And everywhere, tiny pit sprites streaked through the air leaving trails of black smoke and white ash.

As she neared the base of the cliff, she spotted a new threat: a dozen or more Dracu closing in on her father, their movements even faster than usual, leaving a trail of Huntsmen in their wake. Their aim was clear: take out the king.

Fear pulsed in her temples, and everything inside her seemed to rush too quickly. The Dracu soldiers moved with implacable purpose, their green eyes glowing in the dark. Some wore helms, but most went bareheaded to show their sharpened horns. She could see strands of hair plastered to their faces.

A prickle of warning sparked at the back of her neck, making her scan for further danger.

From about twenty or so yards away, a Dracu watched her

with unblinking attention, even as he swung his weapon with deadly effect. He moved like water, even more graceful than the best-trained Huntsman, as three Sylvan opponents tried to take him down. Horns flared out of his shaggy dark hair. He wore a leather cuirass, his arms bare, covered in gashes that ran red with his blood. But it was his glowing stare that raised the hair on her nape. She felt his hatred as a physical thing, a pressure in her temples and against her throat. His mouth opened, but his shout was lost in the din.

She put a hand to her neck, grabbing the vial given to her by Veleda, and pulled the cork out with her teeth. She gulped the brew, taking comfort even as she grimaced at the awful taste. With it, her blast radius should be enough to protect her father.

The Dracu hadn't looked away. Was he edging toward her? *Good. The blast will hit you first.*

Her legs shook, but she stood her ground. Where was her father? She did a quick scan, finding him, relieved that he'd kept his seat in Feria's saddle. But something had changed. The Skrattis and imps and Dracu who had been approaching the king were fighting their way toward the base of the cliff. Toward her.

Did they realize who she was? They were almost on her. Out of time.

She called on the gemstone. Every muscle and sinew in her body sent strength toward her hand. The Solis Gemma fought her. It was a battle of wills, hers against the ring. The resistance brought a throbbing ache into her heart until it felt as if it might burst. The first few times she'd made the blast, she'd thought she was dying. But that was the trick. You had to push past that part, then hold, hold. Never release the power too soon. Finally, when the pain was unbearable, the ring yielded.

The blast radiated from her, the pain sending her to her

knees. Amber light blazed like the midday sun. Dracu and Skratti voices howled and screamed. The thuds of enemies hitting the ground was a reassurance that she'd done her job.

That was the fiercest attack she had ever managed, maybe the widest radius as well. If it was not what her father had demanded, if she still hadn't killed with the blast, at least it was more than she'd ever done before. And she might have saved his life. Perhaps for now, it would be enough.

There were Dracu shouts and commands, attempts to regroup, but she had done this dozens of times over the years. No Dracu within range was impervious to the Solis Gemma.

She could barely survive it herself. Every use of the ring took a toll on her. Being so close to the source, she always lost her vision for a few minutes. And the pain in her heart intensified with every blast. She feared one day she would call on the stone, and she would be torn apart by its answer. Maybe, she thought secretly and with shame, that was why the stone hadn't shared its full potential with her. Her own fear made her unworthy.

As she shook with reaction, she reminded herself this was her role. Her duty. Her penance. Her way of making up for mistakes and failures.

The ground rumbled with the hoofbeats of the Huntsmen's horses, the Sylvan cavalry taking full advantage. If Noctua's favor was with them, this would give the Sylvans the advantage they needed. The Azpian hordes would retreat into the cold earth, and she would go back to Scarhamm to her warm bedchamber. There would be a hot bath, spiced nectar to drink, and Thea would tell her how many Dracu had died because of her. Maybe her father would even set her on Feria's back and take her back to Scarhamm in pride and honor.

Perhaps, finally, she had done something right.

39

She felt more than heard a presence beside her. She blinked hard, but her sight was still gone. Her heart did a double beat. She waited for one of the Huntsmen to greet her.

Instead, coarse fingers grabbed her chin in a painful grip. No Huntsman would dare touch her that way. She shrieked and grabbed for her dagger, but found her wrist held. She punched out with her other hand, but that fist was caught, too.

Warm breath tickled her cheek. "Hello, Cassia."

4

It takes cunning to catch a Sylvan.
—Gaxix, Dracu philosopher

His hand clamped over Cassia's jaw, muffling her screams. She kicked and fought as she was pulled along, her feet sliding against the rocky ground, her limbs still weak from using the ring. The ground shifted, and she was yanked into a steeply descending passage, dirt walls tight around her. Her hands scrabbled for a hold, but the enemy held her by her leather breastplate, pulling her into the depths of the earth.

The air was thick with dirt. Her chest ached to burst as her exposed skin was ravaged by rocks and stones, tearing holes in her woolen sleeves and scraping her arms. It was like traveling into a deeply dug grave. The thought pushed her toward panic. Tears streamed from her dust-filled eyes, and her nostrils were blocked by filth.

He was killing her.

Just when she had lost the battle and must take a breath, her knees and palms met a harder surface, and the passage opened around her. She gasped and choked, coughing so hard she gagged. When she felt a hand grab her shoulder, she went for her knife.

He ripped the dagger from her hand. Defenses gone, sight

gone, she scrambled on hands and knees until her feet hit an uneven surface.

As she cursed him, her voice echoed as if she were in a tomb. In a way, perhaps she was. The Cryptlands were so named because they were the burial grounds of an ancient battle, the dead numbering in the hundreds of thousands. Over time, other creatures had taken over these ancient tombs and tunnels, extending them in a labyrinthine maze under the vast reaches of Thirstwood. The trees were above, but they might as well have been stars for all they could do to protect her.

Moments before, she had let herself celebrate a small win. And now she was in enemy hands. Which meant the ring was in enemy hands. She couldn't fathom how bad this was. The magnitude of her mistake.

Her pulse crashed in her ears, making it nearly impossible to think. Would the promise of ransom keep her alive? Thoughts flitted through her mind, churning up options and discarding them. If only she was as fierce in hand-to-hand combat as Enora and Thea, she could kill him without a weapon.

But she *had* a weapon. The Solis Gemma. It shook her to the marrow that this one Dracu hadn't fallen to the blast.

He came near her again. She could smell the brimstone of pit sprites on his clothes. Her hands were grabbed, her wrists bound together with rope.

"Get up," he said, hauling her up by her shoulders.

Once she was on her feet, she took a breath. She could run, but where? When he put his hand to her back and gave a little shove, she moved, her steps uncertain since she still couldn't see.

"They'll hunt you," she said, taking satisfaction in the idea. "My people won't rest until you're dead."

He laughed. "No one will come after you. You could have run

off for all they know. You wouldn't be the first Sylvan to turn tail in battle."

"Liar." If only she hadn't spent the power of the ring, she was sure she could use it to killing effect for the first time.

He spoke thoughtfully, but there was an edge beneath. "That's the worst insult to a Sylvan, isn't it? As if you don't lie."

"We don't." She spat the words.

His voice gained a hard edge. "You lie to yourselves first, so the words sound like truth to your own ears. What's wrong with you, anyway? I've seen drunk imps fly a straighter line."

I will kill him, she told herself. *If I learn how to kill with the ring, he'll be the first Dracu to die by my hand.*

When a cacophony of voices approached, he pushed her into an indentation in the wall. As shapes materialized from the dark, she realized her sight was returning. A procession of creatures rounded the nearest corner, their torches illuminating them. Tusked Skrattis in clanking armor swatted at pit sprites, smashing their bodies into powder and laughing with loud, wet snorts. Winged imps with bulging eyes floated past, followed by lizardlike drakes with fins as sharp as swords on their backs. Though nothing was as scary as the poison on their tongues. She pressed herself tighter against the wall as they slithered past. Finally, the noise of feet and scales faded, and Cassia heard her own panting breaths, her heartbeat fluttering in her throat.

"A merry group of marauders, don't you think?" her captor said. "They're celebrating our win."

"I say again, you lie," she said, turning to face him. With a shock, she saw that it was *him*. The Dracu who had stared at her with such hatred on the battlefield. His features were sharper up close, his glowing eyes even more disturbing.

He took her upper arm and marched her on through the

tunnel. "I didn't hide you back there for my sake. You see, I would only have to say one word: Deathringer. And they would have swarmed you, torn you to pieces with their teeth and claws."

Cassia knew he was trying to scare her, but it had the opposite effect. He could have let those creatures have her and didn't. So, he must not plan to kill her. Yet.

She lost all sense of time as they traveled on, most of her focus on keeping her feet as she encountered roots or rocks or large bugs that crunched underfoot, making her shudder.

"Are you taking me to your queen?" she asked. Perhaps some bargain could be struck.

"You really do wish to die tonight, don't you?" he replied.

She didn't know what he meant. That the queen would kill her? Or *he* would if she kept asking questions? She'd heard that the queen was mercurial, benevolent one minute and ruthless the next. But the Dracu didn't seem less threatening. Given the choice, she would brave the queen.

After a while, the walls changed, growing wider and taller, more finely finished. The tunnel floor shone with clay tiles. Hanging lamps lit the passage, illuminating painted scenes on the walls. One depicted a group of Dracu slaughtering the Sylvan king. The artist had used moonstones for stars and carnelians for the blood of the Sylvans. She shivered at the violent beauty of it.

Finally, the Dracu stopped at a nondescript wooden door and opened it, pushing her in. It was hard to determine the room's size. A few candles were placed haphazardly on the floor, leaving the corners in darkness. Stone slabs like altars were placed along one wall. A trestle table held neat rows of vials, bowls, and bottles. The smells of crushed herbs and blood filled the air, as well as other things Cassia couldn't identify. Crates and boxes were pushed against the walls. A rickety wooden chair sat next to a cooking pot on a tripod over a brazier with glowing coals.

The space reminded her of the Seer's workroom at Scarhamm. But without the benefit of Veleda's reassuring presence, the smells of death and potions alarmed her. Her pulse beat in her temples, urging her to run, but her wrists were still bound, the Dracu's hand at her back.

"The Court Seer's room?" she asked.

"Not exactly. But don't get ideas. Selkolla's services can't be bought. In case you were thinking of bargaining."

A chuckle sounded behind them. "It has been a long time since I struck a bargain. Perhaps it would be interesting."

Cassia turned to the doorway. A woman stood at least seven feet tall, thin to the point of gauntness, with a severe bone structure that was close to beautiful, but not quite. Her eyes were an odd silver—not pale gray like Enora's but the shade of a cold fog swallowed by moonlight. She moved with the grace of a scarecrow, all angles and elbows, her tattered robes sweeping the floor. Cassia stared up in mute wonderment.

The Dracu dipped his head in respect. "Selkolla."

"You succeeded," Selkolla said, a smile curving her lips. "I confess I doubted you, Dracu."

"You shouldn't have," he said coolly. "I told you I'd bring her to you."

"This was planned," Cassia said, swallowing against the fear thickening her throat. She'd assumed her capture had been nothing more than a seized opportunity.

"Everything that happens is part of a plan," Selkolla said. "It is only a question of whose. Let me see your hand."

"A little difficult," Cassia said, her jaw stiff with fear and anger, "as I'm bound like a brace of pheasants."

— 45 —

Selkolla tsked. "Untie her, Dracu. Her ring has no effect on me."

As her bonds were loosened, Cassia looked the woman over. Her ears were hidden by her long hair, but she had no horns, no tail, no wings. Nothing that would mark her as an Azpian of any kind. The ring's blast only worked on creatures who couldn't bear direct sunlight.

"I am not an Azpian," Selkolla said, smiling slightly as if reading Cassia's mind. "Though, like them, I have not seen sun in many an age."

That was odd. Only Azpians lived in the Cryptlands. "Are you a Seer?"

"Seer. Witch. Mother. I have had many names. How does yours suit you?"

Cassia's hands came free, and she stepped away from the Dracu.

"*Deathringer*," the Seer went on. "An ancient title, given to one who felled thousands with the ring. It must be a burden to wear a legend on your small hand."

"It's an honor," Cassia shot back, disliking the woman's knowing gaze.

Selkolla's eyes seemed to glow as she looked at the gemstone. "It is ugly, some say. A simple cabochon, an uncut stone with no brilliance. I have always disagreed." Her eyes met Cassia's. "Unfinished things can be beautiful, don't you agree?"

"Can we get on with it?" the Dracu said. "When the hordes return, we'll have a hard time keeping them from picking their teeth with her."

"In good time, Dracu," Selkolla said, her eyes steady on Cassia. "Look at me, Sylvan king's daughter."

As Cassia stared up into eyes colder than snow under a blue

moon, she found her mind turning sluggish. The Seer inhaled languorously, and a brine-scented wind swirled through the room, making crates and baskets rattle. Murmuring filled the air, disembodied voices speaking a language Cassia had never heard. A summoning? Without runes or candles? She had never seen it done with so little preparation. And the voices! They were like wisps in her mind.

In a few moments, the voices quieted and the wind died. Cassia felt like she'd been swept into a tornado and spit out into an unfamiliar landscape.

"The answer is clear," Selkolla said, turning away. "The girl cannot be harmed."

Silence filled the air for three quickened breaths.

"You're not serious," the Dracu said in a tone of subdued rage.

"The Solis Gemma is an artifact of the Ancients, and its magic is as chaotic and unpredictable as the Ancients themselves. The spirits tell me the gemstone has formed a bond with the Sylvan king's daughter. Its strength is uncertain, but if you kill her, you could destroy the ring and its power."

Cassia stared down at the gem, which glowed with a dull amber light. A bond between herself and the ring? It felt like something she should have known, should have understood all this time.

"Fine," the Dracu said brusquely. "I'll just cut her finger off."

Cassia's head snapped up, her nostrils flaring as she sent a killing look at the Dracu.

Selkolla merely sighed. "A warrior thinks to solve every problem with a sword. I would not suggest taking the ring by force. The spirits say it must be given freely."

The Dracu looked like he wanted to hit something. "That *can't* be true."

As he turned on his heel and prowled, his restless movements shrank the dimensions of the room. Cassia jumped as, without warning, he kicked a crate, sending it crashing against the wall next to her. The wood splintered, its contents spilling and rolling onto the floor around her. A turnip came to rest against her boot.

"A childish display," the Seer admonished.

Cassia silently agreed.

"Fine, then," the Dracu rasped, running his hands through his hair. "Do whatever ritual you need to. Just get the ring."

Cassia measured the distance to the doorway, calculating her chances in the maze of tunnels.

But the Seer moved to the door before she could, saying something about preparations. "Heed me well, Zeru. Do not harm the girl. I'll return soon." She left behind the lingering scents of salt and rain.

It took a moment for Cassia's fatigued brain to register the name.

Zeru.

Her eyes met the Dracu's as raindrops of memory fell over her, chilling her skin. Zeru was the name of the boy.

The boy who had given her the ring.

"What is it?" he asked, his deep voice too smooth, too silky. "Does the sound of my name make the blood drain from those delicate Sylvan cheeks?" He grabbed the rickety wooden chair and dropped into it, his hands folding over his knees. His unblinking attention made her feel like a trapped animal.

She found her voice, speaking slowly, making sure what she said was true. "I don't recognize you."

A mock sadness darkened his eyes. "I gave you a precious gift. And you don't recognize me?"

She could no longer picture the Dracu boy's face in detail.

She'd worked hard to forget. But something in his movements, his eyes, and the way he spoke ignited embers of memory.

He leaned forward to pin her with his glare. "I gave you the ring, along with my friendship." His voice roughened. "The second is gone. But I'm taking the ring back."

5

> To break a Sylvan, merely keep it in the dark long enough.
> —Gaxix, Dracu philosopher

Cassia studied the Dracu. He watched her silently as if waiting for her verdict.

Could it really be him?

She'd tried so hard to forget everything about the boy. Once, she'd obsessed over why he'd given her the ring. Had it been a lark, a trick gone wrong? Had he known it would bring his queen's wrath down upon her? Had he known it would lead to war? But war had hurt his people, too. It didn't make sense. It had been her father who'd finally supplied the answer, one of those rare times he'd come to check on her.

"Your daughter's fretting is slowing her recovery," the healer had said in a hushed whisper as Cassia lay nearby, only half-asleep. "She persists in wondering about...the Dracu. She asks why he would give her the ring. I remind her the Dracu are never to be trusted, but she insists on trying to make sense of it."

"There is no need for a reason," her father had said in a scathing voice. "The ring comes to her by right of fate. It is ours now. That is what matters."

The healer had paused. "Her preoccupation could be seen as

dangerous. She wonders if the Dracu was harmed that night, too. She . . . worries for him."

Cassia had felt the king's wrath vibrating through the chamber. "Worry for an enemy who delights in chaos?" He made a sound of disgust that made her shiver. "He gave it to her in the hopes it would overwhelm her. Kill her. A weaker Sylvan would have been overcome. Tell her to forget him."

A weaker Sylvan would have been overcome. Cassia had clung to those words. That a Dracu's motivations were never pure had been drilled into her by stories. She'd been a fool to trust one. She'd tried to forget the boy.

But he had not forgotten her. How could he? She was the Deathringer, thanks to him. She'd been using his own gift, an artifact of great power, against his people. She had helped kill his kind. She didn't know how many.

His fault, she reminded herself. The moment he'd given her the ring, he'd guaranteed they'd be enemies forever.

"Well?" he said, leaning down to pick up an item from the broken crate.

"How do I know you're the one who gave me the ring?" she asked.

He watched her as he took a loud bite from whatever food he'd picked up. Cassia winced, expecting it to be some disgusting Dracu food, but as he raised it for another bite, she saw that it was only an apple.

"The boy I knew said his name was noble," she added, grasping at any reason to dispute his claim. "He wore fine clothes."

His eyebrows rose, his voice as dry as bone dust. "Those don't fit anymore."

She tried to remember the boy, bringing a hazy picture to mind. "His eyes weren't so green."

His look was a portrait of disgust. "It's pitiful how you try to deny the truth. My eyes haven't changed."

They had, though. The eyes she remembered were mischievous. Playful. The eyes she was staring into now were furious. Vengeful. Accusing. They couldn't be more different.

The Zeru she remembered had been small for his age, his arms no thicker than sticks. The Dracu before her was a fully grown soldier. But his height was no greater than average. His muscles showed a lean strength without bulk, as the boy's might have become with age and training. The twisted horns growing from his head were much the same, except one of them had been broken, ending in a smooth, angled flatness instead of a sharp point. He had a few white scars on his cheeks, which dipped into shadow under his cheekbones, giving him a hungry look. His uniform was well cared for, his boots polished and his sword hilt glinting, but he didn't have any signs or insignia showing rank that she'd expect to see on a nobly born Dracu.

But she had to admit, it could be him.

He hurled the apple core across the room, watching as it exploded against the wall. "Why would I bother lying?"

"I can't fathom. But I'm not stupid enough to trust you at your word."

"Trust isn't something I require from you. You had mine once, and you killed it in one night."

Her lips parted at his gall. She hadn't even accepted his identity, and now he unfairly claimed *she'd* somehow betrayed *him*. "I didn't ask for the ring. *I* was the one nearly torn apart by the queen's vassals."

He leaned forward. "My family lost *everything*." The word seemed to echo off the walls. "And you gained more than you ever dreamed. How you must have gloated when you realized what I'd handed you. The key to destroying us."

If only that were true. She'd have ended this war long ago. She swallowed, watching him warily. "I had no idea what it was."

"You figured it out soon enough."

She hadn't, but her father had. "What did you expect?"

"I expected you to give back the ring when the queen demanded it from you. When I practically begged . . ." He shook his head, a bitter smile curving his lips. "I was so trusting. So innocent. I bought everything you told me about the honesty of Sylvans."

"Sylvans *are* honest," she said. "We despise untruths."

"A Dracu lie is more straightforward than a Sylvan truth." He lounged in the chair like it was some sort of throne, his words edicts. "Your deceit is disguised, covered by a velvet mantle of truth with nothing of substance beneath it. Dressed up with pleasant looks and a soft manner, the better to trick the unsuspecting."

"Nonsense," she said. "You say that to justify your own deceptions. What about me? An important hostage should be taken to the queen. Instead, you keep me here so you can get the ring for yourself. You're the one scheming."

"My schemes, as you call them, are to right a wrong. To fix my mistake." He watched her with calculating eyes. "And speaking of mistakes . . . even Selkolla, as wise and powerful as she is, isn't infallible."

Cassia was struck by his change of expression as much as the change in topic. He was looking at her with too much intent. "What do you mean?"

"The ring." He stood in a rapid movement. "She claims it can't be taken forcefully. I'd like to see for myself."

Before she could react, he'd grabbed her hand.

⌐ 53 ⌐

"No!" she shouted as he grasped the ring between thumb and forefinger. Not only would she die before giving up the ring, but she'd also tried to remove it countless times and—

She screamed in agony. If felt as if her insides were being torn out, her soul yanked from her body.

At some point, he must have let go. She came back to awareness on her hands and knees, her stomach heaving. A part of her wanted to lie down on the cold, packed earth and sleep forever. Her throat tightened. That might yet happen.

She found the strength to sit back on her haunches, pushing the hair from her face.

He stood a few feet away, looking at her with an unreadable expression. "That was either genuine pain," he said slowly, "or you are an excellent pretender."

That was it. Too outraged for reason or doubt, she held up the hand that wore the ring, called on its power, and put all her focus into producing a blast of light. It wasn't much, just enough to brighten the room for one satisfying moment. *A paltry display*, her father might say. But even that should have been enough to make the Dracu double over in pain, being so close to the Solis Gemma.

Her sight returned more quickly this time, probably because the light had not been nearly so bright as usual. As she blinked her eyes open, her enemy was staring back at her. *How in the nine realms of the Netherwhere did this Dracu resist the blast?*

Her curiosity was cut short as he took a step forward. He looked as if he would enjoy his retribution.

Acting on instinct, she snatched something up at random and threw it at him. He grunted as a turnip connected with his cheek, then hit the floor with a dull thud.

Everything went still. His expression turned from bemusement to anger. Cassia's mouth fell open. She couldn't believe she'd done that. Foolish. Ineffectual. Guaranteed to ignite his wrath. He would kill her now, and it was her own cursèd fault.

But then, as he took a step closer, she decided to go down swinging. She picked up another turnip and wheeled it at him. Enjoying his astonishment, she did it again. She threw another and another, launching the projectiles with precision and speed.

"You're not," he said, blocking a turnip with his forearm, his face a mixture of consternation and awe, "seriously trying to kill me"—he deflected another volley—"with vegetables?"

It occurred to her, strangely at this crucial moment, that her sisters might find some humor in this. Instead of bravely fighting with weapons or even fists, she was using root vegetables to keep a trained killer at bay. If she lived to tell this tale, Enora was going to make a story out of it that would bring the great hall down in howls.

Thinking of her sisters gave her courage. Her pulse jumped, and her energy returned. She wouldn't sit here and be insulted, waiting quietly while her fate was decided. What would Thea do? The answer came swift and sure: Thea would kill the enemy.

But Cassia had never killed anyone in hand-to-hand combat. She had no hope of it without an actual weapon.

The door beckoned.

Hang it. She would run.

She launched the last three turnips in a row, sprang up from her crouching position, and leaped toward the door. Her captor rushed after her, but the floor was covered with rolling objects. She heard a thud and hoped that meant he'd fallen.

The tunnel was as dark as spilled ink, but she ran, a glow from her ring providing enough light for each step. If she remembered correctly, the next bend should bring her to a branch in the tunnel. If he didn't see which path she took, she'd have a chance.

～55～

Rounding the corner, she crashed into something spiky, like running into a thornbush. Gasping, she stumbled back and saw the twin glow of Selkolla's eyes. Standing in front of the Seer was a squat creature half Cassia's size. It appeared to be some sort of shrub with eyes like smooth gray pebbles, and branches for limbs. Its moss-covered body of vines and leaves could have passed for a topiary. Roots coiled to the floor to form springy feet that made the creature bounce ever so slightly. Stems and sticks stuck out of its head like hair. Something about it was eerie and unnerving in the extreme.

"Dracu, you are careless," Selkolla chastised as the sound of approaching footsteps came to a halt behind Cassia. "The Sylvan king's daughter would as soon be a meal for a drake, and the Solis Gemma could be lost forever."

"She wouldn't have made it far," he answered, venom in every word.

His raspy breathing spoke of pent-up rage, but the creature in front of Cassia took all her attention. It was a forest-dweller by its appearance. But those were all familiar to her—dryads like her mother who lived in the trees, delicate pixies with lacy wings, sleek-haired naiads and nixies from lakes and rivers, tiny wood sprites that were so small, it was rare to see them. This creature was unlike any of them.

"Have you never seen moss folk, child?" Selkolla inquired in her richly textured voice. She wore a proud expression as she looked down at the shrub.

Cassia had heard of moss folk, of course, but as far as she knew, they hadn't been seen in Thirstwood for hundreds of years. She'd always heard them described as gentle creatures who'd lived in harmony with Sylvans. This sinister plant wasn't what she'd imagined.

She eyed the tunnel, wondering if she could still run.

"I wouldn't advise it," Selkolla said, as if reading her thoughts.

"At least bring me to the queen as a hostage," Cassia said, deciding the risk was worth it if she could escape her furious captor. "My father will pay ransom for me."

"The Dracu queen is as unpredictable as smoke. She might consider ransom. Or she might tear out your neck with her perfect white fangs. As you are Deathringer, my guess is the latter."

"But," Cassia said, faltering, "you said my death would destroy the power of the Solis Gemma."

The silver eyes softened. "Even I can't tell what she may do."

Cassia swallowed. If that was true, going to the queen was possibly a literal dead end.

Selkolla turned back toward her workroom. The moss creature shambled after her with a sound like leaves shaking in the wind.

With no choice, Cassia retraced her steps, conscious of the Dracu on her heels. When they were inside the workroom once more, Selkolla spoke a word, and the candles flared brighter. Cassia had never seen any Seer, not even Veleda, perform such a feat.

As the Dracu started pacing, Selkolla eyed him. "Slow your frantic rush," she said irritably. "You make the spirits themselves nervous."

"I care nothing for the spirits," he all but snarled.

The Seer shook her head. "You burn through the days like they are wood, but you gather none of their heat. Slow down lest you miss what is important, Zeru."

As Cassia heard his name again, something inside her gave in. Acceptance had never felt more like a kick to the stomach. He *was* the grown version of the boy who had given her the ring. Zeru had made her into Deathringer. He hated her for everything she had done to his people. For all she knew, he could ignore Selkolla's warnings and kill her for the satisfaction of revenge.

"What are you willing to do to get the ring back?" the Seer asked.

Zeru's answer was fierce. "Anything."

"Then trust me."

"I trust no one," he said. "I learned that lesson long ago."

The Seer's gaze was knowing. "Your kind despise me for my Sylvan heritage, but you know I speak truth."

Cassia glared at Selkolla, not wanting to accept that she was Sylvan. It was worse, somehow, that one of her captors was from among her own people.

If she went home without the ring, life would be unbearable. Her sisters would pity her. The loss of hope for her people was too horrible to calculate. Not to mention her father's wrath. Worse, his disappointment. Cassia shuddered.

Better to die here than return home without the ring.

Zeru nodded toward the moss creature. "I've heard rumors you are making scuccas."

"Never use that word to me," Selkolla spat, leaning toward Zeru with dangerously bright eyes. "My moss children are not evil spirits. They are peaceful."

Cassia glanced at the collection of vines and moss. She knew how gentle those thorns were. She had never heard of a scucca.

Zeru shrugged. "It makes no difference to me."

Cassia was caught off guard as Selkolla stepped close and took her hand. When she tried to pull away, the Seer said, "Calm yourself. I only mean to show the Dracu something." As the Seer's hand passed over the ring, red filaments sparked around the gold band, with a few small gaps between rays. "This is a mystical attachment," said Selkolla. The filaments caught and held

58

the candlelight. "A bond like this grows stronger over time. If the threads surround the ring, the girl's own life force will be fused with the gemstone's, making it impossible to remove without destroying both."

Cassia couldn't help but be fascinated by the idea of a connection between herself and the Solis Gemma, regardless of this information coming from an enemy. She'd learned more about the ring since her capture than in the ten years she'd worn it.

Zeru made a sound of frustration. "How long before the ring can't be removed?"

Selkolla stared at the Solis Gemma. "I can only guess. Wards and boundaries are thinned under a full moon, but under a new moon, they grow stronger. A month from now, the ring could be bound to her forever."

Zeru glanced at Cassia with thinly veiled impatience. "I see no reason to wait."

Selkolla shook her head, her eyes lit with an unsettling intensity. "This is an old magic at work. It doesn't bend to my spells. But just as every curse has a cure, every bond has a weakness. You need to find out more about this bond and how to break it." She touched her fingertip to one of the filaments and drew it back as if burned. "There is a place, a sanctuary of the Ancients that still harbors their magic. And you are fortunate, Dracu, in that I can send you there."

His jaw set. "Tell me where it is, and I'll go."

There was a short pause before the Seer answered. "Have you heard of a place called Welkincaster?"

6

To outwit Sylvans, merely bide your time.
Their overconfidence will be their undoing.
—Gaxix, Dracu philosopher

Something about the word *Welkincaster* tickled Cassia's memory, but she couldn't place it.

"No," Zeru said irritably. "Is it in human lands?"

The Seer's lips curved in a knowing smile. "Elevate your thoughts."

He turned his brooding glare on her. "I hate riddles."

"And yet you seek to break a bond. What is that if not a riddle to solve?"

"Selkolla." He said it with a warning bite.

The Seer shook her head. "So impatient. It was a place once known to all the folk. The knowledge has faded, but the place still exists. There are two parts to the key that will take you there. I have one. I believe the ring is the other. If I'm correct, Welkincaster is its true home."

Cassia looked between them, her chest so tight she thought her ribs might snap. They wanted to take her to someplace so remote it was unknown to her people. "I'm not going."

"You don't have a choice," Zeru said.

Nausea twisted her stomach. She crossed her arms, trying to hold herself together.

"Careful, Dracu," the Seer warned, her expression less amused. "An Ancient artifact is bent and shaped by whoever is wielding it. The girl is scared, untrusting. Her feelings could affect the Solis Gemma."

"What are you saying?" Zeru asked.

Selkolla paused before answering. "I'm advising you not to test the ring's ability to protect its wearer. These artifacts are known to have protections of some kind. If you plan to take the girl to Welkincaster by force, you might find your plans going awry."

Cassia's head went light with triumph. The Seer's explanation was guarded and vague, but it sounded as if the ring's power might work against them if they tried to make her go.

Selkolla turned to her with a softer expression. "What would persuade you to go on this journey? A bargain perhaps?"

"Nothing," Cassia said succinctly.

The Seer tilted her head to one side. "What has it been, ten years since the ring came into your possession? And still, you haven't mastered it. You have barely scratched the surface of what the Solis Gemma can do."

Cassia swallowed, hating that the Seer knew her weak spots. Worse, she had no defense that wouldn't reveal how perfectly the arrow had hit its mark.

Watching her closely, Selkolla said, "The answers to the power of the ring are in Welkincaster. If you go, you, too, will have the opportunity to find them."

Zeru made a frustrated sound. "And why would I agree to let her search for information on *my queen's ring*?"

Selkolla gave him a pointed look. "Because this is the only way she will go."

"Stop," Cassia said. "I haven't agreed. Why should I? In fact, why should I believe anything you say? You're working for my enemy."

Selkolla's mouth curved in a small, almost sad smile. "I do not lie, child." With a long-fingered hand, she tucked her hair behind her ear, showing its pointed tip. "Using magic for a long time changes a person. But I was born of the trees, and I still feel the connection to my own. Far away in the human lands, but it still grows. When it is someday culled by a human axe, my spirit will go to Noctua to be with the goddess."

Cassia exhaled slowly, a knot easing in her chest at the proof that Selkolla was Sylvan. At least there was one person here who would not lie to her. "And this . . . Welkincaster. It has the answers I need?"

Selkolla inclined her head. "I believe it must. As I said, it is the true home of the ring."

Gooseflesh rose on Cassia's arms. She was inclined to believe the Seer. Because she wanted to? Or because her instincts were leading her to the truth?

"The answers are there," Selkolla assured her. "Whether you find them will be up to you. If you choose to go."

"And if I don't?" Cassia crossed her arms, staring unblinking into the Seer's eerie eyes.

"If you do not," the Seer said, pausing for a moment to shift her gaze to Zeru, then back to Cassia, "you'll remain as you are. In the hands of an enemy, with no more knowledge than you have now."

Cassia let out her breath in a gasp. "You're not going to help me. A fellow Sylvan?"

"I wish I could," Selkolla said, the mark of honesty in every word.

Zeru regarded the Seer with a suspicious look. "You wish you could help *her*? Selkolla, she has used the ring to help kill or maim"—he shook his head—"thousands of Azpians. Despite your origins, the Dracu queen has given you sanctuary all these years. Do you have no loyalty to her?"

"Enough, Dracu," Selkolla said, not backing down. "My allegiance is as it ever was. And you must see that this is the girl's choice, whether you like it or not. If she stays here, her life remains at risk, and so the fate of the Solis Gemma. The gemstone, above all things, must be preserved."

"Why is it so important to you?" Cassia challenged. "You're allied with the Dracu queen. You don't seem to care what happens to us Sylvans. What does the ring matter?"

Selkolla turned to face her. "The Solis Gemma is an artifact of great power. There are precious few relics of the Ancients left. Its fate, along with the fates of your peoples, lie in the choice you now make. Even the spirits cannot see what comes next. Are those not reasons enough to make me care?"

Cassia's stomach grew more leaden with every word. She had always hated the burden of responsibility she carried with the ring. It felt too heavy, meant for someone stronger. Now she had the additional burden of choosing wisely at this moment. The risks were so great, she could hardly bear it.

As the Seer spoke to Zeru in low tones, she blocked them out and tried to think. If she stayed here, she had no real hope of rescue. The Huntsmen might use the hounds to track her. They might already know where she'd entered the Cryptlands. But it was unlikely they would risk entering, even for her. Her sisters might want to, but her father would never sanction it. Sylvans who went into the Cryptlands did not come out. But...if she could escape, if she watched and waited until there came an opportunity to outwit her captor, and if the Ancients were on her side and she made it through the tunnels unharmed and actually found a way above, if she could find a way up into Thirstwood, the trees would protect her as she made her way home.

But.

She still wouldn't know how to use the ring. She had improved her performance in the recent battle, but by how much? Only a little. And she'd had to get so close to the enemy that she'd been captured. Maybe she would do a little better next time. And the time after. But if her father found out she had been offered this chance and refused? A shudder shook her spine. Scarhamm's walls would tremble with his wrath!

Wishing she knew what to do, she opened her eyes to see a poisoned glare aimed her way. Zeru stared at her as if he could intimidate her into choosing as he wished.

If only she could say, "I choose to go home." To watch his face fall as Selkolla helped her escape. She could imagine Zeru's rage, taste the satisfaction of it, and the relief she'd feel at being home again.

But that would be favoring the safe path, the well-worn path. She was choosing a well-lit garden over the night-dark woods. Why? The last time she'd risked everything, sneaking into the forest at night as a child, she'd brought home the ring. Yes, she'd suffered for it. But this was about her people. Her role in her family. Her duty.

If all went well, she'd return home as a victor with a bounty to share. A warrior triumphant. There might be a revel in her honor. Her father might even...praise her.

"Sylvan," Zeru said, and her eyes snapped back to his. "Do you plan to dither until I die of boredom?"

"Is that a possibility?" When he merely glared, she squared her shoulders. There was only one decision that made sense. "You offered to bargain. If you agree to my terms, I'll go."

"*I* didn't offer," he said, his eyes narrowing on her. "What terms?"

She thought quickly. Bargains were a Sylvan tradition tied to their reputation for honesty. Everyone knew you could agree to a Sylvan bargain confident that the offer was at least truthful, if not beneficial. Terms could be negotiated, of course, but once struck, they were not agreements adhered to by whim or choice. The Ancients always found a way to make you keep your word. Everyone understood this, even Azpians. Which meant Zeru should keep to his side.

She could demand that he leave her unharmed. But the Dracu saw the retrieval of the ring as his path to redemption. She didn't think he'd risk killing her. No, it was getting home that concerned her. Without clear terms, he could hold her indefinitely, unable to take the ring but unwilling to let her go. This new location could become her prison.

She spoke carefully. "If I use the ring to go with you, you have to vow to return me home unharmed before the next full moon."

"No," Zeru said without hesitation. "I don't know anything about where we're going or how long it will take to get the ring."

Selkolla put a steadying hand on his arm. "Zeru, this task will not be accomplished without compromise... Perhaps an adjustment of the terms?" She turned to Cassia. "Three months?"

"One," she said firmly.

Zeru shook his head. "I won't make a vow I can't keep. I'm not ready to surrender my spirit to Noctua just yet."

Cassia felt a pulse of relief. He knew the sacredness of a bargain. Once agreed upon, he would hold to the terms.

"One month," she repeated, digging in.

"And if I don't have the ring by then?" he snarled.

"Even so." She stood her ground, though her legs shook.

"And that part about being 'unharmed,'" he said. "Suppose that killing you is the only way to get the ring? That part of the bargain will tie my hands."

Selkolla sighed. "You are your own worst enemy, Dracu. You have gained a concession from her. Go to Welkincaster. Find a way to remove the ring before the month is over. If you do not, you do not deserve it."

He looked as if he wanted to smash things, his eyes a green fire in the dim room. "Fine. Do you need a blood pact, Sylvan, or is my word enough?"

"Blood," she said, though that was an old practice, seen as unnecessary when words were binding enough. But if he was offering to bleed, she wouldn't say no.

He pulled a dagger from a sheath at his waist. She turned her head away before she could see the blade meet flesh. "If you go with me *willingly*, I swear to let you return home by the next full moon."

"Unharmed. Say it."

"I swear to let you return home, unharmed by me or from any orders of my own, by the next full moon. You can't refuse that addition, Sylvan. If you die by your own stupidity, I won't be held responsible."

She couldn't think of an argument against that. She could be hurt through no fault of his, and it was natural of him to adjust the wording to protect himself.

"Fine." Swallowing her misgivings, she put out her hand. "Give me your dagger."

He handed it over with almost insulting casualness. Didn't he worry for even a second that she might turn his weapon on him?

She took the dagger, noticing the handle had a fox embossed on the steel, and the sides of the hilt were crafted to look like feathers. It was a beautifully made weapon, more ceremonial-looking

⁓ 66 ⁓

than practical. But the blade was sharp as she cut her palm. "As you've made a blood oath not to harm me, and to return me home to Scarhamm by the next full moon, I'll go with you to Welkincaster willingly."

Zeru took the dagger back, wiped the blade on the dark fabric of his sleeve, and sheathed it. She didn't miss the flare of triumph that briefly shone in his eyes.

Selkolla went to her worktable and gathered some herbs, pressing them into Zeru's hand and then Cassia's. "For healing," she said.

The sting lessened almost instantly.

"Now what?" Zeru asked, casting the herbs aside.

Selkolla pulled something from inside her robes and held it up. Dangling from a finely wrought gold chain was a flat metal disc inlaid with precious stones. "An amulet. An artifact of the Ancients I have held in my keeping for a very long time."

Zeru stepped forward to examine the disc. The Seer hesitated briefly before placing it in his hand. "It is yours now. Wear it."

He placed the amulet around his neck, his eyes thoughtful as he let it fall into place below his collarbone. "What do I do with it?"

"Think of the amulet as the lock," Selkolla said, gesturing to where it rested over his leathern breastplate, "and the Solis Gemma as the key."

The Dracu and the Sylvan looked at each other. Years of enmity brimmed in his eyes, and Cassia knew her expression was full of the hatred she felt for him.

"The ring." His brusque tone raised her hackles, but her eyes were on the amulet. Up close, she could see the precious stones formed two great wings.

"Is it that difficult to figure out?" Zeru gestured to the center of the amulet, where a circular indent clearly matched the ring in size.

She was tempted to see how the stone could bruise his face. She lifted her hand and pushed the amber cabochon into the amulet's hollow with enough force to make him grunt. There was a click as metal met stone, a flash of light, and a scent that reminded Cassia of a cool grove on a summer's day.

She dropped her hand and turned to see tree roots appear in the air before her. They were bluish-green and transparent, as if they did not truly exist in this realm. Their ends moved like feelers, pulling apart to create a large oval—a swirling glow of warm light with a darker portion in the center.

"A doorway," Selkolla explained.

It was the size and shape of a full-length looking glass, with glowing roots framing it. But instead of a reflection, a forest of dark green shimmered as if seen through water. Relief surged through her. If Welkincaster was in Thirstwood, she would surely be able to find her way home. The trees were loyal. They'd protect her.

But looking closer, the leaves in this forest were all green, not bloodred like many of the trees in Thirstwood. And their trunks were twisted, their lower branches barren. It wasn't her forest at all. Suddenly, she didn't want to step through into this other wood. It was too different. Unknown.

But Zeru had no patience for her hesitation. "Go," he barked, the threat implicit.

A strange feeling came over her as she passed through the doorway, like she'd stepped through a waterfall without getting wet. Her feet crunched on a bed of fallen branches and pine needles, her nose filling with the scents of soil and peat. She turned to look back as Zeru stepped through behind her, and the doorway dissolved in a flash of light.

7

Azpians crave darkness and small spaces.
To be in air and sunlight is their greatest
agony.
—EXCHARIAS, SYLVAN POET

As Cassia stared at the place where the doorway had been, she put her hand to a tree trunk, craving something solid and familiar. The rough bark helped ground her, but she couldn't sense these trees the way she could in Thirstwood. It made her nervous and a little hollow inside. This forest was another unknown. And there was an eerie sense of waiting, as if the forest had eyes that watched them in silence.

She glanced at Zeru, his face a paler blotch against the greenish black of the forest. Though the moon was full, scant light made its way through the canopy. There was a golden glint where the amulet hung around his neck. If she placed the gemstone in it, would it open a doorway back? It would be comforting to know she had an exit. But an exit to where? Back to the Cryptlands, most likely. Anyway, that wasn't the problem at hand.

There was no discernible path, no direction that looked safe or inviting. She turned in a circle until she spied a break in the growth. Zeru must have seen it, too. Knife drawn, he pushed his way through the tall underbrush. As she watched him disappear among the trees, her lips parted at this evidence of his arrogance. He just assumed she would follow.

As he moved farther away, she could breathe and think. The forest was her realm, not his. She didn't have to trudge along after him, following his every order like one of her father's hounds. She could search for answers on her own, maybe even lose him in the woods. If the Ancients were on her side, he'd be hopelessly lost while she found . . . whatever it was she was looking for here.

She threw herself into the undergrowth. The plants were dry, not as thick as they first appeared. This might not be her forest, but it was similar enough that she moved with efficiency. In a minute, she was yards away and widening the gap with every step.

Rustling was followed by a howl of rage. She moved faster.

It was hard work moving through the thick plants, especially in the gloom, but Sylvan instincts, her experience in the woods, and a hearty dose of fear of the Dracu who was crashing after her made her keep pushing on. She had a flash of memory: running through Thirstwood with her hand in Zeru's. Now she was running from him.

After a few minutes, the noises behind her faded. She'd lost him.

Gradually, the trees grew farther apart, and morning light filtered in, though everything seemed strangely gray. Twisted pines and oaks gave way to a stunted, near-dead orchard. Past the withered apple and pear trees, a dilapidated stone wall begged to be explored.

She had made it . . . somewhere.

The celebratory feeling lasted until she heard a clearing throat. Her breath caught as she turned. Zeru stood in the shadows at the edge of the tree line, leaning against an elm. Her shoulders slumped. He must have been moving with equal speed along another path, and they'd both ended up here. She was on the balls of her feet, ready to run, when she realized he wasn't moving.

Dawn. The rising sun would prevent him from leaving the shadows. She let out her breath. Then, deeming it safe, she smiled.

His face registered the taunt with a silent, angry glare.

Matching his stance, she leaned against a withered pear tree. "Good morning."

His eyes went heavy-lidded. "Your sense of safety is misplaced."

"I don't think so." Either he would step out into the light and fall to the ground writhing in pain or he'd have to stay in the forest until dark. The sky was brightening by the moment. She'd have a whole day to explore without him. She lifted her face. "Looks like it'll be sunny today. Sylvans can survive for weeks on sunlight and water alone, you know."

"Good for you," he muttered, levering himself off the tree. His hands were fisted, but still he didn't step forward.

She knew it was ill-advised to continue taunting him, yet she couldn't help herself. It was too delicious, this reversal. She watched the angle of the sun with anticipation.

He was watching it, too, his eyes flicking from the growing brightness to her. "If you're hoping to slit my throat while I'm laid low, think again."

She raised her brows, disappointed in herself that she hadn't thought of that. "What I'm thinking is, I don't need to stand around while you hover at the edge of your greatest fear."

His jaw firmed. "I am not...hovering."

She took a few steps away, keeping him in her peripheral vision. "I'll leave you to it."

He slammed his hand against the tree so hard it made Cassia wince. "You are not going to explore while I'm trapped here."

"It seems like that's exactly what I'm going to do."

With an angry noise, he stepped out of the trees.

She gasped. She hadn't expected him to do something so stupid.

He tensed as sunlight fell on his face, the warm rays of dawn unhindered by shadows. She waited for him to cry out, to fall.

They blinked at each other.

He breathed audibly as he lifted his hands, looking at one, then the other. "It was a theory," he said in awestruck tones. "Your ring never affected me. I always wondered, but..." He shook his head. "I can walk in sunlight." He said the words reverently, like it was something impossible that had come to pass. And then he chuckled, low and satisfied. It made her stomach turn.

"No," she muttered. The one small advantage she'd had, taken away. She squeezed her eyes shut, wondering if the Ancients were against her.

When she opened her eyes, he was moving toward her, each step more relaxed and self-assured than the last. She looked around for an escape.

"Please give me a reason to hunt you down," he said.

She crossed her arms. She would not run. She waited for him to grab her, yell at her, something.

He looked her over, then nodded in the direction of the wall. "You first."

Shakily, she led the way, telling herself at least she'd had a few minutes out of his company.

The stone wall was more decorative than protective, perhaps, with an arched opening leading into a courtyard. Clay pots littered the area, some broken, others full of weeds. Spindly trees and climbing plants poked between the flagstones, twisting this way and that as if searching for sun. A haze hung in the sky like a blanket of cobwebs. Maybe that was the reason Zeru had not fallen from the sunlight.

Or maybe there was something very wrong with this place.

On the other side of the courtyard, a set of steps led to a building covered in vines. It was so overgrown, it took a second to take in the extent of it. To Cassia's surprise, it appeared to be a castle with four towers, each topped with what once might have been gold spires. The haze in the air must have prevented them from seeing it from a distance.

Zeru climbed the steps, pulling away vines to reveal a set of double doors, each bearing feathers made of copper, silver, and gold. Together, the two doors made a beautiful pair of wings. He grabbed one of the handles and the door opened with a grudging creak.

Cassia looked around. Again, she considered running. But if Welkincaster held answers, they seemed likely to be inside this place.

Following Zeru, she found herself in a dark entrance hall. Dust filled her nostrils, gray light creeping through gaps in shutters that covered the windows. Doors led off into dark rooms and a staircase led up to a balcony. She could barely make out a chandelier hanging from the rafters. The flooring looked elegant underneath its layer of dust, wooden inlay painted copper and gold in a diamond pattern. A cracked mirror hung above a massive hearth.

Cassia headed for the stairway. Zeru followed on her heels.

On the second floor, they found various empty rooms including a ballroom darkened by shutters. On the third floor was a portrait gallery. Cassia stopped to stare a painting of a distinguished-looking man in yellow robes. Sprouting from his back were dark wings that looked like those of a bat, with a claw at the end of each segment. She shuddered—they reminded her of an imp. Every painting seemed to show the same type of creature, a winged being of unknown variety.

"We shouldn't be here," she murmured, voicing a bone-deep uneasiness.

Zeru's voice close behind made her jump. "You sound scared."

She opened her mouth to deny it but found she couldn't. Of course she was scared. Turning away, she continued down a hallway, the floor creaking with her every step.

"I have spent only a few hours in your company," Zeru said as he walked next to her, his footsteps somehow making far less noise than hers, "and already I have no fear of you. I expected the Deathringer to be a hardened soldier, as cold and efficient as the rest of the Huntsmen, her senses honed by training and battle." He gave her a once-over, insultingly dismissive. "It seems all you have is the ring. And even that doesn't work on me."

She considered whether she was fast enough to grab his dagger and skewer him before he could stop her. His words stung. She reminded herself she'd been abducted, subjected to the magic of a powerful Seer, and sent to a strange, neglected landscape with no idea how she'd get home, all in one night. But that did not change the fact that she had done little to try to best this enemy. What would her father think? He would expect her to show strength and cunning, to make the enemy fear her. If only she knew how to do that.

"There's something wrong with you," she said, striding after him as he continued on. "Every other Azpian falls under the ring's blast."

"That 'something wrong' has saved me every time you used

the ring." His mocking laugh grated on her nerves. "For all the fear your name brings, you have nothing without the ring."

Give me a dagger, and then we'll see, she thought. What he didn't know about her was that she never gave up. She might not be Thea, able to kill with her bare hands, but her determination was boundless. She would let him underestimate her, she decided, and wait for her chance.

At the end of the third-floor hallway, they found a dilapidated set of stairs. Treading carefully, Cassia reached the top to find a door to a tower room with windows facing the barely visible outlines of the forest. A wooden four-poster bed dominated the chamber, its mattress bare but for a blanket of dust. She stepped in and looked around, sneezing as dust assaulted her nose. She turned in time to see the door slam behind her. She grabbed the handle and pulled. Locked? She wasn't strong enough to budge it. She pounded on the door. "Dracu, you are not leaving me here!"

"It seems that's exactly what I'm going to do," he replied, his voice muffled by the door.

Furious, she pounded on the door until her hands ached. Until it was clear he had gone. She slumped against the door. She'd let her guard down, and this predicament was her own cursèd fault. If he kept her locked in here, she'd never find a way to master the ring's full potential. She needed to be able to move freely about the castle to search for information. Without any immediate ideas for how to achieve that, she assessed her surroundings.

In a word, disgusting. Cobwebs everywhere, dust an inch thick. Something in the corners that might have been animal droppings. She moved to the window. The rusty latch gave way, and fresh air poured in. The stone sill was wide enough to sit on, so she hopped up, putting her head outside. The drop was vertical and far. She eyed the moldy curtains. Even if she tied them together, they wouldn't be long enough to make a rope. For a while, she watched the scene from the window, noting the twisted, sickly trees and wishing she could speak to them, ask them for help.

The click of a key turning in the lock came a second before her door opened. As Zeru strolled in, a pulse of fear tore through her, making her fingers and toes tingle, the bargain not to harm her insignificant with the open window at her back.

"Please, Sylvan," he said, leaning against one of the bedposts, "you'll only dash your brains out. Surely it hasn't come to that."

"I wasn't going to jump." She gave him a dark look and hopped down. "Worried I'll scratch the Solis Gemma?"

"If it could be scratched, I'm sure you'd have managed it by now. Can you read?"

She blinked at the unrelated question. "Of course I can. I had excellent tutors."

"Can you read Runic?" he asked. "I understand that's a requirement for higher born Sylvans."

She frowned. Having good tutors did not mean she'd been the best pupil. "A little."

He gave her a knowing look. "A very little, I'd say, by the look in your eyes. What about Old Sylvan?"

She eyed him suspiciously. "Yes. My father insisted his daughters be able to read the old myths and histories. Why?"

"I found a library." Without another word, he strode out.

It took a second to sink in. That could be what Selkolla had sent them to find! She hurried after him, down the tower stairs, along third-floor hallways until she caught up to him at the foot of another set of twisting stairs that led to a chamber filled with books.

She had a sudden, quicksilver pulse of hope. Information about the ring could be in this very room! She marveled at the floor-to-ceiling shelves crammed with scrolls and codices. Scarhamm had a library with dark-paneled walls, cubbies jammed full of maps and scrolls, and a dented wooden table for reading them. Her father's purpose there was always practical: researching his enemies and planning how to destroy them.

But this was cozy and inviting. An upholstered seat stretched below the arched window. White and gold side tables held dusty piles of books, and a red velvet chair sat in one corner. She turned in a slow circle, taking in the shelves. "It'll take months to look through all these," she murmured.

"That's why you're here." Zeru was studying the room with a look she could only describe as acquisitive awe, as if all of this belonged to him. "By the glint in your eye, Sylvan, I can see I need to spell out what I expect from you."

She was growing tired of his contemptuous tone. "Yes, please tell me what a person is supposed to do in this room. Juggling? Winemaking? Perhaps some light swordplay?"

He ignored her. "I expect you to read every day until it grows so dark that your Sylvan eyes fail you, and then I'll ask for your report. When I ask if you've read anything relevant to the ring, you'll answer me truthfully. It'll be a yes or no question, with no room for prevarication or Sylvan deception. If you say yes, I'll look through what you've been reading, and I'll find the information myself."

"Oh, I see." She shook her head at his arrogance. "What if the book is in Old Sylvan?"

"Then you'll translate it for me."

She leaned in the doorway, crossing her arms. "And if I refuse? You can't hurt me. Your own word prevents you."

He dropped into the red chair, picking up a book from the table next to it. "Then I'll consider how best to strike at others you care about." He turned a page. "Your family, perhaps."

Protective rage roared up inside her. But his threats were empty. He couldn't get at her family.

"You can't force me to share information," she said, clipping each word out like a poisoned dart. "You can ask, but I won't answer."

He watched her for a minute, his frustration palpable. A muscle moved in his cheek. "Then go." He motioned her out, returning his attention to the book. "You're no use to me."

You're no use to me.

Her eyes burned as she remembered her father saying those words. *A Deathringer who brings no death is no use to me.*

She looked down at the Solis Gemma, which sat dull and innocuous looking on her finger. It was the reason she'd come here. The Dracu was making no concessions, but what did that matter? She'd find a way to take what she needed. In her own time, in her own way, despite his insults.

Blinking hard, she walked to a shelf. Grabbing two books at random, she stalked back to the door, preparing to sweep out.

Zeru spoke sharply. "You're not leaving with those. They stay here."

She turned slowly to face him, meeting his eyes and hoping he could see the fury in hers. "You expect me to sit here with you and read? As if it's nothing."

He stared back, green glare implacable. "If I can do it, so can you."

She swallowed her anger. It was a challenge. A test of her strength. She could not show weakness.

She went to the window seat and made herself comfortable, or as much as possible with tension tightening the muscles of her spine. The book was written in Old Sylvan. She relaxed a fraction. Maybe it had the answers. Regardless, she would get to leave this place soon.

8

> Sylvans have no sense of history. They live in the present,
> flitting among flowers and sipping morning dew.
>
> —Gaxix, Dracu philosopher

Hours later, Cassia set the book down and rubbed her eyes. The meandering history had a few references to artifacts and famous weapons of the Ancients, but she'd seen nothing about the Solis Gemma. She looked up at the walls, the shelves so full they were practically bursting. This would take an age. Her stomach rumbled, reminding her she hadn't eaten since the night before. She'd sat in the great hall with her sisters, barely able to eat a few bites because she'd been so nervous about the coming battle. It seemed so long ago now.

Zeru said without looking up, "What have you found?"

She wondered if his tone would improve if she threw the heavy codex at his head. "Nothing. I'm going to look for food."

He slammed his book closed, looking up with a suspicious glare. "You're not going anywhere alone."

She reminded herself he couldn't hurt her. "You don't dictate my movements, Dracu." She was halfway down the stairs when she heard his footsteps behind her. As she pulled the entrance door open, she felt him crowding her back and turned to face him. "We need food and water. Surely you can see that."

His face was drawn in hard lines. "A brief search for water, then."

Not needing any more encouragement, she descended the steps to the courtyard, Zeru keeping pace. As they went through the archway into the withered garden, the bare fruit trees mocked her hunger. The haze in the sky made it seem later than early afternoon. Shadows seemed to pool in corners. There was a strange quality to the emptiness, as if creatures might be hiding, ready to spring out at any moment. She reminded herself they didn't know anything about Welkincaster, and she should remain on guard.

"Aren't you hungry?" she asked as they crunched along the path. She hated how close he kept to her, crowding her, forcing her to remain on edge.

"Land folk don't need to eat every day," he scoffed. "A Dracu can go a week without food. You told me yourself a Sylvan can go longer with only water and sunlight."

"That doesn't mean I want to." She wagered he was as hungry as she was. "There's not even a kitchen here," she added, following the path beyond the archway. "No storage rooms for food."

"Stop talking about food."

She smirked. "I'd love a mushroom pasty." She watched his nostrils flare, and added, "Or maybe a spit-roasted boar seasoned with parsley and thyme."

He looked sidelong at her, annoyance darkening his eyes. "You are pathetically obvious."

"Grilled pheasant," she went on cheerfully. "Honey cakes. Do Dracu like sweets?"

"No," he said through gritted teeth.

She leaned toward him. "Your face when I said *honey cakes*. I bet you like those the most."

He said nothing, but she was getting to him. She could tell.

She smiled, considering how far to push him. Did this work toward her plans or against them? Tormenting him was too satisfying. She touched a branch on one of the fruit trees. "An apple would be welcome right now."

"So you can throw it at me?" Zeru said. "There's nothing here. We're going back."

But she'd caught sight of something. "Look." She pointed to where a silvery glow wove between trees. "A river?"

Zeru paused, stepping forward. "We must have walked past it in the dark."

His eagerness was apparent, and she shared it. She imagined drinking, bathing, washing her clothes. She quickened her pace, but with his longer strides, Zeru soon left her behind. His form was swallowed by a mist that thickened into fog. She slowed her steps, treading carefully.

She didn't see Zeru until she nearly stepped on him. Or rather, his hand, which was clinging to a tree root, his fingers white. The rest of him was somewhere below, presumably, lost in the mist. *He must have stepped over a cliff.* She would have, too, if he hadn't gone first. Pulse thudding jerkily at the near miss, Cassia knelt, waving the mist away with one hand. It dispersed in little swirls, enough that she saw Zeru's ashen face turned up toward hers, its harsh lines drawn tighter in shock.

He was dangling off an edge, but an edge to what? Maybe the river had carved a gorge into the land, and its waters were rushing below him. She couldn't hear it, though. The place was eerily free of sound.

Even Zeru made no noise. His eyes were wide as they stared

up into hers. And it occurred to her: She could...let him fall. She would be free. She had wished for revenge, and here it was, wrapped like a gift. She only had to walk away.

Then again, if there was a river below him, it could break his fall. "Can you swim?" she asked, wondering if there was deep water in the Cryptlands. She had never thought about it.

His eyes were wide as they clung to hers. "Not a river. Nothing below me but sky."

She watched his fingers as they gripped the roots, waiting for one of them to slip.

He grunted in frustration or pain. "You're going to let me fall?"

She reminded him of his own words. "Someone once told me, 'If you die by your own stupidity, no one else is responsible.'"

"You're misquoting me," he said, but his voice lacked its usual contempt. He seemed to be struggling to breathe.

She took a seat on the rocky ground, crossing her legs.

"This must be a great spectacle for you," he snarled. Though he tried to cover it, he sounded afraid. He might have realized that his fingerhold on the roots was not enough. She was glad, once again, that he had rushed headlong ahead of her.

"Can't you pull yourself up?" she asked. Dracu tended to be stronger than Sylvans.

"Too slippery. The mist."

She had an impulse, a natural tug of conscience, to help him. Her mother used to tell her, *"If you see a creature in need, you should always try to help."* She had probably meant forest creatures, though, not Dracu. Not an enemy.

"Cassia." Zeru's eyes met hers with a force she could feel. "You don't have to come any closer. Just grab a vine and throw it to me."

"I'm not afraid of the edge," she snapped. "I have no reason to help you." But it occurred to her that she did have leverage. She stood and searched until she found a sturdy vine that held when she tugged on it. She returned to Zeru, staring down at him with the vine in her hand. "However, in the spirit of Sylvan generosity, I'll offer you a bargain. If you vow to let me and the ring go forever, I'll help you up."

His terse reply came without hesitation. "I can't do that."

He hadn't even considered the offer. "Maybe you need more time to consider your situation here."

His eyes closed. After a moment of silence, his voice came out harsher than before. "If you have any scrap of feeling, you will tell my family what happened to me."

"I don't see how I could." She heard the hoarseness of her own voice. She hadn't thought about him having a family, and how they might feel if he died.

His eyes opened. "Next battle. Just tell . . . any Dracu. They'll get word."

Cassia nodded. "I can do that."

He stared at her, and she stared back. At any moment, he would lose his grip and be gone. She waited for some lie, some manipulation to try to get her to help. But none came.

"Keep your word, Sylvan."

It was said in a breath, no more. But it acted on her like the shock of jumping into the Scar River on a cold morning. Maybe it was the fact that he'd mentioned his family. Maybe it was some flaw in her character that made her weak to an enemy's distress. She didn't know why, but she found herself throwing the vine. He grabbed instinctively, his palms wrapping around the thick cord. He slid before the vine jerked taut. Cassia only had to pull him forward a few inches before he was able to get a better hold on the edge. When his upper body gained solid ground, he hauled himself to safety. His eyes opened, meeting hers. His skin was waxy, his dark hair and clothing a stark contrast to the frothy mist all around. He was breathing heavily, and she was, too.

Finally, he spoke. "We're on a cloud."

That didn't make any sense, so she turned to peer down, but it was impossible to see past that white veil. "I don't know what you mean." She moved toward the edge, her heart slamming her rib cage.

"Have you no sense?" he growled.

But she was careful to keep her knees on solid ground. Finally, she saw over the edge. Her mouth went slack. Sky. Nothing but sky. An endless wasteland of sky. Birds wheeled about below them, a mountaintop in the distance. It was breathtaking and awful. Her head spun. It did appear as if there was nothing beneath them. And this mist... it was like...

"We are on a cloud," she confirmed. Slowly, carefully, she crawled backward.

When she found her feet, Zeru was glaring around as if he wanted to destroy everything he saw. "I'm going to kill Selkolla."

"I don't think you can kill your way out of this." Cassia turned in a circle, looking back to the abandoned castle—an abandoned castle in an impossible realm. "Welkincaster," she said, testing the word and the idea. "The welkins." She put a hand to her head. "How could I forget?"

"What are you babbling about?" He toyed with the hilt of his dagger, some of the color returning to his cheeks.

"Don't you remember?" She gestured all around them. "The stories? A sky realm of floating kingdoms made by the Ancients. I told you when we—"

When we were children, she'd been about to say. When he was her friend. When she used to tell him stories.

She hated that she remembered that. More, she hated that he *knew* she remembered.

"So." His eyes narrowed. "You didn't forget me."

"Not entirely," she admitted, turning her back on him. "Not for lack of trying."

"Wait," he said as she moved toward the trees. "We should follow the mist. It marks the edge of this...place. Then we'll know the perimeter." He hesitated, his eyes sliding to hers and away. "Maybe we'll find something to eat."

Was that a small concession? Her stomach was so painfully empty, she would take it.

They walked along a narrow area between forest and mist. With careful steps, they traversed the entire edge of the cloud in less than three hours. It was small, smaller than she'd thought when they first arrived. They must have arrived in the center of the forest. The trees felt too close together, the shadows too thick. There was a sense of waiting that she couldn't understand. She found herself turning her head, trying to catch things out of the corner of her eye. When she reached out to the trees, they shivered like neglected things that had gone too long without touch. There were no flowers, no evidence of new growth. An air of stagnancy permeated these woods. A heavy sadness crept into Cassia's heart. The forest was ailing. She wished she could help.

Zeru was silent the entire time. She wondered if he was still rattled by his brush with death or if he was more thrown off by this place than she was. Things were certainly not going as he'd planned.

As they returned to the garden of withered fruit trees, she stopped in her tracks. A flash of bright color caught her eye.

An apple. A red, ripe apple.

"Was that there before?" She pointed and turned to Zeru.

He swept the orchard with a narrow-eyed glance. "I don't think so."

"How could we have missed that?" It easily stood out among the gray-brown branches.

Zeru reached up and plucked the apple from the tree. He sniffed it, examined it, then shoved it at her. "Take it."

She took the apple, regarding him warily. Why didn't he want it?

He left her and went up the steps. "Hurry. We've wasted enough time."

Cassia weighed the apple in her hand, wondering if giving it to her was an act of generosity or sabotage, and whether it was worth the risk. Her hunger won the argument. She took a ravenous bite. The fruit was sweet and delicious. She chewed thoughtfully as she entered the castle.

And almost ran into Zeru's back. He had stopped inside the entry hall, his drawn dagger catching rays of sunlight that slanted in from between the shutter slats.

"You dare threaten me in my own home?" a voice demanded.

Cassia saw green and brown, the colors worn by Huntsmen, and her heart did a double beat.

But the person wearing them wasn't a Huntsman, or even a Sylvan. And he did not look happy to see her.

9

> There is nothing so beguiling,
> so deceptively charming,
> as a Dracu with a plan.
> —Excharias, Sylvan poet

A SMALL MAN STOOD IN FRONT OF THE HEARTH, HIS fists raised in a defensive posture. He was wearing a pointy green cap atop a shock of unkempt white hair, his snowy beard flowing down over a brown tunic and coming to a point past his knees. His nose was red, his eyes a brighter red, and his cheeks...well. Cassia wondered why his hat was not also red.

"You dare enter the sacred realm," he said, his eyes shifting restlessly around the room. "Intruders!" he shouted as if there were someone to hear him.

Cassia put the apple in her pocket, stepped forward, and offered a bow. "We didn't mean to intrude. We were sent here against our will. Or at least I was. We mean no harm."

She went to step closer, but Zeru's arm came up to stop her. "It's a kobold," he said. "They're small but dangerous."

Cassia swallowed. She had never seen a kobold, but she knew they were Azpians, creatures who dwelled underground most of the time. And as such, the stranger was even more dangerous to her. She wondered briefly what an Azpian could be doing *here*, but the place seemed to defy all logic.

"That's right," the man agreed, his eyes burning. "If I had my bow, you'd already be dead."

Zeru put a palm up in a peace gesture and sheathed his dagger. "You startled me, that's all. I didn't mean to scare you."

The man's lips drew back to show sharp teeth. "Outsiders are not welcome. How did you even get here?"

"As the Sylvan told you, we were sent," Zeru said. "We have a task to complete, and then we'll go."

The kobold looked at Cassia in horror. "A Sylvan?" He said it the way one might say *pickled sheep's brains?*

She frowned. "He's a Dracu. Is that any better?"

The man put his fists, hardly larger than two walnuts, to his forehead. "Did the wards fail? Did that worthless Summoner forget to reinforce them again?" He dropped his arms and peered around the room. "And what in the cursèd forest happened to my castle? You've . . . you've . . . wrecked up the place!" His face twisted into a grotesque scowl. "I'll be dismissed! I'll be given some horrible task for eternity. Sorting grains of rice from a pile of ashes maybe. Noctua will think of something awful for me this time."

Zeru cleared his throat. "We did not . . . wreck up the place. We arrived last night and found it as you see. We need only learn something from your library, and we'll leave again. Maybe you can help us?"

"Help you?" The man looked outraged.

Cassia searched for a less fraught subject. "You mentioned Noctua. Are you . . . one of the Ancients?"

"Don't be ridiculous!" the man snapped. "My people are long-lived but mortal. I was a hero in life, and the Ancients rewarded me by bringing me to guard this sacred realm."

"You're saying you're the spirit of a kobold hero?" Zeru asked, not without skepticism.

⁓ 89 ⁓

The man's eyes burned with a proud fire. "With my bow, I killed ten giants in one battle defending my lord's lands. My aim was the truest of any archer who lived. Surely you've heard of me."

Cassia hesitated. "You haven't told us your name."

"Gutel!" he said, as if she should know that already. "Gutel the Great."

As he waited expectantly, Cassia almost wished she could lie.

The kobold waved a hand. "It matters not. Hrimgrimnir will bludgeon you to jog your memories."

"Who or...what is that?" Cassia asked.

"Oh, you'll see." The kobold watched the doorway behind them, practically rubbing his hands in anticipation. "You'll see soon enough."

They waited, all silent. After a minute or so, Cassia asked, "Is Hrim..." She trailed off.

"Hrimgrimnir," the kobold said impatiently.

She nodded. "Right. Is he quite large?"

"Indeed, indeed. Taller than the trees. You can't miss him."

"The thing is," she said tentatively, almost sorry to dash his excitement at their impending bludgeoning, "this place is empty but for us. You're the first person we've seen since we arrived."

The kobold's chest rose and fell for a few moments. "That can't be right." He looked between them, his eyes settling on the amulet around Zeru's neck. "Where did you get that?"

"It was given to me," Zeru said, a hint of warning in his tone.

"That's not for a Dracu to wear!" the kobold said. Without warning, he leaped forward and snatched for it.

But Zeru merely sidestepped him. He put a hand to the man's green hat as his arms wheeled in frustrated grabbing motions.

"It belongs to the welkin!" Gutel shouted. "Give it back!"

Zeru looked at Cassia, as if she would know how to handle this.

"Why don't we tell you how we came to be here?" she suggested. "Is there somewhere we could sit?"

After a few seconds of unsuccessful vying for the amulet, the small man gave a shout of frustration and dropped his arms. "Very well. Since Hrimgrimnir is taking his blessed time about it." He gestured toward a doorway. "In here will do."

In the end, none of them sat. Zeru stood by the window. The kobold took a place in front of the parlor hearth, his chin high, his hands behind his back as if ready to pass judgment. Cassia settled for leaning against the wall.

It was a sitting room containing a small hearth, shelving, two wingback chairs, and a low table with a game board of some kind. Plates, which might have once lined the shelves, now covered the floor. But they were made of metal—gold, silver, and copper—and were not broken. Unlike the ceiling beam that had fallen in one corner.

Zeru explained in succinct terms how they'd come to be there: A Seer in the Cryptlands had given him the amulet, and it was used with the ring to create a doorway that led here.

"The ring? The Solis Gemma?" the kobold asked, perking up. "Where is it now?"

At Zeru's curt nod, Cassia held out her hand.

The kobold gasped. "A Sylvan wears the sacred stone." He passed a hand over his eyes, his expression aggrieved. "How?"

"It was an heirloom passed down in my family," Zeru explained.

"Impossible," the kobold declared, his suspicion palpable. "The Solis Gemma couldn't have become a Dracu heirloom."

Zeru gave a sidelong look at Cassia before adding, "The queen knew of the artifact, but she left it in my mother's keeping as one of her most trusted confidants. Prophecy said the Solis Gemma would help the Dracu win the war against Sylvans, but the queen had not yet been able to wear the ring."

"That's not true," Cassia put in, refusing to let his lies go unchallenged. "The prophecy says the ring will end the war, not who will win."

"Our Seers say otherwise," Zeru replied, his expression defiant. "Every full moon, my mother would take the ring from its hiding place and see if the queen could wear it. But she couldn't bear to be near the ring. After every failure, my mother would put it back into safekeeping." He paused, seeming to calculate what to say next. Finally, he shook his head. "Anyway, I didn't know all that until it was too late. When I first saw the ring, I thought it some hideous old thing my mother would never miss. And for some unknown reason, I gave it to *her*." He indicated Cassia with a slight lift of his chin.

She was stunned. All this time, she'd imagined the most nefarious of reasons for Zeru giving her the ring. Her father had insisted that Zeru had hoped it would kill her. Could it really have been a simple mistake? Then again, he might be lying. She also hadn't missed the fact that he'd given her something he thought was hideous.

"Why did you give it to the Sylvan?" the kobold asked incredulously. "Are Dracu and Sylvans not enemies anymore?"

"We very much are," Zeru assured him. "I was young and easily duped. I thought the girl was my friend."

Cassia's teeth ground together. "The important part," she said, as evenly as she could manage, "is that I came to have the ring. And now the Dracu wants it back. However, the ring can't be removed." *Plus, I'll die before giving it up.*

"Not until I find out how to weaken the mystical bond

between the Sylvan and the ring," Zeru said, his eyes hard and determined. "Though it was an heirloom in my family, the magic of it belongs to my queen and I must return it to her."

But the kobold was shaking his head. "No. It belongs here. In Welkincaster."

Cassia and Zeru exchanged a look. The kobold's intentions didn't fit with either of their plans.

"How long has the ring been in your family?" Gutel asked.

Zeru's answer came quick and challenging. "At least two generations. My mother said it was her mother's."

Gutel's face showed signs of an inner struggle. "Then regardless of *how* the Solis Gemma was lost to Welkincaster, it has been a long time since the gemstone was here in the sacred realm. A long time without its power, which kept the castle in good repair and the forest healthy." He looked around the room, a heaviness about his expression. "A long time for me to be asleep." He said no more, but his head hung low.

Cassia hesitated, her mind snagging this new information. "You're saying the ring does all that? Keeps this cloud in good repair?"

The kobold raised his eyebrows. "What else?"

She glanced at Zeru. "It's been used ... as a weapon."

Gutel glared. "Yes, in the Ancient Wars. A great corruption of the ring. But that's in the past."

Zeru cleared his throat. Before he could say more, Cassia broke in. "And the others?" she asked gently. "There were more spirits here with you before?"

An almost imperceptible sigh moved the kobold's small frame. "Many others. I do not know if they still sleep and can be woken or if they are gone to Noctua's kingdom, to the land of the dead. After enough time, all spirits return there."

93

"Where were you?" she asked. "We didn't see you when we arrived."

Gutel shrugged. "Asleep in the hearth. You wouldn't have seen me, as I was not to be seen. When the ring is in residence at Welkincaster, it used to mean the Lady was in residence. Perhaps the gemstone's arrival here woke me."

"And by Lady...," Zeru prompted.

"Lady Solis. Even the Ancients need a place to retreat sometimes. That is why the welkins were created. The stories tell us these places were once filled with laughter and song. Many of the Ancients visited one another on the welkins, even bringing great champions such as myself to visit." His chest expanded as he took another long pause, his eyes unfocused. "But the Lady hasn't been here in a long time. I myself have only seen her once, when I was brought here long ago. This place is to stay in readiness for her return."

Cassia swallowed. If that was true, she was standing in the place of an Ancient. A truly sacred place. But it was neglected. That much was clear. As if something sinister had grown where laughter and song once lived.

"It sounds like we shouldn't be here," she said, darting a look at Zeru. She had told him as much, and he'd dismissed her.

"We're not leaving until we find out how to remove the ring," Zeru said, his eyes warning her not to contradict him. "Gutel, can you read Runic?"

The small man stood taller. "Of course! That's my written language."

Zeru looked far too smug. "That is excellent news. What about Old Sylvan?"

That elicited a sour face. "I had no desire to learn. I've always found Sylvans to be an insufferable lot." His eyes shifted to Cassia.

"With their self-righteous claims of honesty and their endless hunting. If you ask me, kobolds would still be living peaceably in human homes if it weren't for Silvanus leading his Wild Hunt, luring humans into his traps—"

"That is not true!" Cassia snapped. A shiver ran through her as she realized she did not know her father's full history, and therefore might not have spoken the truth. She amended her statement. "At least, not until after the humans began hunting us."

A glint in Zeru's eye told her he was enjoying her discomfort. "Have your people gone to such lengths to forget their past? Your father is known for his violent nature."

Cassia's voice was hoarse with loathing. "It was your queen who promised war. I heard her myself."

Zeru's eyes narrowed. "She only wanted the ring back so that your people couldn't use it against ours. Instead of offering a pact, your father relished the idea of war. He wants to wipe us out. Or rather, he wants you to do it. With my ring."

Overwhelmed by everything she'd heard, she turned and headed for the door. She couldn't let him confuse her. It felt treasonous to even listen.

"Run, Sylvan," Zeru taunted. "That's what you do best."

She halted at the door, her back to him. "If I were scared of a challenge, I wouldn't have come. It was my willingness to be here that allowed the doorway to open. Don't forget that."

She slammed the door behind her, feeling the reverberations run through her body as her breath heaved in and out.

Through the closed door, she heard Zeru speaking to the kobold. "You see why I need your help. The Sylvan is not going to cooperate, and I need to find answers by the next full moon. I was forced to make a vow to return her home by then."

Cassia waited for the kobold's reply, which came after a short pause. "I'm as determined to get the ring back to its rightful place as you are. More so, I'm sure."

Did Zeru realize Gutel's endgame didn't match his own? Now there were three people with different ideas of who should have the ring.

But it was the reminder of the full moon that ran through Cassia's body like ice water. This would be the first full moon without her there to help. She could not return home without learning how to use the ring to kill. And she had precious little time to do that, considering she still had no idea where the knowledge was hidden.

A new purpose in her step, she returned to the library, making a pile of several likely books. After flipping through a couple of volumes, she found a section about some of the Ancients. She read until the light faded, ignoring—or pretending to ignore—Zeru's grim presence when he finally joined her. As stars began to appear outside the window, she sighed and rubbed her eyes. If only she had Dracu sight like him, she could probably keep reading with a bit of moonlight. As it was, she would have to continue in the morning.

"Did you find out anything about the ring?" Zeru asked sharply as she turned to slip out.

She stiffened in the doorway. "No," she said, hating that it was the truth.

"Anything it all?" he pressed, clearly not satisfied with her answer.

She turned to face him. "Nothing. Happy?"

"Not especially," he said, returning his attention to his book. "Don't think I didn't notice you trying to conceal that small book under your arm."

"It's a book about flowers," she said bitterly. "Are you worried I'll garden you to death?"

"Hardly." He turned a page, his sharply angled face catching highlights on his cheekbones, forehead, and the curving blade of his nose. "I'm worried you'll damage one of the books."

Her hands curled into fists, but she forced herself to turn away, planning to have the final word for once. "If you're implying I'm careless, I might remind you that you were the one who nearly fell off the cloud today."

She'd taken several steps before his parting shot drifted to her. "And you were the fool who helped me up. Why did you squander what could have been your only chance to rid yourself of my presence?"

A direct hit that nearly made her trip on the stairs. It felt like a wound that might fester. Why *had* she helped him? She hadn't let herself think too hard about that particular failure. His words still rang in her ears as she tried to sleep. And in her dreams, she was the one falling through an empty night sky.

10

A Dracu never hesitates to deal a killing blow.

—GAXIX, DRACU PHILOSOPHER

THE NEXT MORNING, IT TOOK CASSIA A SECOND TO remember where she was. She yawned and stretched, groaning at the discomfort of having slept fully clothed, and sat up to run her fingers through her hair. She was cold and hungry. The apple had not been enough to sustain her. She would kill for a comb.

Maybe she could speak to the kobold alone, asking about food and water without Zeru's grim presence darkening the atmosphere. She could show him that Sylvans weren't so bad.

The idea of searching the castle brought a pulse of anticipation, not only because she was certain the answers to the ring's power lay here. She couldn't help an unwilling fascination with Welkincaster, even though she had an instinctive fear of this forest. If what Gutel said was true, it hadn't always been so somber and neglected. A sanctuary of the Ancients? Spirits of heroes being given new life as guardians? It was beyond her wildest imaginings. Sylvans were drawn to curiosities, and this one beckoned to her with promises of rich secrets and untold wonders. She remembered the nursery tales of a cloud realm. Her mother had read her those stories every night when she was little. That was before the ring, before her mother retreated to her tree somewhere in Thirstwood. To heal, they'd said.

But then her mother had never come home.

At first, she'd asked her father when her mother would be back. He'd treated her to a cold silence that told her clearly not to ask again. So she'd asked Tibald. He'd said things like, "When she is well," and "Be patient, Sproutling." Over time, Cassia had stopped asking.

The answer, perhaps, was never.

Her breathing hitched, and her eyes misted dangerously, so she shut those thoughts out and forced herself to her feet and to her door. A massive tome written in Ancient Sylvan would eradicate thoughts of anything else.

As she reached the top of the tower steps to the library, she stopped short.

Zeru was slumped in the red chair, asleep.

She stilled, her breath suspended. He must have read through the night and finally succumbed to fatigue. His soft, even breathing was all she could hear. His head lolled back, leaving his throat exposed. Her eyes widened as they fell on his dagger on a nearby table. Could he be that careless?

She'd wasted her opportunity when she'd pulled him to safety rather than letting him fall off the edge of the welkin. He'd mocked her for it. Her own conscience had tortured her all night. Maybe the Ancients were giving her another opportunity to be free of her enemy.

Her heart thudding violently, she stepped with excruciating care toward the dagger. The floorboards remained silent, giving credence to her idea that the Ancients were on her side in this. Perhaps they blamed Zeru for this invasion of their sacred realm. Cassia could rectify that injustice.

Her hand reached out for the dagger, closing over the hilt. The blade slipped from its sheath with no sound. She took a step toward Zeru. Another.

She stared down at him. His mussed hair fell in feathery spikes over his brow, his lashes dark fans against his pale cheeks. He looked younger asleep. It was easier to see him as the boy she had once known.

No—she had to do this. The ring *must* remain hers. She had to learn to master it before the Dracu found a way to take it. The only way to guarantee her own safety and success was to kill him now. End the threat.

A quick swipe across his throat and it's done! Do it! Now!

Her hand gripped the blade harder as she looked down at him. He was helpless.

Maybe it shouldn't matter. If she were truly as bloodthirsty as he supposed her to be, she wouldn't care.

But she wasn't. And there was something dishonest about it. A Sylvan didn't sneak around stabbing enemies while they were asleep. Which meant...She squeezed her eyes shut, her face twisting. Was she really going to let her enemy live? Again? Her arm went slack before the thought was even clear in her mind.

She couldn't kill a defenseless opponent. She just...couldn't.

Her throat tight with self-directed rage, she went to the window seat, placing the dagger next to her. She opened the Sylvan history and tried to read. But the words kept swimming before her eyes. What was wrong with her? What would her father say about her aversion to killing? She'd never had any trouble playing her part with the ring. But...that was different. She'd never had to look her enemy in the eye. Regardless, her father would say she was weak, craven. She put her forehead against the cool window as shame heated her cheeks.

Zeru's voice broke into her thoughts. "Why?"

She startled upright. The book fell from her lap and thudded to the floor.

In the sunlight, his eyes looked like green glass. He was staring at her with such a serious expression. There was anger and something else, a kind of furious inquisitiveness.

She found herself saying, mostly to get him to blink, "Anyone could have slit your throat while you were snoring."

It wasn't a lie because she hadn't actually said he was snoring. He did blink, finally. "I wasn't snoring."

She retrieved the book and set it back on her lap. "How do you know?"

"Because I wasn't asleep."

It was her turn to stare intently. "I don't believe you."

"You're not that quiet, you know." Back in the safe territory of insulting her, he seemed to relax. "You came in, saw my dagger, padded over to it like a child trying to steal a honey cake from under the cook's nose, and stood in front of me. Then you sighed, went to your seat, and started reading. And I say again, Sylvan, why?"

"I don't think I sighed," she said, a new shake in her limbs. It had been a test. Nasty, awful Dracu. "What if I *had* decided to slit your throat?"

He glanced at her from under heavy lids as if she'd said something truly ridiculous. "I'd have had time to eat my morning meal before catching your wrist."

"Then what were you going to do? Use my failed attempt to kill you as an excuse to kill me?"

"I can't." He tapped his fingers against the chair arm in an agitated rhythm. His lean face caught shadows under his cheekbones and chin, his eyes resentful, suspicious gleams half-hidden by the hair falling over his forehead. "Not to mention your death could destroy my ring."

"*My* ring," she corrected, fury roiling in her gut. "Why test me like that?"

He stood, his mouth a hard line. "Because you let me live." He glared at her as if she'd committed an unpardonable offense. "Worse. You saved my life."

Her eyebrows rose. "Do you want an apology? I think I can manage it. I'm starting to feel genuinely sorry for that decision."

"At first I thought it was this." He lifted the amulet around his neck and let it fall against his collarbone. "That you were afraid you wouldn't be able to leave this place if I fell. But I wanted to know for sure. I still want to know."

How she wished she could lie. She wanted to say, *Yes, that's exactly why I saved you. For the amulet.* But she hadn't even thought about it. How embarrassing. She hadn't even considered what would happen to her if that vital artifact had fallen out of reach.

Instead, she answered coolly, "I'm glad you've sorted out my motivations."

"Except I haven't." He slashed a hand in the direction of the dagger. "Because you could have tried to kill me and taken the amulet. Why would you waste a chance like that?"

She stiffened as his interrogation began to remind her of her father's lectures. "Maybe I realized you were awake."

"Did you?"

She bent her knees, making a show of getting comfortable. "I don't have to answer."

He came a step closer, his hands fisted. "Did you help me to save the amulet? Yes or no?"

To hide her unease at being cornered, she turned her head to look out the window. Was that a bird flying above the treetops?

If so, it was the first she'd seen here. She heard the Dracu's frustrated exhalation but did not turn back to face him. He couldn't goad her, no matter how his nearness set her nerves jangling. There was no answer she could give that wasn't potentially disadvantageous. If she implied she had saved him because of the amulet, that might reduce his sense of obligation—what she hoped was a growing idea that he owed her his life. However, if she told him she hadn't even thought about the amulet, he would ridicule her. She wanted him to underestimate her, but that didn't mean she relished the idea of inviting open contempt.

The Dracu's earthy scents filled her nostrils as he moved right up into her face and asked, "Did you save me because of the amulet?"

Swallowing, she met his eyes. How strange to see her enemy so close. She wanted to put her hands out and push him away but knew he wouldn't be moved easily. For some reason, he seemed to need this answer. She hedged with a different truth. "The amulet has more value to me than you do."

But he clearly knew that for the nonanswer it was. "Did. You." He forced out each word. "Save. Me. For. The. Amulet?"

He looked as agitated as she felt, his chest rising and falling, his eyes snapping. A battle of wills. But Cassia had already lost to him too many times to give in on this.

"What do *you* think?" she asked, her eyes burning with the need to blink.

Anger flared in his eyes, but he turned away, pacing to the bookshelves and staring at them.

Cassia waited, her senses on alert. She prepared herself for the verbal assault that was sure to follow.

But when he spoke, his voice was quiet. "I don't understand you." And that was all.

I don't understand you. It was something her father had said to her. She waited for that familiar feeling of contraction, of getting smaller and smaller. But it didn't come. When her father said it, any attempt to explain herself would make him angrier. But with the Dracu, she could say what she liked.

She realized how true that was. He couldn't kill her. He'd promised not to harm her. She didn't care what he thought of her. She could say whatever she wanted to him.

But all that she could find was a question. "Why does it matter to you?"

His hand rose as if to pluck a book from a shelf, then dropped to his side. "It doesn't."

Without another word, he left, his feet somehow silent on the normally creaky stairs.

Cassia stared after him. "I don't understand you, either." *Nor do I wish to.* She opened her mouth, but a tightness in her neck prevented her from saying the words. Almost as if they might stick in her throat.

11

> Change is rarely accomplished without pain.
> —Gaxix, Dracu philosopher

Gutel appeared in her tower doorway the next morning at dawn, a haughty angle to his chin. "We have a visitor." So saying, he turned to clomp down the stairs without waiting for a reply.

"What visitor?" she asked, taking care on the rickety steps as she followed. "Here?"

He didn't answer, leaving her to imagine and discard possibilities as he led her down to the first floor, through the entryway, and to the door to the sitting room.

"In you go." He gestured imperiously for her to enter, his red eyes sharp with distrust.

Remembering her plan to win him over, she managed a smile. "Who is it?"

Gutel put a finger to his chin, his face screwing up in exaggerated confusion. "Hmm. How could we find out the answer to that question?" He snapped his fingers, his expression brightening. "I know! Maybe you could go in and see for yourself!"

Her teeth ground together. So much for being nice. She had an urge to grab him by the hat and toss him into the fireplace he came from. Resisting that temptation, she stepped inside to find the room transformed. The shutters were open to reveal a view of murky gray sky. The fallen ceiling beam had been removed, the floor swept, and rubble cleared from the fireplace. The gold, silver, and copper plates sat neatly on shelves. The kobold had been busy.

Running out of ways to avoid looking at Zeru, she finally met his eyes, where dark things swam, making her stomach twist. He sat slouched in a chair next to the fireplace, his feet resting on a side table. He nodded toward a corner behind her. "Summoner, meet the Deathringer."

Cassia turned to see a dour-faced man wearing a gold medallion over blue robes. His long features gave him a solemn air, but his eyes were sharp and assessing. She saw no traits to mark him as Sylvan nor Azpian but thought he must be among land folk. She caught the scent of swamp. A water dweller of some kind, perhaps. His hands were clasped, his fingers tinted a deep shade of purple. The scents of spell craft permeated the air, cloves and ashes and unnamed things.

She turned back to Zeru. "A Seer?"

"Gutel told me of an ancient sect of Summoners and offered to contact them. Magus Xoden was kind enough to offer his services." He gave Cassia a slow perusal before adding, "He's confident he can remove the ring."

No! She hadn't expected anything like this to happen, at least not so soon. Her first urge was to run, but where would she go? She turned to the stranger. "How did you come to be here? My father has employed many Seers and none of them ever talked of the welkins. It isn't common knowledge."

"Not to you, perhaps." Xoden spoke as if she should be grateful for his condescension. "An elite group of Summoners has always upheld the wards in this place. Do you think because the land folk have forgotten the welkins that everyone has? It is not for the average dabbler to know."

106

Cassia huffed. Veleda would not like being dismissed as a dabbler. More importantly, she distrusted people who used insults to shift attention away from themselves. "I thought only the amulet and the ring could open a doorway to this place."

"You were mistaken," Xoden said, lips pursed as if considering things beneath him. "If called properly by the steward of a welkin, a doorway forms, and I can step through it."

Bells of opportunity rang in Cassia's head. "Is your medallion the way back?"

"No need to answer that," Zeru cut in. "Sylvan, don't hurt yourself making escape plans. Xoden has to be sent back by the steward of the welkin. Which is Gutel."

"Forgive me," Gutel said, stepping forward with a short bow. "But I am not the steward." His hands were clasped in front of him, his voice tight with distress. "The steward is always a Zerian. I'm...let us say, the *acting* steward until the other guardians awaken."

"What's a Zerian?" Cassia asked.

Gutel put his hands to his hat. "What is a Zerian? Might as well ask, what's a Sylvan? Zerians are the rightful guardians of the welkins." He aimed a pitying look at her. "It's clear to me you learned nothing in your youth, girl. Did you grow up in a tree?"

Her nostrils flared. "You know, Kobold, if you were in my father's household, you'd be reprimanded for your insolence, which could involve basting you with honey and roasting you on a spit."

Gutel replied with a sharp-toothed grin, "And in my household, we marinate Sylvans in a mixture of vinegar and spices."

Xoden looked between them, a frown making deep brackets next to his mouth. "This is a conversation for another time, surely."

"Quite right, Magus," Zeru said, getting lithely to his feet.

"There is no end to the chatter of a Sylvan. The tower is ready."
He made a smooth gesture toward the door.

All hospitality and welcome, Cassia thought bitterly. The way
Xoden looked at her, like she was a problem to solve, made the
hair prickle on the back of her neck.

"You can't possibly trust him," she said, catching Zeru's eye.
"What do you know about him?"

The Dracu's bland look made her long for a weapon. "You just
don't want him to take the ring."

"Of course I don't." She wished she could surprise him, ren-
der him insensible with a few well-placed attacks, as her sisters
would. "This was not part of our bargain."

"But it has always been my intention." His eyes were as flat as
stagnant marsh water. "And it turns out, you don't have a choice."

She couldn't believe he'd do this so soon after she chose not
to slit his throat. "And if I refuse?"

"I'll carry you if it comes to that. You decide."

Her breaths came shorter, her palms growing damp. He had
no gratitude that she'd saved his life and then spared it. "I should
have killed you when I had the chance."

His eyes glittering coldly, he gestured for her to go first. She
kept her head high the whole way to the tower. *Chin up*, as Thea
would say.

Earthy scents of herbs and a hint of acrid ash hit her as
she stepped into the empty tower. The room had been cleared
except for a table covered in vials and bowls. Shutters covered the
window, weak bands of sunlight squeezing through the cracks.
Candles burned from pewter holders placed on the floor. Two
concentric circles with symbols between them had been drawn
with white powder on the floor. A sick, crawling sensation gripped
her stomach as she recognized the rune for fire.

"What are you planning to do?" she asked, wishing she had paid more attention to Veleda's rituals.

Xoden's robes swished as he moved to the table. "You'll have answers soon enough. Step into the circle."

Cassia was familiar with summoning circles. They acted as a contained gateway between realms so the spirits could commune with the Seer without coming into the living world. Some spirits were benevolent. Others were hostile, like the one that had broken half the vials in Veleda's workroom.

What destruction could a spirit wreak if she was trapped inside the circle with it?

Xoden picked up a mortar and pestle and began to grind something that released a sulfurous cloud, inclining his head toward Zeru, who was leaning against the wall. "You may leave us now."

Zeru crossed his arms. "I'll stay."

The Summoner frowned. "That's not advisable. I work with volatile forces. Keeping them in check requires complete concentration."

Cassia disliked him more and more. "There's no harm in him staying."

It felt wrong to argue for the Dracu, but she didn't want to be alone with this stranger. He'd made no bargain not to harm her.

The Magus didn't deign to look at her as he answered. "The spirits I call are reluctant to be summoned and therefore easily provoked. Another presence could cause a failure of the entire spell."

Zeru turned a stony look on him. "You could have explained this before."

"I do humbly apologize," Xoden said with a bow. "I promise the end result will be worth your trust in me."

Zeru hesitated. "I want the ring immediately, the moment you have it."

"Of course," the Summoner assured him, bowing again. "The very moment."

Cassia's stomach clenched as Zeru gave her a final inscrutable look before leaving the room.

As she eyed the symbols, trying to remember the meaning of various runes, Xoden poured powder into one of the vials. "Step in, girl. The Dracu shared the terms of your bargain with me. I have assured him you will not be killed."

Her lip curled. There were a multitude of things she didn't want to endure aside from her own murder. "What are you planning to do?"

Xoden watched with satisfaction as the contents of the vial bubbled over. "Your ring is bound to you with a mystical attachment, and spirits are more connected to that kind of magic. Where the living failed, the spirits will succeed."

"You're going to put me in there with a spirit who will try to break my bond with the ring?" Her heart lurched into a rapid beat. "Absolutely not. For one thing, I've seen hostile spirits. I know the havoc they can wreak."

"I will call an entity familiar to me," he assured her. "Stay calm and do not agitate it."

"I don't want to stay calm," she snapped. "I will fight, and if I'm harmed, the ring will be destroyed."

"That is one theory," he said, focusing on the potion. "I'm not convinced."

"And if you're wrong," she said, "the Dracu is likely to gut you. I hope you're prepared to die for your failure."

But Xoden remained unmoved. "Think of this as a test of your self-discipline. I know your father values that quality."

110

She watched his preparations with increased suspicion. Of course, Zeru must have shared that her father was the Sylvan king, but the Summoner's tone made her wonder if this was more than a casual mention. "What do you know of my father?"

He met her eyes, his own sharp with some emotion. "It happens I once worked for him. He wanted more power over the trees of Thirstwood, and I had proven myself in the field of persuasive summoning."

Her brow furrowed. *Persuasive summoning?* She translated that to mean Xoden could make spirits do his bidding. But what did that have to do with Thirstwood? Her father didn't need spirits to control it. It was his great strength and connection with the trees that assured the loyalty of the forest.

"What are you claiming to have done?" she asked, ready to refute his lies.

"You don't know?" His smile was proud. "I bound some of the hungrier spirits to the strongest trees. Deprived of true life, those spirits have a need for blood. They find it where they can. Animals. Humans. Azpians. The blood of forest folk is forbidden to the trees, of course, making it safe for your people. A perfect defense, don't you think? It is through my efforts that the forest became, in essence, the largest legion of Huntsmen in the Sylvan king's army."

Cassia's head spun. He had to be lying.

"If your story were true," she said, "that would mean you've forced hostile spirits to take over the trees belonging to Sylvans." She shook her head, finding no words for how horrifying that was. "What would happen to the original spirits?"

Xoden's smile was cold. "Perhaps they were consumed by the new spirit, in which case they live on as part of something else."

Cassia couldn't hide her disgust. "If I believed you, I'd say you deserved death for what you've done."

~ 111 ~

"I see you are as small-minded as your father," Xoden said, his lips twisting. He stepped closer, making her take a step back. "After all my work, all my toil, he dismissed me."

"As he should have," she said, revulsion turning her stomach. "The trees belong to the Sylvans. Some of those trees house the spirits of our dead. Some hold the living, Sylvans who have gone into their tree to rest or heal." Cassia's blood ran cold. "My mother."

"A beautiful woman," he said, his smile revolting. "A shame what happened to her."

"What are you implying?" She found herself shaking and gripped her upper arms. "That you hurt her?"

"Not at all. Her illness came long after I was gone. Whether it had something to do with a hungry spirit finding its way into her tree, I couldn't say. I merely admire the subtlety of revenge. Your mother never liked me. I did not grieve her absence." His scrutiny made her skin crawl. "You remind me of her in a way."

"Let me assure you," Cassia warned him, inching back as he advanced, "if you harm me, my father will hunt you."

His smile sharpened. "Why do you think I came to the welkins? He can't find me here."

Her heart became a pebble thrown into dark water. Xoden was without scruples or fear of consequences. And she was at his mercy.

Giving her a shove into the circle, he tipped the contents of the vial, igniting the powder. She found herself inside a ring of misty white flames.

She'd barely drawn breath when a creature materialized inside with her. It appeared both birdlike and reptilian, with a beak and feathered wings, its lower body covered in scales. It appeared to be made of bright smoke with flames like feathers. When she took a step back, it came for her. Contrary to its wispy appearance, its talons were sharp and solid, drawing blood from her arms. It went for her left hand, for the ring.

"No!" Her cuts burned, but she cried out more from fear than pain. With each slash, a burst of bright red light lit the room. Severing her bond?

"Don't scream, you foolish child," Xoden called from outside the circle. "You will only enrage it."

She couldn't think with this thing on her, its wings flapping as its claws shredded her skin. Her hands and arms were covered with slashes. No matter how she blocked it, the thing kept coming at her. She wanted to call out for her mother. Enora. Thea. Her father. Anyone! She even thought of Zeru.

No one is here to help you. Think!

In desperation, she recalled the one powerful thing she had: the Solis Gemma. She had no idea if it had any effect on spirits, but she called on the stone with every fiber of her will, making it a command, a plea, and a prayer all at once.

Before she could release the blast, a second creature was in the circle with her, a fox-like animal with huge, pointed ears, copper-brown fur, and a bushy tail. It rushed at the bird-lizard, its softness brushing her skin as it dashed past.

The two creatures snarled and shrieked, the low rumble of growls interspersing the rip of claws. The fox seemed to be... defending her. It tore at the bird-lizard, making gashes in its smoky form that seeped darkness. With each slash, it grew less distinct until it disappeared altogether. With a final look at Cassia, the fox creature disappeared, too.

She blinked a few times and saw that the shutters had fallen open, leaving the chamber bright. She was trembling, but still standing. The border of flames that held her trapped burned away, revealing the Summoner's face contorted into a mask of rage.

⁓ 113 ⁓

The door crashed open. Zeru strode in, and she met his eyes, her chest burning with rage. His furious gaze darkened further as he stared at her bleeding arms.

"It was working!" Xoden shouted, an accusing finger aimed at Cassia. "My thrall was severing the bond when she—"

Zeru came at the Summoner like a charging wolf, clasping him around the neck and slamming him into the wall so hard the table shook. "You promised she wouldn't be harmed!"

"A few scratches," the Summoner choked.

Zeru's grip tightened. "She's *bleeding*."

"As if you care," Cassia said with soft-voiced loathing, stepping from the circle on unsteady legs. Her cuts throbbed with every beat of her heart.

Xoden's skin was turning blue, and apparently, Zeru wasn't quite ready to kill him. He released the magus, letting him slide to the floor.

Zeru stared down in disgust. "Thralling a spirit is forbidden. You said nothing about that plan when you promised to get me the ring."

Cassia's eyes widened at the contempt in Zeru's tone. Sylvans honored the sacredness of spirits, with strict rules for Seers in their summoning. Spirits were never to be held captive or forced to do the bidding of the living. But she hadn't known the Dracu held to the same ideal.

The magus had no such qualms. Rubbing his throat with his stained fingers, he spat, "Don't pretend you cared. You wanted the ring 'by any means necessary.' And rightly so. What is the value of one common spirit compared to the glory of retrieving an artifact of the Ancients?"

Something clicked in Cassia's mind. "You were planning to

keep the ring. You were never going to give it to the Dracu." She laughed. She couldn't help it.

"Be silent, girl," the Summoner hissed.

Zeru's face was suffused in fury. He grabbed the Summoner's robes and slammed him bodily against the wall once more. "Is that true?"

"I told you not to trust him," she said.

Xoden choked out, "Let me try again. This time, I swear I'll get the ring for you."

"The way you swore she'd come to no harm?" With a violent shove, Zeru sent Xoden crashing into the table covered in vials. Glass shattered, and liquid spilled in hissing pools onto the floor. "Take your things and go before I throw you off this cloud myself."

Xoden raised an open hand in a gesture of defiance, his hate-filled eyes on Cassia as he chanted a spell. Zeru grabbed his arm, shoving it behind his back. "What do you think you're doing?"

"Give me my revenge," Xoden choked, panting. "Do you know how long it took me to make that spirit my thrall?"

Zeru twisted the mage's arm, eliciting a sharp cry of pain. "While she wears the Solis Gemma," he enunciated, "she is under my protection. Do not return lest you wish to make an enemy of me. I assure you I'll oblige."

In the charged pause that followed, Gutel appeared in the doorway, his red eyes steely. "May I be of help?"

"Yes," Zeru said, shoving the Summoner toward the door. "Send this filth back where he came from."

Xoden stumbled, grabbing the door for support before turning a killing look on Cassia. When Zeru strode toward him, his eyes widened at whatever expression he saw on the Dracu's face.

As the Summoner swept out and clattered down the tower steps, Gutel gave Cassia an inscrutable look before following.

When Cassia swayed on her feet, Zeru took a step toward her.

"If you come any closer," she said, steadying herself with a hand on the wall, "I will make you sorry. Somehow, I will. Don't make me vow it."

The chamber went deathly silent.

"He swore not to harm you." Zeru's rough voice scraped along her nerves.

Using the wall for support, she moved toward the door, turning on the threshold to face him. "And you believed him?"

Zeru blinked, his lips tightening a telling fraction.

Cassia shook her head. "My people have a saying: *Tell the truth lest you choke on your lies.* Admit it, Dracu. You didn't care if he meant to keep his promise. Because you didn't care what happened to me as long as you got the ring." She didn't need his admission when she saw the truth in his eyes.

Suddenly, she wanted him to know. Needed him to know. "I didn't think about it."

"What?" Zeru asked, his brow furrowing.

"I didn't think of the amulet," she said. "I saved you from falling because . . . I couldn't do otherwise."

She barely had time to see his reaction as she turned away. But it stayed in her mind's eye as her feet scraped down the steps. It seemed she had finally surprised him. Pity she could not enjoy it.

It wasn't until she was alone in her tower bedchamber with the door shut that she let herself shake.

12

> Strange spirits are best left alone.
> —Excharias, Sylvan poet

As Cassia lay in bed, her thoughts kept returning to the Summoner's claims. He'd sounded so proud of binding hostile spirits to trees, creating the bloodlust of the forest. And that he'd done so under orders from the Sylvan king... it was impossible.

It was said the Sylvan king knew the mind of the forest as if it were his own, and that was why the trees were loyal. But was there another truth, a darker side to it? Her father was always looking for ways to increase the Sylvan advantage over their enemies. Was he capable of sacrificing the spirits of his own trees to protect his people?

There had been blood trees for as long as Cassia could remember, but she had never asked *when* they'd become that way. She only knew that it was long before their war with the Dracu, when they'd faced an even greater threat: humans.

Unlike Sylvans, who gathered dead wood and fallen branches for carpentry and kindling, humans came to the forest with axes that felled the greatest of trees. Only the Sylvan king stood in their way, protecting the ancient forests. Over time, the human population had grown, and the Sylvans were forced to retreat deeper into the wilds. The trees had become bloodthirsty out of protectiveness toward the Sylvans. That's what she'd always been told.

But perhaps it was time that she learned more about the origins of Thirstwood so she could assure herself the magus was lying. Once she was home, she would ask Veleda or one of the older Huntsmen like Tordon. Whether they would *answer* was uncertain. She was starting to realize there were a great many things that weren't spoken about in Scarhamm.

Like her mother. Could *her* tree have become bloodthirsty? If so, what would have happened to her mother's spirit? Even Xoden hadn't seemed sure. Would her mother be trapped inside her tree with a hostile entity? Or could her spirit have been consumed by the thrall? The thoughts were so disturbing, her breathing shallowed, her nails digging into her palms. She reminded herself she had no reason to think any of that had happened. She had to focus on getting home before she could worry about saving her mother.

She shifted her attention to another mystery: the fox-like creature that had defended her from Xoden's hostile spirit. It had appeared right after she'd called on the ring. Were the two connected?

The door swung open, interrupting her thoughts.

"I'm here to bandage your wounds," Gutel announced, his tone reluctant.

"Kobold," Cassia said in warning, "if you set a single toe in here, I will pitch you out the window."

His red eyes darkened, but he didn't take a step forward. "I told him you'd refuse. He is too softhearted for his own good."

"Are you talking about Zeru?" She laughed bitterly as Gutel retreated, slamming the door behind him.

As night fell, she longed for the escape of sleep, but the mattress was lumpy, and her cuts ached. She wanted fresh air and wind in the treetops. The moon rose, beckoning through the window. Finally, she sat up, groaning as her body protested. She went to her door, her hand hesitating on the knob.

Unlocked.

A mistake? Regardless, she would take advantage.

She moved through the dark castle by feel, opening one of the heavy wooden doors carved with wings and stepping outside. How stark and beautiful the night was. The haze that covered the sky couldn't mask the brightness of the moon, which shone like a pearl hanging from an unseen chain. Around it, the black velvet sky was sewn with seed-pearl stars. She almost reached up to see if she could pluck one with thumb and forefinger.

She followed no particular path into the darkened woods. Though the forest was small, it felt vast, opening around her like a book filled with countless stories. Wind shook the treetops, rustling dry leaves and making shadows run across the ground at her feet.

After a while, she found herself in a clearing where a small lake shimmered in the moonlight. Water! Finally! As she approached with eager steps, moon sprites burst into existence, rising from the surface. Drunk on moonbeams, they dashed from tree to tree, winking like tiny exploding stars. One of the sprites settled on her fingertip, its tiny gossamer wings barely visible. She almost had the sense it was regarding her, too. After a moment, it flew away. It must wonder what sort of fool would stand in the path of a moonbeam and not bother to fly.

The lake beckoned, its glassy surface calm and inviting. She sat on one of the rocks and cupped her hands, taking numerous mouthfuls of water. Thirst sated, she poured water over her arms, soaking her ripped shirt, then splashed her face and neck. Instantly, the pain of her cuts eased, her senses opening. She could hear the forest with something more than her ears, a sense woven into her bones. The trees had brought her here. The forest recognized one of its own and knew what she needed. She was one of them, after all.

A branch cracked in the silence. Cassia straightened, alert to the depth of darkness and what could hide in it. *There!* Movement by the edge of the clearing.

Breathless, she pulled each leg from the water and set her feet on the rock. As she watched, a figure emerged, the size and build of a man, though she couldn't see what kind of creature he was. He didn't move closer, merely stood there, regarding her.

No horns, so not a Dracu. Though tall, the stranger wasn't big enough to be a Skratti. A Sylvan, perhaps? Here? The thought was enough to keep her from running.

Her pulse drummed in her ears, but she pushed resolutely past her fear. "Who are you?"

She sucked in a breath as a pair of massive wings unfurled from his back, their clawed edges like that of a bat or an imp. Not a Sylvan, then. She thought instead of the winged votaries she'd seen in the portrait gallery. Maybe Welkincaster wasn't as empty as they'd first thought. Gutel did say more guardians would soon be waking.

"Do you live here?" she asked, trying to ignore her fear. When no answer came, a thought struck her. "Can you understand me?"

"Yes," he said, his voice a quiet scrape of tree bark against rock.

She took a step closer, trying to see him better. "We didn't see you when we arrived. Are there others like you?"

He said nothing.

She didn't know what to make of him. "My name is Cassia. What is the custom here when you meet someone new?"

⁓ 120 ⁓

The stranger paused. "I haven't...met someone new."

She watched him doubtfully. The welkin had been uninhabited for a long time. Perhaps there was an explanation. "Have you been to see Gutel yet?"

"What is a...Gutel?" said the stranger.

That made her smile. "It's the name of the kobold who lives in the castle."

"Hmm," he said, as if he didn't much care.

"You should report to him," Cassia said.

But the stranger didn't seem to be listening. His intense, silent regard made her nervous enough to take a step back.

Either he didn't like her suggestion or he took that as an end to the conversation. He bowed at the waist before opening his wings, then took off with a leap, launching toward the treetops. As he cleared the canopy, his broad and elegant wings opened wider, all sharp edges and grace, until his form was obscured by the haze in the sky. And then he was gone.

Cassia's heart calmed as the moon sprites returned with a gentle glow. But the night's hush felt different, full of unseen things. An owl hooted, the first bird sound she'd heard in these woods, evoking thoughts of Noctua, goddess of spirits, whose animal form was the nocturnal hunter. She didn't know if it was a good omen or a warning.

Senses alert, she made her way back into the castle, climbing to the third-floor portrait gallery and using the glow of her ring to illuminate the people in the paintings. All of them had wings. Some of their faces were stern, some less forbidding, but their eyes were all piercing and lifelike. She shivered as she looked at them, imagining they were examining her, too.

In any case, she was convinced that the stranger she'd seen in the woods was one of these winged votaries.

As Cassia entered her bedchamber, she found Zeru standing by her window, his back to her as he stared out. His arms were clasped behind his back, his pale claws curving over his fingertips. His twisted horns were silhouetted against the dawn like knives on pink satin. For a second, she wondered if she'd chosen the wrong tower and she'd blundered in on him. But no, he was in her chamber, acting like the entire welkin belonged to him.

"Get out," she said, too angry to guard her tone.

Zeru turned to face her. "I sent Gutel to bandage your wounds. You sent him away."

She crossed her arms. "I told him I'd pitch him out the window if he set foot in here. It's not my fault he's sensitive and took that as a no."

He pulled something from his pocket, and she drew back. He sighed at her reaction, making a show of spreading his hands to show her what he'd retrieved.

She eyed the scraps of linen that lay flat over his open palms. "Rags?"

"Bandages." He took another step toward her. "Will you stay still?"

"No. Leave."

"Please," he said, but it was his serious expression that made her pause.

For some reason, she nodded, though she eyed him with great suspicion. As he drew close, she could see each individual thick black hair of his eyebrows, drawn together in concentration as he bent his head to stare at her arms and hands. She looked away as she heard him swallow. Did he feel bad about her injuries?

Worried he'd broken his vow not to harm her? *Good.* As far as she was concerned, he had. He had sanctioned everything Xoden did.

"You washed your wounds." He reached out slowly to touch a cut on her upper arm.

She flinched at the contact, and his eyes came up to hers in a moment of mutual observation and calculation.

"I need to rip the sleeves," he said. "May I?"

She looked at her shirt, which was full of so many cuts and slashes, you could see the linen undershirt through it. It would be no great loss to shred it further. She offered her arm.

With efficient tugs, he ripped the sleeve from the seam at her shoulder. Cool air hit her skin. She felt tension in every part of her but didn't move away. His lashes hid his eyes as he took one of the rags and wound it around her arm. The linen was soft against the raw skin. She tried to feel a cynical rush of hatred. She should tell him to go. But the cut felt better once it was covered, and she couldn't repress a tiny sigh of relief. She offered her other arm.

He tore her other sleeve off and bandaged another cut. Her muscles hummed with tension at his nearness. His gentleness was unsettling.

When he was done, the only cut left was on her ring finger.

Zeru stared down at the ring. Days before, he had tried to take it off, causing her terrible pain. What would he do now?

"I'll have to bandage around it," he said. Carefully, he used the scrap of fabric to cover the cuts on her finger and hand, tying it securely at her wrist. It felt snug and sure. Like it would stay.

"There," he said with a slow nod, almost like a bow.

At the same time, she said, "I hope you don't expect a thank-you."

"No," he said. "I don't."

He was standing too close. She didn't know how much longer she could bear this strange tension. She was almost ready to run back into the woods when he drew the dagger from the sheath at his waist. Her eyes widened as he offered the hilt, his fingers carefully pinching the flat of the blade. "Here."

"Here, what?" She should stick it in his gullet as payback for the Summoner.

"Take it."

She watched her hand reach out and take the blade from him.

He pushed his sleeves up to his elbows, offering his bare forearms. His veins were visible, pushed to the surface by cords of muscle. "Cut me the way you were cut."

Her lips parted. "Is this some sort of bizarre Dracu apology?"

He moved his arms closer to her. "Maybe."

She dropped her own arm. "I'm not going to cut you. Don't be ridiculous."

His eyes held hers. "You want to."

"Of course I want to." She had no trouble speaking this truth. "I wanted you dead the second you handed me over to that Summoner."

He flinched, barely perceptible but she saw it. "So do it."

"No." She lifted her chin. "That won't make me feel better."

His green eyes glimmered as if he was trying to figure her out. "Then what will?"

A laugh escaped her. "I don't know. A comb? Food? Being treated with respect?" *Might as well ask for the moon.*

His lids fell again, hiding his eyes. His arms dropped. "If you're sure."

She shook her head, wishing her sisters were here to witness this. They'd never believe it. A Dracu offering to submit to injury? And her refusing? An enemy was practically baring his throat for her attack, and she was turning him down. Then again, she was glad her sisters weren't here. They'd never understand.

But she had no desire to hurt him back like this. There'd be no satisfaction in it when he'd invited the pain.

She looked up to see him staring at her with an expectant look.

"My dagger?" he said, raising his eyebrows. "I noticed you're not giving it back."

"Oh." And suddenly, she knew the atonement she preferred. "You asked what would make me feel better. I'd like to keep it." She hesitated. "And I'll take the scabbard, too, please."

"It's been in my family for generations," he said, his lips bloodless.

Oh, yes, this was the real Zeru. He would not trust her with a weapon, and he certainly wouldn't give her something of great value. He would only offer an apology on his own terms. She waited until he looked truly nauseated before she handed the blade back.

Zeru took it and slid it into the scabbard. After a moment's hesitation, he took a breath, then with a hasty sort of grace, held them out to her with a bow of his head. "They're yours."

Her heart gave an unsteady beat. Another test? Another trick?

His tone sharpened. "Take it."

With alert care, she took the dagger in its scabbard, winding the leather around her waist. Her heart calmed at the reassuring knowledge that she once again had a weapon to defend herself. As she struggled with the buckle, he moved forward. She held still as he deftly secured it, his hands brushing her waist. He nodded as he looked her over.

"It looks well on you," he pronounced.

Something warmed in her chest before she had a chance to stifle it. Their eyes met. She couldn't read his expression.

125

"I'll be in the library." With a stiff nod, he walked out, his stride less graceful than usual.

Cassia held her hand to the cool metal, reassuring herself it was real.

What a strange thing. He must have felt worse than she'd realized about what had happened with the Summoner. But to bandage her wounds? To give her a dagger that meant so much to him? She unsheathed the blade and stared at the fox embossed on the hilt.

It looked like the creature that had protected her in the summoning circle. With everything that had happened, she hadn't made the connection. And she hadn't even thought to mention the winged creature she'd seen by the lake in the forest.

But first, she needed to digest Zeru's change toward her. Something had shifted, something small and insubstantial, but perhaps important. She was starting to have trouble thinking of him as her mortal enemy.

And that scared her more than anything.

13

We, the folk, were once the guardians of the land.
Humans worshipped us, giving us offerings of gold and food.
—FROM *THE ORIGINS OF THE LAND FOLK*

CASSIA WENT TO THE LIBRARY AND FOUND IT empty. With no one around to stop her, she picked up a volume on the history of the land folk and took it outside. The previously eerie silence was broken by a few birdcalls. And to her surprise, the apple tree was now full of red, ripe fruit. Delighted, she picked one, taking a bite and sighing with satisfaction at its taste. She picked another, then returned to the courtyard and found a stone bench that wasn't broken. As she ate the second apple, she looked around. The haze in the sky seemed to be lifting. A touch of sun made the neglected courtyard seem more inviting. She curled up on the bench and opened the book, resting the heavy tome on her knees.

Much of the history was familiar to her. She knew that Sylvans traditionally depended on revelry to keep themselves healthy and long-lived. But one thing she hadn't understood was the reverence humans had once had for Sylvans. Hailing them as the rightful custodians of the forests, humans had left them offerings of gold, food, armor, even weapons. They would even drop precious items into lakes or streams as appeasements for the spirits who protected those waters. Cassia knew from stories that land folk of that time were prouder, more demanding. They would take revenge if humans used their water or land without giving offerings.

Her mother, Cassia recalled, had a fountain named after her in human lands. Sometimes she forgot that her mother was old enough to remember the time the folk had fled to Thirstwood. As the light failed, she closed the book and returned to her tower, feeling sad. Thoughts of her mother made her melancholy.

As night fell and Cassia still couldn't turn off her thoughts, she gave up trying to sleep and returned to the woods. The sense of being watched was stronger in the dark, the silence more menacing. She had a conviction that these woods were hungry, crying out for help. She wished she could speak to the trees the way her father could. Ask them questions and understand the answers. But all she had was a vague sense of wrongness, of things not being what they should.

The gibbous moon was enough to show her a path, but the shadows were deep, making her neck prickle. She was too curious to turn back. The winged creature had to be a guardian of Welkincaster. She needed to know more about him. Maybe he had the answers she was seeking.

Before long, she found herself in the clearing with the small lake. The glassy pool reflected moon sprites in a glittering array, like gently rippling stars. A shift in the air alerted her that she wasn't alone. One minute, the winged stranger blended in with all the other forest things. The next, he was there, standing out.

Though he was tall and muscular and moved with the care of a predator, the moon sprites moved closer, hovering around him in a welcoming cloud. More reason to think this was a guardian spirit. Though moonlight didn't much penetrate the canopy, she could just make out strange markings on his face, swirls like a painted design on his forehead and one cheek. His hair was tipped with gold as if he'd been basking in the sun.

Instead of greeting her, he picked up a large fallen leaf from the rock and twisted it in his hands, staring at it as if he could puzzle out some mystery in its veins.

Cassia tried to calm her racing heart. "What's your name?"

He looked up from the leaf, speaking softly. "Aril."

"I'm Cassia," she said, folding her arms to hide their tremble. It didn't matter how curious or determined she was. If he was a defender of the welkin, that meant he was dangerous. She only hoped her instinct was right that he wasn't dangerous to *her*.

He inclined his head in greeting.

"Are you a guardian of Welkincaster?" she asked, wanting confirmation.

"What do you mean by guardian?"

She fought the urge to step back. If he wasn't a guardian, what was he? "Zerians like yourself keep this welkin safe from intruders. More should be waking soon."

Aril inclined his head. "What sort of intruders?"

She had no idea. "Come to the castle tomorrow morning for instructions." She lifted her arm and pointed. "It's that way." She waited to see if he would fly away the way he had last time she'd mentioned reporting to the castle.

Instead, he nodded and moved closer, stopping at the water's edge. She had the sudden thought that this clearing might be his spot, and she was, in fact, intruding.

"I hope you don't mind me being here," she said.

"Not at all," he said. "You are welcome."

She relaxed at the sincerity in his voice.

"Is the water not cold?" Aril asked.

Cassia chuckled softly. "Not for me. My sister Enora says I'm like a wood sprite. I never mind the cold."

"You are of the forest." His eyes caught the moonlight as he looked her over. "I can…smell it on you. The forest breathes and lives in you."

A strange fluttering filled her rib cage. She was touched, and a little surprised and unsure how to respond. Her sisters showed affection through teasing. Her father never praised. Perhaps spending most of her time at the outskirts of battles waiting to be called on as a weapon of last resort didn't leave much opportunity for admiration.

"That was a great compliment to a Sylvan," she said, her throat tight.

"What is a Sylvan?" he asked.

Her eyebrows rose at his question. But then she remembered Gutel saying Sylvans did not come to the sacred realm. "We're forest folk."

"You live…in trees," he said, as if half remembering something.

"That was once true. We each still have a tree we're connected to." She felt a familiar pang of longing. "What sort of creature are you?"

He turned his head away, his profile in silhouette. The curve of his nose was somewhat birdlike, but it was hard to see more than that. She waited, but he didn't answer. Did he not know or did he not want to say? Her curiosity about him was piqued.

"Do you swim?" she asked, searching for a neutral topic. "I wish we had a small lake like this back home. My sisters and I swim in the Scar but it's more of a battle against the current."

"The Scar?" he asked.

"A river," she said. "It's near my home."

"Where is that?" he asked, his face in shadow.

"I'm not sure. Somewhere below this cloud."

He cocked his head to the side, looking more birdlike than ever. "Is that why you have no wings? You don't live in the sky?"

She smiled at the surprise in his tone. "No. I dream about flying sometimes." Lately, she dreamed of falling.

He was quiet for a minute. Usually, silence felt awkward, but Cassia found this peaceful. "I like it here," she said finally.

"Yes," Aril said. "I like it here, too."

Something in his tone made her cheeks heat, and again she wondered if she was being naive to be so trusting of him. "I should get some sleep. I'll see you again."

"Very well," Aril said, bowing deeply from the waist. With a light movement, he sprang up, his great wings spanning the sky. As he disappeared, Cassia found she had a lump in her throat. Maybe because Aril seemed a bit lost. Or maybe she envied that he could leave whenever he wanted.

After her midnight wanderings, Cassia slept well past dawn, her eyes opening to her view out the tower window. In the light of day, Aril seemed almost like a dream, something she had created out of loneliness. Her curiosity about him would not be denied, though. She found Gutel alone in the library, perched on a stool facing the bookshelves, his chin resting on his hand. He turned briefly, his eyes cooling as they fell on her, then turned away again.

She moved determinedly to the window seat. She wouldn't be scared away by the grumpiness of a hearth-spirit. Glancing around, she said, "I thought Zeru would be in here."

"He brought you the bandages, I see," the kobold said, choosing a book. "Sure you didn't throw him out the window?"

Cassia fought a smile. "I thought about it."

Gutel snorted.

"He gave me his dagger." Cassia angled herself so he could see the weapon at her hip.

"Why would he do a fool thing like that?"

She frowned at his clear disapproval. "I think he felt bad about the Summoner. You know, the one who set a hostile spirit on me and left me slashed to ribbons?"

Gutel had the grace to look abashed. "That should never have happened. Xoden is a plague. I wish you'd thrown *him* out the window."

Finally, a little softening toward her. "Is he not like the other Seers you've hired to reinforce the wards of this place?"

The kobold made a sound of disgust. "A few of them know what they're doing. Some are plain worthless. You can guess which category he falls into."

This civility was a good start. If she offered him information, he might offer some in return. "I think I saw a Zerian," she ventured.

He swiveled to face her, his eyes wide. "Where? When?"

"Last night. By a lake in a clearing in the woods. He looked like those creatures in the portrait gallery."

"You're sure it wasn't a bird?" He eyed her with obvious doubt. "A sprite or a shadow? You Sylvans don't see well at night."

She breathed in for patience. "There was enough moonlight. It wasn't a bird. Or a sprite. And we spoke to each other."

"So," Gutel said, and might have smiled under his beard. "The spirits of Welkincaster are waking."

Cassia drew the dagger from its scabbard, showing the winged fox on the hilt. "Speaking of spirits, a creature that looks like this protected me in the summoning circle."

Gutel's mouth dropped open. He looked more surprised by that than her mention of a Zerian.

"What is it?" She offered him the hilt and he took it, hefting it experimentally before staring at the design.

"A beautiful piece," he said, handing it back carefully. "Quite old and well-made. Keep it safe."

She took it back, returning it to the scabbard with care. "You clearly know something about this and how it's connected to me." When he didn't reply, she sighed. "I'm being open with you. The least you can do is share information in return. Or don't kobolds believe in fairness?"

He eyed her resentfully. "I believe in Sylvans being too curious for their own good."

She shrugged. "Then you know I won't stop asking. In fact, consider me your new closest companion." She took a spot on the chair next to him, putting her hands on her knees and leaning toward him. "I'll follow you everywhere. I won't leave your side until you share what you know. You'll likely never sleep again. Won't this be fun?"

His eyes widened. "I had no idea you had such a cruel streak." He put his hands to his head and adjusted his hat. "It's called a Vozarra. One of the creatures of the welkins."

"Why did it appear in the circle with me?" She toyed absently with her ring.

Gutel nodded, his eyes on the Solis Gemma. "Because you were in danger."

"I've been in danger for days. Why now?"

The kobold wiped his forehead with the back of a hand. "It's hard to accept. You came to the ring by accident. I'd assumed it was meant for someone else. That you were merely a temporary aberration in its history."

— 133 —

Cassia's jaw clenched. *Temporary aberration.* Not that she hadn't had the same thought herself. "And what do you think now that the Vozarra defended me? And spirits are waking?"

"It pains me," Gutel said, his eyebrows drawn together. He stood and began pacing, his hands making helpless gestures. "But it appears to mean that the welkin has...accepted you...as its rightful caretaker." He tensed as if bracing for something. "It recognizes your stewardship of the ring, and therefore your power to bring life and protection to this sanctuary."

Cassia sat in stunned silence, his words echoing in her mind. *Rightful caretaker. Stewardship.* Bringing life and protection to this impossible realm she hadn't known existed. And the sacred, ancient magic of the place had found her worthy.

That was perhaps the most shocking thing of all.

She'd had little choice in coming here, but now it felt like fate. If the kobold was correct, it meant she'd had a connection to this realm in the clouds from the moment she put on the ring. The ring she'd been told was nothing but a weapon. It was so much more.

"I still say it may be temporary," Gutel said quickly. "Rightful stewards have always been Zerians."

Cassia paused at that. Perhaps she *was* an aberration. But if Gutel believed she was a rightful caretaker, she could use that to her advantage. "Well, I'm not a Zerian. Don't you think it's time you accepted that and did your duty as one of the guardians of this realm? I need help. Are you going to refuse me?"

"All right, all right!" Gutel cried. "Enough! If I wanted to be shamed, I'd visit my mother's spirit in the Netherwhere. Honestly, you are merciless."

"Thank you," Cassia said, smiling. She waited, letting him catch his breath.

"Let me go back to the beginning," he said more calmly. He pulled his stool closer to her, his red eyes lively. "How much do you know about the Old Ones?"

"Not much," she admitted, determined to be a better pupil now than she had ever been for her tutors.

Gutel cleared his throat. "The Old Ones were giant spirits who sprang forth when the world was young. They heaved rocks in a constant shaking of ground, made winds that lifted great waves that swallowed continents, blazed lightning over the skies, and poured lava from the mountains. They played that way for an untold time, making our world into the shape it is now. But after ages, they became bored and longed for someone to appreciate their handiwork. They longed for children. Brought forth by their longing, the ones we call the Ancients came to life. Noctua, Nerthus, and Solis, among them. Of course, there were more than the three sisters, but I don't have time to tell you everything."

Cassia tried to hide her Sylvan curiosity and merely nodded. "Go on."

"Over time," he continued, "the Ancients themselves wanted more creatures to share the lands with them. But the three sisters realized that nothing would grow if wind and lava and lightning kept destroying everything. So, they bespelled their primordial forebears into sleep."

"Nerthus made a lute of slumber!" Cassia said, delighted to remember something of relevance. "And then she helped to put the wind and rock and lava giants—the Old Ones—to rest. I liked that story when I was a child."

"It's not a story," Gutel snapped, pointing to her hand. "The Solis Gemma you wear on your finger? Is that a story?"

"Fine, I liked that *history*," she corrected.

He gave an approving nod. "Each sister had an artifact that

they used to bind the Old Ones into a long slumber. Nerthus fashioned a lute from a branch of the most beautiful tree in the world. Noctua harvested silver from the moon and had it made into a cup of forgetfulness. And to maintain the life force of the sleeping forebears, Solis chose a rock that glowed like the sun, and had it shaped into a gemstone. It was called the Solis Gemma."

A chill swept over her back as she looked down at the amber cabochon on the gold band. Surely not. The ring on her finger was used to *maintain the life force* of the Old Ones? How could something so important end up in Zeru's family? Or on her own unworthy finger? It made her stomach churn. It was as if a thread tugged on her, leading all the way back to Solis. And if she broke that thread, she would be destroying history. Angering the Ancients. Upsetting the balance of the world. The ring bore down on her with the weight of an anvil, heavier than ever.

"Some accounts say the Solis Gemma brought joy, hope, or freedom from darkness," Gutel went on, watching Cassia carefully. "Solis wanted the Old Ones to sleep in peace, and the Solis Gemma provided that."

"It sounds like the ring was meant for good," Cassia said, wishing she didn't have to take these warm stories into darker places. "But the ring was used in the Ancient Wars. The wearer was called Deathringer."

"The ring's theft and corruption into a weapon happened much later," Gutel said, lifting a palm. "As I said, the Old Ones slept, other creatures came to be, and the Ancients nurtured them. Perhaps too well. From barren to fertile, the land exploded with life. There were so many creatures vying for dominance in places that had once held only trees and birds and other small creatures that the Ancients could scarcely rest. Over time, the Ancients craved peace from this ever more crowded land. That's when they harvested power from the primordials and used it to create the welkins. Slowly, carefully, so as not to wake the Old Ones, they took some of the old magic from deep within the earth and spun it into the sky. From here, they observed the land of mortals, both the very long-lived land folk and the short-lived humans, as well as the eternal spirits who roamed the air."

"If I hadn't seen this place for myself," Cassia said, "I'd never have believed it."

Gutel looked pleased. "Indeed, it is impossibly beautiful here. Or it used to be. The Ancients were entranced by what they'd created. But they weren't finished. They needed votaries to guard this realm. They chose creatures they deemed worthy and bestowed wings on them. Any of the land folk could be chosen. So the Zerians came to be."

"You don't have wings," Cassia pointed out.

"Of course not!" His eyebrows snapped together, and he pierced her with a sharp glare. "I'm a hearth-spirit. I guard the hearth, the walls, and the rooms inside. I have no need for wings. And the Zerians were long established by the time I came here."

Seeing she had upset him, she changed the subject. "Are those the people in the portrait gallery? The past stewards?"

Gutel nodded. "There were many welkins, many Zerians, back then. Much art and revelry and song. It was a different time. But yes, through most of its history, the ring was worn by a Zerian."

"Was the ring passed by right of succession when a steward died?"

"There is no right of succession. Stewardship was passed on by choice. The lore says the wearer must be of good character, but also strong enough to bear the magic of the Old Ones. It is an honor to wear the ring, but also a burden. Acting as the bringer of

⌐ 137 ⌐

life and vitality to this place takes a toll. It takes energy and life force from whoever wears it."

Cassia took a shuddering breath. That was the first time she'd ever heard anyone acknowledge the fact that the ring was a burden as well as a great power. "I think it pulls from my strength when I use it."

Gutel nodded slowly, his eyes understanding. "Over time, a bond is formed so they can work in harmony. But if the wearer isn't strong enough...well, it can kill someone who doesn't have enough vitality to handle its power."

Cassia shivered. Did that mean the ring would eventually kill her, take all her life force as she'd feared? She bit her lip before asking, "A Seer in the Cryptlands said there is a bond between me and the ring. Does that mean I'm worthy?"

The kobold looked at her hand. "I'm no Seer. But if the bond is complete, then...yes."

She sighed. "The bond isn't complete. She said it might be one day soon. Can someone steal the ring before that happens?"

The kobold wrinkled his nose. "I don't know that much about the magic. But my understanding is that the bond can only be broken by choice of the wearer, by gifting the ring to someone with a close connection to the wearer. This is the way the magic is supposed to be passed on, only to someone trustworthy who will be a good steward to the welkin."

"But trust can be misplaced," she pointed out.

Cassia felt a prickle on the back of her neck and turned sharply to see Zeru in the doorway. She wondered how long he had been there.

Zeru took his spot in the red chair, leaning back and resting an ankle on his knee. "Don't stop on my account."

The kobold cleared his throat, clearly sensing tension. "The three sisters fought. Nerthus, Noctua, Solis. They razed cities, uprooted forests, and made the land barren in their conflict."

Cassia tried to block out Zeru's presence. "What were they fighting over?"

"Dominance. Power. And most importantly, life for their favored people. Nerthus preferred the humans and hated how some of the land folk hunted them." His eyes shifted to Cassia, and she remembered what he had said about the Sylvan king hunting humans. She steeled her spine and gave him a warning look.

Something flickered in the kobold's eyes, and he continued. "Noctua favored the ephemeral spirits, beings of air and fire who roamed freely and took what they wanted, passing between the earth and the Netherwhere—a place of chaos and instability. Solis preferred the land folk like Sylvans and Dracu, declaring they had the right to hunt humans or any creature. They fought, and thousands upon thousands died. Before the Ancient Wars, there were many more of us land folk. So many more."

"I'm confused about Solis," Cassia said. "She was kind enough to want to bring joy to the Old Ones, but she believed humans should be hunted?"

Gutel nodded in understanding. "You might think by the creation of the ring that Solis was peaceful by nature. But she had no compunction about killing those she saw as beneath her. She found a champion who learned to use the ring for ill. That was the Deathringer of legend."

"Who was the Deathringer?" Cassia asked, leaning forward.

Gutel paused, watching her before answering. "That was before my time. There have been theories, but all agree the Deathringer was described as a creature with horns."

"An Azpian, then?" Cassia asked.

139

"Couldn't have been," Zeru said. "The ring was used against Azpians, I assume, as it only affects us."

"Not solely," Gutel said. "It isn't light that kills. It is a surfeit of life force, pushed into a body too small to contain it."

"You mean," Cassia said slowly, "the ring could kill Sylvans, too?"

Gutel gave her a hard look. "I don't see why not. Might want to think about that when you're deciding how to use that gemstone. At any rate, only a creature with enough life force can wear the ring."

"Too much life force is what makes it a weapon," Cassia breathed. The revelation that Sylvans could be harmed, too, was terrifying. But she was also closer than she'd ever been to finding out what she needed to know.

"A corruption, but an effective one," Gutel said darkly. "Solis's champion caused much destruction." He paused, cleared his throat, and looked away. "It turned out, however, that his slaughter of many thousands wasn't enough to win the war."

"How was the war won?" Zeru asked, drawing Cassia's attention. "I have heard too many different answers for any one of them to be true."

"It was neither won nor lost but ended by a bargain," Gutel said. "The sisters realized their war was destroying everything they themselves held dear, so they made a pact. Each would govern a realm and leave the others alone. Noctua governs the Netherwhere and agreed to keep her ephemeral subjects from entering the material realm, though of course Seers have found ways to summon and contain spirits for short periods. Nerthus watches over the humans, though not many of them worship her anymore. And Solis is the goddess of wild, uncultivated places, still guarded by the land folk, though their numbers have dwindled. When the bargain was struck and the war over, the Cryptlands were dug."

He shifted his attention to Zeru. "A burial place for all who had died during the Ancient Wars."

Zeru nodded. "And the Dracu, creatures of water and earth, chose it when their wetlands were taken over by the humans. Many creatures already lived there, like the drakes and Skrattis." He glanced at Cassia. "We'd been closer allies with the Sylvans, once. The Dracu were caretakers of the roots of trees."

Cassia laughed, then bit her lip as the kobold looked at her with a scandalized expression. "The Dracu cared for the trees? You can't possibly think I'd believe that."

"Your excellent tutors didn't teach you that, I suppose?" Zeru didn't try to hide his animosity, which almost made her wonder if she had imagined him bandaging her wounds and giving her the dagger.

"Much changed when the land folk were forced to move from their natural homes," Gutel said. "Friends became enemies."

"How was the ring lost?" Cassia asked, not caring to dwell on past friends turned enemies. "I know it came here after the Ancient Wars and was worn by Zerian stewards. But when did that end? How did the ring end up in the Cryptlands?"

"That I don't know," Gutel admitted. "The last Zerian steward was Xerxunia the Wise, or so she was called in my time. At some point, I went into my slumber and much more time passed than should have. But I can tell you, at one time, our Zerian caretakers moved freely between here and the lower mainland." He shook his head. "Somehow, it was lost in the Cryptlands."

"I wouldn't call it lost," Zeru broke in. "As I said, the ring has been in my family for generations. I don't know who last wore it, but I know my mother was tasked with keeping the ring safe." His eyes met Cassia's. "Unfortunately, she didn't tell me that until after I gave it away."

"If you got your hands on it as a child," Gutel said, "your mother failed in her task."

Zeru's jaw hardened. "Careful, Kobold."

Gutel held up his palms. "It's a thing of great power, vital to the upkeep of the sacred welkins, stolen and corrupted to become a weapon of the Ancient Wars. It's an artifact of legend. And you said you found it among your mother's things?"

Zeru nodded stiffly. "I admit it's strange. My mother always swore it was hidden. She couldn't understand how I'd found it."

"Tell me about the fox creature," Cassia said, her head spinning with all this knowledge. "What did you call it, a Vozarra?"

"Ah, yes." Gutel sat forward, his eyes bright. "When the wearer of the ring is in mortal danger, a spirit is summoned. It's believed that each of the artifacts has a protective spirit connected to it. In the case of the ring, a Vozarra."

Cassia looked at the dagger. "I've been in danger before, and nothing ever came to defend me."

"Then perhaps the ring had not yet accepted you. Or you were never in mortal danger," Gutel said decisively.

"I was," she said, feeling heat rise to her face at his dismissal of the most terrible experience of her life. "Starting with night I put on the ring. The Dracu queen's vassals tried to kill me." Cassia looked down at her bandaged hand. Even before the attack by Xoden's creature, her hands had been crisscrossed with fine white scars from where drakes had clawed at her and imps had torn at her with their sawlike teeth.

When she looked up again, Gutel's eyes were narrowed in thought. "How did you escape?"

"My father came to my rescue," she said, her chest warming as she remembered. She'd always assumed the trees had alerted him. Maybe, she'd thought, maybe he'd even sensed it through a

⁓ 142 ⁓

bond with her, his child. In any case, he had come to save her. It had meant everything. It was how she knew that she mattered to him. Because of that night.

"To *your* rescue," Zeru said, his voice hard.

She looked up to see his eyes glittering coldly.

"Yes." Her fists tightened in her lap. "You were there."

"I remember it distinctly," he said. "The Sylvan king rode into the clearing, ordered you brought to him, and checked to make sure you had the ring. Then he foisted you on one of the Huntsmen, barely glancing at you. I'm not even sure he knew you were alive. He came for the ring."

The viciousness of his claims stole her breath. "You are vile," she breathed.

"I watched him," Zeru said, relentless in the way he held her eyes, the way he spoke with razor bluntness. "You were insensible. I was fighting to get to you. I saw the way he lifted your arm and dropped it as if you were no more than a container that held his precious ring." His eyes held a fury she had never seen in them. "It was chilling."

14

> Where two or more Azpians are found, mischief is certain.
> —Excharias, Sylvan poet

Cassia was shaking with fury. How dare he—*how dare he* suggest her father cared nothing for her. "Enough," she said, pushing to her feet. "Gutel, you've admitted I'm the caretaker of Welkincaster. I want you to show me what this ring is supposed to do."

Zeru's attention snapped to Gutel. "She's delusional. There is no possible way."

Gutel straightened his hat. "She's right. I'm almost sure of it. The ring sent a spirit to protect her when she was in danger. And she has restored one of the apple trees."

Zeru shook his head, tension radiating from him. "Wishful thinking."

"You saw it yourself," Cassia argued. "I touched the tree and said I wanted an apple and...you know what? Never mind. Your opinion doesn't matter anymore."

Cassia clattered down the tower steps, determination coursing through her. She didn't care what Zeru thought, but it would be satisfying to see him chagrined when she proved him wrong.

As Cassia strode to the withered orchard outside the castle walls, a light breeze ruffled the treetops, a faint pine smell riding the air. When she reached the fruit trees, some of her bravado faded. What if it didn't work?

"Good, good," the hearth-spirit said as he caught up to her. "Did you notice the sky is clearer? And the air isn't so dry. Signs the welkin is already being restored." He went past the apple tree she had already plundered and stopped next to a gnarled pear tree. "Show us what you can do, Sylvan."

She toyed with the ring, suddenly feeling much like she had when her father had ordered her to use the ring's blast in front of all the Huntsmen with no preparation.

Zeru strode into the orchard, his demeanor as foul as a winter storm. "Show us, then, Sylvan. If you're truly what you claim."

She stared at the drooping branches, less confident now that it was time to prove herself. The apples might not have been her doing. The idea that she could use the ring of legend, the weapon that had killed thousands in a bloody war, to grow apples in a barren orchard seemed ridiculous. But Gutel claimed she could. And if she proved that she could use the ring as Welkincaster's caretaker, she might gain the kobold's support. She had to try, even under Zeru's critical eye.

Gutel stepped closer, as if to draw her attention from Zeru, his tone softening. "Nothing to worry about. This is a good place to start." He nodded toward the tree. "Just a touch and a word, Sylvan, that's all it will take. Such is the power of the Solis Gemma."

Her stomach clenching with nerves, Cassia took a steadying breath. She touched her hand to the branch, willing the ring to respond. As she always did, she forced her will against it, feeling power rising and twisting inside of her, fighting back.

"I want a pear," she said, making her voice sound as commanding as possible.

Silence filled the air for several moments as they all stared at the branches. No matter how she struggled to make the ring do as she wished, no fruit appeared. She made the mistake of looking at Zeru, whose smug expression made her want to pick up a stick and whack him with it.

Gutel's brows were drawn together in consternation. "I don't understand. Try again."

Taking a nervous breath, she willed the ring to respond, feeling its power growing before she touched the tree. Light flared, a crack rent the air, and the branch she touched fell, bouncing off the kobold's shoulder on its way down.

Gutel grunted, and the stormy look that rolled over his face made her swallow.

She closed her eyes. "I'll try harder."

"Please don't," he said irritably, rubbing his shoulder. "The poor tree only has a few more branches."

"This calls your theories about her into question," Zeru said.

Gutel held up a hand and turned back to Cassia. "What exactly do you do when you speak to the ring?"

She pursed her lips. "I force my will against it, pushing through when it fights back."

"No, no, no." He waved his hand dismissively. "You're trying to use it as a weapon. The ring focuses the power of the sun, the power of life, and mixes it with your will for growth. There's no need for fighting it." He shook his head. "No wonder you've struggled."

Cassia stared at the branch, a pressure in her temples as she tried to accept this new way of thinking. She had been using the ring one way for so long, she had never considered there was another. Had she been going about it wrong? Maybe Enora was right that she took everything too seriously. Maybe the key was relaxing and trusting that it would work. Swallowing the knot of worry in her throat, she placed her hand on the bark and closed her eyes. Then she spoke to it, Sylvan to tree, just as her mother had taught her in the garden. She had always said, *You only have to ask the plants to grow, and they will.*

"A pear," she said softly. She felt a burst of warmth in her chest. Not painful but powerful. Somehow...pleasant.

Hearing a gasp, she opened her eyes.

A tiny bud that had not been there before grew and blossomed into a flower, which in turn grew into a firm, golden pear that hung enticingly from its stem. The breath left Cassia's chest. After so many years thinking of the ring as a weapon, it was strange to realize it had been something else all along. And that something else came...naturally to her. An unfamiliar feeling bubbled up inside of her. It took her a second to identify it. Pride.

Gutel picked the pear, gave it a sniff, and bit into it. "Not bad. Not bad. Now for a Vozarra."

"What?" she asked, startled by this sudden escalation.

"Summon your Vozarra." He took another bite, his brow wrinkling. "Say, 'Vozarra, attend me.' Be imperious about it."

"You said the spirit is only summoned when I'm in mortal danger."

"That's one way," Gutel said. "And truthfully, I think the Vozarra would only appear in the lower mainland if you were. But here, in the welkins, it can be summoned without a great need. There was never a ban placed on spirits here. You can even call several at once if you're strong enough to do it. I've seen it."

Was she strong enough to call even one? She hated that she hadn't had time to mentally prepare. But she supposed it would either work or it wouldn't.

"Vozarra, attend me," she said firmly.

A blur of brown and copper swirled in the air, materializing into a fox-faced creature. One second, it was made of sunbeams, the next it stood before her, as solid as the trees around it. It had a furry head with a narrow muzzle and huge, fur-tufted ears. Golden eyes blinked quizzically, and a pink tongue flicked out to lick sharp teeth. Cassia blinked. The Vozarra blinked back. Its nose twitched. It looked at Gutel, then Zeru, its watchful stare resting on the Dracu.

Gutel chuckled. "It does seem protective of you. Let us see if you can approach it without getting a bite."

"I'm not rushing the creature," she said, heart still racing. She couldn't get over that she had called and it had appeared. The Solis Gemma was more complex than she'd ever suspected. So much more than a weapon.

The kobold offered his hand. The creature butted it as if in approval. "It knows me well enough. Might be one that has been here before. There's no telling if it's the same spirit every time."

Zeru reached out a fist for the creature to sniff. Two leathery wings snapped open from the Vozarra's back, unfolding like a paper fan. Cassia stepped back, and Zeru jerked in surprise.

Gutel laughed heartily. "You didn't notice those wings, did you? I was waiting for that!" He held his stomach.

Zeru kept his hand extended to the Vozarra, allowing it to get used to his scent. When he brushed its neck, the creature allowed it. When he dropped his arm, it dipped its head and butted him, demanding more. Zeru smiled as he scratched it behind the ears, his battle-scarred hands half-concealed by thick fur. If he had been anyone else, Cassia might have thought it sweet.

"Stop trying to win over my Vozarra," she said, annoyed at how the creature seemed to instantly warm up to him. Stepping forward, she offered her hand. The Vozarra sniffed delicately, its golden eyes wide, and tilted its head to one side. Its eyes were gentle. Cassia felt something inside herself soften in response. She had to swallow before she could speak. "My name is Cassia."

"Careful," Zeru said, his voice grave. For a moment, she was surprised that he would caution her, then realized he was talking to the Vozarra. "Trust her at your peril."

She ignored him, turning to Gutel. "What do we do with it now?"

"Let it be," he said simply. "It will go where it likes. Oh, and if you get any ideas about riding it, either of you, know that a spirit can't go to the lower mainland because of the ban. It would disappear on the way down and you'd find yourself descending rather faster than you'd like."

Cassia winced at the image of falling from the clouds, discarding the escape plans that had already been forming. She petted the furry head with a slow, careful stroke. "Oh, you're soft. And so pretty. The prettiest thing I've ever seen."

"Now who's trying to win it over?" Zeru accused.

Over the next few hours, her hope grew until she was giddy with it. She touched trees and asked for fruit until the branches groaned with the weight of their burden. Gutel produced a basket, and soon it was overflowing with a colorful harvest of apples, pears, and apricots. The trees stood straighter once they started bearing fruit. The gravel path looked neater and more visible the more she walked over it. Cassia moved along, touching trees and asking for things, and generally feeling more powerful than she ever had in her whole life. It was heady. Intoxicating. She could do this forever.

"Slow down," the kobold cautioned her, but she was beyond restraint. Whatever was happening was like fruit wine pumping through her veins. Nothing could stop her.

Her feet crushed tall grasses and underbrush as she neared

the forest. Looking down, she realized that mushrooms had popped up at the edge of the path as she stepped lightly along it. She laughed and heard how wild she sounded. But she could cackle all she liked. She was the bestower of life.

"I said slow down, you fool Sylvan," Gutel's voice said, but the trees beckoned, their twisted trunks seeming to cry out for her help. She obliged. She fell to her knees next to one of the trees and placed her hand where one of the roots curved into the ground. Or the cloud, in this case. The power rushing through her was so heady, she almost wanted to laugh.

Live, heal, grow, she thought, bringing to mind every word she could think of that might help the forest of Welkincaster.

Unexpectedly, she felt the other trees, too. One root system. Like one great tree. The forest might look small, but in life and need, it was overwhelming. So thirsty. Too much. She could feel the life force being pulled from her heart into the ring and then out into the trees, and she couldn't fight it. Her face froze, her throat closing before she could cry out. She was trapped in a state of endless giving, generosity gone amok.

Someone was shaking her shoulders, but that didn't help. *Stop!* She tried to say the word but could only choke. *Stop!*

Zeru's voice shouted in her ear. "You heedless twit of a tree-dweller, damn your eyes!" His apple-tart breath was in her face, his hands gripping her shoulders too hard. "If you weren't dying, I'd strangle you!"

The pain in her heart was indescribable. The fear she'd always had, that the ring would one day tear her apart, was coming true. The trees were taking the blood right out of her. Her pulse slowed.

And stopped.

Suddenly, the Vozarra was there. She felt its fur against her hands and face, heard its snarls and the snapping of its teeth. And somehow, somewhere in her mind, she understood. It was warning the trees to stop taking. She heard the grind of the creature's teeth sinking into bark, and the tree recoiled, its root twitching violently under Cassia's hand, like a snake stung by a wasp.

And she was free. Flat on her face in the dirt, but free. As her heart started up again, she groaned.

"Addlepated, thoughtless, rash..." Zeru was still going.

Head spinning, Cassia put her hands against the mossy ground, careful not to touch the tree again. "You didn't have to drop me in the dirt," she said hoarsely, folding herself into a cross-legged position. When she rubbed her eyes and opened them, three sets of eyes stared back. Gold, green, and red.

The Vozarra was the first to blink. It sat and licked its paw as if nothing had happened.

Gutel glanced at Zeru, then back to her. "I've never seen the like," he said in a kind of hollow daze. "I'm going to check the cupboards for some ale or cider. I don't even care if it's three hundred years old." He wandered off, his green and brown clothing blending with the foliage.

Zeru's emerald glare didn't move from her. He looked as if he wanted to shake her again, at the very least.

"I think I might have overdone it," Cassia admitted, pushing her hair off her face. "With the ring."

"You think?" he snarled.

"Can you help me up?" she asked, as much to break the angry silence as anything.

Part of her knew it was wrong, for a multitude of reasons, to ask the Dracu, but she ached in ways she hadn't thought possible, particularly in the center of her chest. Every breath hurt. The rest of her felt bruised, too. If she could sleep for a year or so, she'd be as fresh as morning dew.

"Help yourself up," he said, standing with an angry movement. Without another word, he turned away and strode down the path. He was just . . . leaving her. *Miserable Dracu.*

Putting a hand to her head, she bit her lip to stop it from trembling and tried to make a plan that would start with her on the ground and end with her standing.

A furry head butted her cheek.

Cassia turned gratefully toward the Vozarra, burying her face in its soft fur until her breathing calmed. She was surprised how close she felt to the spirit already. "Thank you for saving me."

The creature sniffed, but she understood the meaning. It was telling her she was fine now, and she should get up and find food for both of them.

She smiled. "As soon as I can. Do you believe that Dracu? Leaving me here. I saved his life, you know. Twice if you count the time I didn't slit his throat. Would you bite him for me?"

The Vozarra tilted its head to the side as if to ask why she'd want it to do that.

She sighed. "Can you help me back to the castle, then?" She put her hand on the Vozarra's back, hoping the creature wouldn't mind taking some of her weight.

"Sylvan."

Cassia's head jerked up at the single, low-voiced word. Zeru stood a couple of feet away. He still looked angry, but he also looked . . . well, resigned.

She tried to look as if she weren't covered in dirt and, truth be told, a bit of drool from when she had lain half-conscious among the roots.

He sighed, came to his knees, and put his hands under her armpits. "Don't fight me, you mad thing."

"I *asked* you for help," she reminded him, holding on to his upper arms.

In a second, she was on her feet, leaning against his side, his arm supporting her back. He felt solid and strong, and for once, she was too exhausted and relieved to be threatened by his nearness. She shuffled one foot, then the other, and got something of a walk going. The Vozarra trailed behind, stopping to sniff and explore along the way.

"What happened?" he asked, holding her to his side.

"I don't know. One minute, I was queen of all life, and the next I was a pond being drained dry. The trees took too much and I didn't know how to stop them." Her lips trembled, so she pressed them together and ground her teeth. She would not cry in front of him.

"I think you have to remember," he said in a dry tone, "that though you wear a ring made by a powerful Ancient, you are not one."

If she hadn't had to watch her feet so closely, she'd have given him a dark look. As if there were any danger of her mistaking that. "Thanks for the reminder."

His voice turned thoughtful. "Maybe there's a way to control the flow of power. If Gutel isn't drunk as a boiled owl by now after what you just put him through, we can ask about it."

We, she thought sourly. As if there was a "we" in all this. Maybe he'd finally accepted that she had power over the ring, so he planned to ingratiate himself. Or at least pretend he didn't hate her as much as she hated him.

"Let him drink," she said, annoyed at how often she found herself wondering what the Dracu was thinking. "I gather the previous caretakers didn't expire while maintaining the gardens."

Zeru gave a little huff, almost a snort. A laugh? Cassia felt a little pulse of satisfaction at the shared humor, then realized he was probably laughing *at* her.

They walked in silence until they came to the orchard. She looked at all the fruit, but instead of feeling accomplished, she regretted trying to do so much at once. "I suppose you can't repair an entire cloud in one day."

"Only a Sylvan would think she could," he said idly. He pulled her tighter to his side as they entered the archway leading into the courtyard.

They reached the steps. She tested her legs and found them to be roughly as strong as wet straw. "I would claim to be able to make it the rest of the way, but I might fall in front of Voz."

"Voz, is it?" Zeru asked, holding her by the shoulders to keep her upright. He gave her an up-and-down appraisal, a line of concentration between his brows.

She glanced away. "You named her."

"Her?" he asked.

Cassia nodded. "The Vozarra speaks to me. I sort of . . . get a sense of her in my mind. She tells me things without words. Right now, I know she's hungry. Apparently when a spirit is in a solid form, they need food like the rest of us." She spotted Voz cavorting in the overgrown garden, her copper-brown fur appearing and disappearing as she leaped and jumped through the tall weeds. "Take me to the dining room and I'll see if this ring will fill a bowl for her."

"No," Zeru answered sharply, bringing her eyes back to his. "You are not using the ring again so soon." When her eyebrows rose, his expression cooled, and he loosened his hold on her shoulders. "She can eat fruit or do her own hunting. I saw a rabbit or two."

She swallowed. "So, the ring really is restoring Welkincaster."

"It seems so." His jaw was tight, and he looked angry. He was the most changeable thing.

As they went up the steps, she was careful to only lean on him as much as necessary. In the cool interior of the castle, the entrance hall seemed brighter, and the chandelier was fixed and hanging from the center of the ceiling. She wished she had time to explore the limits of what she could do here. Suddenly, her chest ached in a different way, with a sense of loss. Her plans didn't involve staying.

But something significant had changed with the ring. Like a box had been unlocked inside her. A new energy hummed through her, and with it, an undeniable sense of confidence in her own power. She felt a connection to the welkin that went deeper than anything she'd felt before, perhaps even rivaling her connection to Thirstwood.

And her perception of the ring had flipped. It was like wearing the same cloak every day for years, only to realize you'd been wearing it inside out all that time. She didn't need to battle the Solis Gemma for supremacy; she merely had to ask and the gemstone would answer. Now that she had *felt* the right way to ask, she could surely do it again. Though she couldn't claim to have mastered the artifact, there was a flow of power that had opened up inside her, like a spigot turned on.

Soon, she would go home to tell her father her discoveries and display her greater abilities. Then she could focus on using that increased proficiency to create an impressive blast of light. Knowing the ring's history would surely help Veleda find more ways to leverage its power.

And she could never have discovered that history or this power anywhere but here. How odd after everything that had happened, she had ended up right where she needed to be. If her life force was strong enough, maybe she would even be able to slay enemies with the ring.

Her steps faltered at the thought—even with her new powers, would she use them to kill?—and Zeru's hand steadied her. "Careful," he said, his voice sharp. Then he muttered something that sounded like "drunken imps."

"What?" She looked up at him, confused.

And then she remembered. When he'd first taken her into the Cryptlands, he'd said that he'd seen drunk imps walk a straighter line. She caught herself nearly smiling and pressed her lips together. Did he really think he could joke about her capture? He had forced her to come here. She couldn't let herself forget that. She couldn't make the mistake of trusting him in any way. Or being grateful that he'd brought her to this place. It had been an accident. And he still intended to steal the ring from her. He'd probably kill her for it if he could.

She glanced at him sidelong. His face was impassive, but his hands were gentle as he helped her up the stairs. Soon, she told herself, she'd get her revenge. She'd use the ring to crush an army of his people. And make her father proud.

She waited for a sense of triumph at the thought. Instead, she found herself swallowing a bitter taste on her tongue.

She told herself it was the taste of victory.

15

> Heed not the pleas of Sylvans.
> Mercy will be your undoing.
> —GAXIX, DRACU PHILOSOPHER

As Cassia stepped outside for her nightly walk, the Vozarra emerged from the shadows, her nose twitching as she sniffed. Cassia bent down and petted her soft head, her throat thick with a sense of wonder. As she ruffled the fox's ears, Voz pawed at them, and Cassia felt the creature's annoyance.

She couldn't help smiling at the Vozarra's accusing look. "Sorry. I guess you don't like your ears touched." She made a mental note not to do that again. "I was going to walk in the woods. Would you like to come with me?"

The fox didn't hesitate, trotting along ahead of her on the path. Cassia smiled as she watched the fox's white-tipped tail appear and disappear among the underbrush as she sniffed her way along. After a while, Voz led her to the clearing with the small lake, perhaps scenting the water. As the fox lowered her head to take a drink, moon sprites rose from the water's surface in a glittering cloud. Thirst sated, Voz jumped down and stalked into the trees on the trail of some scent. Cassia watched her, taking a seat on a flat rock at the lake's edge.

She felt the air change, and knew she was no longer alone.

She caught sight of Aril a moment later as he emerged from the trees.

"Good eve, Aril," she said, less nervous now that she knew he was probably a guardian of Welkincaster.

"Cassia," he said simply, inclining his head.

"How are you?" she asked, feeling awkward. Back home, whenever there were visitors, her sisters were the ones who handled the small talk. She didn't have the knack.

"Well," he replied. "And you?"

She thought of her recent progress with the ring. "Better and better. Did you go to the castle yet?"

Aril shook his head.

"You have nothing to fear from the kobold," she reassured him. "Your people are the rightful guardians of this place. Gutel will be happy to see you."

"I am not *scared* of the kobold," he said, his voice as rough as a shagbark hickory. He folded his wings around himself like a cloak.

She thought she might have stung his pride. "Why, then?"

"I am a spirit. I belong in the open air." His tone told her he'd tired of that topic. "Tell me more about your people. Your home. Where is it?

Cassia smiled at the obvious subject change, a pang in her heart at the thought of her sisters. "I live in a fortress in a bend of the Scar River. In what Gutel calls the lower mainland."

"Do you like it?"

She looked up at the moon sprites making patterns against the night sky. Did she like Scarhamm? She hadn't thought about it. It was her home. Her sisters were there. The fortress was dark, but it had a somber elegance when it was decorated for revels, although those were extremely rare now.

158

"I like it well enough," she said, shoving away the maudlin thoughts. "Do you like it here?"

He hesitated a moment. "I don't think I'm in the right place."

She looked at him quizzically. "What do you mean?" When he didn't answer, she asked, "Where do think you come from?"

"Somewhere else," he said simply. His answers were cryptic at best, and though she tried not to let it bother her, curiosity was starting to get to her. The shadows hid his expression, but she felt his sadness. "Are there more Zerians here yet?" he asked.

"Not yet. Besides me and Voz, it's just Gutel and a Dracu."

"What's a Dracu?" Aril asked. "Do they have wings?"

"No," she said. "They live underground. They have no interest in creatures of the air."

Her chest tightened as she realized that she didn't know if that was true. She was trying to protect Aril from Zeru, but she couldn't think of a credible reason to do so. Zeru would have as little interest in Aril as she had in an imp living in the Cryptlands. The Dracu's purpose was the ring, and he didn't seem to care about the welkin or its spirits at all.

"Would you like to fly?" Aril asked, surprising her into a moment of stunned silence.

She hadn't been hinting. To be sure she wasn't misunderstanding his question, she said, "I don't have wings, remember?"

"I mean...with me."

She stared up at Aril, weighing his words. "Are you...offering to carry me?"

"You told me you dreamed of flying."

Cassia was touched that he'd remembered. But...would she be safe? She sensed only gentleness from him. But she glimpsed his talons catching the moonlight, and her stomach flipped. Those talons could tear flesh.

159

The question was, could she afford to refuse an opportunity to see the welkin from the air, maybe even find a way home?

"All right," she said breathlessly. "Yes, I'd like to go."

"It's colder up there," he said. "You should wear something warmer."

"This is all I have," she said, spreading her hands to indicate her drab Huntsman's garb, her now-sleeveless tunic over linen trousers. She tried to imagine what Gutel would say if she asked to borrow a cloak. She didn't want to find out. "I'll be fine in this."

"If you're sure," he said, reaching out to put his arms around her, enveloping her. "Hold on to me."

She gripped his arms, his chest solid and steady at her back. "Ready."

He bent his knees and launched them up, and Cassia let out a squeak as her stomach dropped to the Cryptlands. Above the canopy, his wings flapped, creating their own wind. Exhilaration kicked in, and she half laughed, half screeched.

"Scared?" he asked, tensing. "Should I land?"

"No!" she cried, looking around. The forest was a dark blanket beneath her, the castle a pale shape in the moonlight. She could see where the welkin's edge frothed out, flowing like an overpoured tankard of ale. Beyond, the moon touched cloud after cloud, a whole world she had never imagined she would see. It was dizzying. "This is incredible!"

"Oh," Aril said. "Good."

He did a loop over the forest, the sharp angle making her head spin.

"Welkincaster looks even smaller from above," she said breathlessly. The silvered treetops bent and bowed in the wind, waving at her like hands raised in greeting. For a few minutes, Aril allowed them to glide with the breeze.

⁓ 160 ⁓

"How far can you fly?" she asked, staring at the edges of the cloud. "Can you leave the welkin?"

"I haven't tried," he said. "We should go back."

He turned in a wide arc and headed toward the clearing, easily visible because of the moon sprites glowing like moving stars above the lake. His great wings spread wide, pumping to slow their descent. Cassia braced for impact, but he alighted gracefully.

"Thank you," she said sincerely. She turned to face him, aware that his arms still held her, but not feeling any need to move away. "When will you take me again?"

In the dark, she could only see the upward curve of his lips and the sparkle in his eyes. "Tomorrow?"

She nodded, telling herself it was time to step away from him, though she had an urge to move closer to his warmth. She sighed. The last thing she needed was to become attached to a spirit she would soon leave behind. Even as her chest ached with regret, she took a step back.

His hands tightened for a second before he let them fall away. "Good night, Cassia. See you tomorrow night."

After a breakfast of apricots and cherries, Cassia found Gutel reading in the library. The cherries had been a quick addition, more to test her ring than anything.

Setting the book he was reading in his lap, the kobold turned his face away from the light of the window and put a hand to his head. She didn't ask if he'd found the ale or cider the day before. The answer was obvious.

"Why don't we continue with the ring?" she suggested brightly. "I can restore more of the garden."

"Can't you rest for one day?" he said irritably. "You didn't have to nearly kill yourself over a few apples, you know. The ring's presence is enough to restore the welkin if you're patient. You were showing off, that's what you were doing. Showy braggart of a Sylvan."

She crossed her arms, annoyed that he might be at least partly right. "*You* try not to get carried away when you realize your magic ring can make food and bring plants back to life."

"Not back to life. Livelier," he corrected, shielding his eyes from the window. "And don't exhaust yourself. There's fruit enough to feed us. Now sit down. As you're undeniably the welkin's caretaker, Sylvan or no, we have work to do."

Cassia took her seat by the window. "I'm glad you're willing to make do with me."

"There are other welkins, or there used to be," he went on. "I don't know if they still exist. But the Vozarra can fly. Perhaps it would be willing to let you ride on its back." He turned to give her a harsh look. "Don't assume it will let you. They're not horses, you know."

"I didn't think they were," she said, annoyed at the reminder of his low opinion of her. He didn't seem to understand the bond she was forming with the Vozarra. There was something about her that spoke to Cassia's spirit, something wild and free that made her happy to see. And somehow the fox's presence made her feel like she belonged here. "I'm sure Voz will let me know if she wants a rider."

"Don't name it," he said sharply. "You'll only get attached. They come and go, these spirits. They're summoned here when needed but they might not stay."

Hmm. Maybe that explained Aril and his confusion. He'd probably never been here before. It seemed an inefficient way to run things if you were always dealing with new spirits, but she supposed the welkins had their own magic and rules. Still, she couldn't help but get attached. She looked out the window, trying to catch a glimpse of copper fur. "I like Voz. We understand each other."

"You understand nothing yet. You have much to learn. What's that smell?" Gutel sniffed the air. "Lavender?"

"Gardenia," she corrected.

He eyed her suspiciously. "Have you been using the ring?"

She shrugged but didn't meet his eyes. "Not on purpose. Much."

"Don't do that until you know you can handle it." He sighed, rubbing creases into his hat as he scratched his forehead. "I don't know what I did to deserve this. Every other steward was as sober as a priestess."

"Unlike some kobolds," she put in, drawing a harsh glare. Determined not to be put off by his ill humor, she said, "You explained that the Vozarra would disappear if it were to travel to the lower mainland because of the ban against uninvited spirits in the mortal realm. Is that correct?"

"Yes," he said, his red eyes redder than usual.

"Does that apply to all the winged spirits that come here?"

"It applies to any of the ephemeral spirits that come from the Netherwhere," Gutel explained, putting the book back and choosing another. He opened it to show her an illustration of a person with wings. "The Zerian caretakers of the ring were always an exception, though. As they were created from corporeal creatures, they can go between realms." He looked around the room as if noticing something for the first time. "Where's the Dracu? He's usually here by now."

Cassia was glad Zeru hadn't shown up yet. It was calmer without him around. "Probably skulking nearby so he can leap out and scare us."

163

At that moment, Zeru came through the door, his shirt rumpled, his hair a dark, spiky mess.

"Did I summon you?" Cassia cried in horror, alarmed the ring could have that much power.

"Don't be stupid," he snarled, turning to Gutel. "In case you haven't figured it out, she's asking all these questions because she's trying to escape. Not that she's being remotely subtle."

"I want to go home," Cassia said simply. "I haven't hidden that." As she noticed the kobold's sharp look, she added, "I never said I wouldn't come back." She glared at Zeru. Miserable Dracu, making her newfound ally suspicious of her. "Anyway, what were you doing listening outside the door? Are we so threatening that you need to spy on us?"

Disgust laced every word of his reply. "I was waiting for the two of you to finish your how-to-not-act-like-a-fool-who-doesn't-know-how-to-use-the-ring lesson so I could get some real work done."

Cassia raised her brows and glanced at Gutel, who was blinking in surprise. This was grumpy, even for the Dracu.

But nothing could ruin her mood today. She was on her way to mastering the ring. "Gutel will be instructing me on the duties of a caretaker, so if you find that idea unpleasant, you might want to leave."

"I'm not leaving," he said, grabbing a book and sitting in the red chair. "I have to find a way to take that blasted ring from your benighted finger before the next accursed full moon."

Silence descended.

"You can't steal the ring," Gutel told him with soft warning. "She's the steward."

Cassia sat straighter, encouraged by the kobold's quick defense.

"As I've said, it's not stealing if it's mine." Zeru opened a book and leafed through it. "And anyone can be the caretaker. Anyone who wears the ring. I can be the caretaker if I put the cursèd thing on."

"Don't call it cursèd!" Gutel shouted, hopping to his feet. "And not everyone can wear it!" As abruptly, he sat and held a hand to his forehead as if it were a door with broken hinges. "Not only does it have to be given freely, but it also has to be accepted freely and... well, someone unsuited to be steward wouldn't be able to bear the magic. Its magic uses the life force of whoever wears it. It would kill someone too weak to bear it." Gutel lifted his chin at Zeru's skeptical look. "I believe that's why the ring wouldn't come off when you first gave it to her."

Cassia gasped. "You mean, it felt that I was strong enough?"

"That you have enough life force," he said, turning to her. "Otherwise, the ring would have come right off again."

"This is all speculation," Zeru said. "You're bending your logic into knots now that you've decided she's the steward."

"I'm sharing what I've learned from reading the lore," Gutel said haughtily. He wagged a finger. "Don't dismiss the magic of the ring. Respect it, Dracu. Otherwise, you'll never figure out your role in the welkins. I'm convinced you have one. I don't think it's random that your family held the ring in safekeeping. Nor can it be an accident that you gave it to the Sylvan as a child. There are greater things at work here."

Cassia didn't know how she felt about his claims. But the important thing was that the kobold believed them, and therefore, he would support her. "What do you suppose would draw the ring to some people over others?" she asked, enjoying the stiffness in Zeru's posture as he listened to these unwelcome revelations.

Gutel shrugged. "Every steward I've ever known has been good-hearted and trustworthy."

Zeru snorted, making it clear he didn't think the current wearer of the artifact had those admirable qualities.

Gutel took his hat off and inclined his head to Cassia. "Which I suppose must mean that I judged you harshly when we first met. And for that, I apologize."

Drawing in a surprised breath, she dipped her chin. "Thank you." His kindly tone brought a twinge of guilt. "I'm sorry I threatened to throw you out the window. And implied you'd be marinated and roasted if you came to Scarhamm."

He put his hat back on. "Forgiven."

"I'm glad you're both so fond of each other," Zeru said, tossing the book onto a side table. "Gutel, explain to me why a Seer *I* hired would tell me to come here to get the ring back, when all being here has achieved is to make the bond stronger?"

"Perhaps your Seer didn't know," Gutel said. "I didn't believe the Sylvan would be able to wield the magic. But she can. She has proven it."

"And how do you know I wouldn't be able to do the same?" Zeru asked.

Cassia leaned forward, curious. "Did you try?"

"To put on the ring?" Zeru scoffed. "No. The moment I saw it, I had it in mind for you. Fool that I was."

"Ah, see?" Gutel clapped his hands together. "The ring was telling you who the true wearer was. And Sylvan or no, Lady Cassia is the caretaker, so we must—"

"*Lady*," Zeru broke in. Cassia thought she'd never heard a word spoken with so much scorn.

"It's the title for the caretaker," the kobold answered stubbornly. "You'll use it, too."

A glitter entered Zeru's green eyes. "I will not."

Gutel's eyes darkened with warning, and he started to get to his feet.

"He doesn't need to and neither do you," Cassia said, feeling awkward at the kobold's sudden shift to deference. "My father hardly uses titles, unless they are military in nature."

"Well, I'm not calling you by your given name alone," Gutel cried. "You're the caretaker! You deserve respect!"

Touched by his new loyalty to her, she smiled. "I'll feel respected enough if you call me Cassia. Truly."

He scrunched his face up. "Very well. Too bad, though. If we're not using titles, I don't suppose you'll call me O *Magnificent Household Spirit*, as Xerxunia did." He sighed. "I liked that. She was a steward above the rest."

"It is a bit of a mouthful," Cassia said, considering.

Gutel pushed to his feet, his hand still pressing against his head. "We can discuss it later. Tomorrow, I'll show you the portraits and tell you all the titles of past caretakers. For the present, I'm going back to bed."

"Rest well," Cassia said, adding, "noble Kobold."

He showed an alarming number of pointy teeth and bowed, sweeping off his hat. She inclined her head, still smiling as he left the chamber. If only she'd known a few days ago how much things would improve.

"Tell me one thing, Cassia the Cunning," Zeru said, his bitter tone making her shoulders tense. "How did you manage to turn things around so quickly?"

"What do you mean?" she asked, knowing exactly what he meant.

He spoke with studied calm. "When we first arrived, you had no power, no advantage. No hope. Now you have the kobold on your side. You've gained some control over the ring. Somehow, you've twisted everything to your advantage. Maybe the ring has more power than I realized."

She told herself to take the compliment, but his implication that she was using magic to manipulate things bothered her. She turned to face him with a lifted chin. "It's not magic, Dracu. I simply never give up. Sometimes I fall on my face. And sometimes I succeed."

Mostly she fell on her face. She thought of all the many, many times she'd failed to use the ring the way her people needed. Her disastrous attempt to impress her father with her knife skills. Her dangerous experiments with concoctions that had nearly poisoned her. But the Dracu only knew the times she'd bested him. Even when it wasn't intentional.

"You succeed too often for it to be a matter of chance," he observed, his eyes going to the ring.

Well, she did seem to get the better of him, at least sometimes. Maybe he was an exception in her life of failures. Maybe he would be the one creature who would never know how inadequate she felt.

"It's your own failures that bother you," she said defensively. "Your Seer said you craved redemption. Why don't you focus on how you can make up for your mistakes rather than blaming me for them?"

His eyes registered a direct hit before his face darkened with savage contempt. But she'd seen the moment of hurt. Strangely, she hadn't enjoyed it.

"I hope you remember this moment," he said, eyes sharp and knowing, "when I take the ring from your unworthy finger. I won't hesitate to crow over my victory." Then he bent at the waist, treating her to a courtly bow, a mockery of the kobold's kind gesture, before leaving the room.

Cassia couldn't move for a good minute. It was as if he'd read her mind. *Unworthy.* How often had she herself thought that?

Her mood was still bitter when she made her way to the gardens later. "I want a pear," she commanded, touching a tree.

A blossom appeared and grew into a piece of fruit. But the skin was gray and spotty, and when she took a bite, the flesh was rotten.

16

> An Azpian who reaches for the sky must
> inevitably fall.
>
> —Excharias, Sylvan poet

As she spent the next several days considering ways she might get home, Cassia did her best to avoid Zeru. He spent most of his time in the library, no doubt searching for a way to weaken her bond with the ring. Sometimes she sensed his eyes on her when she was in the courtyard below the library window, and she would look up to see a brooding scrutiny that made her pulse jump with an instinctive sense of threat. But Gutel had assured her that only someone she trusted could be the recipient of the ring. Anyway, she was too busy honing her power to concern herself with his plans. After a few days, she could almost forget he existed.

Every day, Gutel taught her more about caring for the welkin.

Together they restored the castle and gardens, sitting in the courtyard whenever they tired. Citrus fruits began to grow in the ceramic pots, and flowers budded and bloomed in stone urns. The haze in the sky had completely disappeared, and the castle's alabaster exterior sparkled, its windows gleaming like crystal.

And every day, she felt the power of the ring growing. She felt happier, more powerful, and more useful than she ever had in her life. Something about using the Solis Gemma to grow things felt right to her. She found herself using the lessons her mother had taught her at Scarhamm. Day by day, she grew more plants, the bushes, flowers, and shrubs reminding her of her mother's beautiful gardens.

More animals appeared in the forest, which Gutel called the Welkinwood. Whenever Cassia went exploring, Voz followed, her keen nose working, her long ears sticking out of the underbrush as she tracked chipmunks or hares. Gutel couldn't go into the forest, which he explained was too far from the hearth for him to remain comfortable. His boundary was the wall around the castle. The steward was responsible for the rest of Welkincaster.

Most nights, Cassia went to the clearing with the lake. Aril was always there, and they spoke more each time.

Cassia told Aril about the world as she knew it—Thirstwood, the Cryptlands, and what she'd learned about Zerians from Gutel. He was curious about everything. It was a welcome change from the dark, brooding looks of a certain Dracu. Gutel had become her ally, but he grew brusque if she didn't immediately learn whatever he was trying to teach her. And sometimes he was grumpy simply because he was Gutel.

Aril was...well...kind. And there was something about him that made him feel separate from the rest of her life. He was hers alone. He asked questions and actually listened to her answers. She couldn't remember the last time someone hadn't interrupted her or talked over her because she was quieter than her sisters. Aril cared what she thought and admired the things she created. And she could tell she had begun to mean something to him, too.

She didn't want to admit to herself how much she would miss him when she left the welkin and returned to her life of training, battles, and being the Deathringer her father always wanted.

It was also getting harder to imagine life without Voz. Gutel had said that spirits would come and go as needed, but Voz stayed. She followed Cassia everywhere, happily exploring the renewed forest, even flying in through her open bedchamber window at night to sleep on the edge of her bed. The creature had a sense of when Cassia was using too much power. When she overdid it, she'd often feel the nudge of a cold, wet nose on her arm. Maybe that was why Voz stuck around: to protect her from herself. She wished there was some way to keep the spirit with her when she went home.

One night, as she sat with Aril by the lake, she was watching the white tip of Voz's tail as she hunted at the edge of the clearing and realized the lake was showing her a reflection of a waxing crescent moon...which meant she had lost track of the days. She'd been so busy, her life on the welkin so full, that the time had flown—more than a fortnight gone! She had to get home before the full moon and another Dracu attack.

Her stomach twisted with guilt. How could she have been so selfish? She needed a way home. Zeru's amulet wasn't a viable option. He no longer wore it, probably worried she would try to steal it. She assumed he kept it locked in his bedchamber, which was in one of the other towers, but she hadn't found a way past his locked door.

If she couldn't get the amulet, she needed another way home. She looked over at Aril, his face a barely visible shape against the night. He had taken her flying a few more times, but he had never gone past the edges of the welkin.

"Want to fly?" she asked. It was a calm night, perfect for flight. "Maybe you could take me beyond the edge of the cloud this time?"

"It's not safe," he said immediately, his tone sharper than usual.

⌒ 172 ⌒

"We'll be careful. I want to see what's below." If she could get a glimpse of some landmark, perhaps the glint of moonlight on the Scar River, she might get an idea where they were.

He blew out a breath. "A short distance only."

She nodded, hopping to her feet and smiling. She caught the flash of his smile in the dark, as if he were amused by her excitement.

His arms stayed tight around her as they crossed the foamy edges of the floating island. Light from the waxing moon made ghosts of the clouds, their wispy forms as insubstantial as memories. From above, the castle looked like a pale confection dusted in sugar, the golden roofs of its spires iced silver by moonlight. A candle flickered in the library window. Gutel always retired early to his hearth, so it had to be Zeru reading late into the night. Cassia smiled at the evidence that he hadn't yet found a way to take her ring.

Her elation lasted precisely until Aril left the welkin behind and she saw black sky beneath her. Her stomach swooped as fear gripped her.

"You're scared," Aril said, a note of concern in his soft, rough voice.

Her back was pressed to his chest, so she couldn't hide the fact that her pulse was wild with terror.

"Going back," he said.

"No, please!" She wanted a glimpse of the land below. "A little farther."

But he was already flying in a wide arc that led them back over the Welkinwood. As they descended, she had to bite her tongue to keep from snapping at him. His protectiveness was no doubt part of his role as guardian of Welkincaster. She told herself it wasn't his fault, but it was difficult not to order him back into the air. She was sure he would comply if she insisted. But he was so kind to her, she hated the idea of ordering him to do something he didn't want to do.

They landed in the clearing. Cassia brushed off her clothing and took a breath. "Thank you, Aril. Good night."

"You're angry." A note of hurt deepened his voice.

She wanted to deny it but couldn't. "I wish you didn't worry so much about me."

"Why?" he asked, his tone stiff. "I'm a guardian of this place. You told me that. You are part of this place, so I also protect you. What is wrong in that?"

Tears sprang to her eyes, though she fought them. "What I need to be safe is to see the land below." She hated this, but finding a way home was more important. "I needed more time."

"Why?"

She looked up into his face, wishing she could see him more clearly in the dark. Perhaps when the moon was full...but by then, she would be gone. The thought made her more irritable.

"What's wrong?" Aril asked. "Is the Dracu being unkind? The kobold expecting too much of you?"

Cassia grimaced. Maybe she shouldn't have complained to Aril. "No, nothing like that." But the mention of Gutel added to her guilt over the possibility—no, the certainty—that her departure would hurt him. Which was ridiculous. What did the hearth-spirit matter? He was no more than an Azpian ghost, given form and life only here in this place filled with the impossible. Nothing here could exist in the world below. Which meant none of it was real. Including Aril.

"I'm sorry, Aril, I have to go," she said, turning toward the castle before she could break down in front of him. She had walked this way so many times, it had become a clear path with mushrooms and flowers lining the edges. Thanks to the ring...which

⁓ 174 ⁓

she would soon take with her, leaving the welkin to decay once again. She hunched her shoulders against the guilt. "I'll see you tomorrow night."

"Cassia," said Aril.

She stopped but didn't turn.

His hand came to rest on her shoulder. "You're in pain," he said, his voice barely more than a whisper.

She reached up to pat his hand, hoping he couldn't hear the tears clogging her throat. "I'll be fine. Don't worry."

"But I do."

She squeezed her eyes shut. This was what she'd feared. He was becoming too attached to her. "Don't worry about me, Aril. Please. Find your own way."

"You want to leave here," he said. "Don't you?"

Why did he have to be so perceptive? "I'm going to the castle to sleep."

He made a sound of frustration in his throat. "I mean you're planning to leave the welkin."

Her heart twisted, pulling strings tight in her chest. The time for prevarication was over. "Yes, Aril." She forced herself to turn to face him. He deserved her honesty. "And you're going to help me."

He put his hands to her cheeks, his rough voice soft and soothing. "I won't. Tell me what's wrong, and I'll fix it."

She released a shaky breath, agonized by his tenderness toward her. "You can't fix what's wrong. There's only one thing you can do to help me, Aril. And that's to fly me home."

He pulled in a shocked breath, his hands falling from her face as he took a step back. "No."

Her lip trembled, but she took a breath and squared her shoulders. "Please, Aril. My family needs me. I . . . I wouldn't ask this of you if there were any other way."

He closed his eyes for a minute. Finally, he opened them with a sigh. "I can't refuse you."

Relief coursed through her. She reached out and gripped his arm. "Thank you."

He looked down at her hand, placing his own over hers. "When?"

"Tomorrow night." She made the decision at that moment, knowing it was right, not only because she'd been away from her sisters too long and worried almost constantly about them. To stay any longer would be unfair to Aril. And to herself. She had no energy for the internal battle she was fighting. She had to save her strength for the battles in the real world below.

As she let her hand fall, she looked up at him. His eyes glittered as they shifted in thought. "You'll come back."

The pain in her chest grew until she pressed a hand there to ease it. She doubted she'd return. For one thing, she didn't have the amulet to create the doorway. "Maybe."

His voice dropped lower, but the force of will behind the words was as clear as an order. "You will come back."

She reached up and put her palms on either side of his face, feeling the new growth of facial hair. "I wish you could remember who you are," she said. "You feel lost because you don't know. You think you need me. But you don't."

His eyes closed as his palms came to rest over the backs of her hands. "If I remember, will you stay?"

Her chest ached as if a thorn were stuck somewhere deep inside. She had left herself too open to him. Vulnerable when she had to be strong. She forced herself to pull her hands from his face, tugging when he held on. "Let me go, Aril. You said you don't belong here. Neither do I."

"You're happy here," he said, a hard note entering his voice, though he released her hands. "Happier than when you talk about your home."

She had no answer for that, so she shook her head.

He stared at her, his shoulders rising and falling in agitation.

She almost stepped toward him. Almost took his hand. But she had no words of reassurance. And she could not afford to let her resolve weaken. "Tomorrow, Aril. You agreed."

He inclined his head formally. Something about the movement made her stomach twist. She wanted to change her mind and stay. But before she could weaken, with a leap, Aril shot toward the sky, opening his wings once he'd cleared the canopy.

She looked down at the ring and saw that it pulsed. Her chest hurt, but she didn't know if it was the magic that pained her or her own weak heart.

17

To trust a Dracu is to dance with chaos.
—Excharias, Sylvan poet

Cassia stood in the ballroom, the one room in Welkincaster she'd so far avoided. It was a long, high-ceilinged room with a dusty checkerboard floor, tall, grime-darkened windows, and crystal chandeliers covered in cobwebs. In the corners of the room, three marble statues, presumably Solis, Noctua, and Nerthus, stood in various poses, gathering shadows.

But it was the walls that had always kept her away. Every plaster panel was carved with the likenesses of Azpians.

There were imps grinning, imps scowling, imps sticking out their tongues. There were Skrattis with faces that might be upside down or right side up, depending on how you looked at them. Their features were exaggerated and varied to the point of being comical, stretched and flattened and twisted, all of them slyly mischievous and cheeky, as if they were inviting you into their joke.

Cassia grimaced. The Ancients must have liked Azpians. But there had been nothing to make her want to come in here. The scene reminded her too much of the Dracu queen's vassals.

However, she'd be gone soon, and for some reason, she didn't like the idea of leaving the restoration unfinished. The wilted plants in stone urns dotted about the room seemed to be crying out for her attention.

Turning her back to the grinning walls, she stepped to a drooping fern, lifting its limp fronds.

As the plant turned from sickly yellow to healthy green, a pleased flush warmed her cheeks. She was going to miss this aspect of Welkincaster, the way it made her feel powerful. But this place, and her pride in restoring it, would have to live in her memory—a bright, impossible thing to lighten the dark days of battle ahead.

Through the window, she saw Gutel outside in the courtyard with Voz at his feet basking in the sun. The weather was warm and fine, as it always was now on Welkincaster. She could be out there with them if she hurried. She moved to another plant, touching it with the hand that wore the ring. Its leaves lifted almost instantly, a bud of some kind forming.

"Very impressive," Zeru's voice said from the doorway.

She stiffened but didn't bother turning, concentrating on sending life into the plant.

Zeru remained silent but she could feel his presence like the hum of bees. With a resigned sigh, she turned her head toward him. He was leaning against a pillar, his arms crossed over his chest.

"Did you run out of books?" she asked, still sending her magic into the leaves.

"I came to congratulate you," Zeru said.

Having only seen him through windows or at a distance for over a week, she was surprised at his transformation. His hair had grown longer, falling raggedly over his forehead, and he looked like his only comb had been fingers running through it. A layer of stubble darkened his cheeks, which were sharper and more sunken than she remembered. And he had dark smudges under his eyes, making them look hard and bright like green diamonds.

"On what?" she muttered.

"On restoring the welkin." He dipped his head. "I've watched your progress. I couldn't help being impressed."

"Unwillingly."

"Of course." He gave her a bland look that made his next words all the more surprising. "When we arrived, this place looked abandoned. Almost everything was dead. Now it's bright and flourishing. Even the kobold's wilted flowers are thriving. I've been forced to conclude that he's right. You are the caretaker of Welkincaster."

She'd never expected him to acknowledge that. Somehow, she felt more threatened than reassured by this display of humility. "You expect me to believe you've accepted that?"

"No." He paused. "But I came to say it anyway."

She watched him as he wandered the room, looking around it with interest. "Sylvans love dancing, do they not?" When she gave him a narrow-eyed look, he lifted his brows. "Isn't it part of what sustains you?"

"I didn't realize a Dracu would know that." What game was he playing?

"You tried to teach me once," he said. "Do you remember?"

She paused, reluctant to admit it. "Yes."

"This could be the last time a Sylvan and a Dracu ever dance together," he mused. "I can't see there being any occasion for it in the future."

She let her hand fall from the plant and straightened. "Don't say that."

His eyebrows twitched up. "Why does that bother you?"

She opened her mouth, closed it, and pondered the idea that

their peoples would be at war forever. Would never share anything besides battles. Yes, it did bother her. "There could be some kind of peace."

"The kind of peace that comes with using that ring to wipe out my people?"

As the truth of his words hit home, she gasped, shocked that she hadn't considered this. Hadn't let herself. She could not—No, she could not think about it. "You don't know how I'll use the ring."

"Your father will have ideas about what you should do with your newly mastered power."

It felt like steel bands were wrapped around her chest. Whenever the war entered her mind, she found some distraction to quell it. "I don't even know if I'll be proficient at that side of it."

"The killing side, you mean?"

She felt her face stiffen, every part of her saying no to the reality of that. Unable to speak, she nodded.

"Cassia. You're deathly pale. You can't even talk about it. How are you going to kill us if you can't even talk about doing it?"

"Stop. Just stop." She hadn't killed anyone with the ring, and maybe her father would see its potential for other uses and change his mind about its purpose. *Ha!* A hysterical laugh bubbled up at the thought. The king would not let her use the Solis Gemma to *garden*.

Zeru cleared his throat, drawing her gaze. She hadn't even noticed him move to stand in front of her. Her pulse was racing, her palms as damp as if she were facing an enemy. Which she reminded herself she was.

"I had a thought," he said, his lean face serious. "Maybe a Sylvan and a Dracu could dance together one last time."

She watched him warily. "Why would you want that?"

He looked up at the ceiling as if something there required his immediate attention. "Sylvan power is replenished by dancing. I just thought..." He met her eyes with studied casualness. "If you don't want to, just say no, Sylvan."

He'd been talking about her using the ring to kill, and now he was offering to give her more power? "You don't want to do that. Giving me more power is contrary to everything you want."

He shrugged. "The ring can't hurt me. All you can do here is make the flowers grow."

He probably thought that was true. He considered her safely trapped here. "But why?" she persisted. "Why would you want to even test that theory?"

He looked around. "I don't know. We're in a ballroom. We are in a realm so separate from our homes that nothing here will seem real once we've left it. Maybe some rebelliousness has taken hold of me. Or it would make me laugh to do something so ludicrous. What does it matter why? It won't hurt."

Never trust a Dracu. The phrase ran through her mind.

He leaned in a fraction. "Be brave, Sylvan. No one will ever learn your shameful secret, that you danced with a Dracu. I could even vow not to tell."

She swallowed, wondering why she was even considering this. "I don't see the point."

He shook his head, taking a step closer. "I've watched you tend flowers for weeks. Does everything need to have a point?"

She lifted her chin, defensive of her hours spent in the garden. "Flowers have a purpose. Beauty."

His lips curved up a fraction. "Maybe the memory of our dance will linger in this place, never quite dying, no matter how faded it becomes. That's a kind of beauty."

The breath locked in her chest, but she couldn't let him see that his words had affected her. "You've been reading too much. You're getting poetic."

He grinned. "Just one dance." He offered his hand, palm up. "What could it hurt?"

Without letting herself think, she reached out and placed her hand in his. As he caught his breath, Cassia couldn't help but feel she had made some small but grievous miscalculation. A little decision that would lead to big regret.

"I had no tutors to teach me formal dances," he reminded her, a hint of defiance not quite covering his insecurity. Up close, she could see the short dark hairs on his chin and a muscle jumping in his cheek. She didn't know what he was feeling, but this wasn't the cold, indifferent Zeru of the past few weeks. Which somehow made her fear him more. "But you tried to teach me once," he added. "Let me see if I remember."

Zeru bowed, then stepped closer, then back, holding himself stiffly. She recognized the steps of a Sylvan dance, which brought a sudden memory of them cavorting together as children under the light of a full moon. Zeru hadn't been so tense and formal back then. Her throat felt thick. She should turn away now and walk out. But it made something twist in her chest to see that he was trying.

"You have the first part right..." She put one of his hands to her waist, sucking in a breath at the intimacy of it. She lifted her other arm, nodding at him to do the same. Their hands clasped so that they were brought closer as they turned in unison, their chests almost touching. Cassia swallowed, her breaths coming faster at the attentive look in Zeru's eyes. They turned to face forward, moving in a promenade with joined hands.

183

"This seems a great deal like walking," he pointed out.

"You're not supposed to march," she said, giving him a wry sidelong glance. "Where's your Dracu grace?" If there had been other couples, this would have been the time to walk around them on the outside. "Imagine there are other dancers," she reminded him.

"Of course," he said. "Other Sylvan dancers, ready to gut me as I prance by."

She couldn't help a grin. "Killing a dance partner is considered bad manners."

His eyes narrowed thoughtfully. "I could try that on the battlefield. Start twirling around and see if that makes the Huntsmen think twice about ending me."

Cassia's laugh echoed around the room. "That would certainly confuse them."

They were both smiling as they came to face each other. She held out her hands again, and he took them, moving forward and back in a repetition of the earlier movements. He had learned all the steps now. But he wasn't quite dancing.

"Loosen your shoulders," she instructed. He did. But the rest of him was as tense as a bowstring. "When you're fighting, you move like water. Why can't you dance like that?"

He looked up, eyes widening as his hand came to her waist for the turn. "Like water?"

She tried not to be so aware of how close his chest was to hers, and the heat that was creeping up her neck. "You're a spectacle of destruction."

His eyebrows lifted. "Thank you."

"That wasn't meant as a compliment."

He grinned. "Then you're doing it wrong."

The turn kept them locked together, and her pulse did something funny when he smiled. "You were fighting even as you stared at me," she added, not knowing why she would bring that up. She took a breath as they faced forward and began the promenade. "On the battlefield."

As their hands fell apart and they walked past the imaginary couples, he replied, "I recognized you. And the reason I move smoothly when I'm fighting is that I'm relaxed."

"Hmm," she said, turning to face him again. "Nothing more calming than maiming and disemboweling your enemies."

His eyes glittered as his mouth quirked up on one side. "Exactly my feeling."

"So, pretend I'm about to kill you," she suggested, her hands finding his. Warmth traveled up her arms from where their palms met, making her pulse beat faster.

"Ah, that may work." He spun her so that her back was pinned to his chest. He leaned into her, his hair brushing her cheek. "Now I have the advantage. Your arms are trapped."

Tricksy Dracu. Her pulse slammed. She hadn't seen that coming.

"Oh yes, very conducive to dancing." It was almost an embrace. She could and should extricate herself. Now.

But he was swaying back and forth, his breath warm against her neck. "I like this better." His voice was low and soft in her ear. "Almost as good as dismembering enemies."

His right arm lay across her chest, gently trapping her while his left found her waist. Why didn't she move away?

Her pulse was mayhem. What was happening?

"This isn't really dancing," she observed, her voice shaky.

"Cassia," he said, his voice low and entreating. "Do we have to be enemies?"

Panic started somewhere in the back of her neck and radiated out from there like a shower of sparks. "You of all people ask me that? Of course we do." She turned to face him. "What deception is this?"

His eyes held hers as securely as his hand, a warmer green than she'd ever seen them. "No deception." The afternoon light painted him in gold, making his eyebrows and eyelashes look darker by contrast. "You have no reason to trust me. I've given you none."

Suspicion was firing like arrows in her mind, and yet she still wanted to hear what he had to say. "So far, we're in agreement."

"But...maybe there's a way we can work together. For the common good."

"The common...good." She waited for her mind to catch up with everything being thrown at her. "There is no *common* good. Not for us. There is good for you or there is good for me. They're at odds."

"What if they weren't?" He sounded so serious. Almost as if he weren't playing a massive game with her, which he had to be. "What if we could find a way to help each other?"

She heard her own breathing. "Did you find something in one of those books?"

"That's not why I'm asking. I'm asking because..." He squeezed her fingers. "You love it here. Anyone can see that. You are...happy." He swallowed. "When I first found you on the battlefield—"

Found her? "Captured."

He dipped his head. "Yes. I thought you were the Deathringer in truth."

"I *am*..." She said it through her teeth, trying to tug her hand free.

He watched her without expression. "I'll let you go if you listen to what I say next."

"I'm listening." Did she have a choice?

186

"I thought you were ruthless. Bloodthirsty. A trained killer who reveled in the blood of Dracu. That's what the stories said. What I assume your father wanted my people to believe. But you're none of those things. You wield the ring because... because I gave it to you, and then your father knew of its potential as a weapon, and he tried and failed to teach you how to use it—"

Failed! He might as well have been slapping her, his words stung that much. "You know nothing—"

"I have eyes." He moved closer. "These past weeks as I sat in the library watching you and Gutel restore the welkin, you transformed. I can see. I see *you*. You've found another purpose for the ring, and you revel in it. You love healing things and making them grow. You bask in tending and nurturing. You didn't kill me, though you had more than one chance. You are not a killer, Cassia. You weren't meant to be one. Why pretend to be something you don't want to be?"

She looked at him, wondering how he could stab her so successfully with only words. *You are not a killer.* Even her father had never said something so damning and so final. Zeru might as well have said, *"You will never have the love of your father,"* or *"Accept your failure as a forgone conclusion."* Nothing could have acted upon her more like a douse of frigid water.

"I like growing things," she said succinctly. "And I've enjoyed restoring Welkincaster. But I also love my people, who are under threat from yours. If I have to kill a few thousand Dracu with this ring to keep my family safe, I will do it." Her neck tightened painfully, but she forced out, "That was my whole purpose in coming here. To find a way to master this ring so I could use it to protect my people." That was true enough.

Something dark slid behind his eyes. "If you would vow not to use the ring against us—"

But she wasn't done. "You only came to me with your parley when you had no other options left. Nothing has changed."

She'd moved her gaze to his chest because she could no longer bear to look into his eyes, which were filling with things too complex and uncomfortable to see. And there around his neck was the chain that held the amulet, tucked under the collar of his shirt once again.

"Something *has* changed," he said. "I've realized I was wrong. Your life was thrown into chaos by the ring...as mine was." His voice came out more hoarsely as he added, "You were right when you accused me of blaming you for my own mistakes. It wasn't your fault. Though I still hate what's happened to you, I see that you were only trying to survive."

"You claimed that you fought to get to me that night," she scoffed, desperate to poke holes in his story. Her gaze flicked back to his, watching his reaction. "You were probably too busy laughing."

"I was beside myself with fear for you." His nostrils flared, and something in his eyes made her breath catch.

"I..." She wanted to say she didn't believe him, but her throat closed up. "Then why didn't you help me?"

"My father was holding me. I begged him to help you."

Cassia stared blankly as her thoughts tangled together. A thin layer of sweat broke out over her skin. She didn't want to hear this. Didn't want to forgive him for that night. Didn't want to think he had tried to save her. That he'd been a victim, too.

She especially didn't want to think he might be telling the truth about her father.

He was making it sound as if being the Deathringer her father wanted would be a betrayal of herself. And though it made her furious, she sensed truth when she heard it. Those soft words, that insight from an enemy, threatened to overwhelm her. Swallow her whole.

His kindness might have touched some vulnerable part of her, but that made it more dangerous. She was so close to becoming what her father, what her people, wanted her to be. Weakness of any kind was her greatest enemy now.

"I don't want to hurt you again," he said, his voice earnest. "Can you hear the truth in what I'm saying?"

She made herself look at him. If only she could read what ran under the surface. He looked back with serenity, but something dark lingered behind his eyes. And she felt a connection to that darkness. That pain. A strange, unnamed, intangible shift was happening. Was in danger of happening. And she had to put a stop to it.

"But you will if you have to." Why he'd had this sudden attack of conscience, or whatever this was, she had no idea, but she could not afford to be pulled around by concern for him.

"Yes," he said in a flat voice. "I have a family, too. I'd do anything to protect them."

She felt her shoulders relax. This was familiar ground. She dipped her chin in a single nod. "Now I see that you are capable of truth."

As they stared at each other, she had the sense she had passed her own test. Her enemy had tried to weaken her, and she had resisted softening toward him. But it felt utterly necessary to do something to prove to herself that he had in no way swayed her. There was an opportunity she could not ignore. A way to get home even faster than she'd planned.

Following an impulse, she put a hand to his cheek and heard his indrawn breath.

Her enemy was...not immune to her. The knowledge went to her head, more intoxicating even than using her magic. Warmth had traveled from her palm into her arm. A breath stayed locked in her chest. Zeru blinked, something in his eyes showing recognition, a need for her to acknowledge that he wasn't alone.

He wasn't. Touching him was a sweet fire, making her pulse hum and her head light.

His eyes dilated as she brushed her fingers over his cheek, and his breathing quickened. When she cradled his jaw, his eyes fell closed, and his head dipped down toward hers. It gave her a heady sense of power, so strong it made her tremble.

Heart pounding, her free hand slid to the chain at his neck and drew out the amulet.

His eyes snapped open. "What are you doing?"

She placed the curve of the Solis Gemma into the groove in the amulet. *Click.*

No doorway appeared. Nothing changed. Nothing except a look of stark betrayal coming into Zeru's eyes.

Cassia let her hand fall, sickness twisting her gut for reasons she didn't care to examine. "It was worth a try."

He stared at her for a few more moments before he spoke. "Selkolla told me the amulet is like the ring: It'll only work if I will it." Though his expression had smoothed, his voice was laden with heavy things. "I suppose you didn't hear that part."

"No," she said, straightening her back. "I didn't."

Zeru inclined his head in a formal nod. "Now I see that you are, indeed, capable of deception." His cheekbones looked sharp in a face as cold as the marble statues. "Well done, Sylvan. I couldn't have done better."

18

> Every Dracu has two faces: one beautiful,
> and one true.
> —Excharias, Sylvan poet

Cassia left the castle before midnight, more than ready to leave Welkincaster. Not, she told herself, that she was fleeing Zeru after what had happened in the ballroom. No, she was eager to get home and show her family what she'd learned about the ring. As she walked the neat path to the clearing, passing green, lush trees on the way, it gave her a sweet sense of accomplishment to have restored the forest to a state of health. Or perhaps a bittersweet one. It was almost certain she would never see the Welkinwood again.

She would have preferred to return home with the amulet. She should have stolen it instead of trying to use it while Zeru was wearing it. She kept remembering the look in his eyes, the way his head had bent toward hers, how he'd seemed so trusting until he'd realized what she was doing. She forced a sharp breath, angry with herself, not only for the failure but because she couldn't help feeling as if she'd done something wrong.

He had thrown her off balance, almost making her question her purpose with the ring. It was time to leave this place behind, along with her doubts.

When she reached the clearing, Aril was already waiting, the tops of his wings visible behind his shoulders, his hair ruffled by a strong breeze, even in the protected haven.

She smiled at him as she approached. "Windy tonight."

"Yes," he said in his rough voice. "Might be too windy to fly."

She frowned. "No, it's not. We're going."

Although she spoke with confidence, she didn't know what she'd do if he refused. When Aril nodded in agreement, she let out a relieved breath.

They prepared as they always did, his arms going around her as she hung on with both hands. She shivered as she felt his warmth at her back, drawing comfort from his familiar strength.

"Are you sure?" he asked, his head bent toward hers. "I wish you would change your mind."

"I'm sure." Once she was home in Scarhamm, she could put any doubts behind her.

Aril took off as before, the force of his jump launching them to the treetops. But a northerly gust gripped them as soon as they left the shelter of the trees, an updraft lifting them higher while he fought to control their trajectory. As they steadied, Cassia looked around.

The moon rose above the castle, painting its alabaster exterior silver-bright in a velvet, indigo sky. The four gold-tipped spires, so pretty in the sunshine, became sword points, reminding her of the spikes where her father displayed Dracu heads. Mist frothed over the edges of the welkin, sparkling and ghostly. Beyond the boundary, dark skies stretched into forever.

"Don't get too near the castle," she cautioned, even as the wind steered them closer. A candle was burning in the library window, and she didn't want Zeru to see them. Aril's wings pumped furiously, but instead of leaving the castle behind, they were heading for it.

"Not that way!" Cassia said worriedly.

He didn't respond, flying to one of the towers and alighting on its spire. There was hardly any room to stand, only a small flat square at the top where the pennant was secured. As Aril turned to face her, Cassia hung on to the pole in desperation.

"What are we doing up here?" she asked, her pulse slamming. Something was not right. Aril wouldn't even look at her. "You're supposed to take me home. Down to the lower mainland."

"Am I?"

The wind gusted, nearly taking her off her feet. "Yes! You agreed."

"Maybe I lied."

Her breath caught. Aril had never spoken to her like that. His strong arms, his raspy voice, his forest-laden scent. She knew him. But he wasn't himself.

She shivered from cold and fear. "Explain this. Why did you bring me up here?"

He furled his wings behind him, staring down at her from so close, and yet he seemed as far away as the stars behind him. "You wished it."

"I definitely did not."

"You wished me to remember. Cassia. Look at me."

Her eyes snapped to his. The light was so much brighter atop the spire, delineating his features. It was the first time she'd had a clear look at him.

And what she saw made her feel as if she were falling through the air with no one to catch her.

It wasn't possible. She turned her head away while her stomach crawled into her throat.

"You know who I am," he said, his voice so forceful it shook her to her core.

Her eyes filled with tears as she fought the oncoming storm of recognition. "You told me yourself. You're Aril."

"An *aril* is a part of a seed, Cassia. For some inexplicable reason, I couldn't remember my own name, but when I looked at you, I remembered the parts of a seed. You taught them to me when we were children. Don't you remember?"

Her breath came in little gasps as she pressed her face to the cold metal of the flagpole. She did remember. She wished she didn't.

"I grew up in darkness underground," he said. "I had no need for wings. But when we came up here, into the clouds, I transformed. Every night, I've taken this shape. Every day, I've returned to myself. The one had no memory of the other until you put your hands on my face and wished me to remember who I was." He dipped his head closer to her, his hair lifted off his face by the wind. "How could you not recognize me?"

She shook her head, denying, disbelieving, ashamed at missing all the signs. Rather than accepting his identity, she felt like she was looking at a stranger. "It was dark. You have wings. No horns." She forced herself to really look at him, noting that his features hadn't changed as much as she'd thought. His winged form had more muscle, which added to the impression of height. But she said defensively, "You have markings on your face. You're larger. Your voice is rougher. Softer." She shook her head. It was more than that. Aril's demeanor had been so open.

Without seeing him clearly, how could she have known it was Zeru?

"You didn't want to see," he said scathingly, the rasp in his voice more pronounced. "Because you wanted to use me."

Her eyes snapped up to his. "You think I'd just wait around for you to figure out a way to take my ring? Put yourself in my place!"

~ 194 ~

"I tried to find common ground with you yesterday. What a warm reception my attempts received."

"Common ground? You realized you can't get the ring, so you were trying to win me over onto your side. As if I'd ever trust you."

"Then you are the clever one, Sylvan." His talon jabbed toward his own chest, a breeze lifting his dark hair. "As Aril, I trusted you. If you knew what I'd have been willing to do for you. How I waited for you with breathless anticipation, how I hung on your every word." His laugh was so bitter it made her want to put her hands over her ears, but she was gripping the flagpole for dear life. "I should have known you only meant to use me to escape. You taught me the same lesson when we were children, but I didn't remember enough to avoid the same mistake. I'll remember now, though. Never trust a Sylvan."

"I trusted *you* as Aril! I told you everything, about my home, my family! And what did I ever do to you as a child?" Rattled by his claims about the depths of his feelings, she leaped on the unfairness of his accusations. "What have I *ever* done to you?"

His eyes burned green fire. "You. Lied. You said you'd meet me every full moon. You were the one who didn't show up after the night I gave you the ring. I returned for you every full moon for a year."

Surprise silenced her. A whole year? She felt a pulse of sympathy for that boy who had come to meet her again and again, only to be disappointed, likely at great risk to himself after everything that had happened. But a memory of how broken she'd been rose up to strengthen her. "Did you really think I'd go back into Thirstwood alone? Aside from the fact that my older sisters watched me like birds of prey, it took weeks for my wounds to heal, years to stop having nightmares. I was terrified of my own forest!"

He took a shuddering breath, the sound almost lost amid

the wind and the whipping of the flag above their heads. "I was scared, too. But I never forgot you, Cassia. Not like you forgot me. And you used a gift I gave you in friendship to help destroy my people."

His bitterness tore at her, but she couldn't let it break her down. She had been right to forget him. How she wished she could believe she'd forget him a second time. A wave of painful loss tore through her like a blade that sliced from her neck to her chest. Aril wasn't real. He didn't exist. She had lost the one friend she'd thought she had. Not that she would show her grief to him. "That's the part that really bothers you, isn't it? The fact that I tried to forget you."

He looked deep into her eyes and enunciated with harsh and perfect clarity, "Yes. You were my only friend. And suddenly, after one mistake, you were gone."

"How could we ever have remained friends after that?"

He swallowed. "I don't know."

They stared at each other, her heart aching. For a second, she was that little girl who wandered into the vastness of Thirstwood to search for her tree and found a friend to ease her fears.

Only in this new scenario, her friend despised her.

"I had no choice but to embrace the role I was given," she said, coming back to the one truth she knew for certain. "You said you understood that."

His smile held no warmth and little humor. "You were a child when you first wore the ring. I understand why you did what he wanted then." He looked away from her, showing his profile against the moon. "But now that you know what the ring is, you have choices, Cassia. Your whole life is about trying to please your father. You choose that above all other things."

He didn't understand. Her mother was gone, her absence like

quicksand that constantly threatened to pull Cassia under. Her father at least paid attention to her, had cared enough to push her to master her power. Making him proud was a need, a desperate wish she had never been able to ignore. But she wouldn't bare that wound for anyone's scrutiny. And who was he to judge her after all he'd done? "I don't regret trying to live up to my potential," she said, the ache of betrayal making her add, "My only regret right now is not being able to slit your throat." In that moment, she meant it.

"What's stopping you?" He nodded to his dagger at her waist.

"I'm so slow, you could eat a meal before catching my wrist, remember?"

"Tell you what. If you can do it, you deserve to keep the ring. If you use my dagger on me, I'll finally admit you are Deathringer in truth." His nostrils flared, his anger palpable, his fingers white where they gripped the flagpole. "And I'll let you go home."

"A bargain?" Her eyes widened at the offer. It was lavish in its terms. Everything she wanted. Did he realize he'd be bound by it?

"A bargain. My word will have to suffice this time. No blood unless you spill mine with your own hand."

Her pulse beat wild in her own ears. "And how will you fly me home once I've stabbed you?"

"You're forgetting the amulet," he said. "If I will it, it'll work. Selkolla said the doorway can lead into Thirstwood. I only need to imagine a spot I know well."

She swallowed, frustrated that she wasn't thinking clearly. He had her turned upside down. "And . . . you'll give me the amulet?"

"No. The amulet is mine."

"What good is it to you?" she asked irritably. "You can't use it without the ring."

"Maybe I want a keepsake. And I don't need to use it with the ring to get home. I have wings, Cassia."

She snarled up at him, more furious than ever. "Which won't help you much once I've gutted you."

"Are you worrying about me?" he mocked. Reminding her he didn't think she could do it. "I'll make this easier on you." He leaned in, his breath warm against her cheek. "I heal faster in this form. One night when I was learning to fly, I crashed to the ground and broke my leg. By the next night, it had healed."

"It's not as sporting if you recover that quickly," she said, relieved at his claim, shivering from his closeness despite herself. Escape was at hand. She just had to hurt him.

He reached slowly, carefully down her body, his hand moving over her arm and to her waist, eliciting a sharp breath from her. But then she felt the cool metal in her palm and realized what he was doing. Handing her the dagger.

Her eyes squeezed shut as she gripped the hilt, her other hand grasping the flagpole. She had to do this. Had to prove it to him. It would get her home. She opened her eyes and stared at his chest. The dark fabric of his shirt rippled in the wind. The amulet's chain glinted on his neck. Its magic would work as soon as she upheld her end of the deal.

"Unsure of your target?" he asked silkily. He ripped the edges of his collar apart. "This better?"

His neck was corded muscle leading into strong shoulders and a firm chest. She had a sudden, startling urge to put her lips to his collarbone. Feelings she'd had for Aril and denied herself because he'd been a lost spirit and she'd have to leave him. Feelings she had briefly and shamefully succumbed to in the ballroom for Zeru. She shook her head to clear it. Stupidity. Folly of the worst kind. Unforgivable distraction. Focus on the bargain. On the opportunity. On the fact that he was her greatest enemy.

198

"What are you waiting for, Sylvan?" he rasped. "A written invitation?"

Her throat felt thick, her eyes starting to run. Cursèd wind. "Stop telling me to do it."

"Do this now or accept that you'll lose the ring to me."

"I won't. You have no way to take it," she said confidently.

"Are you sure about that? Sure of your truth?" His hand came to her cheek, turning her face to his.

Her lips parted. She knew he was manipulating her, but her heart drummed faster, and her skin warmed at his touch. "Yes."

His palm found her nape, resting there possessively as his fingers tangled in her hair. Her eyes closed. When she felt his lips on her forehead, she couldn't breathe. His lips were dry and warm and soft, sliding from one side of her forehead to the other, then down her cheek. She wanted to press him closer.

"So sure of yourself?" he whispered. His breath was like poplar fluff against her skin, light and tickling. His lips settled under her ear against her pulse, and her knees went weak. She wasn't sure of anything. She'd lost track of everything except the feel of him. The pennant pole was between them, providing the only source of sanity available. She gripped it as if it would keep her safe from the onslaught of sensations.

"Tell me you hate me," he said, his breath feathering against her neck. "Tell me, Sylvan. If it's true."

"I hate...," she said. Her throat closed, pain shearing through her at the thought of the lie. She blurted a truth to escape that pain. "Turnips."

He laughed, a low vibration against her neck where his lips were trailing. In a deft movement, he took her by the shoulders and turned her so the pole was at her back, his arm around her.

There was hardly any room to stand, so his hips were against hers, his feet braced on either side. His lips hadn't left her throat. She was leaning her head back, inviting him closer. The hand with the dagger fell to her side, and the hand with the ring found the back of his head. She was all fire and honey, turned inside out with need. How had this happened? It had to be the magic of this place.

She turned her face up to his, giving in to her yearning. "Kiss me, Dracu."

His eyes were as dark as the sky as his head bent and his lips met hers. Hard pressure, soft lips. She returned the pressure with abandon, her head spinning with an off-kilter joy. She made a noise in her throat, a kind of quiet keening. How could she not respond when it felt so good? He took her hand from his hair and placed it against his chest. Hard muscle against her soft palm. Her fingers convulsed fretfully, wanting to touch more of him.

Then she felt his touch on her ring finger. A clang of warning sounded in her mind, but it took a moment to get through the fog of pleasure. "What..."

The ring moved all the way to her knuckle before her reflexes kicked in. "No!"

She curled her hand into a fist that she held to her chest. She looked down to make sure the ring was still on her finger. It was. Relief made her sag against the pennant pole. But the ring had moved! She looked up at Zeru, aghast. His eyes were dark, only a thin rim of green showing around his dilated pupils. She felt a scream climb in her throat.

"How?" she could barely whisper the word.

"Gutel explained it that day in the library," he said, his voice as breathless and uneven as hers. "The ring...can be given if a bond between two people is strong enough. I've proven that we have a bond, Cassia. And that a part of you wants to be free of the burden of the ring."

Her throat closed, horror pouring through her veins like cold poison. "You tricked me."

"I'm merely using the opportunities given to me. Your denial is like a wall I can't break through. I think you feel things for me, even if you don't want to—"

No no no. She couldn't listen to any more. "What happened in the ballroom . . ." Had he been manipulating her with all his warm looks and soft words? Had the moments she had been lost to sensation been calculated to weaken her? "It was all a ploy," she said finally. And waited for him to deny it.

He wore a furious, accusing expression she didn't understand, but it was wiped clean in a heartbeat. "You're right about that, at least. None of this was real."

Something died inside of her. "Then let me end this with some truth."

For the first time in weeks, she used the knife-training skills she'd so diligently honed. Her movement was quick, her strength unhesitating. There was a horrible moment of resistance when the dagger sank into his flesh. His body jerked, his eyes rounding as they stared uncomprehending into hers. His gasp was whisked away by the wind. She saw white and shook her head to clear it.

"Keep to your bargain, Dracu." She pulled the dagger from his side and put it back in its sheath, her stomach roiling. His face was as pale as stone. She felt cold. And more alone than she ever had before.

For a second, she thought he might fall. She grabbed his arm, holding him until he wrapped an arm around the pennant pole for support. Now he was bound to send her home. All he had to do was will the amulet to work, and the Solis Gemma would unlock it. In moments, a doorway would open, and she would step through it. She felt, somehow, as if she already had.

"Better fly down from here while you can," she said, putting her ring to the amulet with a shaking hand. "At dawn, your pretty little wings will fade away."

A swirl of color and light appeared inches from her face, a doorway opening. The trees of Thirstwood shimmered beyond the veil.

"Cassia . . . ," Zeru said, his lips pale.

"Deathringer," she said, though her stomach heaved. "Say it."

His head bowed, whether from pain or in acknowledgment, she couldn't tell. "Deathringer. If that's what you choose."

"I chose a long time ago." Without another word, Cassia stepped through the portal.

19

Sylvans harvest magic from revelry.
A shrewd Dracu interrupts their merriment
at every opportunity.
—Gaxix, Dracu philosopher

As Cassia stepped through the doorway, she found herself in Thirstwood facing an old yew tree, its heavy branches stretching toward the night sky. She stared in disbelief. It was the same tree where she used to meet Zeru as a child.

I only need to imagine a spot I know well. And this was the spot he'd chosen.

She knelt, stomach heaving until it was empty. For a while, she leaned her forehead against the tree, her emotions as wild as a summer storm. When she thought of Zeru, of what she'd done to return here, a heaviness crushed her chest. The memory of the knife going in—

She took breaths of pine-scented air and focused on the comforting familiarity of the woods, and her greater attunement to the trees. Drawing strength from her forest, she stood and started toward home. She could sense which were blood trees without checking the color of the leaves. She touched their bark as she passed, greeting Thirstwood like an old friend.

It was well past dawn when she reached Scarhamm. Scarcely

had she approached the fortress's outer walls than an uproar ensued. The guards pointed, shouted, and her sisters rushed out, their arms pumping, hair flying behind them. Enora reached her first, wrapping her in a tight embrace that brought tears to Cassia's eyes. Thea elbowed Enora out of the way, subjecting Cassia to a rib-crushing hug.

Cassia found herself laughing and crying.

When it was Rozie's turn, she burst into gulping sobs. "You were gone too long!" she accused, her eyes glassy with tears.

Cassia's heart contracted. "I agree," she whispered. "I'm sorry I couldn't get home sooner."

Enora's concerned eyes swept over her. "Before we talk, let's get you to a healer to check you over." She started toward the gate, and Cassia fell in step beside her.

"No need." Cassia lifted her hands for inspection. The ring gleamed brighter than ever. "I'm truly fine. Not a scratch." Only an ache in her chest that she hoped would go away with time.

"Where in the nine realms have you been?" Thea demanded.

Cassia looked up at the sky before they entered Scarhamm's main gate. "You won't believe me." But as they traversed the inner bailey, she told them.

Despite their shock, Enora and Thea pestered her with questions, Rozie looking annoyed she couldn't get a word in. Cassia tried to keep up, though her answers were always interrupted by another question.

When it came to Zeru, she prevaricated so much it made her throat want to close up. But she could not share certain things. Dancing in the arms of her enemy? Not recognizing a winged creature as that same enemy? How he'd almost taken the ring?

No. These were not things her family would understand. She didn't understand them herself.

She was explaining her newfound abilities with the ring when a tall figure emerged from the fortress, his antlers burnished by morning light.

Everyone seemed to sense the king's presence, all the Huntsmen turning to watch the scene. Her sisters went silent, their faces somber.

Thea stood straighter in the presence of the king, but her soft words were meant for Cassia. "You'd better go. Veleda has been working night and day to scry your location. He's been beyond frustrated at her failures."

Cassia stepped toward her father, not knowing what to expect. Every breath in her lungs seemed too shallow, every step too slow. Would he show relief that she was safe? Perhaps even... embrace her? She wasn't sure she'd know what to do if he did. When she was a few feet away, she halted.

"Hello, Father," she said, her neck aching as she lifted her chin to look him in the eye.

His dark, solemn stare took her in, settling on her hand. On the ring.

"You're home," he said gravely. After a pause, he added more firmly, "I'll need your report."

Cassia's lips parted. She couldn't believe he hadn't said anything about being glad she had returned. Zeru's words came back to her, his description of her father's callousness when she'd been injured by the Dracu queen's vassals. *It was chilling.*

Cassia straightened her shoulders. The Deathringer did not need coddling. She gave her report in clipped replies, answering each question as briefly as possible. When she told him about her progress with the ring, his eyes shone with anticipation.

Finally, he gave a single curt nod. "Go rest. There will be a banquet in your honor tonight."

He turned away, striding back toward the fortress. So, that was his welcome home.

For the first time in five years, the great hall of Scarhamm was decked in festive splendor. Garlands of pine cones, berries, and golden-green vines festooned the columns and trailed down from ceiling beams, forming green archways. Long trestle tables were draped with silver lace and set with porcelain plates, wooden trenchers, and pewter goblets. Bouquets of roses, daylilies, and lavender suffused the air with a sweet smell. And every torch, candelabra, and lantern in the fortress had been lit, brightening the halls to a cloudless midday at the height of summer.

Cassia hovered in the doorway of the great hall, awed but uncomfortable with all this fuss over her.

Excitement hummed in the air. Revels had waned with the slumber of the queen, but it seemed the Huntsmen were ready to embrace their return.

Everyone knew the Dracu would attack on the night of the full moon when the wards were thin. And Cassia would be expected to use her newfound mastery of the ring to kill.

Suddenly, she wanted to be alone.

Before she could fade back out of the great hall and send her excuses, Rozie stepped lightly in. She wore a blue dress edged with scalloped lace at the hem and sleeves. Her curly copper hair, woven with bluebells, was making every effort to escape its pins.

"I love your gown!" Rozie said, eyes aglow with gleeful appreciation. "Butterflies everywhere!"

"Thank you, Sproutling." Cassia lifted the overskirt so the starched lace butterflies appeared to fly. "It used to be Enora's."

"When you get tired of it, I'll take it." Her grin faded as she leaned in to add, "If Thea asks, tell her I claimed it first."

"I'll be sure." Cassia smiled as she tucked an escaped lock of ginger hair behind her sister's ear. For a few minutes, they watched the room fill with Scarhamm's residents, admiring the finely made breeches, jackets, robes, and gowns. A number of forest creatures had also been invited, adding color and life to the earth-toned hall. Cassia spotted two lutins, elusive forest-dwellers like kobolds, but smaller and more delicate, their hats red rather than green. A group of diminutive pixies capered through, gently moving their gauzy wings, which looked much like the butterfly wings on Cassia's skirt. They breezed through the open doors to the garden, tittering at some shared joke. Cassia liked the carefree way they wore their pastel finery, and how their hair, both straight and curly, dark and light, was left loose and natural. Pixies were rarely seen, even by Sylvans, so this was a special honor. Through the polished windows they could see river nixies playing in the fountain, their shining curls and braids decorated with water lilies.

"Now that you have the ring figured out," Rozie said happily, "Enora says the war will be over soon and we'll be able to have revels like this all the time!"

Cassia swallowed. Enora's faith was heartwarming, but it was also a reminder that the ring's new powers weren't battle-tested. They could still make things grow—the withered trees in Scarhamm's neglected gardens had proven that. In the hours before the banquet, Cassia had spent her time trying to restore some of her mother's garden. She'd lovingly poured her life force into each plant, encouraging leaves and new growth, filling out the sicklier-looking shrubs. Even the nearly dead rosebushes had started to bud. She'd found a heady satisfaction in using her new powers at home, in restoring what her mother had once planted and tended with great care. And she'd been relieved that the abilities she'd acquired in Welkincaster were just as strong here.

She only hoped the ring's blast would be impressive. Enora had warned her their father expected a demonstration of her new power in front of the guests.

The mood changed to hushed reverence as the Sylvan king made his entrance. His antlers sparkled like fresh snow under sunlight, contrasting with his black clothing. When he turned his solemn gaze around the great hall, every head bowed in respect. Cassia kept her head bent as the king folded his large frame into his throne, the wood creaking as if it, too, contained an ancient spirit. When he was seated, the guests took their places. Cassia sat with her sisters at a table near the dais.

Veleda, in a rare appearance in the great hall, occupied her seat near the king. Her carved wooden chair had a back shaped like an owl for Noctua, goddess of spirits and prophecy. Though it was less impressive than the throne, it was still a place of honor. Veleda's white robes were pristine, her brown hair tamed into braids down her back, her dark eyes taking everything in. The Seer nodded to Cassia, who smiled back at her looking so stately and regal, accustomed as she was to seeing Veleda in bloodstained work clothes.

Cassia couldn't help but remember her mother on her own high seat next to the king, its back carved into an elegant bower made of branches and leaves. That seat had been removed from the great hall years ago, almost as if her mother was not expected to return. But maybe, maybe now that Cassia was learning to control this artifact of the Ancients, she would find a way to wake her mother from her long slumber. She allowed herself a moment to imagine her mother there, her smile warmer than the light from the oil lamps. Cassia blinked and the image was gone. *One thing at a time*, she told herself.

The king nodded to the First Huntsman and the festivities began.

Cassia toyed with her silverware and glanced up at the dais, wondering what her father was thinking. Other than a brief, almost imperceptible nod in her direction, he hadn't looked at her once. She ignored the ache in her chest and focused on the food that was being carried in, massive bronze platters overflowing with delicacies. After eating mostly fruit for a month, it was no hardship to sample the feast of walnut-stuffed partridges, roast boar, dandelion greens, baked pears dressed with nectar, and dozens of other dishes. After a few minutes, she could almost forget that her father hadn't even said he was glad she was home.

Once everyone was finished eating, the court moved to the side of the hall cleared for dancing, and the doors to the garden were thrown wide. One of the Huntsmen asked Cassia to dance. While her feet moved through the steps, she had a flash of memory, her hands in Zeru's as he'd tried, stiffly but determinedly, to mimic her movements. The way he'd spun her into his arms. His lips on her forehead, her cheek . . .

She shut the thoughts down, smiling brighter.

After two more dances, she was about to go out into the garden when a throat cleared behind her. Cassia turned to see Burke, the Second Huntsman, smiling down at her. His golden hair was brushed to the side, his strong jaw clean-shaven. His deep bow gave her time to hide her surprise. He had never paid the slightest attention to her, though she'd snuck many glances at him over the years.

"Hello, Burke," she said. His hazel eyes had an inner rim of green, almost like—

She shut that thought down, too.

～ 209 ～

"Well met, Deathringer," he said, holding his arm out for her. "Welcome home. Join me for a stroll?"

Cassia put a hand on his arm and told herself not to show her nerves at this unprecedented show of interest. They stepped from the great hall into the dark garden, with only a handful of fruit trees lit by moon sprites. Not nearly as many as in the clearing in the Welkinwood. She looked up at the moon, expecting it to be the bright disc she'd been used to seeing. Instead, it was covered by clouds. She looked away, frustrated with herself.

"So I hear you've mastered the ring," Burke said, inclining his head toward her hand. "You've tested it?"

"Of course. See the changes in the garden? The forsythia is flowering, and the roses are blooming. The willows need tending, but—"

"No," he interrupted, "I mean have you tested it on an Azpian?"

She halted midstep and looked up at him. "No. How could I have done that? I've barely been home."

His pale brows lifted. "I heard there was an Azpian household spirit where you were taken. It seemed logical that you'd turn the ring on him."

Cassia pictured Gutel. She thought of his dedication to the welkin, the hours they'd spent sitting in the courtyard as he'd explained her role as steward, his endearing boasts about his heroic past. Then she thought of using the ring's blast on him, and she drew her arm from Burke's. "It seems my stories have spread. I didn't expect anyone to interrogate me so soon."

He bowed low. "Forgive me. I didn't mean to imply you were negligent in any way. You had to do whatever was necessary to survive. Perhaps an opportunity never came."

For some reason, the heat of anger was creeping up her neck.

"Why are you asking me this, Burke? Is it...Did my father ask these questions?"

The Huntsman's lips tightened. "If he had, I wouldn't mention it. That would be indiscreet."

Which was an answer. "Of course."

When Burke resumed walking, she went along with him, but a quiet fury had ignited in her rib cage. She'd barely arrived home, and already her father was questioning her loyalty and judgment. Instead of asking her directly, he had voiced his displeasure to one of the Huntsmen.

As they passed under the heavy branches of a huge old elm tree, Burke took her elbow, making her turn to him. "Cassia."

"Yes." Her heart kicked an annoyed rhythm. Was it too much to expect him to be silent for a minute so she could sort out her thoughts?

"You must have seen my admiration."

She looked up at him in shock. He'd never shown the slightest interest in her. She would have noticed. He was one among a number of Huntsmen she truly envied because they never seemed to make mistakes.

She was tempted to ask if he'd developed this sudden regard for her around the time she returned home. Instead, she said politely, "I had no idea."

"You are quite beautiful, you know," he said, and she was amazed to realize he seemed genuine. She couldn't tell if her pulse was jumping from his flattery or nerves when he touched a fingertip to her nose and declared, "Your freckles are enchanting."

A rustle came from the branches above, and something thudded to the ground. Probably a walnut being dropped by a squirrel, or a piece of fruit now that she'd encouraged new growth on some of the trees.

Burke moved closer. "You haven't paid attention to anyone else, so I'm not worried I have competition. Maybe you've never given a thought to your own happiness?"

His tone was soft and inviting. When he put his hands on her shoulders, she didn't move away.

"Maybe," she said. It was true her happiness wasn't something she thought about. She'd always been too caught up in trying to grow into the role her father had set for her. That was the future she'd always wanted.

"All I'm asking is that you spend time with me," he said, his eyes persuasive. "Let me get to know you, and get to know me. Would you allow me that honor, Cassia?"

It was a flattering question. But the whole thing seemed irrelevant and ill-timed considering they were on the brink of battle. The full moon was just over a week away. Over the next few days, the Huntsmen would check to make sure the wards and walls were secure against the expected Dracu attack. She was about to give a noncommittal answer when he bent and kissed her cheek. His lips were soft, brushing her skin in a way she found not unpleasant. She remained still as he kissed the other.

Their eyes met. His were keen and attentive, but for some reason, not the eyes she wanted to see. When she realized she'd prefer to see the green of high summer, she lifted her face in defiance of that image.

Burke pulled her closer, then suddenly jerked away, swearing roundly. "What—something fell on me." He shot an irritated look at the dark branches. "A piece of fruit?"

Cassia's mouth fell open as she stared at the "fruit" that had rolled to a stop at the base of the tree. A turnip. There were no turnips in the gardens at Scarhamm. Her chest seized at a memory of throwing them at Zeru in Selkolla's workroom.

He couldn't be here. The last thing she'd done was stab him. He'd once threatened to hurt her family. Had he come to carry out that threat?

One word and she'd have every Huntsman at the revel here in seconds. She would be safe from the Dracu who'd given her the ring, who'd done everything he could to get it back, who might, for all she knew, still be out for revenge.

But the turnip seemed more like a message than a threat. A way of telling her that he was here without alerting anyone else.

"We should go back," she said, turning away from the tree to draw Burke's attention. "My father wants me to demonstrate the ring. You know how impatient he is."

"You should have said." Burke rubbed his head, on alert as he looked around the gardens. "I thought I caught a whiff of pit sprites." He patted Cassia's arm. "I'd better not leave you alone."

"What Azpian can stand against my ring? I'll be fine." She put a hand to the center of his back and pushed. "Assemble the others for me, will you, please? I need a moment to prepare. Alone."

It was the best she could come up with, and thankfully Burke accepted her request. As he bowed and kissed her hand, Cassia was painfully conscious of the tree behind her. When he turned and went off along the path, she breathed a sigh, then rushed to the base of the massive elm.

Her heart slammed her ribs as the light from garden torches caught the leather of wings. Seeing Zeru in the form she'd known as Aril was confusing her sense of danger. She wished she knew which version of him was real. Strangely, part of her was weak with relief that she hadn't managed to kill him. She hadn't real-ized the reason for the knot of dread in her stomach until now.

But that didn't mean he had forgiven her.

"There are about a hundred Huntsmen at the other end of the

⌒ 213 ⌒

garden," she told him, trying not to let her wild mix of emotions show in her voice. "I could call for help and they'd be here in a few seconds."

"Why call for help when you can just finish what you started?" Zeru pointed out, his tone sharp-edged and openly challenging. "Kill me with my own dagger and set my head on your father's gate with the other dead Dracu. Wasting time, Sylvan, if you plan to do it."

She drew in a breath, exhaling slowly. "Have you come for revenge?"

He made a gently scoffing noise. "If you thought I wanted you dead, why did you send your Huntsman away?"

The darkness and branches made it so that she could only see hints of him here and there. The moonlight on his cheek. The white of one eye. The fingers of one hand as he grasped a branch. "Burke is not *my* Huntsman."

"Is that his name? It's very stolid. Suits him." He shifted positions, moving forward so she could see him a little better. "To be honest, Cassia, he seems the sort who needs a turnip dropped on him. So earnest. I could barely hold my bile."

So, he was choosing humor. She could do the same. No matter how odd and unsettling it was to have him here. "A turnip, Dracu?"

"That alone should answer your question. Murder rarely begins by pelting someone with vegetables. Unless they are launched by your own sweet hands."

She was amused at the memory, which no longer included a sense of fear. It was almost surreal how differently she saw him now. "How did you get past the guards?"

"With great care."

She closed her eyes at the full weight of the danger he was in.

214

No, she would not call any guards. And she did not want his head on the gates.

"You should go," she said.

"Your problem, Sylvan, is that you state the obvious. I have every intention of leaving. After all, at dawn, these pretty little wings will fade away."

Her crossed arms tightened as if she could protect herself from the memory. Had it only been a day since she'd stuck him with his own blade and said those things? "I'm glad you're alive," she said, hoping the catch in her voice was drowned out by the sounds of the revel in the distance.

"Are you?" he asked with soft curiosity, skepticism, and a hint of something deeper. A need to know that she meant it, perhaps.

She answered in all seriousness. "Yes."

"Is that an apology?" he asked, the challenge returning.

She wasn't sure how to word one. *Sorry for stabbing you?* "You didn't give me much choice."

He was silent for a few seconds, then a sigh wafted down from the boughs. "No. I didn't." After a pause, he added with smooth aplomb, "Gutel was all sympathy and bandaged me nicely. Said I'd been deemed worthy to be a guardian and that his instincts about me were correct. He went so far as to tell me some Zerian heritage might explain my natural resistance to your ring. And perhaps why my mother's family were keepers of the Solis Gemma."

That must be why he had transformed. The welkin had deemed him worthy and claimed him as a guardian. She didn't know how she felt about that. It was as if the ring had chosen them both.

"Why did you lose your memory? And your Dracu horns, for that matter?"

"Gutel thinks it has to do with early transformation, and that I'll have more control over my form in time."

She stared up into the spreading branches, wishing she could see him better. Wishing she could understand why he'd risk coming here. And why she was so terrified that he was in danger. And why they were having a casual conversation instead of saying... whatever it was they should really say to each other.

"Did you enjoy the kiss?" he asked. "Your Huntsman's, I mean."

Her mouth fell open at his audacity. "You dropped a turnip on him before that could happen."

He smiled. "I should have trusted my impeccable timing. Really, though, so soon after ours? Sylvan." His tone was chastising. "You have little regard for my sensitive feelings."

Waves of conflicting emotions tore through her, eroding her sense of stability like an undertow. Was he saying their kiss meant something to him?

She swallowed the question, instead asking dryly, "So, you're saying I shouldn't call him back here to continue what we started?"

"Why don't you?" he asked. "Call him back and point me out in this tree. I'll have no defense. I'm your mortal, sworn enemy. Why not kill me now and be done?"

He was challenging her again, the way he'd done atop the spire when he'd dared her to prove her ability to hurt him. She swallowed past a knot in her throat and shook her head.

Denied an answer, he spoke the words for her. "Because we have a bond."

Her forehead met the reassuring solidity of tree bark. She was tempted to bang her head there a few times to see if she could find some sense. The truth was, she had missed him. Only a day since she'd seen him, and she'd missed him. Aril or Zeru, she'd grown attached. And she was starting to admit to herself that those two people were one and the same. Aril was merely the side of Zeru that he would never show an enemy.

She could discern the outlines of a crouching figure, his wings hidden by leaves. "You really have to go. I'm about to demonstrate the ring. If the blast is as strong as I hope, you could be knocked out of there, natural resistance or no."

"That's some confidence you have, Sylvan. Give me some credit. Anyway, your demonstration will provide me with a moment to leave unnoticed. When do you plan to use it against the rest of us?"

"On the night you attack," she said defiantly.

"As I imagined. But...there's a complication," he said, his voice low and serious. "What I came to tell you. I returned to the Cryptlands after I healed. Something isn't right. Selkolla is... curse it! Your friend is coming back."

She heard it, too. Footsteps approaching. She spoke with quiet urgency. "Tell me!"

"It's Selkolla," he said. "Remember the creature with her?"

"The moss child."

"She called it that," he said, "but the moss folk are gone. Hers is a scucca—a replica made from plant material and a trapped spirit. She has hundreds of them. Maybe thousands. The queen found out, and the Seer claimed to have made them for the Dracu army, but I don't believe it. Selkolla controls them like puppets. They're not truly alive, so I'm not sure they can be cut down by a sword."

Creatures impervious to a blade sounded very, very bad. "How do we fight them?"

"I don't know. But I wonder why Selkolla sent you to

⌐ 217 ⌐

Welkincaster. Did she want you—and the ring—out of the way? I'll find out more and meet you—"

Burke came around a corner a few yards away, his feet crunching noisily. "They're ready for you, Deathringer!"

"Meet where?" Cassia whispered. "When?"

But the boughs were empty. As she turned away, moonlight fell on a small, pale object at her feet. She bent and picked it up.

A fish-bone comb.

20

A Dracu, once dispatched, is best forgotten.
—Excharias, Sylvan poet

Minutes later, Cassia took a deep breath, willing her nerves to settle. She stood tall, head up, the center of attention among a group of Huntsmen, and around them, their assembled guests filling every corner of the garden. They lolled on the edges of the fountain, sat atop shrubs, and stood on the bases of statues. The Huntsmen were somber. They'd seen her fail before and knew how much their success depended on this. By contrast, the forest-dweller guests watched with festive anticipation, as if they were there for the spectacle alone. Maybe they didn't realize the Sylvan king's daughter could decide the outcome of the next attack.

Cassia was excruciatingly aware of her father's expectant regard. He stood head and shoulders above everyone else, his dark stare watchful. Closing her eyes, she took a breath.

Solis help me, she prayed. *Don't let me fail this time.*

She thought of sunlight, water, the seeking of roots, the pulse of nutrients through veins in leaves, the sprouting of seeds, anything that made her feel powerful and alive. But then her mind drifted to the image of Zeru's green eyes, their verdant color and the frenetic, restless life behind them, which he seemed barely able to contain. Strangely, the ring glowed brighter. So instead of tearing her thoughts away, she thought of dancing with him, the feel of his arms around her, his breath warm on her neck. She thought of him risking his life by entering the Sylvan stronghold to warn her about a threat. To insist they had a bond that was not broken by time or distance or the cut of a blade.

The ring glowed as emotion built in her chest, feeling upon feeling, wave upon wave until she felt like an overfilled container. She opened her eyes, preparing to set the light free. As she was about to let go, she spotted Rozie sitting atop a statue. No doubt she'd scrambled up to get a prime view. Her copper hair was wild, her grin wide. She lifted a hand to wave, lost her balance, and nearly toppled. In an ungainly scramble, she saved herself at the last moment. While Cassia breathed a sigh of relief, Rozie gave her a wide-eyed look as if to say, *"Wouldn't that have been embarrassing?"* Cassia grinned as amusement bubbled up, overflowing her internal well.

The Solis Gemma set the magic free.

Her gasp was lost in shouts of surprise. The pain in her chest was minimal. Opening her eyes, she found her sight already returning, though it took a second to realize it. What she saw made her jaw drop. Scarhamm's gardens were lit with the radiance of a thousand lamps, brighter than a cloudless day. The forest-dwellers squinted or shielded their eyes, some of them shrieking in delight or terror. The pulsing glow extended even over the walls, painting the treetops of Thirstwood. Cassia wondered whether Zeru had seen it. Then again, she hoped he was underground, safe, not suddenly visible in the brightness she had created.

As the light faded and night slipped back over Scarhamm like the drawing of heavy curtains, the forest-dwellers laughed, some of them taking up a spontaneous dance in celebration. Her breath locked in her throat, Cassia looked up at her father.

What she saw etched on the harsh lines of his face stunned her. Pride. Unmistakable pride.

In his deep rumble of a voice, he said, "Good."

And dipped his chin to her.

Frozen by shock, she managed a single nod, her mind reeling with the magnitude of this moment.

The blast was everything she could have hoped for.

She was, finally, finally, enough.

Good.

The word rang in her ears as she made her way to the war room.

After so many years of hope and failure, it was almost more than Cassia could bear. Elation and relief fizzed through her veins like strong wine or the sparkle of sunlight on water. She felt as if she were walking on a cloud. She almost laughed at the thought that she had actually walked on a cloud. And that had led her here, to this glorious place of finally being enough.

Enora came to walk beside her, speaking softly so only she could hear. "Are you all right, Cass?"

Cassia grinned. "Never better."

Her eldest sister looked at her skeptically. "You pulled off that incredible display, and all you got was a 'good'?"

A little of the effervescence left her. Enora wouldn't understand. She had always had their father's approval. But this had been the first time Cassia had seen it. Directed at *her*. "It's more than enough for me."

Enora shook her head. "Our father doesn't know how to give a compliment."

As they reached the war room, Cassia took a moment to look around. The room was still large, shadowy, with weapons on the walls and the long, scarred oaken table running down the center. But it appeared darker and grimmer to her eyes. She longed for windows. She missed the cheery brightness of Welkincaster.

Frustrated with herself for wanting what she couldn't have right when she was on the cusp of becoming everything she'd always longed to be, she stood arrow-straight as the king took his spot at the head of the table, glad he couldn't see her ungrateful thoughts. His antlers were lit by the flames from the fireplace behind him, his eyes serious as he regarded the small assemblage of Huntsmen. To his right stood his First Huntsman, Alof. Then Burke, who watched Cassia with an avid expression. Next to him was Tibald, and then Tordon, the Third Huntsman. On the Sylvan king's left, Enora, then Thea, who gave her a wink. Cassia didn't respond, not wanting to do anything that would jeopardize her father's approval.

"Cassia," he said, gesturing with one of his massive hands. "Your place is here." He indicated the spot where ... where Enora stood next to him. Her eldest sister's expression registered shock before she inclined her head obediently and shifted closer to Thea.

Cassia couldn't breathe, completely thrown off balance. Her pulse beat in her temples and her throat felt tight. Take Enora's place? Was it a temporary or a permanent change? She glanced at Enora's face as she moved farther down the table, her stomach twisting. She hadn't wanted to supplant anyone. She'd never imagined trying to compete with or outdo her eldest sister.

But you didn't say no to the king. Her palms damp, Cassia

moved to the now-empty place and tried not to look as out of place as she felt.

"Alof," the king said with a brief nod.

The First Huntsman didn't waste time. "We've scouted the area. There is little sign of activity. But we don't know how many Dracu could be guarding the entrance on the inside."

"We believe their presence is minimal," Burke said as he unfurled a map and held it open with both hands. He turned a look on Cassia. "We'll need the Deathringer to be near the front as we enter the Cryptlands in case we need to make use of the ring."

Enter the Cryptlands? Cassia looked to her father, hoping for an explanation.

"You are to use the ring for protection of our forces only," her father said, his usual sternness offset by a new respect in his voice. "If possible, save your energy for the night of the Dracu attack."

More confused still, she fought not to quail under his iron gaze. Though his manner wasn't harsh, it made her feel small looking up at him. "Aren't we planning for the Dracu attack we expect on the night of the full moon?"

"We still expect that to happen," he said, determination burning in his dark eyes. "But tomorrow, we carry out our own strike against the Dracu."

Blood rushed in Cassia's ears, and the ring seemed to pinch more tightly. She was so shocked she could form no reply. In the meantime, the First and Second Huntsmen resumed their discussion. It was clear this had been planned at length. Thea was staring down at the map showing no sign she thought this was reckless or impossible or ... complete and utter nonsense.

Alof pointed to a spot on the map. "Here is our entrance point in Thirstwood. A hill with a hidden door into their tunnels."

223

Her skin prickled. The thought of going back into that dark, labyrinthine place made all the muscles in her back tense. "How did you find a way in?"

"The Court Seer," Alof said simply. "Veleda drew a map of the tunnels leading from that doorway to the nearby settlements."

Burke must have seen Cassia's confusion. "Veleda has been helping us plan this ever since your capture," he explained. "Her Seeing, her use of spirits, has been vital. It was unfortunate she could find no trace of where you'd been taken by the Dracu, though as she focused her efforts on the Cryptlands, she came up with other useful information about the enemy's lair."

Cassia nodded, sifting through this new information. It made sense that Veleda hadn't been able to scry her whereabouts in another realm. She wished she'd had time to talk to Veleda, but she'd been so busy reinforcing the wards, Cassia hadn't wanted to bother her.

Waiting until Alof completed his briefing, she gathered her courage to ask, "Why are we invading?"

After a thick silence, the Sylvan king answered, his tone implacable. "A Dracu abducted my daughter. If I allow that to stand without retribution, what further insults will I have to endure?"

Unable to bear the fire in his eyes, Cassia bowed her head. *Retribution?* Was that what this was about? She noticed he made no mention of what insults *she* had endured. Or what *she* wanted as recompense for them. Even as she stood in Enora's place at the table, her feelings didn't matter to him. Was she foolish for thinking they ever would?

The conversation moved on to specifics: who would lead, who would guard the passage ensuring safe egress. Enora and Thea would be left to guard Scarhamm while a group of two dozen Huntsmen went on the mission, with more nearby in the woods.

The plan was straightforward: They would enter through the hill and travel a short distance through the tunnels to a settlement. The Dracu homes there would be burned.

"Is this a civilian settlement?" Enora asked in her measured voice as she examined the map. "That is unusual."

"This is not random," Alof said. "The settlement is connected to the Dracu who abducted your sister."

Cassia shivered. *Zeru.*

They were going after Zeru's family.

She almost betrayed herself then. She wanted to shout that they couldn't do this! Killing Zeru's parents for something their son had done was wrong.

But that would destroy the newfound approval she had worked so hard to earn. And she had the feeling that if she spoke, if she said anything at all, her voice would shake, and everyone would know her secret: that she had let herself care for a Dracu.

But could she go along with this? Could she live with herself if Zeru's parents were killed and she could have prevented it?

While she wrestled with herself in agonized silence, Thea spoke with her usual clear confidence. "We've never taken a force into the Cryptlands. Not only is it dark and more airless the deeper we go, it presents challenges to the movement of our troops." She pointed to a spot on the map. "The distance between our front line and our rear guard will lengthen as the tunnels narrow to single file. Do we have a plan for this?"

"That's precisely why it's a small force," Alof said. "We strike fast and get out. Veleda assures us the distance is minimal."

"There's also the question of the Seer Cassia encountered in the Cryptlands," Enora added.

Alof had an answer for that, too. "Veleda will be there to counter any magical attacks."

Cassia found her voice, remembering the vital piece of information Zeru had given her. "Selkolla had a kind of creature constructed of sticks and moss. I heard it called a scucca. I have reason to believe she's made many more, perhaps hundreds or thousands."

Silence fell over the table.

"Hundreds or thousands," the king said critically. "Have you seen this for yourself?"

She held his eyes. "I...no. I've seen one. The Dracu mentioned more."

"Dracu lie," the Sylvan king reminded her, venom dripping from the words. "Or have you forgotten?"

She shook her head. To redirect his attention, she asked, "What is a scucca?"

When the Sylvan king said nothing, Tordon, the Third Huntsman, answered. He was one of the oldest Sylvans in Scarhamm, with a lined face and dark, tight curls worn short against his scalp. "Creating scuccas is an abomination of the natural order," he said. "It requires taking life force from nature and merging it with trapped spirits. Sunlight weakens the magic." His eyes shifted to his king. "Underground, they would be at full power."

The king's eyes burned with defiance. "A few hastily constructed puppets don't concern me. Slay the mage controlling them, and they all fall at once. We have no reason to delay. Be ready to leave at dawn."

Cassia felt a deep conviction it wouldn't be so easy to kill Selkolla. She'd felt an aura of staggering power in the Seer's presence. But how could she convince her father, who was so certain of his victory?

Before she could think of what to say, he'd left the room.

"Let's get on with it, then!" Tibald said, slapping the table in

~ 226 ~

his exuberant way. "Rest, Deathringer, while you can. We've celebrated your return. Now we put you to work!" He grinned at her good-naturedly, and she forced a smile.

Tordon's own smile lifted his craggy face. "An impressive blast, Deathringer. Well done!"

Cassia wished she could enjoy their pride. Tibald had always believed in her, even when she'd shown no signs of ever being able to master the ring. But now that she'd finally achieved her aim, things were not going as she'd thought they would.

As everyone filed out, Cassia stopped Enora with a hand on her arm. "I'm sorry Father made me take your spot at the table. I didn't want to."

Enora's face stiffened, and Cassia realized her mistake. Her sister was proud, and the apology was like rubbing salt on a fresh wound.

"You've earned your place," Enora said woodenly. "Isn't this what you've always wanted? Don't back down now, Deathringer."

Cassia bent her head, fighting tears. She had rarely been at odds with Enora, who was fair and even-tempered in the worst situations. And she hated her sister calling her by the title. She wanted Enora to call her "Cass" as she always had.

When everyone else was gone, Thea remained. She put a hand on Cassia's shoulder and gave it a squeeze. "She'll adjust. As will you. She understands it's not your choice. We might not always want to do what our father requires, but it's for the greater good. Don't be so hard on yourself, Cass. You should be proud. You've never let us down. Not in your heart."

"Thank you, Thea," she said thickly, glad her sister couldn't see the betrayal happening in her heart at that moment.

Stupid. Pointless. A fool's errand.

Cassia berated herself as she followed the familiar paths of Thirstwood. There was no way Zeru would be nearby. There was no way she could summon him. She was not in Welkincaster. He was not, as it turned out, a spirit of the Netherwhere. And even if he were, she was not a Seer with spells to commune with the spirits, living or dead. She should be in bed resting before the planned attack. This was a waste of time.

On the other hand, Zeru was a guardian, and she was the steward of Welkincaster. He'd said they had a bond, and she could no longer deny it. No matter how foolish it made her feel, she had to try.

She had come to the unshakable conclusion that she could not live with herself if Zeru's parents were killed. Not without at least trying to stop it.

She paced the worn paths for hours, all the places where they used to meet as children, repeating variations of the same message. "Summon Zeru. Tell Zeru to meet me in our old spot. By the power of the Solis Gemma, summon Zeru, the guardian of Welkincaster."

At some point in the wee hours, she heard a chuckle. "I knew you liked that ring, but I never thought I'd feel jealous of it."

She froze, the gemstone still touching her lips. Slowly, she lowered her hand. "It worked, though."

"I don't know if you can claim that." Zeru's voice came from somewhere in the boughs above.

"You're here, aren't you?" she pointed out, trying to locate the origin of the sound.

"I had a sudden, inexplicable urge to come here. Were you talking to yourself this whole time?"

"To you through the ring." She refused to feel embarrassed.

"And again, let me emphasize, Dracu, that it worked. You are here. Where I wanted you to be."

A rustle of branches, then a soft thud. The shadows moved and a winged figure came into view. "You admit you want me, then? My dreams realized."

Her heart jumped as she peered up at his shadowy form. She crossed her arms, assessing him as he halted a couple of feet away. "You still don't have your horns."

Zeru ran a hand through his hair. "Did you bring me here to insult me?"

"No." She couldn't help but smile that he saw that as a grievous insult. "But I like that you admit I invited you, and that you accepted my invitation. That's a good start."

His teeth flashed white in the dim light. "Start to what?" When she didn't answer, he went on. "Reminds me of a Sylvan girl I met once in these woods. She liked to give me orders."

Time went backward, and suddenly, Cassia was that young girl full of curiosity and determination to find her tree. Maybe some of that reckless child remained a part of her. "I need to warn you."

"Yes?" He moved closer, his hand coming up to her hair. Her breath caught in her chest, everything suspended as she waited for him to touch her. He pulled a twig out and showed it to her before dropping it to the ground.

"Oh...thank you." She shook her head to clear it, willing her pulse to calm. "There's an invasion planned for tomorrow. I mean today." It was almost morning.

"What are you talking about?" he asked, his tone growing serious.

"Your family. We're going after them." She didn't want him to think she had anything to do with it. "My father found out

229

where your family lives in the Cryptlands and plans revenge for my abduction. Today."

Zeru was silent for a few moments, but she felt his tension like a living thing wrapped around her.

"I'm sorry," she said, wondering if he blamed her.

"No, no, it makes sense. I should have anticipated." His voice was rough with emotion, making him sound even more like the Aril she'd first met in the Welkinwood. Though his voice at night was rougher, he no longer sounded to her like anyone but himself. "Revenge must be taken. I merely thought your people would be too busy preparing for our attack."

"Which you'll be part of?" she asked, seized by a sudden tightness in her throat and chest.

"Of course."

She closed her eyes. "So, nothing has changed. We are enemies."

He moved close, his hands coming to her shoulders. His grip was firm and warm and reassuring. "If we were enemies, would you have come here to warn me? You are not my enemy. I'm not yours. If we're thrown against each other by no will of our own, we're not to blame."

His words were cold comfort. "Who cares about blame if I have to kill you, or you me?" She swallowed, trying to calm herself as she waited for his answer. Why was she so upset, anyway? This is how it had always been. How it always would be.

"I saw your blast," he said, his tone inscrutable. "To call it impressive is an understatement. Was the Sylvan king pleased?"

She recalled the look of pride on her father's face, and still felt awed by it. "I think I could even say it...surprised him."

Zeru sighed, his hold loosening. "It seems you have everything you've always wanted."

"Yes. I do."

He paused. "Does it feel as good as you thought it would?"

Something about the darkness, her fears about the raid, and the knowledge that this might be her last chance to talk to Zeru made her open up. "Everything is…different than I imagined. My father made me take Enora's place in the war room. This invasion…feels…wrong." She shook her head, frustrated. "I haven't felt so unsure of myself in years. And that's saying something." She closed her eyes, shame warming her cheeks. "I wish I hadn't said any of that."

Zeru's reply was soft and hoarse. "I'm glad you did." His hands tightened, and for a second, she thought he might pull her closer. But he didn't. "Thank you for the warning. I am in your debt."

His hands slipped away. She regretted their loss instantly. "You risked your life to warn me about the scuccas. We're even. Did you have a chance to find out anything else?"

"I was barely back in the Cryptlands when I felt your call," he reminded her.

She smiled at his familiar grousing tone. "Like I said. It worked."

"But I did find out a few things. It seems Selkolla came to the Cryptlands after betraying one of the Ancients during their wars. The Dracu queen didn't want to take in a Sylvan, but Selkolla offered her powers as Seer. Apparently, even that wasn't enough. The Dracu queen extracted a vow not to harm anyone under her rule in exchange for sanctuary. If I find out more…I don't know how I'll be able to tell you. Your patrols will be on full alert."

She nodded. "You can't come here again."

His voice took on a grim note. "Cassia, listen. We might be pitted against each other soon, but I will not harm you."

She felt hollow, shaky. She wished she could sleep until all this was over. "You might not have a choice."

"I know. But I can't hurt you. It would be like hurting myself. Worse."

She closed her eyes, her temples aching, her throat tight. He had talked of bonds. She knew as Aril he'd become attached to her. But this was beyond what she'd suspected he felt. Was it real, though? Could this have something to do with his becoming a guardian, and she the caretaker? Maybe it was the magic at work. When she tried to examine her own feelings, confusion fogged her mind. Would she be able to hurt him if it came down to it? She knew she didn't want to. She didn't want to hurt him, ever.

"Why do you even have to join in the attack?" she asked, knowing the dark didn't hide the moisture in her eyes. While she could see nothing more than silhouettes and shapes, his softly glowing green eyes could see so much more. "Go to Welkincaster now while you still have wings. Keep away from it altogether."

"Still trying to order me around." His light tone teased, the affection in it making Cassia's chest ache. "I have to get my parents to safety. And I need to find out more about what Selkolla is planning. I have as much responsibility to my people as you do to yours."

A lump had formed in her throat. She looked down at the ground, afraid of what he might see in her eyes. Regret. Worry. Need. Things she shouldn't feel for him. She took a breath and lifted her chin. "I understand."

He paused, and his teeth flashed. "Besides, battle is the only place I'll get to see you."

She knew that was supposed to draw a smile, but she couldn't. Sadness was like iron flowing through her veins, weighing down her heart.

An owl hooted in the distance. They both looked up, tensing.

Zeru whispered, "One of your patrols is coming this way. I have to go."

She reached out and found his hand, even in the dark. "Be safe, Zeru."

He squeezed her hand, reassuring her with his warm, firm grip for too brief a moment. "Be safe, Cassia."

His lips brushed her cheek before he vaulted into the air and was gone.

21

> Sylvans see not what lurks in shadows.
> There lies our advantage.
> —Gaxix, Dracu philosopher

Morning dew still clung to the leaves when the king and his chosen group of Huntsmen reached the hill, about two hours' march from Scarhamm. Though exhaustion dulled her senses, Cassia recognized the area—a weed-covered mound she must have passed a hundred times without giving it a second glance. At the king's nod, Veleda strode to it, holding her hands high, palms facing outward as she chanted in a clear voice. The earth groaned, a cloud of dust rose from the hill, and a hidden door yawned open.

The king stood next to Cassia, his daunting presence adding to her jangling nerves.

Dread sat heavy in her stomach as the scout disappeared through the doorway, returning to signal it was clear. Alof and Burke filed in without hesitation. After a brief backward glance, she took a breath and followed, Veleda close behind her along with a dozen or so Huntsmen. As the opening was too narrow for him, the Sylvan king remained above with a more sizable guard.

Cassia ran her hand along the rough wall, trying not to think. The earthen floor was sloped, angling down into the root-choked earth, where the temperature dropped as they went deeper. It brought her back to the night of her capture, making her heart kick faster. At least she wasn't alone this time.

But this was still the last place she wanted to be.

After a few minutes, the incline flattened into quiet tunnels where the Huntsmen could walk two abreast. They saw no sign of Azpian enemies, though she was viscerally aware that an ambush could come at any moment. Whenever they reached forks in the path, Veleda pointed the way. It wasn't long before they came to a cavernous space filled with small thatch-roofed houses clustered around a central area with a well. There were no sounds, no light from fires, no signs of life. A hint of acrid smoke lingering in the air was the only evidence of recent habitation.

Burke motioned two of the others to scout with him. They returned in a few minutes, their expressions grim. "The homes are all empty. No one is here."

Cassia's relief was so great, her knees sagged. Zeru must have cleared out the entire settlement.

Alof called out, "Veleda. Can you See where they've gone?"

Veleda nodded, moving forward. "I can scry them for you."

Silently, Cassia cursed herself for not having considered this possibility. If Zeru's family was hiding nearby, the Seer could lead the Huntsmen straight to them. Not only that. If her father got hold of Zeru...

Fear gripped her stomach. It wouldn't be a quick death.

The Court Seer reached into her pack and produced a container of some oily substance, using it to draw a circle on the dirt floor. Carefully, she added runes of protection around the rim, taking her time to be precise. As she finished, she said the ancient words of power and a spirit appeared in the circle, its shape indistinct.

235

"Show us the Dracu who live in this settlement," Veleda commanded. "Show us where they are now."

The spirit's form faded. In the circle where it had been, an image appeared of Dracu gathered in groups in a space that looked much like the cavern they were in, dimly lit by a few torches hung on walls of rough rock. Even in the gloom, Cassia spotted Zeru immediately. He was in his daytime form, complete with horns but lacking wings, strolling through the camp with his usual grace. A child approached, and he crouched down to talk to her, saying something that drew a smile. As he continued on, he received friendly nods.

Cassia couldn't look away. Among his own people, Zeru was relaxed in a way she had never seen. He was obviously adored by those who knew him. She watched with an ache in her chest as he approached two Dracu who had to be his parents. The resemblance between them and their son was clear. His father, whose horns were twisted like Zeru's, looked forbidding as he gave a curt nod and spoke. As Zeru replied, his parents seemed intent on whatever he said. When he finished speaking, his mother embraced him.

Cassia's stomach clenched with envy. It had been years since she'd embraced her own mother. Zeru's father put a hand on his shoulder. By the way Zeru stiffened, Cassia had the sense he wasn't accustomed to this display of affection.

She swallowed against a thickness in her throat. It was clear Zeru loved his parents, and they loved him. She was glad she'd warned him, no matter what happened.

Taking one last look, she mouthed, *Goodbye*, clasping her hands together to keep them from trembling.

Zeru's head twitched and he sniffed the air, turning slowly, his eyes searching the camp before passing over her. He blinked, and his eyes came back to rest on her. She felt her own eyes widen. He looked as if he could *see* her. She was certain that was not how a scrying spell was supposed to work.

Though she couldn't hear him, she read his lips. *Cassia!*

Stifling a gasp, she turned her back to the vision, hoping no one else could see it clearly enough to understand what Zeru had mouthed. "That cavern could be anywhere. We should return above for instructions."

Burke spoke with firm confidence. "We have orders to burn this settlement. When that's done, we can go after the Dracu."

Cassia eyed Burke with sudden dislike. He was a loyal Huntsman, carrying out orders efficiently, but he would never be one to question whether those orders were right. Her stomach clenched as she surveyed the proof of daily life—worn clothing hung to dry on a rope that ran between two houses, a small stack of firewood next to an outdoor stove, a broken pot that had been mended with mud and straw. This wasn't like some areas of the Cryptlands she'd seen, with colorful mosaics and delicate oil lamps—places where wealthier Dracu clearly lived. Forcing the people who inhabited this settlement to rebuild their homes could be a hardship beyond bearing.

"First Huntsman," Cassia said in her most authoritative voice, "the settlement is empty. The targets are gone. Nothing has gone as planned." She lowered her voice to give the impression of imparting valuable advice. "We should return above and report rather than guessing what to do. And guessing wrong."

Guessing wrong was something you didn't risk. Not with the king.

After a moment of thought, Alof nodded. "You're right. We'll go back for orders."

On his word, the Huntsmen retreated through the tunnels. Veleda dismissed the spirit, falling in behind them. She grabbed

Cassia's sleeve, slowing her steps until the Huntsmen were out of earshot.

"If you go back," Veleda said in a low, harsh voice, "your treason will soon be discovered. I can't protect you from this."

Cassia stilled, the breath stopping in her chest. Veleda knew.

The reality of her situation yawned before her like a massive hole. A hole she'd dug herself. Maybe, she thought wildly, maybe if she explained to her father...if she argued her position well enough...if she threw herself on his mercy...maybe he would forgive her.

"I don't expect you to protect me," she said, doing her best to hide her terror.

"And yet that's what I've done all these years," Veleda snapped. "I hope it wasn't a waste."

"Are you going to tell him?" she asked, wishing her voice sounded steadier.

Veleda eyed her. "I'll try to avoid direct questions. But if the king asks, I have no choice. I'm bound by oath."

Her stomach roiling as if she'd drunk poison, Cassia forced herself to move forward. There was only the soft sound of their footsteps until they reached the surface. As she emerged, she squinted against the sudden brightness. Her father's shape was a menacing outline against the light. It struck her how unique and wild his appearance was compared to everyone else. He was taller than any Sylvan or Azpian, any creature except for the northern giants, whom she had never seen. His antlers seemed to span the ages, his eyes as keen as an owl's. Though he was lord of the forest, she had a sharp sense of how different he was, how alone in the world. A familiar pang of longing to be closer to him was overshadowed by fear. If she explained why she'd betrayed him, would he listen?

Before she had time to ponder what she would say, her father barked, "Court Seer! My First has given his report. Give me yours."

"King Silvanus," Veleda said, stepping forward with her hand on her shoulder in salute. "The Dracu have gone into hiding. The spirits have shown me their image, but their location remains obscure. If we return to Scarhamm, I can summon more to—"

"Someone alerted the Dracu to our plans," the king intoned, his eyes roving over the assembled Huntsmen. "Who was it? By your vow of loyalty to me, Seer, tell me truthfully."

Veleda took a breath, her eyes fixed forward. "If you wish, I can ask the spirits now."

"If you know," he said, his tone making the branches rustle nervously, "speak."

The Seer gave Cassia a regretful look before answering with obvious reluctance. "Your daughter Cassia alerted the Dracu to our plans."

There was a brief, explosive silence.

"Did someone order her to do so?" the king demanded finally. "Who was complicit?"

"She is solely responsible," Veleda answered quietly. "No one else."

All eyes turned toward the betrayer. Cassia stood as if pinned by sword point, unable to breathe. Her father moved to loom over her, his eyes storm clouds of condemnation. Something primal inside of her quailed, unbearable tension crawling up her throat. All her resolve that she had done the right thing crumbled as she stared up at him. Revenge was woven into his bones as much as his connection to the forest was. And she had betrayed him.

"Is it true?" he asked, each word a stinging slap of dry reeds hitting stone.

Somehow, this was the most unexpected thing. He was asking her. Asking her instead of telling her what she'd thought or felt or done. If only she could lie. Or stay silent. But she found she could not keep this truth contained.

"Yes," she croaked.

His eyes closed for one beat of her heart. But that flicker of eyelids was more emotion than he had shown since... since he'd glowed with pride when she'd lit the gardens with the light of the Solis Gemma. Now, there was only fury and disgust.

Her cheeks were wet and cold. As she jabbed a knuckle at the offending show of weakness, she saw the ring's glow. Her father grabbed her wrist, pulling the ring into wider view. Cassia wanted to speak, but her throat had iced over.

"You are unworthy," he pronounced. "Unworthy of the title of Deathringer."

Yes, she silently agreed. She had never been worthy of that title, and she'd known it always, always, beneath every hope that she could live up to it. She wanted the killing to end. And it never would. Suddenly, she could see that with clarity. Yes, fighting was necessary to protect the Sylvans and their forest. But her father relished it.

She had shoved her memories of the night she'd received the ring down with all the other things she hadn't wanted to examine. She had dismissed Gutel when he'd told her the Sylvan king was at least partly responsible for human hostility toward their kind, because he wouldn't stop hunting them. He had even made the trees bloodthirsty to add to his power. Silvanus lived to fight, to hunt, to war. She could see now that this, too, was woven into his bones as much as his stag antlers and his bear strength. The only thing he had ever delighted in was battle. And she couldn't stomach it.

Enough death. She wanted no part of it anymore.

He took the ring between his thumb and forefinger. She willed the band to come off, even as a piece of her cried out at losing something that had become intrinsic to her. At losing her connection with Voz. With Zeru. With the land in the clouds she would never see again. Still, she willed the ring off. This was the only way she could escape the role he expected her to play.

But it would not budge. Pain tore through her as her father tried to remove the gold band. Her veins filled with fire all the way up her arm. She gasped, her knees buckling.

"Don't let him take it!" the Seer cried. "Cassia, by the Old Ones, don't."

"Be silent!" the king shouted. "Take the ring off and give it to me," he commanded, releasing her hand.

Head bent, Cassia pulled at the ring with thumb and forefinger, fighting against the dizziness and wrenching pain, her brow furrowed with the effort. But the warm gold was like a part of her, stuck fast. She had a brief flash of memory of the Dracu queen giving her the same command when she was a child, on the night she'd first worn the ring. Now the ring was fused to her even more firmly.

"I can't." A dark realization came to her. The magic knew the truth she had always denied. "I...I do not have a strong enough bond with you, Father."

Suddenly, she felt the weight of a massive hand press against her neck. Fear stilled everything inside her but for her racing heart. Grim death was in his eyes. She had seen him snap the necks of Dracu with no effort at all. Was he really going to kill her?

His hand squeezed.

A sudden flash of light burst from the ring. A growl rumbled next to her ear, and rays of reddish brown swirled into a fox creature with pointed ears and wings. The Vozarra leaped at the king, its glistening fangs sinking into the bare flesh of his arm, forcing him to release her. Suddenly free, Cassia stumbled back in disbelief.

The white markings on the furry head were distinctive, confirming her identity. It was Voz, come to protect her!

Her father reacted with swift and silent brutality. He took the animal by the scruff and tossed it aside as if it weighed nothing. Voz's wings snapped open to fly back at the king, teeth bared, snarling, golden eyes alight with violence. The Huntsmen drew their swords, closing in, but the king needed no help. Despite the blood dripping from his arm, he grabbed one fragile wing and whipped it away from him with punishing force. Cassia gasped as Voz's small form twisted through the air and hit a tree before crumpling to the ground. The sickening crack of breaking bones echoed through the forest. The furry body lay still. It all happened in a moment.

"No!" Cassia tried to run to Voz's side, but her father grabbed her shoulder in a biting grip.

"Leave it," he said harshly.

She looked up at him. It was like seeing a stranger. As if he had stepped out of one of the ancient tomes in Welkincaster, as if he were one of the Old Ones without feeling or mercy. She wondered if she was seeing him clearly for the first time.

"She was trying to protect me," she said unsteadily. "You... you would have killed me." Gutel had told her a Vozarra would only appear in this realm if her life was genuinely in danger.

"Return to Scarhamm," the king commanded, his sharp gesture toward the path stirring the Huntsmen from their frozen stillness. "Now!"

The Huntsmen obeyed without hesitation, falling into line. Burke glanced back at Cassia, but he went without a word. Veleda hesitated.

"Go!" the king shouted.

"You will rue this day, Silvanus," Veleda warned him in a resonant voice. But after a long, hard stare at Cassia, she went, too.

Cassia stood alone with her father next to the hill, the opening to the Cryptlands gaping behind them like a screaming mouth.

She stared at the limp, furry form of the Vozarra curled under a tree. It was wrong to see that lively spirit so still. Could a spirit be killed? She didn't know. Pain ripped through her. The grief was like a key unlocking all the rage she'd held inside. Years of pain she'd pushed down so no one would think she was weak. Years of fury at how unfair her father was to her, demanding more and giving less than he did with any of her sisters. He treated her like she didn't matter. No, as if she didn't exist. As if she were nothing but an extension of the bit of metal and stone she wore on her finger.

Her ring. In that moment, she felt the truth of that, too. It was *hers*. She had suffered for it. It was her burden. Her gift to use however she saw fit. And he had killed the spirit of it. The spirit of *her ring!* Her protector when he, her own father, would have taken her life.

Something inside her snapped.

"You cursèd monster!" she shrieked, flying at her father like a maddened animal, hitting his chest with her fists. It was like hitting stone, the pain in her hands adding to her fury. "That creature was trying to protect me! You were going to kill me!"

His face was blank and cold, but his eyes glittered. "Return home with the others."

Teeth bared like a feral thing, she snarled, "No."

Wind gusted, and the sky darkened overhead.

"Return home now," he repeated.

"No!" she screamed.

"Return. Home." The king said it with the finality of divine judgment. The wind howled, the sky over the hill an ugly grayish green.

She lifted her face as rain pelted down, stinging her cheeks. Let him try to frighten her with a storm, let him bring hail and lightning down on her. She would not comply. "I will not go home! And I will never use the ring to harm anyone again!"

Three times. Three times he'd demanded, and she had denied him.

The king's shoulders stiffened. He turned his head to the side, showing the craggy profile that had been carved in a different time. "Then you are banished from Scarhamm. If you return, you will be treated as an enemy."

Cassia gasped as the sky flashed white, thunder rolling over the forest moments later. "Banished?"

"Do not try to come home. I keep my word." The edict held no emotion, as if he were speaking to a stranger. Without another word, he moved down the path away from her. His dark shape blended with the storm-dim forest, only glimpses of his white antlers lingering between the trees like flitting ghosts in flashes of lightning. And then he was gone.

And she was alone.

She stumbled toward Voz's still form. She fell to her knees, pressing her face against the silky fur as sobs tore her throat. The rain turned to hail that beat at her back and made her shake.

She was not sorry she'd defied her father. She only wished she'd done it sooner. At least then Voz would still be alive. If she could take the ring off, she would hurl it as far from herself as it would go. She would denounce it along with her heritage.

But then who would she be? Who was she without the ring? Without her family? Her people?

She rested her face against Voz's side as cold rain pelted her back, making her shiver. After a while, numbness overcame her, leaving only exhaustion. Craving an escape, she let herself drift into sleep.

In her dreams, she heard was a voice crooning, "Sylvan girl, you are broken only to be reborn. Come now, and I will make you something greater than the Deathringer."

22

In order to be reborn, first you must die.
—SELKOLLA

CASSIA BLINKED IN THE FRIGID DARK. SHE WAS ON her back on a cold, hard surface. The skin on her face and hands felt tight, as if coated with dirt. The earthy scents of soil and moss mixed with the pungency of animal smells. She tried to sit up, but something held her fast. She looked down to see violet bands of light across her chest. Fury surged through her, burning away the sadness.

She turned her head to the side to assess her surroundings. Candles lit the room, some of them melting onto a long table covered in bottles, bowls, and vials. Next to her was a stone slab much like an altar, the kind she'd seen in drawings about sacrifices made to the Ancients. Wooden crates sat against one wall, some of them broken and spilling vegetables. It came to her in a rush of memory—picking up turnips and throwing them at Zeru.

She was in Selkolla's workroom.

Her blood pumped with the need to fight her way free. She could try calling Zeru with the ring, but that would put him in danger.

"Awake? Your face must hurt." Selkolla moved into view, staring down at her with eyes the green-gray of fog. "I had to pull you through the earth to avoid the tunnels. I would say I'm sorry for the scratches, but to my surprise, lies still stick in my throat. It seems I am still more Sylvan than I'd like to believe."

Cassia could hardly think. She struggled against her bonds, but when she moved, shocks like bolts of lightning ran over her skin.

"Calm yourself," Selkolla said. "My moss folk become excited by signs of fear. All that pumping blood. Their spirits have recently been cast into these new bodies, and some of them crave the life force they once had."

A rustle of leaves and the scraping of twigs drew Cassia's eyes to a dark corner. One of the moss creatures emerged from the shadows, staring at her with its cold pebble eyes. Its stick limbs made restless movements like branches touched by wind, its appearance so eerie, an icy chill inched up her neck. Her body trembled, overwhelmed by loss and terror. Voz was gone.

And her father had banished her. Pain arrowed through her as she imagined her future. A future without her family. The world suddenly felt too vast, her place in it insignificant.

But she had no future at all if she didn't find a way out of here.

She took a breath and forced herself to think. "Selkolla, whatever you want, this isn't the way to get it. Free me, and then we can talk."

The Seer's eyes held amused tolerance. "I have anticipated this moment for many years. I will not risk setting you free until we come to terms." Her eyes fell on the ring, and she smiled.

"You want the Solis Gemma?" Cassia tried to stay calm. "But you were the one who said it can't be taken by force without damaging its power."

Selkolla moved to her worktable. "Correct. That is why I hoped the Dracu would be able to freely take the ring from you in Welkincaster." She picked up a stone mortar, holding it with one hand while she gathered herbs. "It seemed a perfect opportunity. The two of you, once bonded by friendship, later connected by mutual hatred, alone in a place steeped in the lush magic of ancient revels." She picked up a pestle and began crushing the herbs.

Cassia stared, almost forgetting the pain tearing through her body. The Seer didn't seem to know her plan had worked, though it had taken her connection to Aril for her to see Zeru in a different light.

"At any rate," the Seer went on matter-of-factly, as if they were having a pleasant conversation over tea and honey cakes, "if all had gone as planned, the Dracu would have been able to take back the ring. However, now that the ring has decided to give you its magic fully, I must adapt. You are part of my plans now, daughter of the forest. As perhaps fate intended for us all along."

Cassia gave her a scornful look. "It's easy to call things destined if you want them badly enough."

Selkolla smiled, putting a sharp fingernail to Cassia's chin. "Sometimes fate needs a push in the right direction. Your transformation had already begun when I found you. Don't you feel it?" Her eyes shone with excitement. "You are becoming what you were meant to be from the moment you received the Solis Gemma." She regarded Cassia with a soft look. "With my help, you will become something more than a mere steward of a forgotten realm."

"Curse your help!" Strength pulsed through her limbs, a need to strike out that was only held in check by the stinging bonds around her chest and arms. Every part of her jolted with the need to smash her way free.

248

"The ring's power is merging with your own, a gift given to one who wears it for long enough," the Seer said.

Cassia recalled Gutel saying the ring would bond with her completely if she was strong enough to bear the magic. But she had no time to consider what that meant. The witch continued, watching Cassia's face with a satisfaction that made her sick to her stomach.

"Even now, you grow stronger," Selkolla said, "your ears keener, your eyes sharper. These are the stages of the transformation. Soon, your mind will become sluggish with the change, and you will be like a newborn babe, impressionable in every way." She added something to her bowl, which made a spark fly into the air. "And I will make you my creature."

Her creature? Cassia struggled, gasping as the bonds stung her. "Let me go, you Ancients-cursed witch!"

Selkolla continued stirring as she stared into the shadows. "In Welkincaster, the ring showed you its true nature. But it was not until you refused to let your father control you that you came into your power. How bitter for Silvanus that only by denouncing you has he made you into what he always wanted you to be."

"And now *you* want to control me!" Cassia said through gritted teeth. "What do you want? There must be something."

"There is no bargain you can offer." The moon-orb eyes shone with a burning significance. "Your father took something so precious to me, I can only restore what I lost with what is most precious to him."

"You heard my father banish me," Cassia said sharply. "How precious could I be to him?"

Selkolla's expression became almost sad. "I speak of the ring. When its magic broke your father, it was lost to our kind."

"What do you mean?" Cassia whispered, unable to stem her curiosity even now.

"In wielding it as a weapon, he took too much from himself. It was killing him." Selkolla leaned forward. "I wish it had."

Cassia stopped struggling, struck by memories of Gutel's account of the Deathringer. A horned champion who had wielded the ring in the Ancient Wars. She had told herself that meant it hadn't been a Sylvan. But she knew that the word for "antlers" and "horns" was the same in Old Sylvan. "You mean...?"

"You didn't know?" Selkolla asked softly. "Silvanus has tried to bury that history. Your father and I were both young, both eager to prove ourselves to the Ancients. Silvanus was the Deathringer, Solis's champion. I fought for Noctua, using the power of the forest. Silvanus saw that he needed the forest on his side. He slew my moss folk to strengthen the hostile spirits he had trapped in the trees." The Seer's eyes were dark with pain. "The moss folk were my children. And he wiped them from this land. I have worked all this time to find a way to bring them back. It is not revenge I seek. It is restitution."

Cassia's stomach roiled. She wanted to refute the Seer's claims. Her father had saved the Sylvans from certain extinction, and he protected every forest creature and the forest itself. That was his role and identity. Not a murderer of innocents.

But she remembered the way his eyes glowed with anticipation when he'd first seen the ring on her finger. The certainty he'd had that it was a weapon. How angry he'd been when she hadn't immediately mastered its use, as if it should have been obvious. Perhaps it had been obvious to him.

"When it was done, he controlled the forest," Selkolla went on. "But it nearly cost him his life. Perhaps the ring took too much from him in the end." She stared into the distance as if remembering. "I never knew who took the Solis Gemma from him, only that it came here, to the Cryptlands. I followed but was unable to trace its exact location. A faint hum of energy, but no more. On the night Zeru gave you the ring, I felt the moment it was on your hand. I told the queen, and we followed the trail of magic to find you. But too late. Silvanus must have felt the same surge of power, reaching you before the queen's vassals could kill you and take the ring. All these years, I have maintained a connection to Zeru, knowing he would turn to me for help in the ring's retrieval. And he did." She smiled. "Now you will use the same artifact that killed my children to bring them back and make them whole."

Cassia breathed heavily, wishing more than ever that she was free, craving time and space to think about everything she'd learned. "The ring can make plants grow," she tried to say calmly. "It can't... bring people back from the dead. You want something impossible."

"Why impossible?" Selkolla asked, her eyes glowing with a yellow light. "I've created bodies from the forest and tethered those bodies to spirits. The ring will merge plant and spirit together to make them truly awake. I'm giving you a chance to create life!"

Cassia hadn't forgotten what the elder Huntsman had said about scuccas. They were abominations that stole life force from the forest to trap spirits in material objects. She wondered if Selkolla had used the spirits of trees to create her "moss folk." These sticks and pebbles with no roots to take up water, no leaves to soak up sun. Xoden had said that trapped spirits craved blood because they didn't have enough life force of their own. They were not alive and couldn't be brought to life.

But she was losing hope that she was dealing with a rational being. Selkolla had a mother's grief and a fanatic's determination.

And while Cassia might wish she could fix her father's past atrocities, she knew she could not do this.

"If I could help you bring them back, I would," Cassia said, meaning every word. "But the spirits you've harnessed...they aren't moss folk spirits. Are they? Which means they don't belong in those bodies. You can't bring them back because it's not *them*."

That seemed to hit a nerve. The Seer drew up taller, her nostrils flaring. "Enough. I had hoped you would share my vision, but I should have known better. You are your father's daughter. I have given you a choice, and you have chosen wrongly. I will have to take control."

The Seer moved to a metal cage in one corner and grasped a squealing rat by its tail. With deft movements, she placed it on her worktable and picked up a knife, stabbing the animal through the heart. Cassia's gorge rose as the Seer poured the rat's blood into a copper bowl, making violaceous smoke spiral from the brew.

"Wait," Cassia said. "Selkolla, we haven't discussed a bargain."

Ignoring her, Selkolla moved back toward her with the bowl, pouring the foul mixture over Cassia's neck and down to her abdomen. With a few chanted words, she sprinkled something on top. Numbness spread from where the potion touched her. In a few moments, Cassia couldn't feel her limbs.

Her heart struck wildly against her ribs, every impulse begging her to fight, to run. But she was as trapped as if she were dead and buried. Desperation made her reach out with all her will. *Zeru!*

She felt no response. She had no way of knowing if he'd heard her silent cry.

"If I die," Cassia said, feeling the numbness creep up her neck, "the gemstone's power will be broken." She stared into Selkolla's eyes, trying to find some vestige of the Sylvan she must have been before grief had twisted her into what she was now.

"If your death were permanent, perhaps," the Seer replied. "But I will give you new life before your last breath leaves your mouth."

As her intentions became clear, Cassia's heart slammed so hard, she thought it might burst. Selkolla planned to make her a scucca, one of those puppets with lifeless eyes. Her body would be alive, but her spirit, her *self*, would be gone.

"Don't do this! Sel—" The numbness reached her throat, freezing her words. There was only one thing she had left, and that was the ring. She tried to summon images of growth and life despite the scents of death all around her.

"You will obey me in all things," the Seer chanted. "As devoted as you were to the Sylvan king, now you will be dutiful to me."

Though Cassia couldn't see her hand, there was no sense of power from the Solis Gemma. Maybe the Seer was preventing her from using it. Or maybe she was too scared, too grieved to feel what she needed to power the ring. Her eyes filled with frustrated tears as a tingling covered her body. Every drop of blood rushed headlong through her veins, chasing something elusively out of reach. She no longer felt in control of herself.

Selkolla leaned over and chanted, "I order you to forget. Forget your home, your family, your past, your very name."

Cassia struggled in her mind. *No!* She wanted to put her hands over her ears, but she couldn't move. She listed the names of her sisters as a defense. *Enora—*

"Obey me," the Seer said, her voice drowning out all thought. "Dutiful girl, do as you're told. Safety lies in obedience. Obey me, and you will be safe."

Thea—

"Empty your mind of all things but this: I am your master, and you must obey."

~ 253 ~

Rozie—

Selkolla waved a burning herb above Cassia's forehead. "I purify your mind. I claim your thoughts. Your very self. You will pledge yourself to me, think only the thoughts I give you, and revel in my orders. Forget all others."

Zeru! Zeru!

"Forget all but me."

She couldn't help but obey. Cassia's last memory was an image of green eyes.

Without warning, Selkolla lifted a knife and plunged it into Cassia's heart. Her body became pain. Shock made her rise from the table against the sizzling bonds. Her heart slowed, each beat a last, desperate bid for life. Her thoughts narrowed to one: This Seer's face was the last face she would see.

She closed her eyes.

Her mind emptied.

"And now you are one of my obedient children," the woman said. "I release you from your bonds. Show me your obedience now, Sylvan girl, and call me what I am: *Mother.*"

Opening her eyes, she found she could see every corner, every crack in the stone walls. She sat up and looked at her hands. Her skin was dotted with tiny gold specks. Her fingers were tipped with short claws. She felt something against her back and reached a hand to touch her shoulder.

Feathers. She flexed and felt the feathers move. Wings.

"You are not what I intended," Selkolla said, "but perhaps you will do. Girl, tell me your name. Who are you?"

She searched her thoughts. *My name . . .* She shook her head.

"From this moment, you have no name," the woman said. "I

am Selkolla, your mother and the Seer who is your master. Look at my face."

The Seer's eyes were like twin moons above a cloud as she said, "You will obey me in all things. My enemies seek to kill me and my children. You must destroy everyone who tries to hurt us. Do you understand?"

She nodded to show she understood.

Mother smiled. "Good."

23

Sever the roots of my enemies!
May they live untethered,
parched and gasping.
—Dracu curse

Mother used her magic to create a tunnel, urging Cassia to follow her. After traveling for some time in the dark, they emerged into the forest, where warriors dressed in brown and green walked a wide path. They turned and drew their swords on her. One man, tall and strong with white antlers, took a step forward.

"Selkolla," he said in a voice that rumbled through the woods. "What brings you above after cowering in the Cryptlands for so long?"

"I've come to take from you what you value most," the Seer replied, "as you took what I loved from me. What do you think of my creation?"

The antlered one turned his head. "What vile creature is this?"

Mother preened. "Isn't she beautiful? I made her. Don't you recognize her?"

The antlered man stared at her with dark eyes, his brows drawn together in consternation, his voice turning hoarse. "She is an abomination."

"You are the abomination." Mother spat at the king's feet. "My moss folk were innocent and gentle, and you destroyed them. Deny that, Silvanus."

He said nothing.

Mother's face twisted. "Murderer. Fitting that I should take the spirits of your Huntsmen to bring my children back to life." She lifted her voice to carry over the thunder rumbling overhead. "I have an offer for those of you here. If you swear your swords to me now, I will show mercy and allow you to keep spirit and body together."

"My Huntsmen will never serve you," the antlered one said. Thunder boomed in the distance.

"Pledge your lives to me as you are now," Selkolla said, "or your spirits will serve me. Who among you will step forward?"

When no one stepped forward, the Seer raised her arms, and the sky turned black.

But the antlered king raised one hand, and the clouds overhead moved away. "Your magic is weak, Selkolla. After these many years, you have not recovered. Scurry back into the hole you've been cowering in. Your time in the world is past."

"And you are but a shadow of your former self," Mother said, her hands fisting at her sides. "Here, you have the advantage of sunlight and the allegiance of your trees. Under a full moon, we shall see who is stronger." She turned in a slow circle, raising her voice to address the warriors. "You have decided your fates. Taste what awaits you when true night falls." She spoke a word, and a moment later, a moss child emerged from the tunnel.

A collective gasp ran through the soldiers. "A scucca," one said with disgust.

Another stepped toward the moss creature, his sword raised. But in moments, a hundred others emerged from the tunnel,

257

followed by a hundred more. They pushed and fell over one another in a green cascade. Swords slashed and cut at the moss creatures, but still more came shrieking up to fight.

The sky darkened again, a crackle filling the air as Mother's eyes glowed brighter. "It is your time to fight. You see the great king with antlers? Kill him."

Without hesitation, she flew toward the king, her wings taking her feet off the ground. Huntsmen came between them, and she hit them with her clawed hands and bashed them with her wings, whirling and striking so they twisted and fell to the ground.

When a dozen of the enemies lay senseless, she reached the antlered king. She stood with knees bent, ready to spring into action.

The battle raged around them. He held his palm up to more Huntsmen, as if staying their hands, and stared down at her, his brows drawn together.

Something about him. She tilted her head, trying to remember.

"Kill him!" Mother screamed.

She slashed out with her claws. The king parried her attack. She struck at the weak spots she knew would spill his blood on the ground.

But he wasn't fighting back, merely blocking her every move.

He whispered a single word. She could barely hear it over the sounds of battle.

Her arms dropped. The soldiers held their swords out but didn't attack. She heard Mother screaming at her, but she couldn't obey. Shame made her face heat and brought a terrible pain to her stomach. She had failed Mother.

Around her, more Huntsmen were slashing at the moss children—a screeching, bloody battle she had to escape.

258

She spread her wings and leaped into the sky. She looked down at her enemies, their swords slashing as an endless river of Seer's children streamed from the tunnel. But the antlered king simply looked up, watching her fly.

The word he'd said meant nothing.

She would fly.

She would hide.

24

I live in the sunshine. I die in the shade.
—from "The Ballad of the Sun Sprite"

SHE LIVED AMONG THE TREES.

She ate berries and slept under piles of leaves. She wandered. Though it was the same forest, it was vast, and she'd flown for hours. Sometimes images flashed into her mind, faces and voices that made her chest ache. She shut them out. Instead, she turned toward the part of herself that truly knew the forest. She opened her mind to the scents and sounds of the woods.

They calmed her.

She sat and listened. She spent all day listening. She could hear the water rushing underground and feel the roots taking water in. She knew when the trees needed sunlight or rain, or when they ached with the effort of new growth. She knew which suffered. They needed water. Some of them craved blood, craved *life*. Someone was taking their life force, and they wanted it back.

On the third night, as she slept under the branches of a spreading elm, a sound came from nearby, something larger than the small animals she had come to know.

She stood and readied her claws.

A shadow moved through the trees and a man stopped a short distance away. Twisted horns grew from the top of the stranger's head. Large, dark wings grew from his back. He looked lean and strong but held no sword.

"Cassia?" he said on a whisper of breath, his eyes wide.

Her heart jumped. She shook her head at him.

He took a step toward her. His eyes were like crushed clover. "Cassia. It's me. Zeru."

Gooseflesh rose on her arms. She was meant to be alone here.

She grabbed a branch from the ground and threw it at him, using the moment to sprint into the forest. The map of trees was so familiar to her now that she slipped between them like water. He wouldn't catch her. But then he appeared in front of her, his wings settling behind him. She hissed, baring her teeth and claws.

He put his hands out, showing his palms. "I only want to talk."

She didn't move.

"Can you speak?" he asked, his brows drawing together. "Do you remember me?"

He sounded... something. Not sunlight. Shadows. He sounded shadows.

They stared at each other. She waited for him to leave. The moon was setting. The sun would rise. He would go before then.

She leaped into a tree, pulling herself onto a branch to wait.

He settled himself on the cold ground. Stillness itself.

But she had the patience of trees.

If he'd twitched, she would have run. But he was so still.

He stared at the ground, but she sensed his attention on her.

When the sun rose, he fell forward, panting. As she watched, his wings vanished. Fascinated, she almost leaped down from her perch to go closer. But after a minute, he shook his head and rolled his shoulders. His clothing was unmarred, as if the wings hadn't been there in the first place. She touched her own to make sure they were still there. He looked up as she did that, his eyes narrowing at the gesture before his mouth lifted up on one side.

"I think yours are permanent," he said. The stranger pushed nimbly to his feet. "Mine disappear at dawn. I've learned to keep these at night, though." He lifted a hand to point to one of the horns that emerged from his dark hair. "Last time I saw you, you commented on the lack. Not very tactfully, I might add."

She watched him as images flashed in her mind of another part of the forest at night. She shut her mind to them.

He lifted his chin as he sniffed the air. "I've always detected hints of the forest about you, Cassia. But there's something more." He paced closer, step by careful step until he stood among the roots looking up at her. He had a way of moving that reminded her of a predator, smooth and graceful. "Something that stays pure over time," he went on, "like gold or sunlight." His eyes were brighter in the morning, his dark eyebrows and hair contrasting with his lightly tanned skin.

She sniffed, curious. She smelled soil, pine needles, leaves, and... him. He was... earth and water. His scent blended nicely with the forest around her.

"I wish I could touch your face and tell you to remember, the way you did to me," he said, his voice thick. His expression made her toes curl. Images of his face in other times crowded her mind. His head dipping down toward hers. She shut her eyes and breathed forest, telling herself this was her life. Here. Now. Nothing before. She stayed still, waiting for him to leave.

The sun was low in the sky when a storm swept in. She wrapped her wings around herself as rain drizzled down, then poured. He was sitting against the trunk of the tree. A shiver ran through his body. For some reason, that made her stomach churn.

When she hopped down, landing next to him, he looked at her with widened eyes before he cocked one eyebrow at her. She jerked her chin toward the place she hid when it rained. He followed her to the scooped-out hollow of a large rock, like a shallow cave, fitting himself into the curved space with deliberately slow movements. She could see the texture of his skin, the flecks of gold in his green eyes. Water dripped from his dark hair. She lifted a hand and let a drop fall onto her fingertip.

He pulled in a breath. She pushed her own wet hair from her forehead and stared at him. He exhaled, his eyes fixed on her.

"I think a part of you remembers me," he said, a little tremor in his voice that could have been from the cold. "The way a part of me recognized you after I'd first taken my winged form. I didn't know who or what I was. I was lost in the woods. I felt so alone until you came along."

Something inside her warned her that it was dangerous to listen. But she liked his voice. It lulled her as the rain pelted down, hitting the ground and sending spray into the protected hollow, wetting her feet and legs. She leaned her head back against the rock and listened.

"I knew you were meant to be important to me," he said, green eyes as bright as new leaves. "Both times. First as a boy, and then as Aril. I recognized something in you, something I wanted to be near. Even as another part of me fought it." His face tightened, and he turned his head away. "This transformation was harder for you, I think. How did it happen? Can you tell me?"

A memory of a terrible pain made her inhale sharply. She shook her head against it, trying to block the thoughts.

"I heard you call my name," he said, his voice low and urgent, his eyes coming back to hers. "I was desperate to get to you, Cassia. But I was too late. By the time I got to Selkolla's room, you were gone. And now you...don't remember me. Or yourself. Selkolla changed you. But I know you're still in there."

She turned her back on him, her fists clenched. She would not listen to that name. Any name from before.

"I'm sorry," he said softly. "I don't blame you if you can't forgive me."

He was silent for a few minutes. Finally, she turned back to face him. She found him hunched over. He sucked in a breath and his hands curled into fists as wings sprouted from his back. She moved as far away as she could in the tight space. First, the wings were insubstantial, made of light and colors. Then they were solid, black, folded against his back as gently as if they were made of parchment.

"It still takes me by surprise," he said with a smile, sounding breathless as he stretched one wing out into the rain, inhaling as if the stretch felt good. "Every night at sunset. Gutel said I might lose the wings if I stop going into the clouds. That's what he figures happened to one of my ancestors." His brows drew together. "There's so much I want to tell you."

She put her hand out to test the rain. It had nearly stopped. They could leave the protected hollow soon. For some reason, she didn't want to go. Not yet.

His eyes went to her hand. "I wonder if the ring still works with the amulet. If it will open the doorway to Welkincaster." He motioned to her hand, then pulled something from his shirt. A gold disc. She drew her hand back. Fear surged through her, though she didn't know why.

"I don't want the ring," he said, all hints of laughter gone from his face as he tucked the amulet away again. "Not anymore. It's yours."

She looked at him, knowing this was important, what he'd

said. Reaching out, she touched one of the claws on the end of his wing segment. He closed his eyes. "That's..." He cleared his throat.

She traced a vein that went from the claw down toward the center of his back. His eyes stayed closed, and his lips pressed together. When he spoke, his voice was hoarse. "Cassia."

She let her hand fall.

"No need to stop." His smile was crooked, his eyes bright.

Her heart was beating faster, but she wasn't scared. She watched his face, noting the way the drops of water traveled over his skin. One had settled at the corner of his lips. She considered wiping it away but decided against it.

"Well," he said slowly, his lips curved up on one side, "we both have wings now. Would you like to fly with me?"

She shook her head, then turned her face away. It was better if he left her as she was. Quiet. Safe. Alone.

"When you're ready," he said. "But someday soon, we have to leave here. You can't stay here forever, Cassia."

She shook her head again.

"I said soon," he added. "Not now."

"Never," she said, stepping out of the protected hollow and striding into the trees. She used her wings to lift her and settled on a high branch.

Surely he would go before dawn.

25

> Memories are images of the past as seen through rippling water.
> —Excharias, Sylvan poet

He didn't go. After the sun rose and set twice more, she accepted his presence like she accepted the weather, as something inevitable.

One morning, Zeru came to her with a handful of berries, putting them into her upturned palm. "Cassia." He spoke her name softly, and she liked when he said it.

"I don't want these," she said, though they were the same berries she'd been eating every day. She was bored of them. She was starting to feel restless in this place.

"Should I find you something else?" he asked. He had offered her cooked rabbit and squirrel and birds, but she had no interest. The sun and plants fed her.

She started to tell him that. "I only want..."

"Turnips?" he suggested, a smirk on his lips. She sometimes thought about his lips while she listened to the trees whisper. His top lip curved intriguingly, and the bottom looked soft.

She narrowed her eyes at the teasing tone.

He grinned. "You love them."

She put her hand out.

"I don't have any." He showed his empty palms. "We could grow them in Welkincaster. In the clouds, you can have all the delicious turnips you want."

She would never leave her trees. "You go."

His smile faded. "You really want me gone?" When she was silent, he said, "You won't miss me?"

She saw the tightness around his eyes and mouth and felt a little ache in her chest. She couldn't help but admit, "I would."

The warmth in his eyes returned. Sunlight on green leaves. "I would miss you, too." His voice was rough like tree bark.

She shook her head, refusing to be moved. "I won't leave here."

He sighed. "Then neither will I."

"Why?"

He laughed, though she didn't see any reason for it. After a minute, he added more seriously, "You have a home, Cassia. In Scarhamm."

Her chest tightened. "Don't say that."

"I don't know if it was your transformation that caused this, as mine did, or if you're under a spell, but something made you forget." He moved closer to gently place his hands on her shoulders. "You have to try to remember. Your sisters must be so worried about you. They love you. Enora, Rozie, Thea."

"Wrong."

He cocked his head. "Aren't those the names of your sisters?"

"It's Enora, Thea, Rozie..." She trailed off in confusion. Those names meant nothing to her.

He nodded, his eyes lighting with approval. His hands flexed on her shoulders. "Scarhamm is your home—"

"No." She pushed him away and stepped back. There was a pressure building in her head, a surge of images she was barely keeping at bay. If he kept talking, she would drown.

⌐ 267 ⌐

He exhaled sharply, frustrated. "Your sisters are in danger. The Seer who stole your memory is—"

Cassia shook out her wings. "No. I don't want to hear."

Zeru looked determined. "Selkolla—"

Her hands fisted, and she screamed, "*No!*"

She rushed through the trees, then launched herself up. He wanted her to fly? She would fly.

"Cassia! Wait!"

Ignoring him, she threaded the trees like a ribbon. When the trunks grew closer together, she rose and skimmed the treetops.

The sun burned down from overhead, warming her back as she zigzagged over the forest canopy. Behind her came the sound of wings. She turned her head and saw Zeru following her, a predator's determination etched on his face. Impossible! He only had wings at night. But she had no time to wonder because she collided with a small branch, careening to the side. She heard her pursuer's wings pump faster. But after a couple of wobbles, she righted herself and shot forward, faster than before.

When she saw the silver thread of a river curving through the forest below, she descended toward it. Too fast. At the last second, she flapped madly, managing to land with only a minor stumble.

Zeru alighted next to her and drew in his wings with a snap, his expression furious. "You have to slow down when you land!"

Ignoring him, she moved back to the riverbank. She fell to her knees and scooped water into her hands, watching it sparkle before bringing it to her mouth. Her reflection stared back at her. She blinked in some surprise, though she didn't know what she'd expected to see. Her face was speckled with dots, some light brown and some gold. Her eyes, a mix of brown and green, had the same gold flecks in them. Her eyelashes were much darker

268

than her hair, which held myriad shades from gold to light brown. Her feathers were a richer gold, almost like metal.

Out of the corner of her eye, she saw Zeru join her, kneeling and putting his hands in the water before drinking from his palms. Wanting space, she waded in up to her knees.

"Careful," he said, his voice still sharp. "The current is strong."

Continuing to ignore him, she used her fingers to comb her hair from her face and gazed at the river as it rushed past. A rippling reflection showed her feathered wings, which looked like they were painted with sunlight. Her hair was tangled, her face streaked with dirt, and it occurred to her that Zeru had been looking at her all this time and never seemed to notice these things. He only looked at her as if she were . . . beautiful.

She heard him slide into the water behind her. He had long since discarded his shirt and boots and walked barefoot like she did.

Suddenly, water hit her in the face, dripping down to wet her tunic. She turned to him with a gasp. He was smiling, his hands cupped as if he'd thrown the water at her deliberately. She looked down at herself. Her tunic was sun-bleached and ragged, the material stained with dirt and berries. Now it was wet and cold, too.

He cupped another handful, but before he could move, she used both hands to splash him. She hit him square in the face, wetting his hair and bare chest.

"Much faster than you used to be," he said, his eyes aglow with admiration. "Almost as fast as me. But not quite."

He splashed her with the heel of his hand against the water's surface. Blood heating, she came back with four handfuls in rapid succession. Each hit him dead on, making him splutter.

He put his hand to his stomach and bent at the waist. It took her a second to realize he was laughing. When he looked up, his dark hair fell over his sparkling eyes. "I guess if you don't have turnips, you improvise."

For some reason, Cassia found herself smiling.

"Do you want to swim?" he asked.

She shook her head.

He slid into the water and moved to where her feet kicked gently. "Swim with me," he said. "It's cold, but that never seemed to bother you."

She stared into his eyes, wanting to join him. Trying to resist.

He put his hands out. "Come on."

With a sigh, she settled her hands in his and let him pull her into the water. Fear pulsed in her chest as her wings dragged her deeper.

Zeru gripped her. "I've got you. Put out your wings like this." He showed her with his own, spreading them over the water.

She tried, but the sudden movement made her slip, and she took in a mouthful of river.

He grabbed her around the waist, pulling her close to his chest. "See? I've got you."

Heart thumping at all the new sensations, she looked around, examining the bulrushes, the sticks and logs and other flotsam that had gathered against the riverbank. When she looked back at Zeru, he was lifting his face to the sun. She stared for a minute, admiring the corded strength of his neck. Then she closed her eyes and did the same.

"Dracu stillness, we call it," he said, his voice as soft as a cattail. "I always struggled to master that. It's like you were born with it. I keep noticing little ways you've changed. You see better at night now, don't you?"

Not interested in discussing her vision, she opened her eyes

270

and looked at him, feeling the solidness of his chest against hers. She put her hands to his shoulders, listening to his breathing change as she touched him.

"You're so delicate," he said, barely above a whisper. "And so strong."

"You're sunlight and water and roots," she said, not knowing quite why.

He blinked. She saw his throat bob as he swallowed.

She raised her hand toward his face and stopped an inch away.

"Touch me," he said, his heart beating against hers.

She placed her palm against his cheek, feeling the scrape of short hairs on his jaw.

He closed his eyes.

Raising her hand, she raked her claws gently through his hair, scraping his scalp with a feathery touch. His mouth opened on an inhale. After a brief hesitation, she put her fingertip to his top lip and traced the bow, then slid it across his bottom lip. "Soft."

When he didn't move, she put her arms around him, her palms coming to rest on his back under the spot where his wings grew. His arms tightened around her waist. She rested her head on his chest, waiting for her heart to calm.

"Your eyes have always been beautiful," he said, his voice rumbling through his chest into her ear. "Now they're stunning. Not just the color, flecked with gold. They're more open. I used to wish I knew what you were thinking, but now I usually have an idea." He went quiet for a few seconds. "I want you to remember, and still look at me like that." He swallowed. "And I don't know if you will."

The fear in his voice made her look at him. "I don't want to remember." There. She'd said it.

"I know," he replied, his eyes darkening with sympathy. "And part of me wishes you didn't have to. That we could stay here forever. But I have responsibilities. And so do you. Your people—"

She pressed her lips to his. He gasped and she froze, wondering if she'd made a mistake. But before she could pull away, he returned the pressure, his hand coming to rest on the back of her head. Sunlight exploded behind her eyes. Dizzy with a thousand sensations, she wrapped her arms around his neck, and leaned into him.

When she pulled back, they both gulped air.

"You taste...," he said, "I don't know...like sunlight and evergreen with a hint of metallic gold." He closed his eyes, his lashes dark against his cheeks as he rested his forehead against hers. "Irresistible to a Dracu who spent his childhood in darkness and stale air."

"I'm sorry," she said, not knowing why. She swallowed, feeling something coming in the back of her mind, a knowledge she'd been keeping hidden. She put her lips to his once again to drive the thoughts away.

As his hands moved over her back, Cassia's fingers sought the hair at his nape. So silky. Soft lips, soft hair, hard chest against the softness of hers. It was like flying. Any moment she could fall.

She sensed him the same way she heard the forest. His blood hummed through his veins like the water that rushed underground. His breath was like a warm breeze caressing her face. The rapid beat of his heart was a woodland creature startled by a predator. *She* was making his heart rush like that, which meant she was the huntress. But he didn't try to run, only to pull her closer. The press of his fingers on her back seemed as desperate as hers. He tasted like the river, pure and sweet, with a hint of clean earth.

Since she was the predator, she gently bit his lower lip, opening her eyes to watch his reaction. He grunted softly, his eyes dark as he opened them. Her hands left his hair to touch his face, her fingertips resting on his cheekbones before sliding down to his neck and coming to rest on his shoulders. The ripple of muscle underneath felt like the current of the river flowing past them, strong and dependable.

She pulled back, and they stared at each other.

Do my eyes look like that? she wondered. She tried to find the words for how his eyes looked: Sleepy. Shining. Dreaming.

His eyes were the woods at dusk. She could get lost in them and still feel at home.

"I'm sorry, Cassia," he said, a vulnerability in his voice drawing her out of her daze. "But...you'll hate me later if I let any more time pass. As much as I don't want..." He shook his head. "I have to do this. It's too important."

"What?" she asked, her stomach twisting at the urgency in his expression.

"Remember," he said, taking her hand and covering the ring with his palm. "Remember."

As his grip tightened over hers, she had an image of him from another time when he had held her hand in a brightly lit ballroom. She would have liked to stay in that memory, but other images soon followed. A fortress. A smiling face of a woman with light greenish-brown hair. An antlered king. Girls whooping as they chased one another in a rose garden. Tall trees at night. A green-eyed boy. A gemstone on a gold band. A queen wearing a dark crown. Battles. Revels. A castle in the clouds. A fox-like creature with wings. The memories she'd held at bay crashed over her, washing away her sunlit peace.

Zeru held her, but she was being carried away from him, too

many sensations rolling toward her, burying her. She doubled over as she relived Voz's death. Her father banishing her. The pain tore through her, as fresh as if it were happening at that moment.

When she thought it couldn't get worse, she felt the stone slab underneath her, smelled the herbs as the Seer cast a spell, saw her long-fingered hand raising a knife. She felt the blade slice into her, tearing the world apart.

Finally, the images flickered away, and she felt Zeru's arms around her, smelled his scent, the water cool against her skin. She had survived remembering. And she was still here.

But with knowledge came the heat of shame. How could she have forgotten her sisters?

After a few minutes, she caught her breath. She tried to stop shaking, but her limbs were out of her control. Realizing she had Zeru in a death grip, she let him go, putting her hands into the river and splashing water on her face.

"Cassia?" he asked tentatively. There was so much hope in his voice.

Finally, she lifted her head to him and asked, "How . . . how did you get your wings during the day?"

He blinked, seeming surprised at her question. His voice was rough as he answered. "I don't know. You ran. I was scared. I wanted to follow you. And they were there."

Her chest tightened. "Your wings appeared . . . because of me?"

He nodded.

She shook her head. She couldn't wrap her mind around it, that their connection went that deep. That her need transformed him. She wished she had time to explore this bond and what it meant.

But she'd wasted too much time already. Hiding. While her sisters were facing a lethal enemy. Suddenly, the water felt too cold, the forest too vast.

"What's happening?" she asked, bracing herself for whatever he would say. "Back home?"

His eyes were the deep green of shaded pines. "Scarhamm is under attack. For all I know, Selkolla might have broken your wards by now. That was ... six days ago?"

Cassia exhaled, a fist gripping her stomach and twisting it. While the seat of her people was under attack, she had flown off, abandoning them. It didn't matter that her father had ordered her to stay away. If her sisters were in danger, she would break any ban to help them.

It wouldn't take long to return to Scarhamm now that they both had wings. One last question before they left. "How did you make me remember?" she asked.

His nostrils flared. His eyes fell to her lips, and there was sadness mixed with longing. "I felt the magic of your ring. It's the same feeling I get when I use the amulet. I recognized it ... and I used it."

Pain thrummed behind her aching eyes. "You used my own magic against me."

"No." His throat bobbed as he swallowed. "*For* you. I knew you'd want to go home."

"It's not my home anymore," she said, taking a steadying breath. "But you're right. I'm going."

26

> Never fall into the hands of a Sylvan.
> They will never let you go.
> —Gaxix, Dracu philosopher

"You're not coming with me," Cassia said in her steeliest voice.

Her back was to Zeru, her toes curled into the reeds at the edge of the riverbank. One last moment of calm before the storm. He stood a few feet away, leaning his back against a tree as he waited. She needed a minute in the place that had been a haven to her after the worst days of her life. She hadn't noticed before, but there were fewer blood trees in this area of Thirstwood, as if whatever magic that had turned the ones near Scarhamm hadn't reached this far. Maybe that was why she'd found it so peaceful.

"I *am* going with you," Zeru said, his tone amused but implacable. "I appreciate your attempt to sound stern, though."

When she turned to look at him, his arms were folded over his chest, and he wore a smirk that should have made her angry. Instead, a rush of feelings tightened her chest, and she wanted to go back into his arms.

"When we get there," she said, stepping away from the rushing river, "you'll have to hide nearby. If you fly too close to the fortress, the archers will take you down."

He quirked an eyebrow at her. "Give me some credit, Sylvan."

"Don't underestimate them," she warned.

"I never do." His jaw hardened as he straightened from his lounging posture. "Your archers have killed too many of my people."

She turned away, a sting in her chest. All the old animosities were still there between them. She couldn't forget that.

A heartbeat later, Zeru grabbed her hand, sending a pulse of warmth through her veins. "I'm sorry. That's the old bitterness. I don't blame you for their deaths, any more than I want you to blame me for the Huntsmen I've killed."

She nodded, the ache in her chest easing. "I understand."

He stepped closer, putting his hands on her shoulders as he looked her up and down, an inscrutable expression on his lean face. "What about you? You look...different now. What if the archers don't recognize you?"

"That might be all for the better," she said, taking a breath, her jaw feeling tight as she spoke the words. "My father banished me. He told me never to set foot in Scarhamm again."

His eyelids fluttered, and he shook his head. "What do you mean? Why?"

She forced herself to tell him. "He asked the Court Seer for the name of the person who had warned the Dracu about our attack."

Zeru's skin lost some of its sun-kissed tone. "You were banished because of me?"

"No," she corrected, "because I betrayed my father's trust. I don't regret it. He would have killed your parents, and their whole settlement besides." She hesitated. "I also told him I would never use the ring to hurt anyone again. Probably worse than the other betrayal in his eyes."

"Did you vow it?" Zeru asked, his face ashen.

She shook her head. "No."

He let out a breath and his shoulders relaxed. "Good. You need to be able to use the ring to defend yourself. It might be the only thing that can harm Selkolla's scuccas. That could be why she sent you to Welkincaster, out of the way."

Cassia realized she hadn't explained that part to Zeru. "That could be part of it. But she also hoped you'd figure out how to take the ring. Then she was going to steal it from you."

Zeru's face darkened. "I should never have trusted her."

"What matters is stopping her now." With one last look around to memorize this haven in Thirstwood, she said, "We should go."

In moments, they were airborne, Zeru with his dark, clawed wings and Cassia with hers covered in velvety gold feathers. The sun was in the west as they flew side by side over the forest, the prevailing wind at their backs helping speed their flight. Zeru knew the way, which was good because she'd been in no state to pay attention to direction when she'd fled. During her first flight, she'd taken breaks, stopping to rest whenever she needed. Now her wings ached, but she didn't want to waste a moment. She needed to get to Scarhamm. She tried not to let herself think about how bad things could be.

As they flew, Zeru shared what had happened after he'd taken his parents to safety. He *had* been able to see Cassia when Veleda had scried their location in the Cryptlands, a hazy image but clear enough to suspect she was near. Later, he'd heard her call for help, but by the time he'd reached Selkolla's room, she'd been gone. After tracking the Seer in the woods, he'd found her and a legion of her scuccas attacking the Sylvan forces as they tried to retreat toward Scarhamm. He'd flown ahead to warn the Huntsmen guards, but the archers fired on him, and he didn't know if they'd heard his warning. That's when he'd left to search for Cassia.

"I found that if I concentrated, I could sense you in some

way—I somehow knew which direction you'd gone. And when I touched the amulet, the feeling was stronger. I could only fly at night, though, so it took a few days to find you.

"What about you?" he asked, a hardness to his voice. "I want to know what happened to you, Cassia."

Where to start? Taking a fortifying breath, she said, "My father killed Voz."

There was a tense silence before Zeru said, "I didn't think that was possible. The Vozarra are spirits."

She shook her head, telling him what had happened to Voz.

Zeru's face was a stiff mask as he listened. "I know the king is your father," he said with rough loathing, "but if it were anyone else, I would swear vengeance against him for destroying that loyal creature."

"I know." She wanted vengeance herself. The thought of what her father had taken from her made her want to put a torch to his entire fortress, leaving his throne on a pile of ashes. But that would only hurt her people.

"What about the Seer?" he asked softly. "Did she take your memory?"

"She used a spell and ordered me to forget. She wanted to use me to bring her moss creatures back to life. She thinks the Solis Gemma is the key to doing that." Her voice grew choked as she told him about Selkolla's attempt to kill her so she could make her obedient.

"She put a knife . . . *in your heart?*" Zeru demanded, his voice more wrathful and hate-filled than she'd ever heard it.

Cassia glanced over at him to see a face she would never want to encounter in battle, the very image of a violent killer. Rather than disturbing her, his protectiveness warmed her.

"She had to stop my heart to gain control," she explained. "It worked. I obeyed her until she ordered me to kill my father." She paused to swallow, not wanting to think about what could have happened. "Even though I didn't know who I was, even though I wanted to follow her orders, I couldn't do it." She could still feel the bitterness of the shame she'd tasted in that moment when she'd thought she'd failed her master.

"Of course not," Zeru said in a scoffing tone. "You wouldn't."

Contrarily, she found herself irritated. "No one thinks I can be ruthless."

His low chuckle was insulting. "Not if they know you."

She glared down at the endless sea of trees below. "I don't think you realize how much that annoys me."

"What?" He looked over at her in surprise. "I'm not saying you wouldn't be able to defend yourself. But to take the life of someone you love? Never. It goes against your nature. You would never take a life without the absolute need to do so. And even then, I don't know if you could."

How his opinion of her had changed.

"I did take lives," she reminded him. "I used my ring, and Azpians died because of me." A surge of sick shame hollowed out her chest. So much death and loss. And it might not have been necessary if her father had been at all interested in seeking peace. If only someone had stood up to him, questioned his decisions. But no one questioned the Sylvan king.

"I know you did," Zeru said in a somber tone. "But I also know how much you hated the role your father forced on you. And that you won't be his Deathringer anymore." He paused. "What are we going to do about Selkolla?"

"I've been thinking about it," she said. "I suspect the ring will work against the scuccas. But how many at once? Once I use the ring, I can't use it again right away."

"We may need to try something less expected." Zeru looked thoughtful. "What about the bargain that binds Selkolla: a safe haven in return for her vow not to harm anyone in the Cryptlands? It was made with blood, powerful and binding. Selkolla can't harm anyone who is under the queen's rule."

"Hmm." Cassia considered this. "So, the Seer can't go after Azpians." She paused, thinking back to what the Seer had told her before she'd tried to transform her, then shook her head. "She says my father killed her moss folk in the Ancient Wars. She's out for revenge on him and his people."

"I don't think that's all she wants," Zeru said, the intensity of his gaze sharpened with suspicion. "She has too many of those creatures if she's only after Scarhamm, though the queen won't move against her without proof. After all, the scuccas could win her the war against the Sylvans."

"There's something to this," Cassia said, her mind working at the problem. "We have to find the right way to use it."

They flew in silence for a while, Zeru's hand reaching out for hers. She smiled, clasped his fingers. Seeing him as she did now, getting used to the connection between them, was both exhilarating and overwhelming. Feelings kept rushing up to twist her stomach or grab her heart. She could sense by the way he kept looking at her that he was absorbing it, too.

Night fell, but with the moon so bright and her improved vision, Cassia could see as well as if it were day. When they stopped to rest, Zeru took her by the shoulders and stared.

"You are so beautiful, Cassia," he said.

"Zeru," she said simply, and slid her arms around his waist, gasping when his lips came to her neck.

"No time," she said, more to convince herself than him.

He sighed, pressed her lips with his, and nodded. As she

followed him into the sky once more, she wondered if they would ever have the time together that they craved.

As the wind caressed her face and Zeru's wings kept time with hers, plans started to form in Cassia's mind. Plans that would turn her father's world upside down as effectively as anything an enemy would devise, but that would also benefit her people.

"I have an idea," she said finally. She wondered if Zeru would think she'd lost her senses. "It involves your queen."

His brows rose. "How?"

"It will take negotiation. And your influence." She felt a spark of mischievous satisfaction as she added, "And...well...lying."

His lips curved up, his eyes sparkling. "You have my attention. How do you propose to lie?"

She smiled at him, struck by how much she enjoyed seeing him happy. "I won't. You will."

"Ah." He grinned. "Far less complicated."

"You haven't heard my plan yet."

She told him as the sun rose over the trees, painting the canopy a fiery orange, much like the small flame that had been ignited in her mind. Someone had to stand up to the Sylvan king. It might as well be her.

When she was finished, Zeru flew beside her in silence for several minutes. "I'm trying to decide if you are brave or just very, very naive. I confess I'm leaning toward the latter."

"You're probably right." She looked up at the clouds, wondering if any might be welkins. "But I don't see any other way."

"Neither do I," he replied soberly. "But I'll be surprised if we make it to step two."

"One at a time," she said. "First, I have to face my father."

When they drew close to Scarhamm, Cassia chose a spot she deemed safe for Zeru, finding a break in the trees large enough for them both to land. As he touched ground beside her, she said, "This is as close as you can go before you risk being met with one of the regular patrols."

He looked like he wanted to argue, but then seemed to think better of it. Stepping close, he squeezed her hands and kissed her forehead. "Tread carefully, *katra*."

She gave him a quizzical look. "What does that mean?"

"It's an Old Azpian word," he said, looking away, his jaw tense. "I'll tell you what it means if we survive step three."

"Step one," she negotiated. "Or tell me now."

His eyes met hers with amusement. "Two, then."

"I'll hold you to that." When she went to kiss his cheek, he turned his head and met her lips, making her dizzy for a minute. His hand stayed on her back, a desperate pressure, as if he couldn't get close enough to her. It wasn't easy to pull away, but she did.

"Stay safe, Dracu." Before she could be tempted to linger, she launched herself up, and didn't look back as she gained air.

As she flew closer to the fortress, she found the perimeter changed beyond recognition. The earth was scorched and the trees blackened, their burned branches like bones in an ossuary. Zeru had described things as he'd last seen them, a panicked clash with scuccas in the forest nearby. The stone walls were intact, but there was no sign of the creatures. What if Scarhamm had already fallen, and Selkolla was inside its walls? But at that moment, one of the Huntsman archers came into view, and Cassia breathed again.

It was odd to see her home from a new vantage point, her view encompassing the fortress, walls, and trees that grew in the garden. It all looked so much smaller from the air, reminding her that there weren't so very many Sylvans left. Aside from Scarhamm, there were only a smattering of villages. If Selkolla won this fight, the forest folk would be effectively wiped from the land.

It was beyond strange to see the Huntsmen archers aiming at her. She was careful to stay outside their range.

"Identify yourself," one of the Huntsmen shouted from a watchtower. With a quick glance, she saw that none of them had been part of the Cryptlands raid, so none of them would have seen her in this form.

"A friend," she called back. "I seek an audience with the king." When no reply came, she added, "I have valuable information about your enemies."

"Who are you and where do you come from?" another demanded. "I've never seen your kind."

She considered how to answer. She could say she was a Zerian, but the word wouldn't mean anything to them. She couldn't admit her true identity. Many of the other Huntsmen had heard her father banish her, and the order must have circulated by now. Thankfully, her lighter hair, the gold flecks on her skin, and her wings must make her look different.

"I've come from far away," she said, which was more or less true. "I've come to help. I will make vows not to harm you. If you let me come closer, we can speak more."

The First Huntsman, Alof, appeared at the top of the ladder, with Burke following him. Cassia's shoulders relaxed a fraction seeing they'd survived the scucca attack. They halted and stared for half a heartbeat before Alof drew his weapon.

"She's Selkolla's creature," he said, using his sword to point. "She attacked the king. If she comes any closer, fire."

Cassia stared at the fortress. How could she talk to her father if they wouldn't even let her come close?

Just then, a silvery head appeared at the top of the watch-tower steps. Enora was dressed for battle in her leather armor, with knives strapped in a line that bisected her chest.

Her gasp was loud enough to hear at a distance. "Cassia!"

Even as the Huntsmen kept their bows trained on her, Cassia had to smile. Of course her sister would recognize her no matter what form she was in.

"Any of you fires on my sister," Enora said, "be prepared to put an arrow through me, too. And Thea. And even Rozie. Those who harm one of us earns the vengeance of all. So unless you want to sleep with one eye open the rest of your lives, I suggest you stand down."

Cassia felt tears rise behind her eyes at her sister's protective-ness. "I think they get it, Enna." A nickname she hadn't used for her sister since childhood.

The bows were lowered, and Alof nodded his assent. Cassia remained watchful as she approached, but none of the Huntsmen dared defy Enora's threatening order. Alighting on the watch-tower, she furled her wings and looked at the familiar faces of people she had known her whole life.

Enora rushed to embrace her, then pulled back to look at her wings. "What in the nine realms of the Netherwhere did you do to yourself?" Without letting go, she turned an angry face on the Huntsmen. "Keep your weapons down!"

"Your father's orders were clear," Alof said, though he didn't look pleased about it. "If Cassia returns, she is to be turned away by force, if necessary." He looked at her, his eyes regretful.

Cassia's heart turned to stone. She'd made the mistake of neglecting to extract a bargain from the Huntsmen not to harm her. They could slaughter her right now.

⏜ 285 ⏜

Enora put herself in front of Cassia, her lean, muscular arms spread to make her body as large a barrier as possible.

"Enna, give me a chance to explain," she said, laying her hand on her sister's shoulder. "Let them decide."

"As long as they decide correctly," Enora said, clear menace in her tone.

Cassia turned and met their eyes, each in turn. How could she explain that she'd been under the Seer's control but no longer? "When you saw me before, the witch had stolen my memory," she said. "She tried to make me into one of her scuccas, but somehow it didn't work, and I was transformed into...this. I didn't want to hurt any of you. I escaped her, and my memories have returned. Under the dirt and blood and some strange new wings, I'm the same person you knew."

As they hesitated, Burke cleared his throat. "If she were still Selkolla's creature, I don't think she'd be asking us to trust her. She'd been trying to tear our heads off with those claws. Scuccas are mindless. They no longer know who they are. Cassia seems like herself to me."

Alof's lips curved up in a barely perceptible smile.

Cassia looked at Burke with gratitude for coming to her aid.

Alof stepped closer. "We still can't let you inside the walls. It'll be our heads if we do."

"He won't know it's me if you don't tell him," Cassia said, realizing she had gained an inch or two of height in her new form and could now see over her sister's shoulder. "None of you recognized me, after all. Let me talk to him briefly and I'll go." Her lips curved up, hoping they could see it was her, the same person they'd always known. "If he asks you later, say you didn't recognize me. It's not a lie."

"It's a bent truth," Enora said, her eyebrows raised as she

turned her head to level a side-eye. "Not like you to be dishonest, Cass." She huffed a laugh. "Not like any of us."

"Well, maybe it's like me, now."

"How do you know he won't recognize you?" Burke asked, his eyes wide as he looked her over. "Different as you are, you are his daughter."

Her smile soured. "But he never really saw me."

"If you're wrong, it'll be your death," he replied, his eyes boring into hers. "And none of us want that." His jaw tightened. "Despite what you've done."

She dipped her chin in understanding. "I'll take the risk. This is my chance to atone." After Selkolla hadn't been able to make her hurt her father, she should have turned on the Seer and fought. Instead, she'd run. For that, she had to make things right.

Burke took a step closer. "It wasn't right what you did. Warning the Dracu about our attack."

Enora tensed, but Alof put up a hand to stay them both. "We hope you had good reasons for what you did, Cassia."

She blinked, a little shocked at Alof considering that she might have. "I did. Though I don't know if you'd agree with them." She looked at each Huntsman in turn, willing them to listen. "Burke, Alof. All of you. This has to stop. The war with the Dracu, with the Azpians, has to end now. We have no chance if we fight each other. Selkolla is the bigger threat. If we can't accept that, we've lost."

The Huntsmen were silent for a minute. Uncertainty wound in Cassia's belly like a coiling root.

Finally, Alof spoke. "What you're saying is hard to accept, and we have good reason not to trust you."

Cassia's chest tightened, expecting them to dismiss her the way her father always had. But Alof added, "But my gut tells me that you believe in what you're saying. If I dismiss it, we could all pay the price. And since you are the one with the most knowledge of the scucca threat, that's worth considering."

Relief poured through her, leaving her lightheaded. First Burke, now Alof. They were listening. "Before I go to my father, tell me what's happened over the past few days. I know Selkolla brought her scuccas to attack."

"They're gone during the day," Alof said, "and come back at nightfall." He cleared his throat. "It might look safe now, but don't step outside the walls. I'm glad you didn't have to approach on foot."

"Why?"

He indicated the perimeter with a jerk of his chin. "Selkolla spelled the ground to be soft when a Sylvan steps on it. It... swallows anyone who tries to leave. We sent out scouts and almost lost two men. The wards are the only thing keeping us safe. Veleda is refreshing the magic constantly. She's barely slept."

"I assume you used fire on the scuccas." Cassia gazed sadly at the blackened area of forest. She could imagine the horrifying scene: burning arrows setting the scuccas ablaze and the trees catching fire.

"We had no choice," Alof said, anger and regret clear in his voice. "There had to be a thousand of them. We cut them apart and they"—he made a gesture in the air—"simply knit themselves back together."

Burke grunted in disgust. "Those things are just... *wrong*."

"Unnatural," Alof agreed. "Fire was the only way to keep them off. But we hated having to use it. The trees..." He stared at the forest with a shake of his head. "They gave their lives for Scarhamm."

Sylvans grieved when a single healthy tree was lost, let alone hundreds. "You stopped the spread of the fire, though," she pointed out.

Burke's eyes warmed. "The river nixies came to our aid, using water from the Scar to put out the flames. But what about next time? We can't keep burning our forest. And Veleda is worried about the full moon. She's not sure her spells can hold the wards."

"What can you tell us that will help us fight these creatures?" Alof asked.

She held up her hand to show the ring. "I have reason to believe the Solis Gemma could work on them. Sunlight weakens them, which is probably why they don't attack by day."

"Hope you're correct," he said. "Because the full moon is tonight."

27

The sharpest weapon is truth.
—GAXIX, DRACU PHILOSOPHER

Enora and Thea led Cassia through quiet hallways. It was a strange experience to walk next to her sisters and have to be mindful of her wings. They didn't seem to notice, though. Or hid it well.

"It's so empty," Cassia said, unnerved by the lack of activity. There were usually any number of Huntsmen and servants passing through. "Did...we lose that many—?"

"No," Enora assured her, giving her a comforting look. "We didn't lose anyone. Not yet. Since they attack at night, everyone tries to sleep during the day. Except for the servants and guards on duty."

A servant passed by, coming to a full stop to stare at Cassia with wide eyes before he bustled on nervously.

Enora looked amused. "No one knows what to make of you."

"I hardly know what to make of myself," Cassia admitted. "How is Rozie?"

Enora's confident stride faltered. "She's not herself." They reached the door to the war room, and Enora turned to face her. "None of us have been." She took a breath. "I'm so happy to see you. But you haven't even told us what happened."

"I'm still not sure, exactly," she admitted. "Selkolla tried to make me into one of her creatures, and somehow it failed." She still didn't know how much of her transformation was the ring turning her into a Zerian and how much was Selkolla's spell. "I'll tell you the rest later."

Thea's frown was forbidding. "Are you sure you want to do this?"

"Yes."

"I'm not leaving you alone," Enora said in a warning tone. "If he tries to hurt you, I'm going to defend you."

"Don't!" Cassia grabbed her sister's hands, distress making her pulse race. "I don't want you to risk yourself for me." The consequences to Enora could be anything from losing status to losing her life. Their father was unpredictable in his punishments, as she knew better than ever.

"I don't care." Enora's face reminded Cassia of a mother wolf she'd once seen protecting a cub. "This is not negotiable. I'm telling you how things are."

Enora opened the door to the war room. "Father...someone is here with information about our enemies."

The Sylvan king's impatient voice rumbled through the open door. "Let him in."

"Her," Enora corrected, holding the door open for Cassia. "She has knowledge of the Seer and her creatures."

Cassia entered the war room, detecting the familiar scents with a keener nose than she'd had before. She could smell the blood from the old weapons that hung on the walls and wondered if the tarnish she'd always thought was rust was perhaps something else.

Thea had given her a pair of gloves to hide the ring, but she still felt its weight on her hand as she looked at her father.

Tordon stood on the king's left, his head coming up in

surprise as Cassia entered. Tibald, who stood at the king's right hand, was staring at a map that was laid out on the scarred oaken table between them. The king straightened to his full height, and Tibald looked up and gasped. The next second, his sword was bare, and he was rushing around the table.

"Stop!" Enora shouted. "She's not dangerous. Tibald, put that away. She's come to help."

The king's gaze moved to Cassia. She swallowed, feeling as if she were staring down her own fate. Without blinking or turning away, the king nodded subtly to Tibald, who sheathed his sword and moved back to his place.

Cassia moved to the edge of the table, her pulse beating in her throat. "The news I bring can't wait. I doubt Selkolla has brought the full force of her power against you so far, and you need to know this now. Before she strikes."

Tibald seemed to recover from his initial surprise, his eyes growing watchful. "Are you looking for payment in return?"

"No." She cleared her throat. "I only want you to listen. You won't like what I have to say, but I assure you, it's worth hearing."

"Don't presume to tell us what we'll like and not like," Tibald said irritably, drawing himself up. "What are you, anyway, an overgrown pixie? I've never seen wings like yours."

Cassia couldn't help but smile at his typical straightforwardness. "Call me an overgrown pixie. It makes no difference to me."

The Sylvan king spoke with his usual brusqueness. "Share your information. We have no time to waste."

She swallowed and met her father's eyes. Any moment, he would recognize her and order her thrown out. Or killed. And even if he didn't, what she was about to say could also incite his wrath. But she was going to say it anyway, though her pulse beat in her temples so hard she worried they could see her fear.

"Selkolla claims that you were once the Deathringer, and that you killed her moss folk."

Aside from Enora's gasp, the silence was so absolute, Cassia could swear she heard a spider scuttling to its web in the far corner of the war room.

"The witch isn't to be trusted," said the king in a scathing rumble. A fine vibration went through the floor, his outrage palpable.

"Maybe," Cassia said, curling her hands into fists under the cover of the table to hide their shaking. She might be in a new form, but she was still scared of her father. "But Selkolla is a Sylvan. She has many sins—I don't think dishonesty is one of them."

"She may be a Sylvan by birth," Tibald said, eyeing her narrowly, "but she has been twisted and warped by her unnatural magic. Who are you, anyway? How do you know the Seer of the Cryptlands?" When she didn't answer, he turned to Enora. "What were you thinking letting a stranger in here?"

"Listen to her," Thea said firmly.

And Thea's word was enough, apparently, to draw all eyes to her. Cassia straightened, her hands clasping together behind her back as if she was giving a report. The weapons master was watching her too closely, the wheels turning in his head. "Long ago, Selkolla made a bargain with the Dracu queen. In return for the queen's protection and a home in the Cryptlands, she vowed not to harm anyone under the queen's rule."

Tibald made a get-on-with-it gesture. "How does that benefit us?"

"Selkolla wants vengeance against the Sylvan king, but it's possible she won't stop there. If she successfully takes Scarhamm, she'll have a stronghold that she can use as a base of power. And from what I've heard, the Dracu queen is worried. She wants Selkolla's creatures to join in the war against the Sylvans, but she fears those same scuccas will be turned on her. That bargain is her only assurance that won't happen."

"A bargain sealed in blood?" the king asked, his expression showing interest.

"Yes. But the bargain needn't apply solely to Azpians in the Cryptlands. It could apply to anyone who vows fealty to the queen." She looked between them, letting the idea sink in.

"I still don't see your point," Tibald said, tapping the table absently with one finger.

Cassia took a breath and forced herself to speak the words that could get her thrown out or worse. "If the Sylvans make a temporary alliance with the Dracu . . ." She ignored the thunderous look on her father's face and continued, ". . . they would be immune from harm from Selkolla and her scuccas."

"That," the king said, slowly and succinctly, "will never happen."

Cassia barely stopped herself from calling him "Father" as she went on. "I say again, when the queen gave Selkolla sanctuary, she forced her to agree to a bargain that forbids the Seer from harming anyone under the queen's rule. A blood bargain. Unbreakable. You can use that to your advantage. What else do you have?"

"This is clearly an attempt to trick us," Tibald said, slapping the table. "Did Selkolla send you?"

"No," she said. "I hate her as much as you do. I want her defeated more than anyone."

"Not more than we do," Tordon said, his ageless eyes solemn.

Enora stepped forward as if she wanted to say something. Cassia gave her a quick warning look. If her sisters defended her, it could make her father wonder why. And she didn't need any more scrutiny. At her speaking look, Enora pressed her lips together.

Cassia turned back to Tordon. "We both want the witch and her scuccas gone. Selkolla's attacks so far probably haven't been that serious. She's been preparing, testing the wards, toying with you. Only your wards protect you. And I hear that your Seer can barely keep them intact."

"How do you know all this?" Tibald demanded, crossing his arms over his chest.

She ignored his question, focused on saying her piece. "The full moon is tonight. Wards will be weaker, boundaries thinner. If you don't find a weapon against Selkolla before that, Scarhamm could fall. Tonight." She checked her father's reaction and saw a face carved in marble.

"Well," Tibald said, waving a hand at her as he shook his head. "Now we see your machinations clearly enough. Oh, of course we'll simply bow down to the Dracu queen. Should we bow to you, too? Why not! Let us all swear allegiance to our greatest enemy and a stranger we have no reason to trust."

"I'm not lying," Cassia said, frustration heating her skin.

"You're not a Sylvan," the weapons master added, "so I have no way to know that." He turned to face the king. "My liege, say the word and I'll get rid of this winged vermin. She doesn't even look like a pixie, now I think of it. She could be some kind of Azpian who lives in the lowest realms."

Thea pushed away from the wall, her tone as commanding as if she were in battle. "If she has information, it doesn't matter where she came from."

"She is right about one thing," the king acknowledged, surprising everyone into silence. "If Scarhamm were under the queen's rule, it would prevent Selkolla from killing our people."

Cassia swallowed and watched him, waiting.

295

"But that alliance will never happen," he finished, meeting her eyes. "Never while I breathe."

"Selkolla is moving closer," Cassia persisted, the heat of anger filling her at her father's stubborn pride. "I heard she has spelled the very ground outside the walls, which means she has already broken the perimeter wards and is probably underground nearby. She's clearly made it past Thirstwood's roots. She's been waiting for the right moment to strike."

He didn't argue, but the flames in his eyes told her he was reaching the limit of what he would tolerate.

She pressed on. "I know you've used fire on the scuccas, but that's a temporary solution, not to mention dangerous to the trees. And we can't assume that fire destroys the creatures. The trapped souls in the scuccas might be able to build themselves new bodies from whatever they find in Thirstwood, for all we know."

"Then we burn the area of Thirstwood around Scarhamm," her father said.

Cassia gasped. "And destroy our...yourselves? All your protection, your life force, your food, everything comes from the trees. Burning the forest would be embracing defeat."

Flames rose in his eyes. "And your plan is to surrender. To submit to an enemy of centuries in the hopes of defeating the threat of the moment."

She shook her head. "The 'threat of the moment' hardly describes what you're up against. Selkolla must have been harvesting souls for years, perhaps taking fallen soldiers in the wars." She hadn't thought about it before, but that made sense. "And if that's so, then everyone who falls tonight will become one of her foot soldiers. Trapped in a body of sticks and moss forever."

"Enough," he said, rattling the table with a blow. "I will not allow my people to swear allegiance to the Dracu queen, even temporarily."

She kept her hands at her sides, her chin up, and her shoulders squared. "I'm asking you to look at the only option left. The scuccas are deathless and could number in the thousands. But this way, they can't hurt you. You could cut them down and they wouldn't be able to fight back. By their master's own vow."

"Then what?" Tibald gestured at the map. "Play this game of stratagem to its conclusion. We live forever as subjugates of the Dracu?"

"No," she said. "The alliance would have clear limits. It would last only until the threat is neutralized. Say, until sunrise."

He laughed. "And the moment the deal ends, Selkolla would return with her forces. Your plan merely delays the inevitable."

"Not if they can all be wiped out at once."

"There are thousands of the things," said the weapons master. "There's no way. Not even with your plan."

Her fisted hands tightened until her nails dug into her palms, drawing blood. She had to convince them. This was the only way. If only she could share that she was willing to help them with the use of her ring. But her father had made that impossible.

"There's another possibility." She took a breath, preparing to expose the next ludicrous phase of her plan. "If you agree to the alliance, I think I can get the Dracu queen's army to fight side by side with you. And Selkolla's vow already protects the Azpians. If her vow applies in Scarhamm, you'd essentially have invulnerable soldiers fighting side by side with you to defend Scarhamm."

"Who *are* you?" Tibald asked again.

But his question was lost as the king spoke. "Dracu within my walls?" His lips drew back from his teeth. "Never."

"Not even to save your own people?" she asked, her voice rising with anger.

"You have wasted my time." The Sylvan king looked at Enora. "Get her out of here."

Cassia stared at her father, knowing this might be the last time she saw him. She could live with that. But she couldn't live with his pride dooming all the people she loved. "If you let this opportunity pass," she said with all the scathing condemnation she felt, "at least you won't live long enough to regret it." And with as much dignity as she could muster, she moved to the door. Enora stood in the doorway, pale and silent. Thea wore a furious expression. Cassia gave them a quick head shake to remind them not to defend her. That would only draw more attention and put them all in danger. But as she stepped through the door, a sharp command stopped her.

"Hold."

A single word. An order. Cassia froze. The crackling fire made the only noise in the fraught hush. She turned back to face her father.

"If the queen makes a vow first," the king said with bruising force, "if she swears not to harm any Sylvan or any forest creature under my rule, and to leave Scarhamm at the next rise of the sun, I will consider."

Cassia nodded once. As she turned away, she saw her own shock reflected on her sisters' faces.

She had survived stage one.

As they left the war room, Enora said, "I will never get over what happened in there. Are you sure you're not a spell caster of some kind?"

Cassia chuckled. "If there was magic used in there, it wasn't mine." She stopped her sister before she could take the stairway leading up to their bedchambers. "No time, Enna. I have to go."

Enora grabbed her hand. "You can't leave without seeing Rozie. She would *kill* me. Or her whining about it would make me wish for death."

Cassia smiled. "Then bring her to Veleda's workroom. I have one last thing I need to do while I'm here. You can all help me."

"Veleda's probably not there," Enora said with a frown. "She's been at the walls almost constantly, reinforcing the wards."

"I don't need Veleda. Just her supplies."

Minutes later, Cassia was in the Seer's dim workroom being squeezed to death by skinny arms, a cloud of ginger hair tickling her chin.

"I missed you I missed you I missed you," Rozie chanted, finally raising her head, her eyes large and pleading. "Also, the cat peed on your bed while you were gone so I threw the quilt on the rubbish heap because I didn't want anyone to know."

Cassia found herself grinning wider than she had in a long time. "I'm not worried about it, Sproutling." She stepped back and gestured around the room. "But if you want to make it up to me, I could use your help. Actually, you can all help me search."

Thea leaned against one wall, her expression one of interest. "What for, exactly? Do you need spell ingredients?"

"No. I need you to turn me into an Azpian."

Thea shook her head wryly. "Already bored with this look?"

Cassia laughed. "Not exactly."

Rozie looked intrigued. "Like a Skratti or something?"

"Like anything that might get me through the Cryptlands without them knowing I'm a Sylvan." Cassia surveyed the possibilities: feathers, bones, herbs, animal horns, twine, bottles of

~ 299 ~

unnamed substances. Surely some of this would work. "Tibald thought I was an overgrown pixie. Maybe you can turn me into an overgrown imp."

"Their wings are different," Thea pointed out. "Dark and... batty."

Cassia shrugged. "Then cover my wings with something. I don't care. Just make me look like something that crawled out of a lower realm."

"We can do better than that," Thea said, looking unimpressed with the contents of the room. "I have a dress I can give you. I was saving it for a revel, if we ever have one again, but... I think it'll be perfect."

While Thea went to retrieve the dress, Enora brought a bucket of warm water, and Cassia did her best to clean up. She wished she had time for a full bath, but she was aware of Zeru waiting for her in the woods. If he grew impatient enough, she wouldn't put it past him to try to sneak into Scarhamm again. And it wouldn't be so easy this time.

"No more excuses, Cass," Enora said once Thea had returned and Cassia put on the dress, her soft gray eyes serious and worried. "Tell us everything, quickly if you must."

Cassia sighed, turning so Thea could lace up the back. "As I said in the war room, Selkolla blames our father for the death of her moss folk." She hesitated. "She claims he was the Deathringer of old and killed innocent forest creatures in the Ancient Wars."

After a stunned pause, Enora said, "No way to know if that's true, but if the Seer believes it, she has every reason to want revenge."

Cassia turned around as Thea finished fussing with the dress. "Selkolla has been planning this for a long time. She's making

300

more and more of those stick things, the fake moss children. She thinks my ring will resurrect them for real." She took a steadying breath, her hands curled into fists as she related the rest. "She tried to kill me and bring me back as her creature so she could have control of the ring. But instead of transforming me into one of her obedient puppets, well...I think the ring protected me. Made me into something else that she couldn't quite control."

"I'll kill her," Thea said, her eyes burning with fury.

"Not if I get to her first," Enora said, her cold anger somehow more chilling. "I don't care if she's an Ancient herself."

"I'll help," Rozie said, her expression fierce.

Cassia's eyes misted at the way her sisters swore revenge. Pretty much an expression of love in her family. "Anyway," she went on as Rozie brought a jar of some dark substance and began painting it on her wings, "the Seer cast a spell to make me lose my memory, and that's why I was gone so long." She bit her lip. "I hid in the woods for days. I didn't even remember who I was, let alone...you. I forgot my own sisters."

"Not your fault," Thea said simply, gathering a handful of small bones. Cassia wondered what she planned to do with them. "How did you end up remembering?"

"Um." Cassia glanced down at the floor as if some extra courage was lying there somewhere. "Zeru came to find me. He helped me remember."

The room went silent.

"Isn't that the name of the Dracu?" Thea asked, her eyes narrowed to slits. "The one who abducted you?"

Cassia squinted. "It's complicated."

"Oh, Cass," Enora said, her face drawn with rueful sympathy. "Do not tell me you have feelings for your captor."

⌣ 301 ⌣

"No! Not at the time anyway. I hated him. But he had... another form. How can I even explain?" She spread her hands helplessly. "We need more time. And we don't have it. I'll tell you later. For now, please help me get ready."

"But I want to hear more," Rozie said, her chin in her hands. "How did the Dracu help you remember?"

As Cassia blushed, Enora seemed horrified but took pity on her. "Enough about that. We have an Azpian to create. Cass, tell us why you're doing this."

As her sisters embellished her disguise, Cassia told them her plan. They listened in silence, though she caught them exchanging significant looks. When she was finished, Enora merely said, "Dangerous. Is there a remote possibility I could talk you out of this?"

"It's the only way we have a chance," Cassia said. "Trust me. Please."

Thea nodded. "Of course we trust you." And to her relief, left it at that.

"Ooh!" Rozie cried, her eyes rounding. "I see eyeballs in a jar! Can I put extra eyeballs on you?"

Cassia laughed. "If you can find a way to attach them."

A few minutes later, Enora finished smoothing Cassia's hair with a final stroke of a boar-bristle brush. "You know, Cass, all those times I helped you get ready for revels when you were little, I never quite envisioned this."

"Well?" she prompted, spreading her arms and turning in a circle. "Am I hideous?"

"Awful," Thea said, "but also kind of stunning. You fill out my dress better than I do. We'll have to be careful how we get you out of here because the guards are going to be terrified when they see you."

302

"*I'm* terrified," said Enora, grimacing. "I hope this disguise actually works."

"You look amazing!" Rozie breathed, her eyes shining with admiration. "Promise you'll come home, Cass."

Cassia swallowed at the worry in her sister's eyes. "I'll do everything I can to come back in one piece. I promise."

28

> Persuasion is a subtler kind of warfare.
> Every word should be planned as carefully
> as an attack.
>
> —Gaxix, Dracu philosopher

When Cassia returned to Zeru, she found him pacing grooves into the forest floor. As she landed, he grabbed her around the waist and looked her over as if there might be a knife lodged somewhere in her person. His eyebrows lifted as he took in her appearance, but his only remark was, "You were gone too long."

She frowned at his chiding tone. "I was as quick as I could be. And I'm fine, thanks for asking."

His eyes met hers with a wry look. "If I hadn't thought you were fine, I'd have come for you, archers or no. I could feel your tension through the amulet, but no great fear. I still worried, though."

"Then it doesn't work that well because I was terrified."

He pulled her close, leaning in so their foreheads touched. "Did you know," he said slowly, as if relishing the words, "that you have Dracu horns?" As her heart thudded in response, he took a strand of her hair and slid his fingers along it, drawing back to stare at the top of her head with a heavy-lidded look. "I gather this is your idea to move through the Cryptlands incognito."

"Yes." She reached up to check that the horns were in place. When Zeru lifted his hand, she grabbed it to stop him, smiling as his fingers curled possessively around hers. "Don't touch. They're attached with hair pins and twine. Also, my wings are covered in some substance that I hope is made from crushed herbs." In the end, green-dusted hair and wings, bone jewelry, and some dark powder around her eyes and under her cheekbones to accentuate them were enough to give her the appearance of an Azpian. For ease of movement, she'd added leggings underneath Thea's form-fitting black dress. Enora had also given her a pair of long black gloves to cover the Solis Gemma. Rozie hadn't figured out how to attach the eyeballs, so she'd settled for making a necklace out of animal bones and twine. All in all, it was a look.

Zeru's hand moved to her chin, turning her face back and forth, his gaze heating. "Were you going for winged Dracu? I can't say I've ever seen one. Aside from myself, of course."

A shiver ran through her at the appreciation in his eyes. "I'm going for 'Winged Azpian of Unknown Variety.' My sisters can't decide if I look awful or amazing."

"Amazing." His lips curved up, his darkened eyes taking on the alert calm she associated with the predatory side of him. "No question."

She lifted a brow as she surveyed his tidied clothing fitting snugly on his lean, strong frame and his dark, finger-combed hair. "You've cleaned yourself up, too."

He made a dismissive motion. "As much as I could."

She looked up at him, not hiding her own appreciation. "I like it."

As she stepped close, his lips settled over hers. Heat rushed through her veins, distracting her from everything else. Risking her disguise, she put her arms around him and clutched him.

He exhaled and shook his head as if clearing it, then slid his hands to her waist. "Dare I ask how it went with your father?"

"Better than I could have hoped." Now that she'd had some time to calm her nerves, her relief was knee-weakening. "My father agreed to consider the bargain if the queen vows not to harm any of his subjects. The deal would last until sunrise tomorrow."

He gave her an incredulous look, shaking his head in admiration. "That's—I'm amazed. Well done. As much as I believe in you, I doubted it was possible to get his agreement. No one recognized you?"

"My sisters did. But Enora threatened messy vengeance on the guards if they told my father. And he ... didn't know me." Why did it still hurt to say that? She wished feelings could be turned off like a spigot on a barrel of fruit wine.

Zeru's expression tightened. "He never did."

She nodded, feeling a bit of weight lift at his words. She felt seen by him. "We'd better go. We still have to make our way through the Cryptlands to your queen."

"Getting to her isn't the problem." He stared hard at her, as if he wanted to ask her to reconsider. "She won't be easy to convince."

"Then you'd better be persuasive."

They entered the Cryptlands through the same hill where Cassia had before. As she stepped into the dark, her whole body prickled with fear, and suddenly, she couldn't move. For a second, even Zeru's hands on her shoulders made her want to run.

But then he said her name, and her eyes snapped to his as she fought her way out of the images of danger crashing through her mind. She had no reason to think that Selkolla would know she was near. Or to suppose that the Seer still had any power over her. But she didn't want to test that unknown.

"It never gets easier," she admitted. "Entering the Cryptlands. I fear I'm not meant to be an Azpian." She smiled shakily, gesturing down at herself.

"You don't have to come with me," Zeru said, worry shadowing his eyes. "It's not too late to change your mind."

Cassia took a breath and straightened her shoulders. "I'm going. If you can't get the queen to agree, then I have something to offer her."

His lips tightened. "Are you sure you want to do this?"

"Yes."

He gave her fake horns a doubtful look. "What if your disguise isn't enough?"

"You said I look amazing," she reminded him pertly.

He exhaled sharply, giving her another once-over. "I'll do most of the talking. Don't speak unless she asks you a direct question. I don't want more scrutiny on you than necessary."

She rolled her eyes, using her best Zeru voice to say, "Give me some credit, Dracu."

His lips pressed together as if he were fighting a smile, and his eyes filled with lazy warning. "A fair imitation of me, I'll admit."

Smiling, he leaned forward, brushing her forehead with his lips. "Ready to go on?"

"Tell me what to expect."

"The tunnels should be relatively empty until we near the queen's apartments. Follow my lead. We shouldn't have any trouble getting in to see her. She might be . . . a little unhappy with me."

"Oh, good, something else to worry about," Cassia said dryly. "Why?"

～ 307 ～

"I...haven't reported to her directly since I left for Welkincaster, though I've sent messages. She takes offense at these things. I'll handle it. It'll be fine."

She hoped he was right.

The path was as quiet as he'd predicted, with only a few imps and pit sprites floating past. As they rounded a corner, a drake stood in their path, its forked tongue flicking in and out as it watched them with reflective eyes. Cassia drew back sharply, but Zeru stepped up to the creature.

"Move your scales," he said in a tone mixing threat with boredom, "or I'll use them to make myself a new pair of boots."

The creature scuttled off with a hiss.

As they went on, the tunnels grew brighter, with lanterns illuminating colorful wall tiles. Guards were stationed at intervals. Her pulse pounded in her throat as their eyes followed her, the oils and powders inadequate protection against their probing stares. But soon she and Zeru reached a large set of elaborately carved doors. The queen's chambers.

Zeru nodded to the guards as if he knew them. "This is my new friend," he said. "The queen will want to meet her."

To her surprise, they were shown in without further questions.

Cassia's stomach clenched, her palms turning damp as she stepped into the Dracu queen's inner sanctum. It was a long, high-ceilinged chamber with white columns, a pale stone floor touched with a gold-leaf pattern of vines spiked with clawlike thorns, and twin tapestries behind a malachite throne.

The queen was even more intimidating than Cassia remembered. Of modest height but stately, her eyes were as green as the bog sprite chandeliers that hung from the shadowy ceiling. Councillors and waiting women flanked her on both sides, some of them standing while others sat on benches upholstered in shades of violet and clover. Imps floated above their heads, their bulbous eyes keeping watch on everyone below. Cassia tried to calm her breathing in the presence of so many enemies. She could only hope her disguise was convincing enough to get her through the next few minutes.

"My queen," Zeru said, stepping forward with a low bow. "Forgive me for not coming sooner."

"My errant lieutenant," the queen said with languidly raised brows, as if she'd just noticed him. "Are you still alive?"

Zeru bent his head to hide a smile, saying in an undertone pitched to be heard, "I suppose I deserved that."

"What finally brings you back, Zeru?" she asked coolly. "I hope you have a good reason for this intrusion."

Cassia hid her surprise, both at the queen's familiarity and Zeru's title of lieutenant. He had said his family lost everything when he'd given her the ring. But she hadn't known Zeru had worked his way back up into the queen's favor.

"I'm sorry you see my presence as an intrusion, my queen," he said with an incline of his head. "I hope to make amends. This is my new acquaintance. I've brought her here because she has important information to share. It might be better if we had . . . a quieter audience?"

This practiced grace was yet another side to him. *Court Zeru,* Cassia decided. As polished as the queen's crown.

"I heard of your return, yet you have not reported in." The queen's displeasure seemed to cause a ripple of tension to flow through the court. "After weeks away when I had no word from you." Her voice held the steam of contempt, like cold water poured over hot stones. "Did you think I would forgive your derelictions so easily?"

"I'm sorry, Your Majesty," he said with smoothly delivered

contrition, "it pains me that you consider me derelict in my duty. I traveled based on Selkolla's advice, my single aim to retrieve the Dracustone for you."

Cassia hadn't heard the Solis Gemma referred to by that name in a long time. It reminded her that the queen had never stopped thinking of the ring as her rightful possession. And here it was in her throne room only feet away from her and with only a layer of fabric concealing it.

The queen's demeanor changed to one of keen interest at the mention of the ring. "Did you retrieve it?"

Zeru cleared his throat. "I have always been grateful that you gave me a chance to get it back, and to serve you when you could have condemned me."

One of the courtiers laughed. "Clearly, he didn't succeed. Empty promises are Zeru's specialty."

The queen's lips curved up, a contrast to the annoyance in her eyes. "Lieutenant, explain this to me. Your reputation and the honor of your family lay in that task, and yet you failed." A furrow appeared between her brows. "How can I trust you with anything if you fail me at the most crucial of times?"

"We can't doubt he tried," the same sneering adviser said. "He has the stink of forest folk all over him." A few chuckles rewarded his remark. "How far did you go in trying to get close to the Sylvan king's daughter?"

Cassia looked at the courtier, wishing she could use a blast of the ring specifically on him. It seemed Zeru had enemies in the court. It also seemed he had had to deal with heckling and abuse over his childhood mistake. Perhaps he was used to it. But she could feel her own anger rising.

"My queen," Zeru said, ignoring the interruption, "there's a greater threat to our people than the loss of the Dracustone. As

I'm sure your scouts have reported, Selkolla's army numbers in the thousands."

She waved a languid hand. "Let her slaughter the Sylvans. The better for us."

As Cassia stiffened, Zeru gave her a quick warning look before turning his attention back to the queen. "The scuccas repair themselves even as they fall." He paused. "If such an army were turned against us, how would we fare?"

The queen shifted on the shining throne. "She cannot harm us. We made a pact in blood." She spoke as if her own words comforted her.

He lowered his voice. "My queen, Selkolla is mentioned in the ancient histories. Stripped of her powers long ago, she sought refuge here at her weakest. What if she has been rebuilding her strength? What if she has searched all this time for a way around that pact?"

"Then we have other Seers to protect us," the adviser said with scathing dismissiveness. "But we won't need them. Selkolla's power is behind the Dracu queen. It's your allegiance I have reason to question, Lieutenant."

Zeru didn't shift his attention from the throne. "Ask Guzzo here how he plans to defeat an army that heals itself. I respectfully request again, my liege. Could we speak in private?"

The queen tapped her chin with a long finger, her nail filed to a sharp point. She nodded her chin toward Cassia. "What is she, Zeru? Where did you find her?"

He took Cassia's hand and made a show of looking her over proudly. "She came from one of the lower realms. Isn't she lovely?"

The queen made a circular motion with her hand. Zeru guided Cassia in a slow twirl.

"Intriguing," the queen said. "She looks like one of us but the wings...Dracu and imp, perhaps? I suppose anything can happen in the lower realms." The courtiers laughed, and the queen's expression became one of amused benevolence. "I could groom her to be one of my waiting women, if you want to keep her close. I'd lend her to you when you need her for...other purposes."

Cassia sucked in a breath, her eyes shifting to Zeru. He had gone straight-backed, his face stony. "That is more than generous," he said with an incline of his head. "But she's here because she brought us valuable information. I promised to escort her home once that's delivered."

The queen pouted. "A pity. She would be an interesting addition to my retinue." After a moment, she made a slight inclination of her head. "Very well, you may have your private audience. Everyone, out. Except for my guard."

"But, my queen," said the adviser in strident protest.

"You as well, Guzzo," she said. As the courtier finally moved to the door with a poisonous look at Zeru, the queen added under her breath, "Especially you."

When the door had closed behind all but her two guards, Zeru said, "Guzzo continues to be himself."

"I can't stop him, short of cutting out his tongue," the queen said. "And his family is powerful enough that I can't dismiss him. I expect he'll try to put a knife in me someday, but I have my own plans for him."

Cassia found her brows rising toward her hairline. No one would speak like this in the Sylvan court. No one would dare.

But Zeru was smiling as if he exchanged quips with the queen all the time. "I anticipate that day with pleasure. But we have no time to waste. My queen, you won't like what I have to say, but it must be said. The word in the lower realms is that Selkolla plans to move on us next."

312

Outrage suffused the queen's face. "Since when have the lower realms taken any interest in the politics above them?"

"Selkolla has dabbled there, collecting ingredients for her scuccas. Apparently, they see her for the threat she is. If the Cryptlands fall, the lower realms are next." He nodded to Cassia. "This girl came to me with a key piece of information about the scuccas."

"What's your name, girl?" the queen asked, her gaze curious. "And for that matter, what are you?"

"Her name is Arozenna," Zeru said, saving her from having to lie. They'd decided on an altered version of Rozie's full name— Rozenna. Her sister had thought it fit her appearance.

"As for what I am," Cassia said, shifting so her wings were more visible, "your guess is as good as mine." Which was true, as she had no idea what to call herself anymore. She blinked her soot-darkened lashes, playing her role of ingenue straight from some nameless pit.

Avarice lit the queen's eyes. "I can see you are unique. Would you like to stay here to work in my service? It's a rare opportunity. Most Dracu girls would kill for it. And many have."

Cassia swallowed. "I thank you, Your Majesty." She saw Zeru tense beside her, but paused as if considering the offer before she shook her head. "But I must decline. I have promises to others that must be kept."

"No sensible creature would break a vow," the queen said with a nod of understanding. "What is your information, Arozenna? If indeed you have anything useful to share."

Pulling in a fortifying breath, she replied, "Selkolla has given me reason to believe that the scuccas have at least one vulnerability: your Dracustone ring."

Tension hummed through the air, invisible threads pulling

tight. "My ring." The queen's fingers drummed on the arm of the throne, her eyes moving to Zeru. "Is this meant as some sort of jest?"

"Not at all," he assured her. "This is vital information. If the ring is our sole weapon against the scuccas, and we don't have that weapon, our best hope lies in killing Selkolla before she moves against us."

The queen leaned forward. "You dare to tell me that my ring is vital in my fight against a traitor in my midst, and yet you were the one tasked with retrieving it. And failed." Her voice grew louder. "I could take your head right now, Zeru. Explain to me why I shouldn't."

Cassia tensed, ready to reveal her own identity before she'd watch Zeru executed. But he made a subtle gesture to hold her fire. "Because I have a plan. The only plan that will end with you remaining on that throne."

"You dare—"

"I would dare anything out of love for you and my people," Zeru said, his words ringing with truth. "Those weeks when I was gone, I spent reading ancient texts in a place beyond imagination, and though I couldn't retrieve the ring, I gained insight. If we don't defeat Selkolla now, she will be a claw in your back for as long as you live." He paused, tensing visibly as he added, "I've looked at this from every possible angle and come to one conclusion: We need to make a temporary alliance with the Sylvans. And before you decide, my queen, ask yourself if I have ever been wrong."

She leaned forward, her eyes burning with anger. "You gave away my ring."

His head bent. "Aside from that foolish childhood mistake."

The queen regarded him with seething disbelief. "Reports tell

~ 314 ~

me you spent weeks alone with the Sylvan king's daughter and you did not get my ring. Now you come to me saying we must ally with them?" She gave him a knowing, narrow-eyed perusal. "Maybe Guzzo is right about you."

"My loyalty is to you," Zeru said.

"Perhaps," she mused. "And perhaps the Sylvan king's daughter has persuaded you that an alliance with them is the only option. You might even believe it. But that doesn't mean she is without guile. Sylvan honesty is legendary, but they find ways around the truth. In their own way, they can be as cunning as we are."

Zeru nodded, ignoring Cassia's irritated look. "I know. It's poison on my tongue to even suggest that we ally with the Sylvan king. But if you let me explain the proposal, I think you'll find it to your liking. It involves the Sylvans..." He paused dramatically, his voice carrying a layer of mischief as he said, "...swearing allegiance to you."

Though her lips curved up, suspicion darkened her eyes. "Why would the Sylvans agree to such a thing?"

"I helped them believe it was their idea," he said, grinning fully. "Did you really think I would form a connection to the Sylvan king's daughter without using it to our advantage?"

The queen blinked, her brows lifting. "I'm listening."

By the time Zeru was finished, the queen's white teeth were bared, her green eyes aglow. "So, the Sylvan king begs my protection. He knows he will be slaughtered without my help." She chuckled to herself, resting her chin on her hand as if savoring the thought.

"Yes," Zeru said. "They have no hope without us."

"Do you swear," she asked, her expression sobering, "that you bring me this proposal in good faith?"

Zeru didn't hesitate. "On my loyal heart. This is the only way I see for us to win against Selkolla and keep the Dracu safe. I swear it."

Cassia watched the queen carefully. The stories said she could be mercurial, her judgments harsh and brutal, but she was obviously pragmatic if she'd ruled for so long. This offer brought her a face-saving reason to ally with the Sylvans, with her in a position of power.

"Tell me this, girl," the queen said, taking Cassia by surprise when she'd thought the queen had all but forgotten her presence. "Do you hate the Sylvans as much as we do?"

Clasping her hands together, Cassia looked up with a mischievous expression. "I don't think anyone hates them as much as you do."

The second's pause as the queen considered that answer felt like a long, dark night.

Finally, the Dracu queen laughed, lifting a hand to wave to one of the guards. "Assemble my generals. We go to Scarhamm."

29

> Dracus in Scarhamm? Never let me see the day.
>
> —THE SYLVAN KING, IN RESPONSE TO A PROPHECY

THE MOMENT THEY WERE ALONE IN ONE OF THE darkened tunnels, Cassia found herself pressed against the wall, her head bent back with the strength of Zeru's kiss. She smiled against his lips, her fingers diving into his thick hair. His hands gripped her above her waist, his palms curving over her ribs. She clutched his shoulders as if she might float away if she let go. The exhilaration of success and the rush of risk blended with the dizzying joy of his kiss made her feel as light as air.

"I can't believe we succeeded," he said when she finally drew away for breath, the excitement in his eyes making her grin. "Your impossible plan has become less impossible."

"I knew I'd be in danger," she said dryly, "but I didn't expect her to threaten *you* with decapitation. I should have remembered your ability to inspire murderous impulses."

He lifted a skeptical brow. "I don't know, you never managed to murder me."

She blinked at him cheekily. "Maybe I wasn't trying very hard."

That earned her another minute of heated bliss. When he pulled away, she was surprised to see irritation narrowing his eyes. "You took your time refusing the queen's offer to stay. I started to think you were actually considering it."

Surprise parted her lips. "I didn't want to insult her by refusing too quickly."

He didn't look mollified. "You could have given me some clue."

"Like what?" she asked. "A broad wink? That would have been subtle."

His eyes narrowed. "Rude, sarcastic Sylvan. I wonder, do you taste as tart as you sound?" His hands slid up her body until his fingertips cradled her jaw, and they didn't speak for another few minutes.

When she pulled away, she observed, "You're closer to the queen than I realized. She seems to like you."

His hands slipped down to rest on her waist. "My family was among the most powerful in the Cryptlands, outside of royal blood." He nodded his chin toward the area they'd come from, where everything was beautifully crafted. "We had servants, lived lavishly. When I gave the ring away, the queen punished us. But...when I showed promise in her army, she couldn't ignore me. Eventually, over the past few years, I've regained some of her favor. She made it clear if I returned her ring, my parents would be forgiven, and everything would be as it once was."

So, that was why it had meant so much to him to get the ring back. "And there I was, standing feet away from her. You could have given me up. Instead, you lost the chance to help your family."

"Give you up?" His laugh rang through the tunnel. "Ah, yes, I could have handed you over to the queen and watched you suffer, maybe die at her hands." The words dripped with sarcasm. "That's definitely something I would be capable of doing." He nodded to himself. "Why didn't I think of that?"

His mocking tone and the censure in his expression for suggesting such a thing made it clear how he felt. She dropped her gaze, humbled at the fervency in his eyes.

He lifted her chin, waiting until her eyes met his before saying, "My family will be fine. And if we pull off your plan, the queen may be happy enough that she rewards us anyway. Without the ring."

"I hope so." She put her arms around his neck, pressing herself into him. "You deserve to be rewarded."

His eyebrows rose. "This is a new, refreshing perspective."

When their lips met, the kiss was sweet, heated with words they hadn't yet spoken. As they finally drew apart, Zeru sighed and put his forehead to hers. "We have to go if we plan to follow the Dracu army."

Cassia nodded, closing her eyes. Danger behind them, danger ahead. She had a sudden impulse to put her ring to the amulet and spirit them both off to Welkincaster. But she would never leave her sisters to fight without her help. Never again.

Zeru added, "Or you could go back to Scarhamm alone. Your wings would take you there faster."

That wasn't an option. "And risk being shot on sight for the second time? No, I'm staying with you." As his arm tightened around her, she added, "You can tell your queen we couldn't bear to be parted."

His grin turned wicked. "I'll try to make that believable. Though she already thinks we're together."

Cassia made a face. "Yes, offering me to you like some sort of perk."

A speculative light came into his eyes. "And like a gallant fool, I refused. Maybe I should have taken the time to carefully consider. The way you did."

319

The warm glow in his eyes reminded her of something. "You promised to tell me what your endearment means if we made it past step two."

"Oh," he said, turning his head to the side. "I didn't think we'd actually live this long." His tone was light, but she felt the tension in his body. "So, I don't actually have to."

"You are displaying what one of my tutors used to call 'Dracu sophistry.'" She punched him lightly. "Tell me."

His face lost expression. "It's something tediously obvious. I don't want to bore you."

She pulled back to look at him squarely. "You're really not going to tell me? You all but promised, Dracu."

A hunted look came into his eyes. "It wasn't a vow. It was a loose agreement at best."

She sighed. "Well, I guess I might never know, then. Because step three of my plan is the most dangerous." She put a hand to his jaw. "I wish you'd tell me."

Though he leaned into her hand, his eyes shifted away. "I'd rather go into battle than risk watching your face fall as I tell you something you don't want to hear."

She tried to turn his face toward her, but he was as immovable as rock. "Tell me, Zeru. Last chance."

He paused for a long time, and her heart swooped as his face turned back to hers. "It means," he said slowly, "'turnip.'"

There was a soft challenge in his eyes, and something vulnerable that made her heart squeeze. She could tell he was lying, and yet she couldn't help but laugh.

Once the sun was low in the sky, hidden by the trees of Thirstwood, the Azpian army set out toward Scarhamm. Cassia and

Zeru followed, staying away from the queen and her advisers, while behind them imps flew among clouds of pit sprites. Zeru seemed perfectly comfortable, but Cassia's whole body felt prickly and alert, no part of her able to relax. It was beyond strange to be marching with Dracu and their Azpian allies, even a few drakes pulled along on chains by Skrattis. The queen and her contingent of advisers conferred while scouts and guards sniffed the air and watched the woods for signs of scuccas. Their rotted-leaf smell lingered, and the ground cover between the woods and the fortress was crushed and churned into mud.

Cassia recalled the Huntsmen's warnings about Selkolla spelling the ground to devour Sylvans, but it stayed firm as they approached. Perhaps she was protected by the Azpian company she was in, or she was no longer quite Sylvan enough to be affected by the spell.

As they drew near, the gates creaked open, and one of the guards motioned the queen and her small retinue inside with a respectful bow. His eyes lingered on Cassia, but she kept her face forward and hoped he didn't recognize her. Likely, she would be a curiosity to everyone wherever she went from now on. She had better try to get used to it.

Zeru bent and whispered in her ear as they passed through the gates, his eyes on the Dracu heads lining the posts. "This feels so wrong. Passing the gates of my enemies."

"How do you think I feel?" she asked, nodding toward the company she was in.

The Sylvan king stood in the inner bailey, the spread of his antlers and his stance proudly declaring the space his own.

"You'd better act as mediator," she whispered to Zeru. "My sister Enora should be here to help...ah, there she is. Coming from the barracks. Silver hair. No-nonsense attitude."

"I see her," he whispered back. With a final speaking look at her that seemed to warn her to stay safe, he moved off toward the Sylvan king. He bowed first to the king, then to Enora as she looked him over. Zeru's voice carried over the hushed assembly. "Silvanus, king of the forest," he acknowledged. "We come in good faith to discuss our shared cause, defeating the betrayer, Selkolla. Is there somewhere we can speak together?"

"Here," the Sylvan king said in his low rumble. "If the Seer is in the ground nearby, let her witness our pact and know she cannot hurt us."

The Dracu queen stepped closer to the Sylvan king, and Cassia was struck by the difference in size between them. But the diminutive queen displayed no fear, her words like a gauntlet thrown in the massive king's face. "I hear your subjects are eager to swear fealty to me."

After a short pause, the Sylvan king replied in a voice lacking all expression. "You are no doubt eager to claim my subjects as your own. But first, the terms. Does your blood pact with Selkolla specify only the lands that were yours at the time? If so, no alliance will help us."

"It includes any people who have sworn fealty to me," she asserted. "I have a witness in your own camp."

The king's eyes grew stormy, the winds picking up in the trees nearby. Someone stepped forward.

Veleda.

Cassia's mouth fell open.

"I was there," Veleda confirmed. Her long, dark curls were wilder than usual, her face showing exhaustion. Her eyes flicked to Cassia and away, so fast that Cassia was sure she'd recognized her.

Veleda had been witness to Selkolla's pact with the Dracu

queen? Prickles of reaction covered Cassia's whole body. How could that be?

The king stared down at his Court Seer. "A traitor in my camp?"

"No traitor," Veleda said, her chin raised. "I was in the Cryptlands at the time of the promise Selkolla made to the Dracu queen. I will explain all, Your Majesty. But for now, I speak Sylvan true when I tell you I heard the terms of the vow. It was sworn in blood with all the proper rites to make it binding."

The pact was made in the Cryptlands, so Selkolla would be bound by it more strongly there. But it should apply here, too, especially if this land is declared the queen's.

Cassia looked at Veleda as if seeing her anew, suddenly remembering how easily the Seer had moved through the Cryptlands, as if she knew the way. She wished she had time to question her. But everyone's eyes were on the Sylvan king, awaiting his reaction.

His eyes sharpened, and a cold, pine-scented breeze blew. "Very well. This declaration of sovereignty will last only until the sun rises. But first, you must vow not to harm any Sylvan or anyone who has ever served me."

"Until sunrise, only," the queen added with a cunning smile. "Very well. I agree to your terms. In return for your people's fealty, I vow not to harm any Sylvan or any subject of the Sylvan king until sunrise. Do you all bow to me?"

After a hesitation, the king nodded. A rough chorus of voices spoke as one, as if they had practiced. "We swear fealty to the Dracu queen until sunrise."

The Sylvan king's expression grew somber, and a dark cloud passed over Scarhamm. He towered over the Dracu queen. "I will make you pay if you betray me, Nienke."

323

"Worry your antlered head about the problems before you, Silvanus," the queen said blithely, surveying the fortress with the air of a conqueror.

Before the sun had even fully set, the Sylvan and Dracu forces took their positions behind Scarhamm's walls. Cassia and Zeru stood together atop the watchtower. Cassia could feel the anticipation of the trees, as if the forest knew what was coming and waited with nervous excitement. The two Huntsmen on lookout gave them space, leaning on the railing and talking quietly at the opposite end.

"Well, Sylvan," Zeru said, leaning his arms against the railing next to her, "by some blessing of the Ancients, your plans have gone well. Dare we hope for more? Maybe Selkolla won't be able to strike Scarhamm, and you won't have to initiate stage three." He rubbed his chin, which was darkened by a few days' worth of growth.

Cassia nodded. Everything had gone better than she'd expected. But the Seer had been planning this move for a long time. "If she does come, at least there are more of us fighting together."

"Yes," Zeru agreed. "That alone is almost beyond belief." He turned a look of shining admiration on her that struck straight at her heart. "You did that, Cassia."

She shook her head, uncomfortable with so much credit. "I couldn't have done any of this without you." If it weren't for him, she'd still be hiding in the woods without even a memory of her name. She still hadn't thanked him for coming for her. It seemed too great a thing to express.

"And I have a feeling my sisters have been working on my father. It seemed as if he'd accepted the alliance by the time we arrived." She looked down at the forest, undeceived by its quiet darkness. The trees' restlessness felt like her own. Or maybe the trees knew more about what was to come than she did.

As if sensing the same tension, Zeru turned toward her. "Whatever happens tonight, stay up here on the watchtower where you're safe."

"No," she said with quiet ferocity. "I can't believe you'd even suggest that."

His eyes were serious, his voice full of conviction. "Selkolla wants the ring. If you are down there in the fray, you'll be an easier target. Don't make it easy for her. If she can reach you, you're playing into her hands."

Cassia turned her head to watch the forest, seeing more in the gathering dark than she'd ever thought possible, thanks to her sharper vision. "Even if she did ... I don't think she can control me anymore."

"I don't, either," he said, tucking a lock of hair that had escaped her braid behind her ear. "But we don't know. Don't risk it."

"It's my choice, not yours," she reminded him.

"I know. I'm trying to persuade you, not order you." He brushed his lips across her cheek. "Does this work better?"

"No," she breathed, turning her head so their lips almost touched, "but keep trying."

Footsteps on the ladder made them pull apart. Cassia wasn't surprised when she saw a silver head followed by a dark brown one. Enora and Thea smiled at her, then faced Zeru as if waiting for an introduction.

"Enora. Thea. This is Zeru," Cassia said simply, warning her sisters with her eyes.

"We've met," Enora said, giving him a brief nod.

⁓ 325 ⁓

"Pleased to meet you," Zeru said with a polite, stiff bow.

Thea merely stared at him, her expression telling Cassia that she'd like nothing better than to take the Dracu's head from his shoulders.

"Where's Rozie?" Cassia asked, trying to break the tension.

"Safe in her bedchamber," Enora answered, "probably trying to bargain her way out here to fight with us."

Cassia could easily imagine Rozie traipsing into the garden wearing oversized armor, determined to defend her home with whatever weapon she could lift. "I hope you left someone firm in charge of her."

Enora lifted a brow, amused. "Two of the staunchest guards I could find. They're probably wondering why they were stuck with the toughest post."

Cassia chuckled, taking a moment to examine the garden below. The rustle and murmur of the Sylvans and Dracu forces blended with the forest's evening sounds.

"Won't be long before we know whether we're getting visitors tonight," Thea said, surveying the woods.

As always, Cassia envied her sister's equanimity in such a tense situation. But Thea was right. The waiting was almost over. None of them doubted that Selkolla intended to make her move on this night.

Zeru made a noise, and Cassia turned to see sweat break out on his forehead. Sunset, she realized. Her hand went to his shoulder as he gripped one of the wooden supports, his jaw firming as light swirled at his back. Then his wings formed, black and segmented, the claws looking like curving thorns against the backdrop of the forest behind him. They opened wide, and he shook them out before furling them at his back. His chin lifted, and he gave her staring sisters a raised-brow look.

326

"Well," Enora said dryly. "That's not something you see every day."

"He's not boring," Thea agreed with a nod. "I'll give him that."

Zeru's slow smile made Cassia's heart thump harder. "Glad I could amuse."

As the garden filled with shadows, the fortress faded to a silhouette. Every indrawn breath brought the scents of burned wood and the familiar pine and peat of the forest.

Next to her, Zeru lifted his chin and sniffed the air.

"Cassia," he said in a warning tone.

She put her hand on his arm, staying his speech. She smelled it, too. Rot and decay. One of the hounds barked as a rumble shook the earth. That was all the warning they had before a hundred thorn-clawed hands dug their way up into the garden.

30

> Darkness is an Azpian's home from cradle to grave.
> Let not your guard down after sunset.
> —Excharias, Sylvan poet

Cassia watched as Zeru flew down from the watchtower, using the rebound of his landing to slice off the head of one of the stick creatures. Another came at him, two branches reaching with thornlike fingers. As he severed the wooden arms, another vine lashed around his ankles. He leaped up to avoid its grasp, hacking another in the same motion. Four more scuccas emerged from the ground, covered in soil. With a quick circular motion, he cut branches and vines in a spray of green. After that, Cassia lost count. The creatures kept repairing themselves, and still more emerged from the ground. Selkolla's creatures were attacking Dracu and Sylvan alike, which meant the Seer was defying her vow to the Dracu queen, as Veleda had said she might be able to do outside the Cryptlands. If she was able to do that, it called their whole plan into question. And they were all vulnerable. Including Zeru.

Cassia climbed the railing, poised to fly down to him.

"No!" Enora cried, grabbing her arm. "The Seer wants the ring. She wants you. You have to stay here, Cass!"

But she pulled against her sister's grip. "I'm not going to stand by and watch."

Enora's grip tightened as she stared at the clash of swords and scuccas. "Thea's already gone to throw herself into the fight. I need to be at her back. But I won't leave you unless you agree to stay here."

Cassia's gut twisted as she watched the scuccas close in around Thea's whirling body in the fray below. As Enora hesitated, she saw that Zeru had help, several Dracu soldiers around him. "Fine! I'll stay."

Enora gave her arm a squeeze before dashing to the ladder and disappearing from view.

Cassia watched the battle with an agonizing sense of helplessness. She had always felt separate from the rest of the Sylvan army, but it had never galled her as much as now. She could see everything and do nothing. Her hand twitched. She ripped off the glove to uncover the gemstone and saw that it was shining like a beacon, almost as if it wanted to be used. Something in her responded, an energy coiling inside her. But she'd get one good blast, and then the ring would be depleted. Not to mention the light might incapacitate their Dracu allies.

She ground her teeth together in frustration.

There was no pattern to where the scuccas appeared. They were like some evil crop that sprouted up no matter how many times they were culled. Several Dracu fought at Zeru's side, splitting and hewing the creatures with ruthless efficiency. But after a few minutes, cuts opened on their arms, their blood dripping down. Zeru's wings seemed to be in the way. He wasn't used to them, had never fought with them in close combat. She put a hand to the railing. She hadn't *vowed* to her sister that she'd stay up here. Surely Enora would understand—

Tibald's distinctive voice boomed out, "Move! Clear the center! Make room for the king!"

⌁ 329 ⌁

Cassia's head jerked up, her eyes finding her father as he strode into the yard, felling the creatures with his sword as he went. Her heart caught in her throat as the scuccas swarmed over him, hiding him from view. But several figures moved alongside him—Enora, Thea, and Zeru among them, along with Alof, Tibald, and Burke. Together, they cleared enough room for the king to raise his arms and speak words in some ancient tongue.

The earth shook and rippled, making the scuccas stagger. Soon, the whole area was obscured by a cloud of dust. There were sounds of choking, the tramp of feet as Dracu and Sylvans scrambled to safety at the edge of the yard, and the scuccas' screeching as they fell into the opening in the earth.

When the dust cleared, a great, jagged scar ran from one end of the yard to the other. Fruit trees that once lined the garden paths were skewed, exposing their roots. The king and the small group of his defenders stood on the edge of a chasm.

Inside was Selkolla. He must have sensed her with the help of the trees.

Cassia gasped as she caught the glow from the Seer's eyes, even brighter than she remembered. Those pale hands had held the knife that slid into her heart. For a second, Cassia couldn't move. When she remembered to breathe, the Huntsmen were already moving toward the Seer.

Hope surged in her chest. Selkolla's death would end this.

But a sudden gale blew the king back. The wind lifted leaves and branches into the air, twirling them before slamming them down. In the eye of this storm, Selkolla rose as if carried by the squall. A soil-darkened whirlwind curled beneath her, lifting her to the level of Scarhamm's wall. Her dark robes whipped around her, her pale hair streaming into the sky like a ghostly, colorless flame. Her silver eyes caught the scant light of dusk. The archers fired a volley of arrows, but they bounced off the misty shield that curved around her.

Scuccas emerged from the chasm, pouring from the earth like ants.

The Sylvan king raised his hands, an expression of deep concentration on his face as he created his own wind to battle the Seer's.

The hairs on the back of Cassia's neck lifted as lightning came into the Seer's hands in a flash of white. As the crackling bolts hit him, the king convulsed, staggering on the edge of the scar in the ground he had made. His palms angled outward, he made the fallen trees shake, their exposed roots growing longer, longer, reaching for the Seer. They wrapped around her, cupping her whirlwind like a hundred seeking fingers. A sharp crack echoed over the garden. Soon, more roots lashed over the others.

The Sylvan king was making a cage around Selkolla.

But almost as soon as it had formed, the roots flew apart, raining wooden shards all over the garden. The air crackled as another bolt of lightning slammed into the Sylvan king, this time with a thunderous explosion. The light was blinding, lasting for several seconds before it faded. When Cassia could see again, her father was on his knees.

Her sisters and Zeru were regrouping from the moment of sightlessness, fighting the scuccas, which were still coming.

Cassia looked at the glow of her ring. Step three of her plan was the most uncertain of all. It involved using the light from her ring on the scuccas, giving everything she had. Her theory was that it would harm the scuccas. If she was fortunate, it could destroy them all at once. Or it might only incapacitate them briefly. Worst case, it might do no damage at all. Then their last defense was gone, and they would have to try to survive until morning and regroup. There was no certainty that they could. It was both risky and a long shot. Still, she had to use it. Now.

But before she could act, the Dracu queen appeared on one of the balconies overlooking the garden, her voice carrying over the yard. "Selkolla, I invoke the blood contract! All creatures here, both Dracu and Sylvan, have sworn fealty to me. By the power of your oath, you cannot harm them. Your own blood binds you."

Red light appeared in glowing circles around Selkolla's wrists—mystical shackles binding her to her promise. Selkolla fought them, her eyes glowing with rage.

The Sylvan king was still on his knees, but his voice rose strong. "I cede Scarhamm and its subjects to the Dracu queen of the Cryptlands until sunrise."

The shackles that bound Selkolla brightened, growing thicker and stronger. Zeru looked up, meeting Cassia's eyes, his own eyes shining. The magic was working. The scuccas seemed confused, fighting with less vigor.

Selkolla kept fighting the binding. The red shackles flashed brighter again, and the wind around her weakened and died.

Her shield was gone.

The archers took advantage, loosing a barrage of arrows. Selkolla screamed as blood spread over her gray robes like red ink blotches on parchment. Then she fell into the darkness below her.

A moment of hushed silence followed. The scuccas were disappearing back into the earth. In seconds, only a few sticks and leaves remained to show that they had been there. Did that mean the Seer was dead?

The Sylvan king was the first to rise and move toward the place where Selkolla had been. Zeru, Enora, and Thea followed. Cassia's throat closed, fear and hope warring for space in her chest.

"Silvanus!" Selkolla's voice pierced the quiet. "This isn't over!"

Wind swirled, pulling the king and his daughters to the edge of the opening. Enora's foot slipped. Cassia jumped onto the railing—

But it wasn't Enora who went into the dark. It was a Dracu with wings who hauled Enora back as the Seer's wind caught him, pulling him in. Zeru used his wings to slow his descent, his sword slashing out, but the earth closed over him with a rumble like a slamming door.

Only smooth ground remained where Zeru had been.

Cassia's body jerked as if she'd been hit by one of Selkolla's lightning bolts. Leaping, she flew down from the watchtower, her wings barely slowing her as she crashed onto hard, unforgiving earth. She slammed a fist into the ground, trying to punch her way through.

She turned to her father, who stood with her sisters a few feet away.

"Open the ground!" she cried, her voice breaking. "Let me go after him! Now!"

He stared at her. Did he not recognize her? Though she'd discarded the fake horns long since, she still had powder around her eyes.

"I'm Cassia!" she shouted, so furious at him her voice shook. "Your daughter! The one you banished!"

As some of the creatures gasped, Cassia's eyes were drawn to the Dracu queen as she stood on the balcony, her face a mask of rage. It was clear the queen hadn't guessed that the Azpian of unknown variety from a lower realm was really the Sylvan king's daughter.

"I know who you are," the Sylvan king intoned, drawing her shocked gaze to him. "I knew you in my war room and dressed as you are now. I will always know you."

⌒ 333 ⌒

As she stared into his eyes, a memory came to her, one she must have suppressed with all the others when she had gone into hiding. Her father staring down at her in her new winged form when she hadn't even known her own name. He had said it. *Cassia.* Perhaps, some part of her had known. Had wanted this confrontation, craved it. But none of that mattered now. All that mattered was Zeru.

"Then help me!" Cassia screamed. "Either kill me or help me! Decide!"

"Please, Father," Enora said.

"Her plan may have saved us all," Thea added.

He merely showed his empty palms as if he could give her nothing.

Cassia screamed, the sound echoing against Scarhamm's walls and through the trees. Something in the air changed, a question floating on the wind.

Need need need? the trees of Thirstwood asked.

She turned toward their voices in her mind. The roots felt the passage of the Seer through the soil, a path traced through the woods. *Open the ground! Make me a path to Zeru! Please!*

The roots responded, slowly, slowly at first, and the ground trembled. Then they pulled the earth apart, and Cassia fell, scrambling and grasping, into darkness.

31

> Even more than truth, a Sylvan values freedom above all other things.
> —Excharias, Sylvan poet

Cassia stumbled on the uneven ground, the steady glow from the Solis Gemma lighting her way. The passage was rough and uneven, blasted from the earth in desperate haste. Exposed roots jutted from the walls, and soil slid down, filling the air with choking dust. Large roots made the way narrower, snagging her wings and yanking her off balance. After a while, her knees and palms were scraped raw. As her cuts bled freely, some of the roots twitched toward her, until she was dodging and rolling to avoid them, her wings a disadvantage in the narrow space. The blood trees did not seem to know if she was friend or enemy. One root snagged her, its root hairs grasping her feathers with the strength of determined fingers. With a fierce yank, she ripped free, gasping in pain as feathers were torn from her body in a spray of gold.

She was a mass of aches by the time the passage came to an end. She had the sense she had stepped into a large open space, though the glow from the ring only showed a few feet around her. The scents of herbs and old blood mixed with the tang of soil. She took a step forward, looking down as something crunched beneath her boot. A pile of vines and sticks. No. It was a scucca with twiglike arms laid carefully by its sides. She moved her hand to search the area by the light of the ring. More scucca bodies. Dead? There were no signs of injuries, no cut branches or torn leaves. Not dead. Never alive. Yet.

This had to be the place where Selkolla made her scuccas.

Cassia found her breath locked in her chest. As she took an instinctive step back, a green glow flared, so bright she raised her arm to shield her eyes. Selkolla stood tall among her creations, framed by roots that hung down from above like columns.

"Where's Zeru?" Cassia demanded, her voice hoarse from the choking dirt.

Selkolla picked her way between the bodies, her gray eyes aglow as she came closer. "Welcome to my birthing chamber."

"Your what?" Cassia took another step back.

"The birthplace of my children," Selkolla said, confirming Cassia's belief that the witch's mind was far beyond reason. "Does it matter that they don't come from my own body?"

Cassia choked on bile. "This place is grotesque. A place where spirits are forced into prisons of sticks and vines. Where is Zeru?"

Selkolla tsked. "Honesty is no virtue when it comes with the bite of contempt." She put a hand to her heart. "Do you have no care for the feelings of a fellow Sylvan?"

Cassia made a sound in her throat, anger building in her chest at the way the Seer toyed with her. "I don't care what you are. Where is he?"

Selkolla waved a hand, and the green light extended farther into the cavernous space. About twenty feet away, a glow came from a cage made of violet bands of light. The bars pulsed as if in time to a heartbeat, emitting a rhythmic hum. Zeru's figure lay on his side, a dark wing half-covering him.

Cassia took a step closer to the cage, reaching for him. A

crackle of energy leaped out, flowing into her outstretched fingers and up her arm, flinging her back as her veins filled with fire. She cried out as she hit the wall behind her, her wings taking the brunt of the collision. Pain zinged through her shoulders and up her neck, blending with the ache in her head. She fought to her feet and blinked to clear the dizziness.

Her eyes snapped to Zeru as if tethered to him. He hadn't moved, not even at her cry of pain. Seeing him limp and lifeless hit her like a blow, a gut punch of grief that reverberated through her body. She had lost so much. Her home. A future with her family. Her place in the world. She couldn't imagine losing him, too. Surely Noctua would not take his spirit when she needed him most.

"Zeru." A hoarse plea that scraped her throat. *Please. Don't leave me.*

From the corner of her eye, she saw Selkolla's face split into a wide smile, as if this were a performance she enjoyed.

A fiery ball of hatred ignited in Cassia's gut. Power built in the ring, making it flare like a bonfire fed with fresh, dry kindling. As the power built, Cassia saw red filaments appear in the air. Lines of red light that led from Selkolla to each one of the scucca bodies. She sucked in a breath, confused. Could those be the bonds that connected the Seer to her creations?

Selkolla's silvery eyes shone knowingly. "Your ring will not hurt me, daughter of the Sylvan king."

Cassia choked out a pained laugh. "Maybe not. But your 'children' like to stay close to you, don't they? I'd like to know what the Solis Gemma does to them." There had to be a reason Selkolla was so anxious to make Cassia into one of her thralls. "I'll make sure the blast is large enough to catch every single one."

Selkolla's smile gained a hard edge. "The moment you do that, Zeru dies."

Despite the threat, the horrible tightness in Cassia's chest eased. That meant Zeru was alive.

She glared at the cage, longing to smash the bars that kept him from her. "Is he injured?"

"Sleeping," Selkolla said with indifference.

"That's no natural sleep." Cassia watched the barely perceptible movement of his chest. "He's under your spell."

"And you are under his," the Seer replied. "Even banishment has not deterred you, it seems. I knew you would come for him."

Despite the pain of that reminder, Cassia refused to spare a single regret for her father now, not when Zeru's life hung by a delicate thread. Zeru, who saw her true nature. Who had tried to get her to accept it, even if it meant losing his opportunity to retrieve the ring and redeem himself. He had seen their connection when she'd still been denying it, offering himself to her in little ways, finding her when she was lost, helping her remember—even though he'd known he might lose her. Her heart contracted as she thought of the way he'd looked at her in the woods, in the stream, when they'd kissed. The way he'd gripped her in his arms in the Cryptlands, as if he wanted to hold on to her forever. The way he'd risked himself by coming into her home, the fortress of his enemies. How he'd trusted her enough to try her risky plans. How he'd helped her protect her people. How he'd risked himself to save Enora.

But what she was feeling was more than gratitude. She felt *right* with him. She was . . . herself with him in a way that was freeing. She wanted him, and she wanted to be with him. She knew it now more than she ever had before, as an ache in her chest and in her throat and behind her eyes. The urgent need to protect him was like a living thing inside her demanding action.

"I always find him." Cassia willed him to hear her words, to wake, to smile at the reminder of what he'd said to her as a child. "How did you know he meant something to me?"

"The moment before I drove the blade into your heart," Selkolla said, "you called for him with what should have been your last breath."

Cassia bit her tongue until she tasted copper. She hadn't realized she'd managed to say Zeru's name aloud. That revealing slip might cost him his life. "What's the point of this, Selkolla? You told us you can't take the ring by force. Do you think I'm just going to give it to you?"

Selkolla smiled. "I don't want it anymore. I've come to realize the ring's sun magic isn't compatible with my own. It's *you* I need."

Cassia swallowed. "You already failed to make me into one of your so-called children. I resisted your orders even when I didn't know who I was. What makes you think you can control me now?"

Selkolla looked down at her from her great height, but it was her expression that conveyed her belief that Cassia should feel small. "You give yourself too much credit. It was the Solis Gemma I underestimated. If the spell had gone as planned, you would have been what you were meant to be, a being of the forest, accepting your lot without question. But the ring chose to protect you. Its power gave you wings, and turned you into the thing you are now. Something the world has never yet seen. A Sylvan Zerian."

Selkolla meant to cut with her words, but instead, Cassia felt a rush of strength remembering the ring had truly bonded with her. It had found her worthy. It had kept her mind and spirit intact.

There was more to it, though, that Selkolla was denying. Even if the ring protected Cassia, she had *still* known herself enough to defy the order to kill her father or harm any of the Huntsmen, despite Selkolla taking her memory.

⌒ 339 ⌒

"The ring may have protected me," she said, her chin lifting, "but I was the one who defied you."

Selkolla's tone carried the bite of a north wind. "Defy me now and Zeru dies."

Cassia closed her eyes. She was cornered and Selkolla knew it. She could not risk Zeru. "What do you want?"

"A simple bargain," the Seer said. "I will allow your Dracu to live if you bring my scuccas back to life in truth."

Cassia let out a long breath. Selkolla wanted the impossible.

"Once you fulfill your side of the bargain, you will be given every consideration. The best chamber in Scarhamm. The queen's apartments in the Cryptlands. All of Welkincaster."

Each of these options appeared like a dream in Cassia's mind, full of color and detail. The final image was of herself and Zeru embracing in front of the castle on a cloud. As if that was all she cared about. The Seer was so wrong about her.

"You're planning to take everything, then?" she asked, marveling at the Seer's ambition. "Scarhamm, the Cryptlands, even the clouds?"

Selkolla dipped her chin. "Never again will I trust the world to be kind to my moss children simply because they are gentle. I will eliminate every possible threat and make the world safe."

"Safe," Cassia said, her fists tightening, "and under your control?"

"Precisely." She gestured down to Zeru. "But I would let him live as a guardian of Welkincaster. He would not be free to leave, but he would be yours."

Cassia stared down at Zeru's still form. If she agreed, he would be safe. Safe and trapped while the world died around them. Because Selkolla saw no value in the living unless they were controlled by her.

"We would be a formidable pair, you and I," Selkolla went on. As she spoke, tendrils of persuasion stole into Cassia's mind like seeking fingers. The perfect full moon promising peace and harmony if she would only surrender her will. Selkolla's magic inviting her to obey, like the moon pulling the tides. "You have the magic of the woods. You have the power of the Solis Gemma. And I have the knowledge of the Ancients and the potential to regain my former status. You could help me, and I would reward you."

A part of Cassia wanted to harken to that inner whisper, to give in rather than face the messiness of her own choices, her own mistakes. A small part. She would rather die than live as a creature without free will. She pushed at the seeking fingers, imagining a mental barrier as strong as the walls of Scarhamm.

"Would you let my father and sisters live?"

She saw the answer in Selkolla's eyes.

"Why do you persist with this misplaced loyalty to your father?" the witch asked in a tone of genuine curiosity. "You've spent your life striving to be the ideal daughter, hurting yourself in your efforts, trying and failing to gain his love. And he banished you for not wanting to take revenge as he would. When will you admit your devotion is foolish?"

Cassia waited for the expected sense of shame at the blunt listing of her failures. Instead, she felt a kind of relieved acceptance. Nothing she had ever done had made her father love her. So she was free to stop trying.

"If I've loved foolishly," she said, "at least I was able to love." Her father, she realized, could never feel as strongly as she did. About anyone. Even her mother's disappearance had barely seemed to affect him. Another thought she'd kept hidden from herself for too long.

"What does love bring but pain?" Selkolla scoffed. "I loved

my moss folk and lost them. I have suffered longer than you can imagine. My new children have not replaced them in my heart." Her voice tightened with pain. "They don't...they can't love me back."

"And yet you want to remake them," Cassia pointed out.

"Because you will make them whole again," Selkolla said. "Let me show you what he took from me."

In her mind, Cassia saw groups of wood folk, creatures that looked like they came from the forest, with bark-like skin and greenish-gray eyes. They played in the sunlight, cavorting among the trees, raising their small faces to the sun. A series of memories came in rapid succession, and feelings came with it. There were moss folk in a twilit glade, dancing arm in arm with Sylvans, raising their hands to catch tiny moon sprites on their fingers, opening their mouths to laugh with a sound like rustling leaves. And the trees loved them. Cassia felt that. She felt the warmth of joy, the affection Selkolla had for these gentle beings, the way they made her feel young again after far too many eons in this world. For a second, Cassia wondered if Selkolla could be an Ancient herself, but the images changed, snagging her attention. The moss folk had grown shy, peeking out from behind the trunks of trees, less willing to come into the sunlight as the forest changed, as a darkness spread over it. Some of the trees were red now. Blood trees. Finally, there were images of the blood trees preying on moss folk, dragging them down with hungry roots.

"No!" Cassia didn't realize she had cried out until the images abruptly stopped. "No. No. My father ordered the trees not to harm any Sylvan." She wished she could believe those mental images were a lie. "That includes all forest-dwellers. His edict should have protected your moss children."

"Hungry spirits and thrall magic require blood, and he chose the blood of the weakest folk in the forest. He sacrificed them for the spell to work. Ask him yourself."

Cassia bent her head. She believed Selkolla. She couldn't even bring herself to point out that the witch was using thrall magic as well. Her father was...a monster. He was the strongest creature of the forest, stronger in might and magic than any in Thirstwood or the Cryptlands. Stronger, certainly, than any Sylvan. But there was a different kind of strength. A strength of spirit. Of conviction. And there, she had strength, too. She was the one with the will to wield the artifact of the Ancients. She had bent, she had tried to be something she wasn't to please her father, but she hadn't broken. She hadn't become his Deathringer. She hadn't become like him. Now, finally, she was glad of it.

Loathing made her heart thrum unevenly, her breath coming in short bursts. Her hand trembled, the ring filling with power. For a few moments, her anger was directed not at Selkolla, not at the scuccas, but at the king of Scarhamm. Her mental walls buckled, her emotions too wild to control. The seeking fingers in her mind gained purchase, sliding into her thoughts, riffling through her memories like thieves.

"Get out of my head, witch!" Cassia shouted, turning her attention back to resisting.

Selkolla laughed. "Call me 'witch,' then. You are not the first."

Cassia shook her head to clear it. "It won't work. The spirits of your moss children are in the Netherwhere. The spirits you've summoned are not them. They won't ever be like the ones you lost."

Selkolla's eyes hardened. "I vowed that I would bring them back to life. A vow to Noctua. I have no choice." The shadow of her long-fingered hand fell over Zeru, and a crackling filled the air. "Do you need to watch him die? Decide now, daughter of the Sylvan king."

"You can't hurt him," Cassia said, putting herself between them. "By your own vow. He's still a subject of the Dracu queen."

Selkolla gave her a pitying look. "When Zeru became a guardian of Welkincaster, he became a Zerian. His loyalty was divided, and divided again when he allowed himself to love a Sylvan. Not just any Sylvan but the Deathringer. One of the greatest enemies to the Dracu. That makes his loyalty to his queen uncertain. Uncertain enough that I should be able to kill him. Shall I test my theory?" The ball of sparks grew in her palm.

Cassia sucked in a breath. There was no time for second guessing. She had to trust each decision as it came. "No. Wait. I'll... I'll try. I agree to your terms. I accept your bargain, Selkolla." As the sparks on the witch's fingers died, she could breathe again. She looked at the bodies of the scuccas, uncertain what Selkolla expected her to do.

As green lights floated in the room, she understood. "Are those the spirits you've summoned?" Her voice sounded thin, the knowledge that Zeru's life depended on her success making her stomach clench with dread.

"I need only merge these spirits with these bodies, and then you can begin your work," Selkolla said, her voice confident now. "Await my instructions."

As the witch chanted, the green lights spread out in the massive room, illuminating it. The cavern was much larger than she'd thought. So many bodies. There had to be hundreds. Thousands? Selkolla must have been planning this for years upon years. It was unthinkable. And each scucca had a thread of light attaching it to the Seer. When Cassia concentrated, she could see them.

Suddenly, the sticks began to move, some of the vines twisting into the air. Cassia swallowed, her stomach heaving at the

344

thought of what she had to do. This was the only way to save Zeru. But at what cost? Would these scuccas be even stronger because of her? Harder to defeat?

Then, the scucca body next to her sent a questioning thought into her mind. *Alive?* it asked.

Cassia stared down at it, shocked. She could sense its mind the same way she had learned to sense the thoughts of the trees. In her time in the woods after Selkolla took her memory, she had spent whole days listening. These moss children, ill-made as they were, were of the forest. They were more like plants than people, perhaps. She opened her mind to them, safe for the moment from Selkolla, who was distracted by the spell she continued to chant, sending more spirits into more of the constructed bodies.

The messages from the scuccas rushed in on Cassia so fast that she put her hands over her ears as if she could block them out like sound. But the images and thoughts kept coming, piling on one another.

They were not all the same. Some spirits were friendly, gentle. Some were spirits of the dead that had lived long and did not want to return to the living world. Others were spirits that were never meant for the living world. Dark spirits of the Netherwhere with dark thoughts, their forms as changeable as smoke, not quite contained by the scucca bodies. These spirits longed to cause havoc among the living. They yearned for it and would follow whoever was most brutal to achieve it. Cassia tried to sort out the different types, to shake off the chill of horror that such malevolent spirits had been pulled into this world. She tried to focus, to sort through it all, and come up with a plan. But their thoughts overwhelmed her.

Whatever their origin, none of them deserved to be shackled to Selkolla. To anyone.

345

"Now," Selkolla said harshly. "Body and spirit are one. Give them life, and I will reward you."

Cassia was only half listening, attuned as she was to the spirits. Some of them *were* moss folk. She focused on their memories as a guide. Closing her eyes, she used the images and her will to shape, shape, grow. The same skills she'd used on Welkincaster, imagining life and health back into the plants. She imagined these moss folk as they once were, beings of the forest.

Selkolla's gasp made her open her eyes. "It's working," the Seer said, her voice hoarse with emotion. "I knew it."

Cassia watched as the ring's light, a gentle flow of energy, worked on the scuccas, raising them to their feet, their stick arms becoming rounder, more like people than constructions. Their eyes shone with intelligence instead of blankness. Selkolla seemed to be barely paying attention to her now. She was too drunk on the joy of seeing her children again.

Cassia continued, feeding life and health into each of them, both the true moss folk and the scuccas filled with dark spirits, pulling from her own energy to keep the flow steady, so much that her own body started to feel the effects. Her mouth became parched. Her lips cracked with dryness. Her pulse, which had been racing, started to slow.

"Enough," Selkolla barked, somehow aware of how much magic Cassia could bear to use. "Enough for now."

Cassia stumbled as she stopped the flow of magic, righting herself with effort. The Seer was riveted by the moss children. Cassia wasn't sure if these creatures were true moss folk, or if she'd made them look similar enough to fool the Seer. But she could read through her bond with the forest that their hearts were pure, their spirits gentle, their thoughts full of gratitude for being given life. They recognized Selkolla. They loved her, and she reveled in it. A genuine smile transformed her face as she embraced them one by one. She was beautiful, Cassia realized, her mind dazed with exhaustion.

With that, she turned to face the cage that held Zeru. Tentatively, she moved closer, her eyes roving over him with the attentiveness of longing, etching every detail into her mind. His lean face, the hollows beneath his cheekbones, his sharply made nose, his dark lashes lying against his cheeks like sable fans. She wished she could see his eyes one last time. Selkolla had sworn not to harm him. No matter what happened to her, he would be safe. What she planned to try next might cost her her life, but he would be safe.

"Thank you, Zeru," she said, her voice nearly inaudible with the tears that were choking her. "For helping me see who I really am, even as I fought it. Fought you. Thank you for . . . everything. I wish . . ." She shook her head, the pain in her chest too sharp to continue.

His eyelashes fluttered, and for a moment she thought he might open his eyes. But the lashes settled back against his cheeks, and his breathing steadied once more. Her lips trembled, but she forced herself to take a breath and do what she'd decided to do.

Gutel had explained that the Solis Gemma gave life, but a surfeit of life force would kill. If she pushed the energy of the Solis Gemma into the bonds between the Seer and her creatures, would they break?

She had given Selkolla's creatures as much life and energy as she could, trying her best to give them awareness. She had restored the few moss folk spirits, making their bodies into moss folk again—or as best as she was able. She had kept her part of the bargain.

Now, she had to be true to herself. Growth was not only a physical thing, but went soul-deep. You couldn't grow unless you had the freedom to do so. She had to free the spirits. *You can choose,* she said, speaking to all the creatures in her mind. *Your spirit can stay or leave. If you want to return from where you came, go!*

With that, she used the rest of her energy, all the magic she could summon from the ring, pulling it as harshly as she had when trying to please her father, when trying to be the Deathringer he expected. But now she did it to help rather than harm. She concentrated on the red filaments of light running between Selkolla and the spirits in the cavern. The Solis Gemma hummed, light crackling as it spread, the color changing to a warmer yellow, then orange.

The filaments that kept the scuccas bound to Selkolla wavered and pulsed. "Be free!" she cried.

As the filaments snapped, a tumult of rustling rose all around the cavern. Some of spirits left the bodies immediately, visible as green lights floating into the walls and out of sight, leaving their empty bodies in woody heaps. Other creatures moved with confused steps, walking in circles as if they didn't know what to do with this freedom. The dozen or so moss folk looked around with wide, solemn eyes, their hands grasping at Selkolla's robes as they murmured in their leaf-rustle voices.

Selkolla's hands went to her chest as if she felt the bonds snapping as a physical thing. When she caught her breath, her silvery eyes were pale with fury. "What have you done?"

32

> Those who break a vow to Noctua
> forfeit life and spirit to her.
> —Excharias, Sylvan poet

Cassia watched Selkolla, a sense of calm flowing into her. For so long, she'd been terrified of making the wrong choices, not living up to expectations, earning disapproval. This choice was so much more dangerous—it might end her life. And yet, she didn't regret it. Everything had led her here: her failure to be what her father wanted, the ring bonding with her, her time with Zeru. Zeru who believed she was worthy if she was herself.

Her inner voice told her that life was nothing without freedom. Without choices. The scuccas needed freedom to have a chance to truly grow. Perhaps they would become like the moss folk that had once roamed the earth. Maybe they would end up being a scourge that the Sylvans would have to deal with. But she had given them the chance to choose, for good or ill. As lightning crackled and grew in the Seer's palms, Cassia was scared, but she didn't doubt herself. She met the eyes that shone like drops of heated metal. Her calm defiance only seemed to enrage the Seer further.

"I made no vow not to harm you," Selkolla rasped, her face twisted with hatred, her voice unrecognizable in its harshness. "You dare to sever the bond with my spirits? Then follow them, Silvanus's daughter. Follow them into the Netherwhere!"

As lightning crackled, ready to strike, the hum of the forest moved through Cassia. If she was fortunate when she died, her spirit would reside in the forest itself, inhabiting one of the trees until one day when it was felled, and her spirit would go to the Netherwhere. Maybe she would finally find her own tree.

But the forest wasn't ready to accept her spirit yet. It felt her need, and she felt its response. Roots creaked to life, reaching down from the ceiling and moving toward Selkolla. The Seer gasped as one wrapped around her arm, yanking it back. The sparks in her hand shot toward the wall, dispersing harmlessly on the soil. Selkolla spoke words in an ancient tongue, issuing her own commands, trying to control the forest.

Pain exploded in Cassia's temples, the force of her will pitted against Selkolla's. Cassia attuned to Thirstwood, leaning into her own connection to the trees.

The Seer was ancient. Powerful. She might have been speaking to the trees, stealing their life force for her scuccas, since the forest was nothing but seeds in soil. What chance did a young Sylvan have against her?

But Cassia refused to die without a fight. Her sisters might not know what happened to her, but if ever the story was somehow told . . . she wanted it to be that she fought until the end. That she'd tried to protect Scarhamm and the land folk.

Expanding her awareness, she focused her will, speaking to the trees. *Grab her! Hold her!* The roots came down from the ceiling once again, swirling like tentacles, converging on Selkolla, wrapping around her in a wooden fist.

The Seer chanted rapid words in a ringing voice, this time calling her scuccas. Some of the creatures fled. Others rushed toward Cassia, baring their thorny teeth.

The moss folk who were huddled around Selkolla opened

their eyes wide. They spoke to her urgently in their strange tongue that sounded like the whisper of a breeze among leaves. Cassia understood their meaning well enough. They were asking her to stop, to let the Sylvan go. To free the spirits. To start anew with them.

Aren't we enough? they asked. *We are enough. Peace, Mother.*

"Listen to them," Cassia said, raising her voice over the scuttle of creatures who approached on all sides. "These moss folk spirits are too peaceful to fight. And half of your scuccas have left you already. More will leave when they see you don't have the power you used to wield. You can't win by force. Not now."

"Curse you to the deepest pit of the abysmal depths," Selkolla swore, spittle leaving her mouth in a spray of rage. Lightning crackled around her. "I will kill you if it takes everything to do it."

"Do you even care about them?" Cassia challenged, furious at the way the Seer was throwing away her dearly bought second chance. She'd claimed to love her moss folk, and some of these spirits were real moss folk—ones she must have known in the past. But she hardly seemed grateful. Cassia's chest tightened painfully. She had never been enough for her father, either. "That is what you said you wanted. A second chance with your children! Is it them you love? Or is it power?"

"Be silent," Selkolla hissed, the lightning growing around her as if she were a storm cloud about to light the darkness on fire. "My future was clear. Safety in power. These moss children are few in number. Not enough to restore what was lost. Not nearly enough! You broke your side of the bargain. You cheated me."

Cassia laughed. Though Selkolla had all the power in this moment, she was desperately grasping at straws. "Noctua herself knows I didn't. I gave everything I had. When I might have died of it, you told me to stop. Because you want to save my Deathringer power for your other plans. But I will never use that power to kill again." She took a shuddering breath. "The forest sides with me. The moss folk are begging you to stop. Choose them, Selkolla. Choose peace. And begin again."

"The forest does not side with you!" Selkolla's face was lit yellow-white with the crackle of energy around her. "Your father subjugated it long ago by trickery. One day, I'll take that from him, too. After I kill every one of his daughters."

Cassia's voice turned brittle as ice. "Threatening my sisters is a mistake. Unlike you, I'd do anything to protect the people I love."

The Seer's face twisted with loathing. "Kill the Sylvan king's daughter!"

Cassia watched as the army converged on her. She was out of energy, out of life force. Out of ideas.

She looked down and saw that Zeru was still asleep. But the cage was gone. It must have been destroyed with her blast. She crouched next to him, determined to protect him if there was even a tiny hope.

The scuccas closed in, crashing against her, their thorns slicing into her skin, into her wings as they covered Zeru. She couldn't see anything but dirt and the whipping of vines, and a hundred thornlike fingers.

"Protect us!" she called to the trees.

The roots twitched to life and began sliding between Cassia and the scuccas, pushing them back. More roots followed, weaving together as the creatures writhed against them. The scuccas thrust their branches into cracks and contorted their bodies to squeeze through. Cassia drew her dagger and stabbed at their hands, but there were too many, slashing and clawing at her.

"Break through!" Selkolla commanded in a terrible shrieking voice. "Kill her!"

The creatures bit and clawed at the wood, hacking it into chunks that they threw or spit onto the ground. They were a sea of vines and leaves and moss. The air was thick and choking with the scent of rotting leaves.

But the lattice of roots proved too thick for the creatures. Through a small crack, Cassia watched Selkolla's cheeks stain red with fury.

"Stand back, my children," the Seer commanded, her voice so low, so dark, it was barely audible. "I will do this myself."

The scuccas fled as lightning flared brighter than the sun.

As the blast hit, everything went white. At that moment, Cassia felt strong arms around her. Leathery wings enveloped her. Soft lips met her cheek. A strange pulsing energy covered her, not unlike the waterfall feeling of stepping through the portal into Welkincaster. As the lightning grazed her, it burned her arms, her forehead. She smelled her own hair burning. And the burning of wood.

But she was alive.

When she opened her eyes, the tree roots were blackened and shredded. Zeru was wrapped around her. Slowly, slowly, his weight eased onto hers. She caught him, tried to hold him up. Called his name. But he was too heavy. She found herself on the ground with him, cradled in his arms.

"What did you do?" she asked, though it didn't sound like her voice, high and thin as it was.

"Protected you," Zeru whispered, his eyes half opening to stare into hers. "My job as guardian. Amulet. I can create protection. For you."

Comprehension came slowly. He had never told her the amulet had a protective side, like the ring. Gutel must have told him. But he'd used it...for her? Her heart wanted to shrivel, wanted to cease beating. If he had saved her at his own expense...

"What about you?" she cried, gripping his shoulder. Shaking. "Did it protect you?"

His eyes fluttered closed, the sable fans resting against his cheeks.

Time stopped. Cassia's breath locked in her chest. His breaths no longer brushed her cheek. "Zeru!"

Her eyes, looking around wildly, met glowing gray. Selkolla was leaning over her, grasping one of the blackened roots, her eyes lit with hatred.

"You broke your vow." Cassia spoke the words, knew their truth, and watched as understanding dawned on Selkolla's face. "You broke your vow not to harm him. I kept my part of the bargain. You didn't. Noctua knows it."

"No." The Seer stepped back. Blinked. Shook her head.

"Yes." Cassia spat the word, clutching Zeru to her chest. "You broke a vow to an Ancient."

The trees sent a torrent of meaning cascading into Cassia's mind. Selkolla had taken too much of their life force for her scuccas. She took and never gave back, drained but never replenished. What the trees wanted now was the life force she'd stolen, which flowed in her blood and in her creatures. Only her Sylvan heritage had protected her from the vengeful forest.

Cassia clenched her hands, speaking to the trees as her father did. Attuning to them, she put all her energy into her connection to the forest. The moment she sensed she had their full attention, she spoke. "This Seer is no longer protected by the Sylvans. Take what is due to you. Take back what's yours."

Cassia felt a shift as the forest listened to her. But another power also hummed in the air, something older, vaster, and wilder than Cassia or even the forest. She had the idea that a greater entity was there with her. The Seer fell to the ground, her shields gone, as if Noctua herself had removed the last barrier that protected her. It was said that if you broke a vow to Noctua, the vengeance would be swift. It was terrifying to see the truth of it.

The root tips whipped out like arrows aimed at Selkolla. Cassia covered her ears against the screams. Branches snapped and soil fell in chunks. Dirt and rocks cascaded down, filling the air with dust.

When the screaming stopped, Cassia opened her eyes. The Seer's robes were shredded to rags, blood making the dirt shine. As she watched, the blood disappeared, pulled into the ground. Satiated, the roots retracted back into the ceiling. Cassia took a shuddering breath.

Then she flung herself over Zeru, her ring hand on his chest. "Live!" she cried, putting the palm of her ring hand over his heart. She poured every bit of life and growth and healing into him, all the energy she could gather inside of herself. What little she had left. Her chest ached, her eyes filled with tears, and for a second, she wondered—if she gave him all the life force she had, would it be enough to save him? "Live, Dracu," she begged. "Please. Please, Zeru."

And because she didn't know what else to do, she put the ring to the amulet he wore around his neck.

33

Never trust a Dracu, but especially never trust their queen.
—EXCHARIAS, SYLVAN POET

AFTER THE DARKNESS UNDERGROUND, THE BRIGHT moonlight above Welkincaster was blinding. Zeru still lay on his back, Cassia half on top of him, his wings crushed beneath. But now they were in the courtyard where citrus trees grew in clay pots all around. A few were broken, the shards littering the flagstones.

"What in the nine realms of the Netherwhere are you doing?" a voice shrieked. "You broke two...no three...of my pots!"

Cassia put her face against Zeru's chest, tears streaming from her eyes. "Gutel! We need help!"

Gutel rushed forward, his hands coming to Zeru's neck. "He's alive. He's alive, but just barely. I don't know...Give him some of your power. Do you have any left?"

Though her heart ached as if it were tearing itself in two, Cassia nodded. Breathing shakily, she sent Zeru everything she could summon from herself. Her own strength was waning, but the ring was more powerful on Welkincaster. If the magic of the Ancients lent her strength, and she gave him everything she had, maybe it would be enough.

When his pulse continued to slow. She gave him more. More.

The power was leaving her body, her life force rushing away. Her eyelids grew heavy. Her pulse slowed. But Zeru's life meant more to her than anyone's, and she would do what she must to save it. "Live," she whispered, her eyes falling shut.

For a time, she floated, flying through a dream. She saw a door made of light, like the one to Welkincaster but brighter. Was it a dream or another place where spirits roamed? She realized she was being given a choice. Much like the choice she had given to the spirits, she could stay or go.

"Sylvan, Sylvan," she heard a voice call from very far away. "Come back. Please come back."

Cassia made her choice. Pain returned to her body as she battled the distance, fighting her way back to him. When she finally managed to open her eyes, Zeru was propped against the wall, crushing her to him, stark fear in his eyes as he stared down at her.

She threw her arms around him and felt his shuddering chuckle. "I thought you were dead," she accused.

"I was worried about *you*," Zeru said hoarsely. "Worried you gave me too much." But then he smiled so wide, it made her head spin. Cassia turned her body toward him, burrowing into him like a small animal seeking shelter. His face was pale, his eyes standing out even brighter than usual, and his skin was covered with dirt and blood. But he was alive.

She wanted to devour him.

But Gutel would not be ignored. "What happened? It seems you've both been in a great deal of trouble, and I want to know everything."

As they gave a brief version of events, the kobold looked increasingly horrified.

"You should have said something," Gutel chastised, pacing in front of them while rubbing his forehead, putting creases in his green hat. "You should have yelled, '*Help!*' as you arrived. I had no idea what you'd been through. The Seer, her creatures." He shook his head. "I guess I don't mind a few broken pots. Are you back to stay?"

She shook her head, the movement making her dizzy. "I have to go to Scarhamm to make sure everyone is safe. Zeru can stay here to recover."

"No," Zeru said, his dark eyebrows gathering like thunderclouds. "If there's any chance the queen is testing the boundaries of her vow, I want to be there to reason with her."

Cassia grimaced. "I'm worried, too."

Thoughts fled as her eyes caught a pointy copper-brown muzzle poking through the arched door in the wall, followed by a pair of golden eyes and large brown ears that twitched. Cassia's lips parted, her breath catching. It couldn't be. It had to be a different Vozarra. She was a fool to hope.

"Oh, right, your Vozarra showed up a few days ago," Gutel said absently. "I think it's that one you call Voz, though I told you not to name it." He shook his head. "It came back in rough shape, even for a spirit. I've been nursing it back to health."

Pushing up onto her knees, Cassia threw her arms around the kobold, making him squeak in protest. "Thank you, Gutel. Oh, Magnificent Hearth-Spirit, Generous Fixer of the Broken, Great Healer of Modest Proportions..." She took a shaky breath. "I'm sorry, I'm not very good at this, but I'll give you a hundred titles, I promise."

"What...what..." Gutel's arms flailed. "Unhand me, Sylvan! Zerian! Lady! Don't make me do violence against a steward. I can't breathe!"

"I'm sorry." Cassia wiped her eyes and pulled back, turning her head to the side to catch another glimpse of the winged fox.

"Oh, Voz, you are beautiful. The most beautiful creature in the world."

"Hey," Zeru said, amused and annoyed at once.

Cassia grinned at him. "Second most."

"I do like 'Magnificent,'" Gutel said, dusting off his green jacket. "We'll work on the rest."

"How?" She turned shining eyes on him as Voz approached, butting her soft, furry head into Cassia's hand, making tears spring to her eyes. "How did she come to be here? I watched her die."

Gutel wrinkled his nose, removing his hat and scratching his head. "She may never be able to materialize in the living world again," he said. "But this is a place of spirits. Welkincaster has its own rules. Haven't you figured that out yet?"

Overcome by relief, Cassia grabbed Voz around her torso, careful of her wings, holding on until the fox sent her a clear thought: *Let me go.* She laughed and released the Vozarra. "Fine, fine, no one wants me to maul them, I guess."

Zeru cleared his throat. "At your service. I just need a few minutes to recover. It feels like I was struck by lightning."

Cassia sat back so she could look at him. "I can't believe you did that."

"Can't you?" He lifted a brow. "I knew the amulet would absorb some of the blast."

"But did you realize it would be too much and you'd get hit with the rest?"

She bit her lip. "You shouldn't have risked your life for me."

"I'm a guardian. You're the steward. There was no question."

"Is that why you did it?" she asked.

He looked away for a minute, and she realized he wasn't going to answer. Maybe he saw her disappointment. His fingers came to

⌣ 359 ⌣

her chin, lifting her face. His eyes were sun-warmed emeralds as he said, "I heard you say you always find me."

She swallowed. "I wasn't lying."

Gutel jammed his hat back on his head, looking like a grumpy green toadstool. "Well, this has been enough excitement. I'm going to find myself some cider and watch the sun rise."

Cassia sucked in a breath. "Sunrise. We need to get back to make sure the queen leaves Scarhamm as promised."

Zeru grasped her chin. "First things first." He bent his head and kissed her hard, a bruising brand that said things without words.

When they stepped from the portal near the gates of Scarhamm, it was clear the Dracu queen had been busy. Dracu soldiers manned the battlements and guarded the gates.

Not a Sylvan in view.

"Exactly as I feared," Zeru muttered grimly. The sun hadn't yet risen, so the Sylvans were still pledged to the Dracu queen. Apparently, she was enjoying her sovereignty while it lasted.

"My sisters," Cassia said, agitated almost to panic.

"Don't worry, we'll reason with her," Zeru said, but that didn't calm her fears.

They found the Dracu queen holding court from her perch on the Sylvan king's throne, her feet dangling off the edge as she spoke to her ministers.

Veleda sat in the Court Seer's seat, a place she generally avoided. Cassia looked at her with a questioning glance, but she merely shook her head slightly as if to say, *not now*. Whatever the reason, Cassia was sure the Court Seer had been given no choice in the matter.

Zeru elbowed his way to the front of the throng, pulling

Cassia with him. "You seem in good humor, my queen. Do you not care to find out the fate of Selkolla? She is dead. Thanks to the Sylvan king's daughter."

The queen's eyes showed relief that turned quickly to anger. "You lied to me. You told me the girl was from the lower realms. You, disloyal wretch, brought the Sylvan king's daughter into my throne room. I should order you hanged."

Zeru inclined his head as if in admission. "I'm sorry for the deception, my queen. I needed her to help me secure the alliance that allowed us to prevail over Selkolla. I should have trusted you with the truth."

"Yes, you should have." After a moment of murderous glaring, her eyes glittered with mirth. "But if you'd done that, I might have gutted her, and she wouldn't have been able to use the Solis Gemma to kill the traitorous Seer." She motioned to his wings, a slight wrinkle on her brow. "Is this some trend brought up from the lower realms?"

Zeru rolled his shoulders. "They're...new." He ignored the chortle of one of the courtiers. "I'll explain all, my queen. First, we need to know where you've put the Sylvan king's daughters."

"All I require is the return of the Solis Gemma," the Dracu queen demanded, her eyes fixed on Cassia. "You have used it to kill my people. If you have used it to save us as well, I will take that into consideration. The Sylvans and Dracu were able to ally for one night. Perhaps a longer peace will follow. But only if you return the ring immediately. I cannot have this weapon in Sylvan hands."

In the tense pause that followed, Cassia's heart seemed to shrink in her chest. She wanted peace above all things. But the ring was part of her. She turned to Zeru and thought he understood what she was silently asking. *Do you want me to give you the*

~ 361 ~

ring? She was certain she could. They had a bond. She trusted him. More than that, she thought he would be a good steward to Welkincaster. He deserved the ring.

But Zeru shook his head, a ferocious certainty in his expression as he stepped in front of her. "The Solis Gemma has bonded with the Sylvan King's daughter. It can't be removed. It belongs to Cassia for life."

As the queen's nostrils flared, Veleda spoke, reminding Cassia that she had been silently following all this. "Queen Nienke, I don't believe Cassia will use it to harm your people ever again. I know you have little reason to trust the Court Seer of Scarhamm, but I'm truthful and I'm rarely wrong." Her eyes met Cassia's. "At least, not about people."

Everyone seemed to be holding their breath, waiting for the queen to fly into a temper. Denying her did not seem like something that was done lightly. But after a long look at Veleda, the queen shifted her small frame on the massive throne. "Perhaps some agreement could be made." Gasps among the courtiers drew a hard stare from their ruler. "Selkolla prophesied the ring's importance to my people, and look where trusting her led? I could never wear it, anyway. Ugly old thing."

Cassia gaped at the queen. She had started a *war* over the ring, and now she acted like it didn't matter? But maybe this was face-saving. And maybe there were other parts of the prophecy that made it easier for the queen to accept this outcome. Perhaps she would never know. She inclined her head to the queen. "All I want is for both of our peoples to be safe."

"Will you swear an oath not to use the ring against my people?" the Dracu queen asked, suddenly deadly serious.

"I won't swear to anything until I see what happens next. But I have no wish for war. I have no desire to be Deathringer unless

I have to be." Though she was barely holding on to her temper. "Where are my sisters?"

After a long pause, the queen seemed to accept her refusal, giving a light shrug. "Here and there."

"And my father?" she asked.

That drew a satisfied smile. "Generally unharmed."

Cassia's felt an urge to wipe off that smug smile with a blast of light. "It's almost dawn. Release them."

"Perhaps you would like a bath," the queen offered. "You seem to have a fair bit of blood splatter about you." She made a circular motion that encompassed both of them, then turned to one of her waiting women. "Onyx, have a bath drawn for my lieutenant. The Sylvan surely wishes to bathe in the river. Or in a blooming lily filled with morning dew."

Zeru made an angry noise, but Cassia shook her head at him. "I'm going to find my sisters," she said, her hands curled into fists. "I assume you locked them in the dungeon?"

The queen put a hand to her chest. "What kind of heartless ruler do you think I am? They're in the stables."

Cassia gave one last look at Zeru, her stomach twisting, not knowing when she might see him next. "I have things to sort out here that might...take some time. Will you...would you be able to help your people find their way out of Scarhamm?"

In a heartbeat, Zeru's demeanor changed. His back straightened, his chin came up, and his eyes took on a glittering quality that made Cassia feel sick. He'd clearly taken her words as a dismissal. *No,* she wanted to say. *It's not like that!* But the queen was watching them with avid curiosity and Cassia was aware of Zeru's enemies in the court. She didn't know how he'd be treated if they knew about his attachment to a Sylvan. If he even wanted anyone to know.

363

"I will do my best, daughter of Silvanus." He offered her a graceful bow.

"Thank you," she said, his formality making her chest tighten. "And thank you for...your help." She put her feelings into her eyes, hoping he could see.

But he'd turned his head to the side, a muscle jumping in his cheek. "It was my great honor to assist you. I wish you good fortune in...whatever future you have planned."

Her lip trembled, and she knew if she stayed any longer, she would cry. "Goodbye, Zeru."

She turned to the queen, lifting her chin and reminding herself this was her home.

"I'd like to go with her," Veleda said.

After a moment, the queen flapped a hand. "Very well. I've had ill luck with Sylvan Seers."

As Veleda fell into step beside her, Cassia turned back for one last look at Zeru and caught him watching her, a look of longing in his eyes that made her want to clutch her chest. She forced herself to turn away. Veleda said nothing as they turned into the quiet halls of Scarhamm.

It wasn't until they reached the open air that Cassia found her voice. "I have so many questions, I don't know where to start."

Veleda's steps slowed. "Since when have you hesitated to ask me for anything?"

"That was before," Cassia said, realizing she had never known Veleda as well as she'd thought. "Why did you first come here? To Scarhamm?"

"Among the forest folk, doesn't every Seer aspire to a place next to the Sylvan king's throne?"

Cassia shook her head. "That's not an answer."

"No," Veleda admitted. "It's not." She came to a halt. They

were about halfway across the training yard, where flowering shrubs had started to grow along its edges. The Seer looked around at the plants and pointed. "See that rosebush? Its thorns and flowers? Roses might seem strong," she continued, "but they need tending to thrive. They can get a blight. They can be over trimmed and die. A plant might grow twisted and refuse to bloom. So much can go wrong."

"I know that better than ever," Cassia said. "What are you trying to say?"

"I'm saying that your mother was gone. There was no one to tend you, no one who understood your nature. Your father was trying to prune you into his own image, and when that didn't work, his answer was to cut you down more. And more."

Cassia nodded, the familiar ache in her chest easing at the sense that Veleda saw her clearly. "But how did you know that? From a spirit?"

"Many signs telling me to come here before it was too late. That the Sylvan king's daughter would save or doom the land folk. I knew it was vital for me to come here."

"Were you truly helping me become Deathringer?" Cassia asked bluntly.

A hint of amusement came into the Seer's dark brown eyes. "What do you think?"

"I think," Cassia said slowly, recalling the years of experiments, the modest steps forward, the tiny improvements that never amounted to much, "that you helped me make small gains that would satisfy my father, however briefly, but not enough for me to be what he wanted."

"Well," said Veleda, her smile widening, "I guess you were paying attention."

Cassia looked away, angry at the Seer and herself for not

suspecting that she was undermining her use of the ring. Even if Veleda's intentions were pure, she'd deceived her.

"I'm sorry," Veleda said, putting a gentle hand on Cassia's shoulder. "I was trying to help you, just not the way your father wanted. If you'd used that ring the way he had, disaster would have followed. Not just for the Sylvans but for all land folk. The signs are clear on this point, Cassia. I tried in small ways to help you see that wasn't your path, but you were so set on gaining his approval."

Cassia nodded, swallowing. Veleda was right about that. But she couldn't wrap her mind around the scope of this. That what she did with the ring affected so much of the future. Her thoughts went to the mystery Zeru had never solved. How did the ring, which his mother had guarded for so long, end up where he could find it?

"Did..." Cassia almost stopped herself from asking. It seemed so outlandish. But then she recalled Veleda admitting she had witnessed Selkolla's vow to the Dracu queen. "Did you have something to do with Zeru finding the ring? Giving it to me when we were children?"

"How powerful do you think I am?" Veleda said with a chuckle that wasn't entirely convincing. "But I will say, if it had been Thea who wore that ring, the outcome would have been very different. One of you was meant to find it, and...it was better that it was you."

Cassia blinked, imagining someone as relentless in battle as Thea using the ring. She shook her head. "We have more to talk about. Much more. And you'll have to answer to my father."

"You should go find your sisters," Veleda said, her tone making it clear she was done sharing confidences. "Your bond with one another is the greatest defense against the coming upheaval."

"What do you mean?" Cassia asked, her head snapping toward Veleda. "What upheaval?"

The Court Seer watched a bank of gray clouds scudding overhead, her eyes narrowing as if she saw something Cassia couldn't. "It's all too vague and too soon to tell. But you and your sisters are in the middle of it." Her brows came together as her gaze shifted to Cassia. "One of you is going to be more powerful than the Sylvan king." Her voice lowered. "It scares me to think what might happen if someone gains that much power and isn't ready for it."

As Cassia reached the stables, four Skratti guards stood watch. Enora sat serenely on a three-legged stool looking like a soldier-turned-milkmaid. Thea leaned against a wall chewing on a piece of straw, apparently unconcerned with the scucca gore that covered her leathern breastplate and green tunic. Rozie sat on the ground weaving something.

As her sisters caught sight of her, their faces lit with relieved smiles. Enora bounced to her feet and grinned.

Rozie threw down her handful of straw and leaped to her feet. "Cass!"

Cassia opened her arms, bracing her legs as Rozie crashed into her. A protective feeling came over her, and she kissed the top of the ginger curls. "Are you weaving a basket?" she asked.

Rozie lifted her face to whisper in Cassia's ear. "It's a garrote to kill Skrattis."

Cassia couldn't help but laugh, drawing the stares of the Skratti guards. "Move aside," she ordered, placing Rozie behind her. "My sisters are to be released immediately."

"Not our orders," one of them growled. "Queen said the king's antlers make it clear he's an animal, and he belongs with the pigs."

The other nodded. "And throw his daughters in with him, she said."

"See that light over there?" She pointed to the east. "I know it's been a while since you've seen sunrise, but unless I'm greatly mistaken, you're going to be very uncomfortable in a few minutes."

"We've taken Scarhamm," the first Skratti said, licking one of his tusks in a way that made Cassia wince. "We'll get used to the sun."

"Will you get used to being pummeled by the Sylvan king?" Thea asked, buffing her nails against her dirty shirt. "Because I think he's waking."

The Skrattis looked at one another. "Maybe we'd better check in with our queen." They weren't as fast as Dracu, but they hustled away in due haste.

"We could have killed them," Thea said, smiling as she watched them go. "If it weren't for that pact. At dawn, things would have been interesting." She sounded regretful at the lost opportunity for bloodshed. Cassia remembered Veleda's assertion that if Thea had worn the ring, things would have gone differently, and couldn't help a small shiver.

"Where is he?" Cassia asked, steeling herself.

Enora nodded to the shadows inside the stable. "Selkolla's lightning had quite the effect. He fell asleep right after you disappeared into the ground." Her expression tightened, her eyes showing worry. "Oh, Cass. I was scared to death."

Cassia knew Enora didn't scare easily. "I'm glad to be home."

"What happened?" Rozie demanded. "Tell us every detail."

"The Seer is dead. We're safe, Sproutling. I'll tell you everything, but first, I want to have a word with our father."

Enora's expression sobered. "We'll go with you."

Cassia shook her head. "I can handle him now." And she realized that was true.

368

With a deep breath, Cassia moved into the stable, her heart beating thickly. She found her father sitting on the floor, his back resting against a bit of wall between stalls. His breathing was shallow, his eyes glassy as he looked up at her. She wanted to ask if he would recover but knew he wouldn't appreciate her pointing out any weakness.

"What of the Seer?" he asked, his voice rougher than usual.

"Dead."

"The scuccas?"

"Released from her power. Some of them are peaceful. Others aren't. We'll have to deal with them as we come across them in Thirstwood."

The Sylvan king stared into the middle distance. "I felt the influx of life. But for a moment"—he looked up at her—"you commanded the forest."

She gave a single nod. She'd felt it in that moment, the entire forest listening to her. Her, and no one else.

Silence fell. Cassia waited for her father to say something, anything. Even threats would be welcome.

"You have nothing to say to me?" she asked.

His eyes shifted. "Words have never been my battlefield of choice."

She drew a breath. "Words don't have to be a battlefield. There are other ways to talk."

"None that I know," her father said.

When he said nothing more, she asked, "Am I still banished?"

"No." The answer was firm but stiff, angry.

Her teeth ground together. He wouldn't apologize. Never. Even for nearly killing her.

"Because of the power I have now?" she asked.

He said, equally firm and angry, "Because you are my daughter."

369

Cassia looked away. She couldn't help but swallow. It was as close to an admission of wrongdoing as she'd get. Though he'd never say it, he regretted banishing her. He'd known who she was even in the war room. But he hadn't acknowledged her. The Sylvan king did not admit to mistakes.

He was inscrutable, so beyond understanding. She sensed that emotion lived somewhere behind those cold eyes, the same way she could understand the trees. And she knew beyond doubt that her father was the loneliest person she had ever known. Maybe that was partly why she'd always longed to be closer to him. For his sake.

She had to accept that she would never understand him. And that there were others who would welcome her love and give it back.

"I know why you forbade the younger Sylvans from finding our trees," she said. "I used to think it was because you were worried we'd go into a long slumber, the way my mother did. But now I know. You didn't want anyone else to have a connection to the forest. You didn't want to risk any rivalry to your supremacy."

His eyes met hers, but he said nothing.

"And I know what you did to the forest," she said, her voice low and fervent. "I met the Seer you hired. Xoden." She waited, but he still said nothing. "He told me you had him trap hostile spirits in some of the trees to make them bloodthirsty. To gain power and control."

The king's nostrils flared. He didn't admit or deny it.

"And my mother?" she demanded, afraid to ask, terrified how he might answer. "Was her spirit one of the ones sacrificed to your greater cause?"

"No," he said succinctly. "I did nothing to harm her. That is one line I would never cross."

She felt the truth in his words, and something in her eased.

⌒ 370 ⌒

"If you ever do think to cross those lines, or to sacrifice any more Sylvan spirits, know this: I will battle you for Thirstwood if I have to."

He lifted his chin. "You plan to fight me for control?"

"It depends. You should think about this war and whether it's necessary. The queen seems to have accepted the loss of the ring. That's a start to brokering peace. If you don't, you might find the roots of Thirstwood less than willing to do your bidding."

"Threats?"

His sneer made her stomach clench, but she wouldn't back down. "Enough war, Father. Enough."

Epilogue

A Dracu loves forever.

—GAXIX, DRACU PHILOSOPHER

ZERU CLOSED HIS BURNING EYES, REELING FROM THE brightness of the full moon after spending so long in the Cryptlands. As he gulped fresh air and brushed the soil from his face, his heart crashed in his aching chest, his eyes scouring the trees. After surviving a month without seeing her, he was starved for a glimpse.

His heart stopped. There. Her golden hair was touched by moonlight as she sat waiting under the yew tree. The same tree where he'd given her the ring. He closed his eyes, trying to get control of himself before he spoke to her. For all he knew, she'd called him here to discuss finer points of the peace bargain. He'd worked tirelessly for it, fighting with Guzzo and the other fools in the Dracu court, knowing that Cassia and her sisters must be working equally hard in Scarhamm. He'd also helped his parents settle into their new, finer quarters, courtesy of the queen's gratitude for helping eliminate the scucca threat.

But when he'd heard Cassia's call, heard her voice through the amulet, everything in him had woken up. And he'd rushed to their old meeting place as eagerly as he had when he was eight years old. No, more desperately. He'd warned himself not to hope that she wanted any more from him than his help brokering peace.

"Dracu, Dracu," Cassia said, a smile in her voice. "I'm a better hunter than I used to be. Don't make me track you."

"As if you could, Sylvan," Zeru said, his heart slamming as he sauntered over to where she sat. "I have wings now, remember?"

"So do I. Care to test me?"

Yes. He longed to fly with her again. But he lifted a shoulder in a negligent shrug. "It's too warm to fly."

She looked up at him, her eyes devouring. His heart was trying to leap out of his chest and into her hands. "Too warm to fly? What kind of sad excuse for a Zerian are you?"

He gave the sky a cursory glance. "If you really want to, I suppose we could."

"No, it's all right. I wouldn't want to drop this." She held something up.

"What is it?" he asked.

"It's a honey cake. I know how you love them."

He swallowed as he took the wrapped package from her hands, careful not to touch her. That would be asking too much of himself. If he felt her skin, he was going to fall apart. "Did you bake it?"

"No. It wouldn't be worth eating. Anyway, you didn't make any of the gifts you gave me."

He took a spot next to her under the tree, his back leaning against the bark. He didn't worry whether it was a blood tree. The pact they'd negotiated said the trees would only harm a Dracu in defense of a Sylvan. And he had no intention of hurting Cassia. Ever. Carefully, he unwrapped the cake and took a bite. Sweetness exploded in his mouth. The fact that she'd somehow known these were his favorite . . .

"Would you like a bite?" he asked.

"It's yours. You enjoy it."

He swallowed. "Just a taste."

She turned her head toward him, her head resting against the trunk. "All right. Feed me a bite."

Her lips parted, their beautiful contours filling his vision. He felt his nostrils flare, the blood pounding through his veins. He broke off a piece of the honey cake and put it to her lips. She took the bite, licking his finger as she did before it disappeared into her mouth. His mind emptied. She was either very cruel, or...

"Good," she said. "But I knew it would be. Our cook is the best."

"I can't argue," he said, wondering how he managed to keep his voice so steady. Maybe his Zerian form gave him preternatural control over himself. Not his heart, though. That was Dracu. It was still base and wild. And hers.

"Now it's your turn, Dracu. Where's my gift?"

"I gave you three," he reminded her, taking a breath for courage before he added, "By Dracu tradition, that assures our bond for life."

She went silent, but lifted something around her neck, showing the holed stone on a string. Then she turned her head to show the fish-bone comb in her hair. *She'd kept them.* "I didn't know that. I guess you don't owe me a gift, then. But I owe you two more."

He closed his eyes. He enjoyed the game they were playing, but it was stretching his patience to its limits. If this uncertainty went on much longer, he was going to start howling like a moon-maddened wolf.

"You do owe me something, though," she added. "You were supposed to tell me what *katra* means."

He groaned. He couldn't help it. Of all the things to ask him now. He pushed to his feet. "Did you bring me here to torture me, Cassia?"

She stood, too. Her brows were drawn together. "No. I missed you. Didn't you miss me?"

"More than I ever knew possible," he admitted, hoping that wasn't revealing too much.

She flew into his arms, pushing him into the tree. He clutched her back as he stared hungrily at her face. "By the Ancients, I have longed for you."

Thankfully, before he could embarrass himself further, she distracted him. Her hand crept inside the collar of his shirt, her other hand on the back of his head, pulling him closer. "Kiss me, you fool Dracu."

Her mouth was soft, her tongue hot, and he wondered if she tasted the sweetness of honey, of her own gift, on his lips.

"I hated being apart for so long," she said, taking a breath before kissing him once more. He reveled in her voracious need for him, his head spinning with a joy he'd started to lose hope he'd ever feel again. When her sharper Zerian teeth drew blood from his lip, she jerked back. "I'm sorry! I hurt you."

"Quiet," he snarled, and showed her that he didn't mind at all. They didn't speak for a long while.

As the moon set, his arms tightened around her. It always surprised him how right she felt there.

"I'm going to be very angry if you don't tell me what your endearment means," she warned him, her hands combing through his hair.

"Oh," he said, nuzzling her cheek. "Right. I guess I shouldn't worry you'll run screaming?" It was still a question.

She gave him a deep kiss, biting his lip deliberately this time. "What do you think?"

"There's no exact translation," he said, holding a palm up when she opened her mouth, "but it means some combination of the words *love, haven*, and *home*."

They stared at each other for a minute. Cassia smiled as her eyes shone with a film of tears. "I *katra* you, too," she said.

Laughter burst from him. No one could surprise him like she could. Though he was dizzy with the meaning of what she'd said, it was too much to absorb at once. Later, when he was alone, he could replay that moment a thousand times in his mind. But for now, he would tease her and laugh. "That's not how you use it," he said. "Poor Sylvan."

She shrugged, her eyes mischievous. "I'm the steward of Welkincaster. I do as I please. Speaking of, I was wondering if you wanted to spend some time there with me. Now that the peace deal is almost done, I'll be free from my duties for a while. Want to grow some vegetables?"

"Only," he said, nipping her gently with his teeth, "if we grow turnips."

She laughed as their lips met and they held each other, their bodies so close together they looked inseparable. As they slept a while later, moon sprites danced around them, wanting to get closer to the winged Dracu and the golden Sylvan with so much sunlight in their hearts.

Acknowledgments

It's been a long road getting here. While I was editing this book, I lost both of my parents just a few weeks apart. For a while, I didn't know if I would ever be able to write again. I have so many people to thank for helping me through this time!

To Suzie Townsend, thank you for going above and beyond to help me finish this book! I would still be paralyzed if not for our calls. Big thanks to the team at New Leaf, especially Sophia Ramos for your brainstorming help, Olivia Coleman for handling so many details, and to Tracy Williams and Keifer Ludwig in foreign rights.

To the team at Little, Brown Books for Young Readers, thank you for being so patient and supportive. Deirdre Jones, I'm in awe of your perceptive edits and excellent eye for honing! Grateful thanks to designers Sasha Illingworth and Patrick Hulse for beautiful concept art and design. Thank you to assistant editor Jessica Levine for handling so many details! Thanks also to production coordinator Kimberly Stella, production editor Annie McDonnell, and copyeditor Starr Baer—I'm amazed at the detail work you do! Thanks to the team in marketing and publicity: Alice Gelber, Savannah Kennelly, Cheryl Lew, Christie Michel, Emilie Polster, Mary McCue, Victoria Stapleton, Danielle Cantarella, and Shawn Foster. Warm gratitude to editor-in-chief Alvina Ling, publisher Megan Tingley, and deputy publisher Jackie Engel. Thank you to artist Micaela Alcaino for creating a cover more beautiful than I could have imagined!

To Molly Powell at Hodder & Stoughton, thank you for

everything, especially the early brainstorming help. Also, to the team at Ravensburger, thank you for patience and support!

Mary Ann Marlowe, Kristin Wright, Summer Spence, and Jennifer Hawkins, thank you for the support, laughs, good advice, and for being the first people to read and to believe in this book. I don't know what I'd do without you! Nicki Pau Preto, Morgan Rhodes, and Maureen McGowan, thank you for being my writerly travel buddies! To the Lady Seals, it means so much that you're always in my corner. And to the Writing Wrecking Crew— Christian Laforet, Ben Van Dongen, and Brittni Brinn—thanks for being there when I needed you most.

Mom and Dad, love you forever. To my brothers, Erik and Mark, love you both for dropping everything to care for our parents with me. Heartfelt thanks to my dear Takaki family for being my biggest fans. Extra hugs to my niece, Zoe, for being the bravest young woman I know, and for being a passionate reader who cheers me on.

Finally, to the people who give me purpose: Darren, thank you for being the love of my life, the one I lean on the most, my haven in every storm. Nicklas, Aleksander, and Lukas: You are my joy. I love you so much.